MAGIC HARBOR

DIMENSION 8 – BOOK 2

KEEPER OF THE WATCH SERIES

KRISTEN L. JACKSON

Black Rose Writing | Texas

© 2019 by Kristen L. Jackson
All rights reserved. No part of this book may be reproduced, stored in a retrieval system or transmitted in any form or by any means without the prior written permission of the publishers, except by a reviewer who may quote brief passages in a review to be printed in a newspaper, magazine or journal.

The author grants the final approval for this literary material.

First printing

This is a work of fiction. Names, characters, businesses, places, events, and incidents are either the products of the author's imagination or used in a fictitious manner. Any resemblance to actual persons, living or dead, or actual events is purely coincidental.

ISBN: 978-1-68433-338-7
PUBLISHED BY BLACK ROSE WRITING
www.blackrosewriting.com

Printed in the United States of America
Suggested Retail Price (SRP) $19.95

Magic Harbor is printed in Garamond Premier Pro

I'd like to dedicate this one to my husband, Glenn. My rock, my muse, my true other half. My *biggest* fan. Your feedback is essential to my writing process, and your steady support is my inspiration. I couldn't complete even one sentence without knowing you're behind me 100%. Thanks for making this crazy 'writing-thing' possible ... and for putting up with my obsessiveness when I'm so totally immersed in writing it's all I can sleep, eat, talk and dream about. I love you!

SPECIAL THANKS TO:

My mom, for your unwavering support my entire life in whatever inspired me at the time. Your support has been a constant in my life, and I thank you for it. I love you!

My sons, Jordan and Jeremy, I'm so proud to be your mom! You both inspired Chase's character in different ways. Thanks for inspiring me every day, in everything I do. I love you both!

My sisters, Kelley and Kim, for your support and love. I can't imagine not being the 'middle' to your 'older' and 'younger'. I love you guys!

My beta readers, Nancy B., Leah U., Mom, Kelley—your feedback is so helpful (each of you in your own way!) to the creation of the final manuscript. I can't tell you how thankful I am that you are willing to donate your time to my writing. Thank you!

My publisher, Black Rose Writing, for once again believing in me and my story.

My editor, Martin Matthews.

Once again, thank you to Laura of Laura Danielle Photography for my amazing author photo.

And finally, thank you to everyone who has supported me by buying and reading my book, leaving a review, offering words of support and encouragement, attending one of my events, or leaving a comment and sharing posts online. You have no idea how much you inspire me to keep writing.

MAGIC HARBOR

Dear Future Keepers,

We've written this down in the hopes that we will survive our year of jumping and pass this information, as well as our watches, on to you—our future ancestors. We pray that you will read this journal and find solace in the knowledge that others have been on the same path you are now only just beginning. Take heart. You are not alone. If you're reading this, it means the hunters have failed in their quest to destroy the remaining watches ... at least on the last jump as our journey has not yet ended. Be on guard, they may be searching for you even as you read this. Preserving the legacy now falls to you—if we have survived the year.

Once you've coupled with your watch, it will become a part of you. Your very lifeblood will power the watch as it pumps through the timepiece, just as it pumps through your own heart, and in fact, your heart will beat in time with the watch while it is a part of you. Embrace it. You will have the unique ability to commune with ancestors who have come before you as your blood mingles with theirs. Your stamina will increase, and your body will not tire due to your heart's steady beat.

Be prepared to jump to each new world consecutively on the following dates only. You will remain in each new dimension until the next date on this list. I'm sure you've noticed that your birthday is listed. That's because all keepers were born on one of these chosen dates. Your destiny has been set since the moment of your conception.

All jumps are automatic—you won't be able to control your departure in any way, so don't even try. You'll find most jumps are ... uncomfortable. Be strong, the pain won't last.

When you've completed your eighteenth year, your journey will end and you will return home with the option of living out the rest of your years in the dimension of your choice. Your status as a keeper of the watch ends the moment you turn nineteen, along with your ability to traverse the twelve dimensions. Your watch will go dormant as it waits for the next keeper in your bloodline. Tuck it away along with this journal until the day comes for you to pass it on.

But you're just beginning. Take care of yourself. Take care of your watch. Add any information you deem important to this journal to continue the legacy. Our family heritage lives on through you. Protect the watch with your life, and remember: things aren't always what they seem. May God bless you on your eighteenth birthday and the year that follows.

Signed,
Alyx Eris & Chase Walker

Keeper Jump Schedule, Year Eighteen:

Jump Date/Dimension/Keeper Family Surname

January 1; Dimension 1; Graham
February 2; Dimension 2; Woods
March 3; Dimension 3; Fox
April 4; Dimension 4; Eris
May 5; Dimension 5; Atlas
June 6; Dimension 6; Walker
July 7; Dimension 7; Roberts
August 8; Dimension 8; Apollo
September 9; Dimension 9; Young
October 10; Dimension 10; Gray
November 11; Dimension 11; Vega
December 12; Dimension 12; Cook

PROLOGUE
ALYX

August 8th, 8:00 a.m. The ticking clock echoed in her head. *Tick-tick-tick-tick.*

Eight minutes left before the jump.

I think we're ready…

Alyx fidgeted with the zipper on the backpack. Up and down, up and down. *Zip-zip. Zip-zip.* Everything was packed. She paced the perimeter of the room in circles, a frown wrinkling her forehead. Chase watched her from the middle of the living room.

They were alone in the abandoned house they had been living in since the victory against the hunters here in Dimension 7—one of twelve parallel worlds, the existence of which remained hidden from most people within those dimensions. Here, they had discovered a post-apocalyptic parallel Earth under the tyrannical rule of two hunters hell-bent on finding the remaining watches, and put an end to their dictatorship. The people here were truly free for the first time in years. A gentle sigh hissed between her teeth.

The watches opened a magical door between twelve parallel worlds, but only watch-wearers known as keepers could bond—or couple—with a watch. Since the invention of the twelve watches by Chase's ancestor, Elias Walker, over one hundred years ago, the two they'd dubbed 'hunters' had made it their life-long goal to steal the power the watches provided. Her eyes took on a faraway glint as she recalled the history she'd been taught since she was old enough the listen. In the beginning, the hunters had tried to harness the power of the watches for themselves—the remarkable ability to travel the twelve dimensions. They soon learned that only a keeper's blood can power the watch itself … and had begun their quest to eradicate all keepers and their watches. Only children born on specific dates (the first day of the first month, second day of the second month, and so on up to the twelfth day of the twelfth month) within specific ancestral lines could jump to a new world each month of their eighteenth year, and even then only if they coupled with the watch after their eighteenth birthday.

Alyx rounded her shoulders, standing taller. It was an honor to be a keeper, and she had painstakingly—calling on all her powers of persuasion—convinced Chase of that when he had his own doubts back in his home world, Dimension 6.

The hunters new goal was clear: to find and destroy all remaining watches ... and their keepers.

Keepers. Us. That's why we have to destroy them first. They won't stop until they've killed us all.

A determined look lit her eyes. Since hunters were nearly immortal, it wouldn't be easy. Hunters aged at a very slow rate. They had been around since the watches' invention but looked like they were in their mid-twenties. Although she and Chase had defeated the hunters in this dimension, she knew they would likely continue to battle the hunters' 'other selves' in each dimension they jumped to. Only a keeper was born solely in one world. Everyone else had the potential to exist in multiple worlds.

At least we don't have to worry about running into our 'other selves' ... I don't think I could survive two of him. Her eyes found Chase and traveled the length of him. His blonde hair with just a slight hint of curls at the tips, cerulean blue eyes that crinkled when he laughed. And those dimples.... At that moment he looked up as if he could hear her thoughts, flashing a smile that showed off that very feature and had her heart skipping in her chest. Her lips turned up against her will. He seemed to have that effect on her. Her shoulders raised with a sigh.

Who am I kidding? He has that effect on everyone.

Breaking her eyes away, she turned and resumed her pacing.

Each event in time caused a shift, creating a ripple effect resulting in a different reality in each world in the multiverse. They had no idea what—or who—they would find in each new world they jumped to. Only the box they'd found hidden in Chase's home world could guide them on their journey. In it: an ancient journal written by the creator and previous keepers, along with currency and some other trinkets they had no idea how to use.

She knew they had succeeded in this seventh dimension to the best of their ability, but still they had failed to complete a big part of their mission. There just hadn't been time to search for the last keeper before the next jump. Originally, there had been twelve watches, one originating in each dimension. Now, all but three had been destroyed by the hunters. Hers. Chase's. And one other. It was their hope to find the last keeper and protect him along with his watch, though they had no idea in which world the third keeper might reside, or for that matter if the next keeper had even been born yet. One thing was sure. If he, or she, resided in this dimension, they would most likely never know it, since this was a one-stop dimension hop. Their time here was up, and they would not return to D-7 again. Even now, they were mere minutes away from jumping to the next world. Dimension 8.

Her hands continued to toy with the zipper as she spoke and her brow creased again. "I think we can assume we'll both jump to Dune Harbor, I just wish we could jump together to the same coordinates."

Chase reached for her hand. "What if we hold hands? Anything we're wearing or holding goes with us, right? If we hold hands, maybe we'll end up in the same place this time."

She tilted her head. "But what if our touching throws everything off? This hasn't been done before, we have no idea if our two transports will be compatible, or if combining them will have disastrous consequences. We could end up anywhere, or worse, not survive the jump. Maybe we should just take our chances and hope to find each other quickly once we get there. Maybe make a meeting point?"

"Easy for you to say. *You* didn't have to see *me* executed. I don't want to risk something like that happening again, Alyx."

She blew out a breath. "Okay. We'll try holding hands. But just in case that doesn't work, meet me at Uncle Charlie's house as soon as you can."

Chase nodded.

She glanced at her watch.

8:05 a.m.

"Ready?" She said.

"Ready."

They stood side-by-side, backpacks on, fingers intertwined. Chase absently rubbed his thumb over Alyx's palm as they waited.

"Three minutes seems like an eternity when you're waiting," he said.

"True."

8:07 a.m.

Both pairs of pupils dilated as the watches began glowing, then pulsing brightly, bathing the room in unnatural light.

"Good luck, Chase."

"I love you, Alyx."

She inhaled a deep breath and looked into his glowing blue eyes. "I..."

All at once electricity filled the room and both of their bodies hummed with power of it, causing the hair on their arms to stand on end. Dual silver ever-changing pools appeared above each of their heads, taking on a life of their own. When they emerged, they were about the size of a coin, hovering over each of them, and then grew before their eyes to the size of a full-length mirror in the blink of an eye. The wavering shapes writhed in anticipation of the passing minute, fluctuating in constant motion as if agitated.

8:08 a.m.

Chase looked at Alyx questioningly. "What?"

"I..." Suddenly, she launched herself at Chase, wrapping her arms around him and holding on. He caught her, stumbling back a step, and returned her embrace, folding her in his arms and hugging her body to his. As always, their bodies fit perfectly together. His hard lines meshed with her soft curves. Alyx squeezed her eyes shut, her head tucked under Chase's chin, so close she could feel his heart beating against her body in perfect unison with her own.

And she waited.

A bolt of lightning streaked through the room as the two shimmering pools bounced off of each other like opposing magnetic forces. His cobalt light joined with her iridescent magenta glow, combining to create a deep mulberry color that ignited their veins and traveled throughout their bodies, as if they had become one unit.

Anticipation turned to attack. The writhing pools above them continued to bounce off of each other, as if engaged in a deadly battle, until a final crash when, accompanied by another bolt of lightning, the two energies united, creating a single shimmering mercurial pool that hung above their heads.

At once the cosmic war ceased, and the mass moved peacefully, as if there had never been discord. A second after the discrete entities joined, the now single larger mass dropped from the air. Both Alyx and Chase were consumed from head to foot in one heartbeat, disappearing instantaneously. The house where they had been present just seconds before stood suddenly vacant. The only trace that anyone had been there was the electrical hum and a faint burning smell left in their wake.

And that's when the pain began.

CHAPTER 1
CHASE

Agony.

It encompassed his body, saturating every pore; every blood cell pumping through his veins seemed to be screaming in anguish.

Fire.

There was no pinpoint of space within or without left untouched by the violent pain that burned through to the core of his being. It was as if his heart had burst out of his chest in flames, his body gasping to breathe through the inferno raging inside him.

I can't...

He clenched his teeth against it, jaw grinding, hands fisted even as his eyes remained clamped shut. Coherent thought was just out of reach, so he turned into himself, searching for some kind of solace, sinking farther into a pool of never-ending blackness. Sanity knocked on the outskirts of his consciousness, but he turned it away, preferring the nothingness. Flames licked along the edges, searching for a crack in the mortar, a tiny hole to find its way deeper inside the well.

Pain.

Can't. Give. In.

Clawing toward the surface, Chase pushed with every ounce of energy inside him to beat back the burning that threatened to consume him.

I survived this once before. I can do it again.

Willing his body to move, he was again denied. It was as if a tractor trailer was parked on his chest, and he was powerless to do anything but lay here, every breath a struggle. The roaring in his ears made his brain hurt, but he shoved back at it, forcing it to retreat with the strength of his will alone.

Alyx. Are you here?

That one thought gave him the push he needed to fight. He cracked one eye, letting the searing light pierce like a dagger into his cerebrum. He lifted his head and looked down. Chestnut hair tinged with purple tips fanned out across his chest.

Alyx.

Not a truck. Alyx lay sprawled on top of him. His head fell back and he closed his eyes again. He willed his arms to move, gingerly wrapped them around her. Second by second, the pain was receding. Now he could die peacefully.

"Ch-Chase?" the muffled voice broke down the rest of the wall, and he rolled to his side carrying her with him. His breathing evened out, and he savored the feel of doing that one simple act.

"I'm here," he croaked through his tortured throat.

"You're … hurting me."

"What?" He forced his eyelids open, and realized he was squeezing her to him in a vise grip. Loosening his arms, he moaned. "Always complaining."

The sound of her labored breathing broke through the fog, and he pushed his body upright.

"You okay?" he asked, watching her eyelids flutter open, her lavender eyes meeting his.

"Better now. It's getting better." She, too, gingerly pushed her body into a sitting position, arms resting on her knees, body hunched over.

"Thank God." He rubbed his hands over his face then into his hair, making it stand on end. "At least we're together this time."

"Yes."

"Two jumps down. How many more times do we have to do that? I can't think."

The corners of her mouth lifted, though her eyes remained strained. "You have ten more jumps. I have eight. I've got three down, and I skipped a dimension, remember?"

He scowled down at her, then looked up for the first time taking in his surroundings.

"Whoa. Where are we?" He slowly got to his feet, taking in the scene before him. "Uh, guess we didn't land at the beach this time."

CHAPTER 2
ALYX

"No, definitely not the beach." Alyx pushed to her feet, bent over with hands on her knees, breathing erratically. Her eyes traveled the area around them, squinting through patchy shade broken with bursts of sunlight, creating a kaleidoscope of colors.

A myriad of green hues invaded her senses. Juniper bled into olive and basil creating an explosion of mossy color interspersed with various browns. Vertical slants in shades of mocha as far as she could see.

The smell of pine made her nostrils flare. A musty scent saturated her senses, and she stood straighter.

"A forest. Do you think this is the same place we camped in Dimension 7? The one near that town? Apple Blossom?" She turned in a full circle. "I think I can find my way out, if it is. I spent a lot of time there," she added.

Chase scanned the area. "Don't know. We're not in the clearing. And I don't hear a stream, at least not close by. It feels … different." His head tilted as he met her eyes. "I thought we'd always land in the middle of Dune Harbor. I didn't expect this. Where's the beach?"

"We have no way of knowing where in Dune Harbor we'll land. It's different each time. Let's check this place out. We'll have to find our way out of the woods if we're going to look for the hunters and begin our search for the last keeper."

"Yeah, and we need to find food. Jumping makes me hungry."

Alyx rolled her eyes. "You're always hungry. Food's the least of our worries. Didn't you stuff your backpack with every packaged food you could fit before we left?"

"And yours is stuffed with weapons." He winked, flashing those dimples. Alyx sighed, a slight smile tugging at the corners of her mouth.

She shook her head, continuing her inspection.

"Never know when we may need to use the Inferno Ray to incinerate something, or the Spark Gun to incapacitate someone for a while. You were happy to use them in D-7."

Crack-snap. Crack.

Both heads jerked toward the sound. They held their breath and stilled their bodies, heads cocked.

Alyx positioned herself back-to-back with Chase, hand inching toward the set of blade discs she always carried in a holster under her shirt. The small weapon could, if thrown correctly, sever limbs or even decapitate a target. Her hands went clammy as she remembered a hunter meeting just that fate in D-7. Alyx could almost hear the sound of the woman's head thumping to the ground; see it launching into a wobbly roll as her body remained standing. At least temporarily. She shook her head to clear the image.

Snap.

"What was that?" she whispered.

Chase held up a hand, palm out.

"Don't move," he breathed. His finger slowly pointed toward the distant left. "Keep quiet and don't move."

She froze, except for the hand that continued creeping toward her weapon of choice, just barely breathing as she slid one of the blade discs out, grasping it between her fingers. Her legs spread in battle stance and she rolled her shoulders. This is what she'd trained for since birth.

Her eyes followed the direction Chase indicated, and at first she saw nothing. Then she heard it. A low rumbling, like an engine idling, continuous and fierce.

When she pinpointed the spot from which the sound originated, her quick intake of breath gave away her surprise. Two eyes glowed out of the shadows as the thing peered from behind a tree, a mixture of light and dark shades of gray camouflaged the creature perfectly in the dark patches of shade. As she made eye contact with the thing, it slinked from behind the tree, snarling. Its dagger-like yellow teeth were bared, lips curled in warning. She saw that the fur on its back stood on end, and its tail was raised and straight.

"A wolf?" she murmured.

"No. Too small. Shh."

She began raising her arm, ready to launch the blade disc toward the animal, but felt Chase's hand on her forearm holding her back. She looked at him over her shoulder, raising a brow.

His hushed words barely reached her ears, "Don't kill it unless you have to."

She gave a slight nod. Her arm relaxed by her side, blade disc in hand and ready if needed.

They remained at a stand-off, no one moving, their breathing amplified in the stillness. Sweat trickled from beneath her hair down the base of her neck causing a shiver to run along her spine, despite the heat of the day. She resisted the urge to swipe it away. Continuously glancing down at her watch's gentle violet glow, she could see the the blood-red minute-hand move notch by notch. They stood as still as the trees surrounding them for what seemed an eternity, though she knew only minutes had passed.

Enough.

Alyx took one step toward the small wolf-like beast. As she drew her arm back, another set of eyes appeared behind the animal. The pup crouched behind its mother, mimicking her stance, though it lacked her size and dominance. The high-pitched growl had one corner of her mouth lifting. The small body seemed disproportionate in its awkward adolescent stage, lanky hind quarters larger than the front. It was covered in fuzzy fur, much lighter in color than its parent. The copper color of its head bled into a gray flank and tail. Its winsome appearance belied any attempt at intimidation.

Once again, she lowered her arm, even before Chase's hushed words reached her ears. "It's just a mother protecting her baby."

He inched his hand toward his jeans pocket, and pulled out a stick of beef jerky. She rolled her eyes.

Of course he has food in his back pocket. Probably in every pocket.

His soothing words filled the silence, spoken softly, making the mother's growl gain volume. "It's okay. We're not here for your baby. Here, I'll share." Gearing back as slowly as possible, he tossed the jerky in the creature's direction, and the treat landed a few feet in front of it with one bounce on the soft turf.

The animal's trembling body lurched at the sudden movement, lips pulling back to reveal dark gums, saliva hanging from its jowls like shoestrings. The pup hid behind its parent, only its head and eyes visible from around her hunched back. The mother's nostrils flared as it picked up the scent of food. It leaped forward in one swift move, snatching the snack and disappearing into the shrubbery, the pup right on her heels.

"Thanks. For not killing them," Chase said.

"I'm not heartless."

He nodded. "Just practical."

"Could have solved your food problem. Wolf-burgers might be good," she teased, returning the blade disc to its holster.

Arms gesturing, he retorted, "I'm not eating a ..." His words trailed off. "Wolf-burger. Good one." He looked back to where the pair had disappeared. "I wonder what that thing was? Not a wolf, exactly. I was thinking coyote because of its size, but its features were wrong. The snout was too blocky. Maybe some kind of a dog?"

"It doesn't matter, it's gone. Now, we can get on with finding our way out of here."

Chase nodded. "We ought to find shelter before nightfall." His eyes scanned the area. "You hear anything?"

She shook her head.

"Shouldn't we hear birds? Leaves rustling? Crickets chirping? An airplane overhead? Something. Anything. It's creepy that there isn't another sign of life."

She scrutinized the area in a 360 degree circle. "Let's move." She started moving away from the place where the creature had disappeared and heard the sounds of his footsteps in the underbrush following.

"How do you know which way to go?" Chase asked.

"I don't." Her eyes remained alert as she continued moving forward.

CHAPTER 3
CHASE

Chase grumbled to himself as he stooped to pick up more firewood, adding it to the thick bundle already under his arm. This wasn't the way it was supposed to go. What could they accomplish stuck here in the forest?

He'd done his share of camping as a boy, so he knew how to survive in the woods. He could probably keep the two of them alive for the month, until they jumped to the next dimension on September 9th. And if they could find a water source, he could always catch fish to feed them. He looked down as his stomach grumbled.

But finding water here was not as easy as he'd first thought it would be, and his brow furrowed when he held up his nearly empty water bottle, sloshing the liquid back and forth. Food and water. That had become their first mission here in Dimension 8.

August 10th. Two days.

They'd been tramping through these woods in the summer heat for two days, and neither one of them had a clue how to get out of here. And worse, he was beginning to suspect that they'd walked in a full circle. Was that the same tree the animal and its pup had hidden behind when they'd first arrived? It had the same slant to its trunk. Hard to say. All the trees were beginning to look alike.

Forty-eight wasted hours.

He sighed, and continued his task.

When his hands were so full it took both arms to wrap around the stash he began backtracking, following the slashes he'd left on the tree trunks as he walked. He'd begun marking their path yesterday, so if they did circle around again they would know it without a doubt.

When he got back to camp, Alyx was sitting cross-legged on the moss-covered ground between two majestic hemlock trees that had to have been planted sometime in the last century. She had something in her lap, and as she studied it her hair fell forward covering her face from his view. The purple tips stood out amongst the greenery, and her head snapped up when he took a step closer, wild violet-blue eyes softening with recognition.

"You're back."

"Got enough firewood to last us for tonight. What'cha got there?"

She held out her hand, palm up. "Some kind of fruit. Recognize it?"

The berries were the size of grapes, round and translucent, seeds visible deep inside them. At a glance, they looked like frozen dewdrops in solid form.

He dropped next to her to get a closer look. "Definitely not. They're kinda cool, though. Where'd you find them?"

She pointed. "Over there, growing up the side of that weird tree."

He turned in the direction she indicated. "Uh, I don't see..."

And then he did.

The tree was bent sideways, its trunk at an angle reaching toward the sun's rays. Now that he saw it, he wondered how he had missed it. Unlike the other trees of this forest, its body was smooth and appeared translucent when viewed from any angle except straight on. It blended with its surroundings so well that he had missed seeing it the first time around. The leaves were a pale iridescent lime green, and also seemed to shimmer into nonexistence into the shadows and light of the forest. Like the berries, they were translucent.

Alyx raised a berry to her mouth, and Chase swatted it out of her hand.

"Hey!"

"You can't just eat every berry you find. You didn't already eat one, did you? What if it's poisonous?"

"How will we find out if we don't eat them?"

"Good question. But I'm not comfortable eating those berries until we do. That's one of the first things you learn in Boy Scouts."

She huffed. "What's Boy Scouts?"

"Seriously? I pegged you as a Girl Scout for sure. It's a kind of a club that kids can join to learn all kinds of survival skills."

"My parents taught me all of that. My training began on the day I learned to walk. I didn't need a club."

His shoulders shook. "Apparently they missed teaching you about poisonous berries."

She sat up straighter, her head lifting a notch. "They taught me how to survive. To protect myself and others. We each have our strengths."

He winked, a slow smile spreading. "You're right. That's why we make such a good team." He leaned over, bumping her shoulder with his. "Good find, though. Let's stash them, and watch the plants and see if anything else comes to eat them. If an animal or bird eats one and doesn't keel over, I guess we'll be okay, too."

Chase reached across her lap to grab his backpack and looked up, meeting her eyes. His smile faded as his expression turned suddenly serious. His eyes focused on her lips, and he leaned forward.

Alyx leaped to her feet.

He looked up at her, crossed his legs, and leaned back on his arms. "I thought..." He looked away.

"Thought what?"

"You were going to tell me something... Right before the jump. Remember?"

"I don't know what you're talking about."

His eyes followed the red climbing up her cheeks, and continued, "You like me, admit it. Like when you stare at me when you think I'm not looking. And how you melt when I kiss you..."

"Ha! Melt? Is that what you call it? We're melting because of the heat, not because of some kiss." She slammed her hands on her hips and began pacing a small path in front of him. "How about we focus on surviving in this place? Finding food, maybe? Or, I don't know, getting out of here so we can search for the two hunters and the last keeper? How about we get our priorities straight."

His eyes followed, aware of her every movement. *Wow. She's something.*

He pushed slowly to his feet and took a step toward her. "Oh, my priorities are in the right order."

She jumped back and assumed a battle stance; knees and elbows bent, arms raised. "I need space."

His arms dropped to his sides and he sighed while taking a step backward. *You're moving too fast, moron. Slow down. She may be eighteen like me, but she's never even had a boyfriend before.*

"That, I can do." He scanned the area, remembering the sound of her laughter when they'd gone swimming on their last jump. "Okay, priorities. Let's make camp. We need to take inventory of our food supply, and as much as I hate to say it, ration it out. Since food is not abundant around here, we need to make sure we don't run out."

Alyx relaxed her pose and nodded. "Too bad you shared some of our supplies with that beast." She frowned. "And I'm almost out of water."

"Me too." He held up his plastic water bottle and shook it back and forth. "Let's try digging for water after we make our shelter. I'll look for large sticks to use as supports, you look for bushes with good-sized leaves, or fallen branches still full of leaves. Who knows, maybe it will rain?"

Splitting up, he wandered around the campsite glancing periodically in her direction, picking up anything he could use to fashion into a shelter for the night. He leaned two long sticks against the tree with the thickest trunk. Using a rock and a spoon from his backpack, he carved a small notch into the wood, then wedged one end of the stick into the notch while pushing the other end into the ground.

"There. That should hold for one night." He repeated the process so the two sticks created a small lean-to at the base of the tree.

Alyx began placing her discoveries on top. She'd broken branches off a nearby bush, and the leaves were thick and wide.

She nodded when Chase spoke, "Those are perfect."

Overlapping them together in a zigzag pattern, he watched as she stood back to observe her work and gave one curt nod. "This will do."

"Perfect. Now for water." Chase squatted, grasping the spoon and stabbing it into the soil. He scooped the earth and dumped it onto a growing pile next to the hole he created. It fell like dust that rolled down the sides of the mound. Sweat dripped a jagged path from his temple to his jawline even though his body didn't tire as he dug.

"The dirt is very dry," Alyx said unhelpfully.

"Well, I'm going to keep trying. I'm not nearly deep enough yet."

"Okay. I'll go check the area for any signs of water nearby."

He nodded, his small mountain of dirt growing as the hole got deeper.

After a few minutes, he sat back and wiped the sweat from his brow. The heat emanating from his body had him pausing for a break. He glanced at his hole, now elbow-deep. Odd. It was still just as dry as the topsoil. In his experience the deeper the hole, the more moist the soil, but this was almost like working through sand.

His tongue was glued to the roof of his mouth. What he wouldn't give for a fountain soda from McDonald's right now. Along with a cheeseburger and fries. A pie. Maybe a milkshake. And a cookie. He scowled at the spoon in his hand before pushing himself back up to resume digging. The aquamarine glow of his watch caught his eye, and he paused to stare at the minute and second hands, for a moment mesmerized by the movement of his very lifeblood flowing through them. His blood: the power source for the watch itself as his heart beat in time with the clock. *Don't think I'll ever get used to this.*

He resumed his monotonous task. Scoop and dump, scoop and dump. The mound grew mere tablespoons at a time.

Why didn't we think of bringing a shovel? He wondered.

The rumbling in his stomach put a scowl on his face.

He barely heard the cracking of twigs off to his left that signified he was no longer alone.

CHAPTER 4
ALYX

Alyx strode away, putting both physical and mental distance between herself and Chase. She rolled her eyes.

Why does he make me act this way? He makes me so...

There were not enough words in the English language, or any native tongue for that matter, to describe her feelings for him. A scowl marred her features. One minute, she couldn't stop looking at him and butterflies fluttered deep inside her. The next moment, he made her so mad she wanted to slam her elbow into his face. It had been that way since they met. She wanted to be close to him, and then when they were alone together she pushed him away. At least they'd jumped to the same place this time. She would just have to figure out the rest as they went. Her pupils dilated as her watch began to glow more brightly than before, so in tune it was with her jumbled emotions.

And, I left my backpack at camp. His fault.

She shook her head, thankful she at least had the pair of blade discs she always carried—and the knife she'd brought to mark her path. She scanned the small clearing up ahead.

Don't think we've been this way yet...

After slashing a diagonal line in the nearest tree with her switchblade, she continued moving forward and took one step into the open area, the sunlight warming her hair at the roots and slowly spreading downward through her body. Despite the temperature, she sighed, tilting her head back to let the warm light bathe her face, as she had done on that not-so-long-ago day at the beach with Chase. A picture of her and Chase bobbing in the waves flitted through her mind. It had been a good day. Sharing a picnic lunch on the sand, she'd been so relaxed with him. She sighed again. *Wish I could get that back.* Her cheeks heated as she relived the saltwater kiss.

Jerked out of her peaceful state by a low rumbling sound, she crouched, holding the knife outward in her fisted hand. Her body froze, in tune with every movement and sound around her. As she scanned the clearing, she inched her hand around to release a blade disc from its holster, then grasped it, too, at the ready. Her lips formed a thin line, eyes wide as she turned in a slow circle.

Her watch amped up its illumination another notch, casting its purple glow on the skin of her forearm, which was covered in tiny goosebumps, highlighting each delicate hair as it stood on end. She almost wished her timepiece would begin vibrating to indicate the hunters were near. Her muscles ached for a fight. Instead it remained still and silent, its fierce violet glow the only indication that this watch was different from any other. Well, along with the fact that it would remain a permanent part of her until her nineteenth birthday...

She inched farther into the clearing, and her body froze.

There!

Across the field, on the far side, she spied just the slightest hint of movement. The growling grew louder, as once again she found herself at a stand-off with the wolf-like creature from the other day. She'd almost missed it, so completely did the beast blend with the shadows of the forest. The pup behind its mother once again; it hunched its back in a feral warning not to come closer.

Alyx had to respect the ferocity with which the animal protected its offspring. She relaxed her pose degree by degree, held up her hands and moved backward, retreating into the protective cover of the trees.

"Lady, I don't want to hurt you, or your baby." She took another step back. "But I will if I have to."

The rumble grew less intense with every step that increased the distance between them.

Too bad I don't have a pocket of jerky.

She continued to observe from across the field. The mother suddenly lost interest in her and whipped its body around so her back was to Alyx, tail held straight and stiff. A ululating howl released from deep within its chest, sending a chill through Alyx's body, despite the heat.

Turning toward the pup, it nudged and yapped, pushing it toward the spot where Alyx stood hidden in the dark patches between the trees, then turned to face a new enemy.

A pack of beasts—she silently counted six of them—slowly approached, the sounds of their feral growling drowning out her own. The mother snapped and snarled, jumping forward and back as if on a spring, and once more turned to her pup to give it another brutal nudge.

Alyx studied the new arrivals from the shadows. Though they appeared to be the same breed of animal, they stood taller than the mother, her head reaching only to their chest. What she lacked in size, she made up in ferocity. Her teeth bared, she blocked every attempt from one of the others to move in the direction of her pup.

Running back and forth in front of them faster than seemed possible, she was a blur in shades of gray. The six were different colors, too. The fur a combination of deep chocolates, whites, and blacks speckled with lighter patches of copper. Except for one. It alone was midnight black, with a jagged beige stripe running along one side.

The pack was closing in on her. The pup, unsure what to do, crouched and trembled, looking from its mother to Alyx. It began body crawling away from the scene, slowly closing the distance between itself and Alyx with each movement forward. The small creature kept stopping to look back over its shoulder, as if undecided whether it should try to help its mother, or flee. The tiny whimper was drowned out by the baying of the pack. Tremors shook its entire body, and Alyx crouched down, arms held out.

"Come on. I've got you."

In two giant leaps it entered the cover of the trees as it ran past, ignoring her outstretched arms, to disappear further into the thickly wooded forest. She turned to watch it disappear in the direction of their temporary camp.

Wish I had a cell phone so I could give Chase a heads-up.

She sighed, turning to focus on the struggle on the far side of the field. She looked through squinted eyes.

I should leave, now.

But her body made a different choice. She stood, taking a step into the clearing toward the battle.

CHAPTER 5
CHASE

Chase jerked around, scalp tingling. He scanned the area, easing to his feet. His eyes narrowed on the mysterious berry tree.

There! About five feet up.

Was that a hint of movement behind it? As if something—or someone—was hiding there. Standing upright.

He inched toward his backpack without taking his eyes off that spot and snatched the bag before backing up against the ancient hemlock tree where he'd made camp. The rough bark scratched the skin on his back through the thin fabric of his cotton t-shirt. He ignored the discomfort and pressed his body closer still. With a slow tug on the bag's zipper, he groped inside, smiling when his hand grasped the cold metal of his old familiar .45 handgun. Thumbing the safety off, he held it pointed toward the treetops, continuing his scan. The weight of the barrel in his hand and the coolness against his skin eased the stiffness in his neck, providing an immediate confidence boost. His keeper's heart beat a steady rhythm, despite the stress of the unknown; likewise his breathing remained calm and steady. Being a keeper did have some advantages.

His back straightened when there was a rustling in the bushes, the jagged tree trunk digging deeper into his skin. He slowly aimed the weapon toward the suspected interloper's hiding place.

Chill, man. It's probably just Alyx.

Still, he remained poised and ready for action, eyes on the almost-translucent tree. Depending on the angle of his vantage point, it shimmered in the sunlight like a mirage.

Weird.

His head jerked to the side when the absolute silence was shattered by a sudden, piercing howl off in the distance. The creature from the other day? He frowned. It sounded like more than one.

"Alyx!" he called, pushing off from the tree to head in the direction he thought the noise originated. "Alyx!"

Two things happened simultaneously. Something ran from behind the berry tree heading the opposite direction, and something else approached, crouched low to the ground, toward him from the other side. The thing running toward him posed the biggest threat, so he turned in that direction, grudgingly losing sight of the other.

He recognized the wolf-like pup almost immediately. As he studied the animal, his head tilted. What strange front legs the little guy had. Something was—off. There were little bumps—one on each side—along his sides at his front hip joints. Strange. He couldn't quite put his finger on what it was ...

Taking one step in the direction of the tree, he shook his head, thumbed the .45's saftey on, and shoved the handgun into the waistband of his jeans. With one more longing look in the direction the other ... person? ... had disappeared, he turned back toward the animal running toward him. His knees popped as he squatted. After a quick scan, he saw that the pup was alone. The animal was running, body low and tail tucked under.

"It's okay, little guy. I'm not gonna hurt you," he crooned.

The pup raced past him and straight into the hole he'd dug.

Chase inched closer to peer inside. The puppy was curled up, trembling and whimpering, and he reached a hand toward it intending to soothe. It snarled and snapped at his fingers, and he pulled back quickly.

He sat on his haunches and sighed. "Hey, hey, just trying to help. You've got sharp teeth, you know. What a scary beast you are. She taught you well, your mom did. Okay. You stay here, I'll see if I can find her. And Alyx." He frowned and looked back over his shoulder in the direction of whatever it was that had run from behind the tree as soon as he'd been distracted.

Laying a branch loosely across the hole for cover, he strode away, following the marks Alyx had made with her switchblade. The growling and snarling grew louder with each step and he broke into a jog, moving as fast as possible while ducking branches and potholes along the way. He tore through the tree-line and into the clearing, body filled with the endless and empowering energy the watch provided. *Wish I had this ability on the football field in school...*

Despite the surge, he froze. A pack of three ... wolves? ... were circling a tree. These animals were more similar in size to true wolves than the mother and pup they'd encountered, but the wide, blocky snout still hinted at a mix of some kind.

His head jerked up at a shout from across the open space. "Chase! Go back. There are still three of them."

"Alyx? Where are you?"

"Up here. We took out three of them, but I have no weapons left. My backpack's at camp."

His eyes tracked across the clearing and upward, and he saw her wedged between branches, the wolf-beasts snapping and jumping at the base of the tree. Pacing a circle around the perimeter. He squinted. Was that something in her arms?

"We?" he asked before jerking his head back to the pack.

The coal-black creature with a slash of beige on its side turned its golden eyes in Chase's direction. The obvious leader.

"Great." He took an involuntary step backward, his shoulders rising and falling on a deep breath. "I'll distract them, you climb down," he called.

With one more deep breath he crouched and began sprinting the perimeter of the clearing.

"Hey! Come get me! Over here!" he yelled over his shoulder.

The alpha broke away from his remaining pack and began stalking him. Not running, just purposefully following, the yellow glow of its eyes intent on this new prey. At its one bark another followed, this one a brindle, heading straight toward Chase. The second one glanced at its leader as if awaiting his instructions.

The third, white and oatmeal-colored fur standing on end, remained at the base of the tree, preventing Alyx's escape.

Chase ran, eyes darting up and down, down and up. Down at the roots that snaked up through the ground. Up tracking both 'wolf-beasts' as they slinked after him, breaking off in two directions. Working together as a unit. It was only a matter of time, he knew. But he had to keep them distracted. For Alyx.

If only she could get free, they could work together just as their enemy was united against them. But a quick glance told him all he needed to know. The white was sitting, head tilted back as it guarded Alyx like a sentinel.

"Watch the black one. He's the leader." Alyx's voice traveled across the clearing breaking through the rhythmic sound of his pounding feet. *Thump-thump-thump-thump.*

Chase didn't answer, lost in this game of cat and mouse.

I have a newfound respect for mice...

His eyes found the brindle and he scanned, searching for the black.

Where are you...?

A tingle traveled from the base of his skull to his spine. He halted, spinning in a circle.

He called to Alyx, "Do you see the black one?"

"No..."

The brindle continued its advance, closing in on him one step at a time. Its lips curved up in a snarl baring its teeth, the four dagger-like canines standing out amongst the others.

Crap.

"Okay. I'll..."

"Don't! Don't say what your plan is. I think they ... understand us."

"What ...? That's ridiculous."

Chase turned to face-down the approaching creature. "Keep an eye out for the black one. I'm gonna take care of this guy. Even out our odds."

"Chase, I told you not to ..."

The brindle stopped, tilting its head, and reversed. Eyes never leaving his, he backed up putting more distance between them.

"Okay, maybe you're right."

Chase began slowly circling around, and the animal continually turned its body so it was always facing him, anticipating his every move. He raised his gun, aiming it at the brindle's chest.

"Chase, look out!"

He spun around in time to see the black alpha emerging from the bushes behind him. He waved the weapon back and forth between the two beasts.

The two began to slink forward as one, closing the distance between them, Chase in the middle.

"The pup's at camp. If I don't make it, take care of it."

Both beasts halted, heads whipping to look at each other. The black gave one quick bark, and the brindle turned toward the trees.

A high-pitched primal moaning erupted from the tree Alyx was hiding in.

"No!" she screamed.

In a blur of motion, something hurled itself out of the tree toward the wolf guarding Alyx.

The mother.

"Alyx?"

"Don't hurt her!" In the next second, everything changed. He saw Alyx launch herself out of the tree, landing directly on the white wolf-beast's back. At the same tick of the clock, the black alpha took off and lunged at Chase. He raised his weapon and got off one shot before the beast landed on top of him, knocking the air out of his chest, the gun sailing through he air. The claws sank into his skin and a burning fire erupted in his shoulder, as if some kind of poison had been injected into him.

The searing pain set his body on fire, but he pushed it back. He kicked his feet into the animal's gut, causing it to lose its balance and they fell in an awkward spiral. Paws and legs entwined in a roll across the turf like an alligator in a death spin.

CHAPTER 6
ALYX

Alyx wrapped her arms and legs around the creature in a vise-grip, feeling the raw strength in its muscles bunched under her arms. Its powerful body vibrated as it bucked, head twisting around desperately first one way then another searching for soft flesh to sink its teeth into. She clasped her hands and hooked her ankles, squeezing her thighs tight in her quest to hold on. Barely.

Her ally—the mother—advanced and retreated, nipping and snarling.

She twisted her head when her ears picked up the sounds of snarling from across the field. A gunshot reverberated throughout her core.

Chase? I can't see...

The distraction was all it took. Her sweaty fingers started to slip apart. Though she grasped them more firmly together, she could feel them starting to slip again almost immediately.

No! Need a plan. Think!

Her eyes landed on a large fallen branch at the base of the tree, and she let go, bracing for the impact of her body with the ground. She squeezed her eyes shut for just an instant, falling with a *thud*.

"Oomph!" She immediately rolled to the side and made a grab for the stick. Using her foot, she broke it in half creating a jagged point at the end of it, and turned to face her attacker.

The mother had other ideas. Taking advantage of Alyx's diversion it lunged forward, its pointed teeth sinking deep into the white's throat, drawing blood. Holding on, it shook its head back and forth in a death shake.

Alyx froze. The whimper gurgled from the beast's shredded throat, but it managed to shake off the mother and back away, blood oozing from its wound, crimson contrasting against the pure whiteness of its fur.

Wielding the tree branch like a weapon, Alyx held her ground.

With one more sideways look, the creature turned and slinked away into the shadows of the forest.

Alyx looked toward the mother. She, too, was bleeding, but seemed to be holding her own. She quickly found and retrieved one blade disc and the switchblade, feeling infinitely more confident having them in her possession once again—though she would have preferred the inferno ray.

"We make a good team," Alyx said, reaching a hand toward the animal. It retreated. "I see, we're only allies in battle."

The wolves were gone. Or at least out of sight. Her eyes were drawn to an unmoving heap where the battle had been.

Her breath shuddered and she broke into a run, her scream echoing across the open space. Chase was lying immobile in the clearing.

She dropped to her hands and knees by his side, hands shaking as she reached toward him. The blood smeared across his face and covering his t-shirt broke through her reality all at once, and a desperate, incoherent cry similar to the wolves' escaped her own lips as her breath stuck in her throat.

No!

"Chase? Chase!" She searched his body for the worst of the injuries. "What can I do? Chase? I need your help. We have to move." She jumped to her feet, positioning herself behind his head. She grasped his underarms, using her weight as leverage until her biceps shook, and he moved barely inches.

I'll never be able to get him all the way to camp this way.

Her eyes scanned the clearing. No sign of the wolf-creatures. Or the mother. So much for working as a team.

"It's gonna be okay. I promise."

She bent over him, placing her lips on his forehead, lingering a moment longer than necessary. With one deep breath, she lurched to her feet and started running.

CHAPTER 7
CHASE

Deep within his mind, Chase was fully conscious. Outwardly, he struggled to move—caught somewhere between sleeping and awake. He lay immobile, even as his mind zigged and zagged in ten directions at once. Deep inside him lived electric energy with no outlet. Her voice reached him as if through a receding tunnel.

When he heard it, he focused all his energy on moving his tongue, forming just a single word with his lips. His vocal cords remained still, though his mind screamed out.

Alyx.

He willed his eyelids to open. Concentrated so fiercely on moving even one muscle in his finger that a roaring white-static noise seared through his skull, and he retreated.

Nothing. Neither pain nor discomfort reached him. He was insensate, paralyzed. Even as he fought it, something deep inside him knew it was to no avail.

I feel like I've been drugged. The wolf-beast?

He heard Alyx, but was powerless to respond in even the slightest way.

Don't go, his inner-self screamed. But again ... nothing. Stillness. Silence.

A different scene played out in his mind than the one before him. Like a theater production.

The black wolf defeated, lying at his feet. Chase running to Alyx. Dispatching the white wolf that attacked her. Pulling her into his arms. A kiss. He could feel her lips moving under his, hear the little catch in her breath as it deepened, smell her familiar woodsy scent. The taste of her filled his mouth. His hands tightened around her just a fraction as she tilted her head to get closer still...

It all seemed so real—a movie with him playing the lead role. An alarm bell broke through the perfect moment, and the mirage dissipated like smoke on the wind. A fictional picture created in his mind alone, conjured for only him to see. The line between reality and fantasy remained blurred, and he sank back into darkness.

Waiting. Wondering. Doubts trickled into his subconscious.

Is it all a dream? Every bit of it?

Being a keeper.

The watch.

Uncle Charlie's death.

Is Alyx even real? Or just a figment of my overactive imagination?

From deep within him, another scene played out. So real and true he couldn't tell where reality stopped and fantasy began. This one was achingly familiar. An internal battle raged. Which was truth? He latched on with his whole being.

Chase bounded up the porch steps and entered the house, tossing his backpack on the recliner, toe-ing off his shoes in the middle of the floor.

"I'm home!" he called.

Uncle Charlie replied from the kitchen, "Don't leave your shoes in the middle of the floor. What time's the game tonight?" He was wearing his favorite Dune Harbor Sharks jersey, the royal blue and black colors emphasizing the paleness of his skin. Though they lived at the beach, he faithfully slathered on SPF 50 sunscreen, giving him the appearance of a tourist despite growing up in this very house.

Chase sauntered into the room, reaching for a banana. Between bites, he answered, "Seven. I'm gonna catch a shower and head out. I'm stopping by Mason's on the way."

"I'll come with you. I'm going with Jean and David, anyway. You have time to eat before you go. I made lasagne." Now that his uncle was retired, he poured over cookbooks and online recipes, filling his time with cooking. A hobby that Chase supported wholeheartedly.

"Always time for lasagne." He reached for another banana.

"Hey! Leave some of those for me! I claim one for my breakfast cereal tomorrow morning. Do I have to write my name on it? Jeez, can't keep enough food in this house," he grumbled. The twinkle in his eye contradicted his words. "Gonna have to start hiding the food..."

This was a replay of a familiar conversation between the two.

"It's football. Makes me hungry."

"Ha! What about when it's not football season?"

Chase winked, a grin spreading across his face. "Hey, you raised me. Must be your fault."

"My fault? Ha!" His laugh broke free, filling every corner of the small room. He continued preparing the garlic bread, laying slices of thick bread side by side on the cookie sheet. He slid the bread into the oven and turned, looking over the rim of his bifocals. "So, the game. Will there be scouts there tonight?"

"Probably. Next week's the big game, but coach said they could stop by any game now."

"You got this, Chase. I'm so proud of you. You're gonna get a free ride at the school

of your choosing. Mark my words. We'll finally have a professional football player in the family. I can't wait to see it!"

"Maybe." Chase stared out the window with un-seeing eyes. He pushed himself off the wall and turned away.

"Oh, remember it's trash day. Mrs. Ruiz says she needs help putting her old sofa out at the curb. Can you stop over there before we go?"

"Can't I do it tomorrow?"

"Nope. It's early pick-up. Needs to be out tonight. It's good to help others, Chase. She needs us now that Mr. Ruiz is gone. Remember that. Someday it might be you who needs the help."

"Fine. I'll do it before my shower."

After devouring the second banana, he pushed out the front door.

• • •

If they hadn't been frozen by some unseen force, his nostrils would surely have flared at the strong scent of ripe banana. This memory, if that's what it was, felt so true and right, like a key finding the right keyhole after being lost under a floorboard for a decade. *This* is reality. The memory of the watch, even now casting its pale blue light on his unmoving forearm and still hand, was fading minute by minute. In this reality, it didn't exist. Had never existed. Breath escaped his lips at a steady pace, and he retreated even further into his subconscious mind.

• • •

Chase squinted at the bright lights illuminating the football field, the rectangular school-building a dark shadow off in the distance. A soft breeze ruffled the blonde curls at the back of his neck as he rubbed his hands together, class ring turning toward his palm. Sighing, he twisted it back around and shoved his hands into the hand warmer he wore around his waist. The crisp air hinted that colder days were coming. Dull-gray bleachers were already filling with early arrivals hoping to claim the best seats. His uncle and the Moores among them. Dropping to knock out his pre-game push-ups, the burning in his muscles as he pumped up and down did nothing to expend his excess energy, nor to calm the pounding in his temples. Blades of grass tickled his nose on each drop-down, but he was oblivious.

He was triggered. Why did people think they could push Mason around? For that matter, why did Mason allow it? Over the years of their friendship, Chase had come to his best friend's defense so many times he'd lost count. Mason didn't bother anyone. But his shy demeanor and chubby build attracted bullies. He'd thought he put an end to all that years ago ... but apparently when Chase wasn't around to defend him, they still preyed on him.

I wish Mason had told me about this. If I hadn't seen it for myself, I never would have known it was still happening. I'll fix it. I just have to make it more clear that if anyone bothers Mason, they'll have to answer to me. What made it worse, in his mind, was that some of his teammates were involved. And the nasty things they'd done...

He gritted his teeth just thinking about it. His fist itched to punch the smirk off Jared's face...

"Chase."

His arms pumped harder. Up and down, up and down. Sweat trickled off his brow, disappearing into the turf below.

"Chase."

The quarterback, his friend Carl, slapped him on the back. "Save some for the game. Coach says the scout from Penn State is here. Let's show 'em what a great combo we make."

Chase pushed off, falling backward into a sitting position, hands draped on his bent knees.

"Yeah. Yeah, let's show them."

"You okay, man? This is probably the most important game of the year. I need your head in it tonight."

"Yeah. I'm good."

"Good." Carl pounded the pads on his back. "Sharks, baby!"

"Sharks." He pushed himself up, squinting into the stands again. As long as Mason sat with his parents, he should be okay.

Better be. Mason was one of the nicest and most genuine people he knew. If only other people could see that, too. I'll take care of it. It'll never happen again, if I can help it.

Still, throughout the game, his eyes kept cutting to the stand, keeping watch.

Right up until he dropped the ball that could have won the game. He'd been wide open. There was no excuse for not catching that perfect pass. That one play had probably ruined any chance he had at the scholarship his uncle wanted for him so badly.

If he was honest, he hadn't been entirely present through the whole game, and it showed in his lackluster performance tonight. And if he was really honest, he didn't even know if football was what he wanted for the rest of his life, anyway.

He'd have a talk with Uncle Charlie after his eighteenth birthday in June. He was thinking maybe he'd try his hand at deep-sea fishing for a living. Save up for his own fishing boat, and eventually have his own business. Stay near the beach.

It could work. He just had to convince his uncle.

Right now, I have to check in with Mason, and make sure he's alright.

As if from a long distance, the sounds of howling broke through his memories, bringing him back to the present. The scene fell away, leaving only blackness. He still couldn't move, but his ears picked up the sounds of approaching footsteps. He heard huffing and shuffling as they approached, but still could not will his eyelids open.

I can't see!

What's happening?

Something wrapped around his torso like a vise, and a sensation of floating engulfed him. Another scene began to play in his mind.

His body gently rocking on the waves, bobbing up and down with the current. Chase tilted his head back and let the sun warm his face.

I could stay here, floating, drifting, forever...

CHAPTER 8
ALYX

Alyx shielded her face from tree branches, oblivious to the checkerboard of angry scratches that crisscrossed the underside of her forearm. Flying through the woods toward camp, her legs pumped at a steady pace. There had been so much blood. Soaking through his shirt, slashing across his face, shoulder and arm.

He's hurt. He needs me. Don't think about that. Just focus on getting the backpack. One thing at a time.

Her family, the Eris family, would disagree. They always had two plans mapped out and a third in the works. It had served them well over the years, but she couldn't think of anything except this moment.

Get help to Chase. Priority one.

She couldn't think beyond that.

Buzz-zzz-zzz. Buzz-zzz-zzz.

Her eyes flew to her watch, the feel of its vibrations against her wrist tickled her skin—which could only mean one thing.

The hunters were near.

Her timepiece had the ability to signal when the hunters were nearby. Unfortunately, the hunters could also track the watches using a golden chrysoberyl crystal they wore around their necks. Most likely how they'd found her lost in the woods. The same enchanted crystal also made it possible for them to send one-way messages to their other-selves—though their communication was limited to those in the next consecutive dimension.

Her feet slammed to a halt and she braced herself on a tree trunk, the jagged bark digging into the smooth skin on her palm. Violet eyes searched the area around her with such intensity they seemed to glow. She held the blade disc in one hand and the switchblade in the other.

Nothing.

Buzz-zzz-zzz. Buzz-zzz-zzz.

Her body jerked at a rustling in the bushes, eyes sharp and alert. She could not locate the source of the sound. Tilting her head, she stood listening. Still nothing.

Neither the wind whistling through the leaves, nor a bird deep in song reached her ears. Only silence. A silence so eerie a chill raced up her spine despite the heat of the day.

Strange.

Even the air around her seemed to go stagnant, as if there was a shift in the very atmosphere surrounding her. Her nose crinkled as it detected a slight electrical scent.

Looking back over her shoulder in the direction she'd left Chase, she took a deep breath.

Go back? Or continue toward camp for the backpack and first-aid kit?

Hesitating just a second more, she took another slow sweep of the area around her before retracing her steps. The two hunters—a man and a woman—could be closing in on her right now. She broke into a jog and headed back toward Chase. Her footsteps crashed through the foliage, reverberating off the static trees and back to her ears in the muted woods.

If the two hunters from this dimension are near, they pose a bigger threat. I have to get to Chase before they do. Unless they've already found him...

She reached the perimeter of the clearing and skidded to a stop. Her mouth formed an 'O' and she took one involuntary step backward, sliding behind the trunk of a tree to observe unnoticed.

What is this place?
What the...?

CHAPTER 9
CHASE

Floating. Drifting. Bobbing peacefully up and down on the waves. Body weightless, arms spread, head back.

Ahh. Home. My happy place.

He swirled his hands in a lazy figure-8 pattern under the surface, the crisp saltwater swirling between his fingers tickling the tender skin, and the sigh traveled the length of him. Such a serene place, the sea.

I wish...

The pressure around his mid-section grew in intensity. A vise-grip crushing his very center, jarring him from his reverie. He gasped as his beloved ocean was ripped away into a charcoal gray void, and all he could do now was feel the intense emptiness and pressure surrounding him.

No!

Sharp daggers dug into his sides, back, and gut, and if Chase had regained even a tiny semblance of control over his own body, he surely would have fought whatever detained him with every ounce of strength he possessed.

He remained immobile. His eyes refused to open, and his limbs hung limply at his sides, swaying willy-nilly back and forth in whichever direction the velocity and wind agreed upon. Bile burned his throat as his body floated along, carried by whatever had him in its grip. His only bodily movement was the involuntary and instinctual act of his lungs expanding and expelling air, his chest rising and falling with each slow shallow breath. He was unable to even budge the muscles in his throat to swallow down the bitter taste.

If I puke now, I'll drown in my own vomit. What a way to go.

This must be hell.

To be aware but unable to change the situation in the least. At the complete mercy of whomever—or whatever—had him in its clutches. Helpless.

Hell.

His mind began to deny the situation, to look for solace from within once again. To shut out the torture and impotence that cloaked him.

Just as the blackness began to close in, he was jerked back by the sound of a scream.

I know that voice. Why is she screaming?

And then, a rubbing wetness on his forehead, cheeks, neck, wounded shoulder.

The ocean? Have the waves come to claim me?

No. This was not the total submersion into a large body of water, but instead the sensation of something wet rubbing against him. Lapping at him.

The rough, sandpaper feel of … moisture.

In a burst of white light, Chase regained control of his arms and legs, trying to sit up only to realize he was airborne. It was not a gradual process, but instantaneous. One second he was immobile, completely at the mercy of those around him. The next, all of his bodily functions returned in a flash of lightning that streaked across the sky. Vertigo erupted in his head.

His eyes opened, light exploding in his brain, and his sharp intake of breath was followed by his hands desperately searching for purchase on whatever had him in its clutches.

Feet.

No, not feet. Claws.

Claws?

It, for lack of a better description, looked down its narrow snout from above him, face framed by velvety russet fur ruffling in the wind, copper eyes clashing with blue. An eternity passed, staring, searching. As if the thing were coming to an important decision. Its triangular ears which sat at ten and two o'clock on its head twitched, and it looked away, dismissing him.

A … fox? I must be hallucinating. This can't be real.

When eye contact was broken, Chase clutched at the feathery legs that carried him, his own limbs flailing in mid-air. His eyes traveled the length of this thing's body, and widened when they took in the multi-colored hazel feathers on its wings.

The creature was flying. Holding him in its … talons?

Why does this beast have talons? Its head looks like a fox, but it has talons? And wings? What the … ?

As they gained altitude, his eyes made the inevitable downward trek.

A shout tore from his very core, mixing with Alyx's scream far below him. His fingers tightened around the thick feathered legs that held the power of life or death.

His life or death.

Oh, man. I'm dead for sure.

CHAPTER 10
ALYX

The scream ripped through her throat, and she charged the clearing on a battle-cry. Two unfamiliar wolf-creatures sat on their haunches, noses pointed toward the sky, for the moment completely focused on the air directly over them, paying no attention to her, despite being mere meters away. Both animals visibly flinched, shoulders trembling as a high-pitched howl trumpeted from the thing directly over them. Lowering their bodies to the ground, they rolled onto their backs with feet complaisantly in the air in a sudden show of submission. Their small whimpers filled the air, eyes never leaving the creature hovering above, bursts of tremors racking their bodies.

Her eyes tracked theirs, and she tilted her head. Another sound escaped her, this one filled with despair.

The beast had Chase's limp body in its clutches, and it flew above them gaining altitude with each passing second.

I'm too late!

As this flying monster gained altitude, her horrified eyes widened when Chase awoke and began struggling with his captor. The thing holding him weaved sideways, thrown off-balance by his struggling, before regaining control. Alyx gasped and fell to her knees, her hand fluttering to her cheek, allowing herself only a moment of despair.

"Chase!" She lurched back up, for once unsure what to do. Glancing down at the knife and blade disc she clutched in each hand. Both insignificant pieces of metal, of no help to her now.

The creature began rising into the clouds, size shrinking with each flap of wings, carrying Chase with it.

"Chase!"

She thought she heard him yell, though it was hard to differentiate between his voice and the pounding in her own skull.

She didn't know how long she stood, head tilted backward. Time returned by slow degrees, and when she finally lowered her eyes, she wished she hadn't. Her eyes narrowed and she squatted into a fighter's stance as the wolves, no longer submissive, methodically circled her. She was trapped.

Her body sprang into action without hesitation. She ran toward one, her keeper's body filled with a surge of unnatural energy, she weaved to the side just as it lunged toward her, teeth bared. On a snarl, it whipped its body around, but she was already halfway across the clearing, though the second beast was close on her heels.

Can't keep evading forever.

She turned and changed her course, now heading directly toward the first wolf.

It crouched, stalking toward her, and still she ran, releasing a blade disc as she jumped sideways yet again. The weapon whizzed past the creature, missing it by centimeters, instead slicing into grass and stopping half-buried in the dirt.

The animal immediately went on the offensive, charging toward her. She ran and pushed off with her feet, leaping over the beast with a mid-air flip. She barely noticed the pain in her upper arm until she landed unevenly on her feet and rolled sideways onto the fresh wound.

"First blood. Score one for you."

I need that blade disc.

Eyes scanning the area, she saw the glint in the grass. Leaping up, she ran back toward it, only to be blocked by the other wolf-creature beside her. She held the switch blade out in front of her, and tilted her head, taking two deep breaths, then charging again, scowling at the thought of the more effective weapons she'd left back at camp.

The two now had her trapped between them once again.

"Is that all you got? Come on." She took a step backward, bracing for the dual attack. Her eyes flew to her left, and she gasped. "Look over there!"

Both wolves' heads whipped in the direction she'd pointed, and she moved quickly, putting distance between her and the animals.

"Ha! Not so smart. Can't believe you fell for that one."

She ran straight for the blade disc, plucking it out of the ground without stopping, turned and released.

The yelp made her flinch as the closest wolf fell in the grass whimpering. The other froze in its tracks, looking between her and its mate. Its lips lifted baring its yellow teeth, thick saliva hanging from its jowl. It began stalking toward her, death in its eyes.

Alyx took a backward step. She glanced again at her knife.

Run or fight?

She took a deep breath and rounded her shoulders.

"Come on. Let's do this."

Buzz-zz-zz.

Her eyes flew to her watch, the purple glow on the petite, metallic, octagonal watch face amping up as it furiously vibrated on her wrist. She took a backward step as the hunter stepped out of the trees into the clearing.

CHAPTER II
CHASE

The treetops were pinpoints in an emerald sea below him, and Chase couldn't stop his eyes from looking down. Clouds fogged his vision, and as he tightened his death-grip on the strange creature that held him, his body began to relax. He didn't know why, but a sudden feeling of acceptance took hold of him, and he began to take in the sights around him.

Off to the left, the terrain became flat and the dense trees disappeared, and he could just make out the rolling sea.

So, we are near Dune Harbor. Probably.

Along with that realization, his body lost the last thread of tension, and a feeling of hope returned for the first time since they'd jumped. His consciousness gave him a poke.

Ha! You're still flying hundreds of feet in the air, carried by some mysterious wild animal that most likely wants to feed you to its family! What's there to be hopeful about?

Still, as his eyes traveled the land below from this bird's eye view, he felt at peace.

But you're separated from Alyx again, you moron!

The contradictory feeling of contentment remained, pushing aside all fear.

And then he saw it. Jutting up above a bustling coastal town with streets running parallel to the beach, it overshadowed everything around it.

The structure stood above the neighboring buildings. *A ... castle?* It was a large, square building, his first impression that of an ancient castle, and in fact did have the rough shape of a stone keep. With an intriguing blend of past and present, four low horizontal walls formed a square with the middle opening into a courtyard with a circular pit in the center, and at the corners four stone sky-scraper 'towers' rising toward the sky, surrounded by opalescent cone-shaped glass enclosing each turret.

This towering building had a unique feel, and though similar to castles he had learned about in its initial appearance, was still unlike any Chase had ever seen before.

The entire structure seemed to shimmer in and out of existence. Much the same quality as the berry-tree back in the forest, the sheer iridescence caused Chase to doubt what was right in front of him. Or more accurately, below.

Chase would have rubbed his eyes, but he didn't want to loosen his hold. Instead, he blinked repeatedly against the biting air, and just as the building came into clear focus, the fox-bird veered the other way and his view was lost.

"Wait! What is that place?" he called to his captor.

It tilted its head, its copper eyes blinked once, and then looked back toward the sky dismissing him.

"Where are you taking me?"

The animal threw back its head, muzzle forming an O-shape. Its howl filled the sky as they veered away from the mysterious disappearing 'castle'. Wind unevenly parting his hair, Chase craned his neck to get one last look, and in its place was now a rectangular brick structure, standing the same height as the surrounding buildings with square windows evenly spaced along the sides. No sparkly castle-building. Gone were the turrets, mystical glass, and courtyard.

A hallucination? Like the dreams before he'd regained his mobility?

His eyes scanned the town as it shrank smaller and smaller with every flap of the powerful wings that carried him. They began a slow decline toward another forest. Or was it the same one?

He shook his head.

Guess I'm about to find out.

CHAPTER 12
ALYX

"You," Alyx hissed through her teeth, changing direction and veering toward Ursa—one of two hunters set on bringing about the destruction of the watches, along with their keepers. In a second's time, Alyx saw this hunter as she'd been in previous worlds—as the other-selves of the woman standing in front of her now. One thing remained constant world-to-world: The hunters wanted the remaining keepers dead. On their last jump, this woman had succeeded in killing Alyx and had stolen her watch—along with her arm—and drank her blood in order to try to use it for dimension travel. Ursa had found out quickly enough that the watches do not work that way. If it had not been for Chase turning back time in D-7 and saving her before that happened ...

Her dark thoughts were interrupted by Ursa's words. Alyx glared in the older woman's direction.

"I do not wish to fight." The hunter held up both hands in surrender.

"Too bad. Because I do." Alyx would soon be on her. The smooth handle of the knife in her palm gave her the confidence she needed. Her eyes burned with hatred as her mind continued to replay the multitude of laws this woman had broken in prior dimensions.

I'm coming for you.

Ursa took a step backward, rounded her shoulders and crouched. "Have it your way. Just remember, I didn't want this."

"Whatever." Alyx threw her arm back as she lunged at the other woman, whose legs gave out from the impact. Both women fell to the ground in a heap, Ursa's fingernails digging into the tender inner skin on the bicep of the arm that held the knife. Alyx ignored the pain, intent on two things. Protecting her watch, and staying alive. And if that meant killing the hunter, then so be it.

They rolled and grappled over rocks and grass, the only sound that of their grunts in the otherwise silent forest. Alyx found herself underneath the hunter, pinned down. When Ursa shifted, she took advantage, bringing up her knee into the other woman's gut with all her strength.

The hunter gasped as the breath was knocked from her, falling to her side and clutching her stomach.

Alyx took the opportunity to jump to her feet, reclaiming the upper-hand. "Where's Pavo? Don't you two usually stick together?"

Ursa followed suit, one arm held protectively in front of her. "Stop this. I want to *help* you," she panted. "And, I'm alone. I've been living in these woods by myself for a long time now."

"I don't think so."

"It's true."

"Liar." Alyx circled the other woman.

Ursa shook her head, her shoulder-length, raven hair swinging. "You don't know me. Not really. You know only shadows of me. My other selves. But that's not me here."

Alyx glowered into the face of a woman who looked to be in her mid-to-late-twenties, when in reality she was much, *much* older. "Sure. And I'm a fairy princess."

Ursa sighed. "You're not safe here, just follow me and ..."

"And you'll lead me right to Pavo, into a trap? I don't think so." Alyx lunged.

Ursa feinted to the left, and Alyx breezed past. Turning, she again charged toward her rival. And missed. The woman was quick on her feet.

I need a game-plan. She's an equal match for me, so it needs to be a surprise ...

Just then a desperate howl broke the silence. Alyx shivered in the heat.

Alyx had just enough time to register the look of panic in her opponent's eyes before the other woman took off into the woods.

No choice but to follow.

CHAPTER 13
CHASE

The landing was anything but gentle. His heart maintained a steady rhythm due to his keeper's status, but that was the only reason it wasn't bursting out of his chest. Chase landed with a thud when, his breath stolen by the impact, the creature dropped his human cargo five feet from the ground and touched-down smoothly beside him, wings automatically folding under to disappear completely from view. If he hadn't seen this creature flying, he'd never know there were wings, so completely were they hidden.

Pushing up on shaky arms, he scanned the area.

More trees.

I'm really getting sick of seeing shades of green. Why couldn't he drop me on the beach?

Shaking his head, he continued his surveillance.

Where's Alyx? Are we destined to be apart when we jump?

He sighed as he pushed shakily to his feet.

Well, we found each other last time. We'll do it again here.

Turning full-circle, he froze to study the creature that had brought him here. Strange didn't even begin to cover it. Here on the ground, he was able to look at the thing's entire body. He took an involuntary step backward, barely noticing when his backward progress was stopped by a tree. His eyes traveled the length of this animal's body. During flight, he'd already seen the fox-like copper head and bird-like front legs that had carried him. But now, his eyes widened at the full-picture before him. Its broad chest was auburn in color, and the muscles underneath the short hair bunched when the creature moved. Its raw strength was evident in every breath it took. This was not an animal to mess with. Though so far it had been gentle with him, he was aware that the situation could change at any moment. He knew nothing about this thing. All he did know was that it had separated him from Alyx, and he had no idea why.

Chase steadied himself on the tree, looking straight into the thing's eyes which were level with his own. It cocked its head, triangular ears pointing up, fox-like copper eyes boring into his own, allowing this scrutiny. Waiting almost patiently.

His eyes moved down its neck, and the longer copper fur bled into short-haired amber, then changed yet again to a tawny shade further down its back. Its tail was relaxed and bushy. The fur had barely noticeable black-tinged tips—and underneath the black, gray intermixed with white.

He once again met the creature's eyes. He had no more idea the identity of this animal than before. If anything, he was more confused now.

"Um. Hello. My name is Chase." He reached out a hand, and the creature looked at it, then flicked its eyes back to his.

"What are you?" he whispered, taking one step closer.

When it remained calm, he took another step.

"Can I ... ?" Reaching a tentative hand out toward the animal, the powerful chest muscles danced under his touch, yet it allowed the contact. The fur was soft as down and smooth to the touch, tickling his palm.

"Wow. We don't have anything like you where I come from," he breathed in awe. "At least not that I know of."

The creature bowed its head.

And then something changed.

It swung its head up as if it had heard a sound that Chase's ears could not detect, and then stomped its feet. The magnificent wings unfurled in a flash of golden feathers, and on a running jump it took off, disappearing into the trees. The howl that tore from its throat was such a high decibel that Chase slapped his hands over his ears, his body hunched over.

"You'll get used to that."

Chase whipped his body around to see someone approaching him from behind. "M-Mason?"

"How? How do you know me?" It was Mason, his best friend from high school, but it wasn't. This version of Mason was reed-thin, his posture straight. His auburn hair was held back in a stubby ponytail, ends curling.

"I ... I just do," Chase replied carefully.

"But I don't know you. Have we met before?"

He nodded. "A ... long time ago."

Mason paused for a beat, hands on his hips. "If you say so. Coming?"

"Coming? Where?" Chase asked.

Mason sighed. "Jeez. Don't you know anything?"

"I like to think I know lots of things. Just not whatever it is you want me to know."

"You're funny. Let's go." Mason turned, walking away.

"But you didn't answer my question. Where are we going? I have to find my friend ..." Chase said.

Mason called over his shoulder, "You'll see. If you don't know, then this is gonna be fun."

"What ... ?"

"Follow. Or don't. I'm going." Mason kept walking.

Chase glanced at the sky above the trees where the creature had disappeared just moments ago, then at his almost-best-friend's retreating back.

There really was no choice.

"Hey, wait up!" He jogged to catch up.

CHAPTER 14
ALYX

Alyx held her arms protectively in front of her as she ran, dodging trees, leaping over roots and rocks. She stubbed her toe, the pain traveling up her leg, and she stumbled forward. Tree branches scraped her already bruised forearms, stinging the tender flesh. The pain stoked the fire building inside her.

Ursa seemed to be heading back in the general direction of camp, which suited her just fine. There were things she needed to retrieve before she began her search for Chase.

I can't believe we're separated again. Despite all our efforts to remain together.

A branch smacked her in the face, the sting bringing angry tears to her eyes. She ripped it from the tree, the splintered wood slicing into her palm and drawing a line of blood. Her teeth clenched. Wiping her hand on her pants, she threw the stick to the ground with a curse, stomping on it with her foot.

It's not fair.

She thought about Chase's lifeless body, hanging from that creature's grasp, and the blood drained from her face.

But he woke up. I saw him. He's okay. I know he is. And I'm going to find him.

With renewed energy, she picked up her pace. Through her clumsiness she'd lost sight of Ursa but could still hear the sounds of her progress through the forest, and she knew she wasn't far behind her enemy.

Once again, a sudden feeling of stillness invaded the woods. Each step she made seemed to echo in the silence, the only sounds traveling through the trees were those created by the two women running across the rough terrain. Each breath seemed to trumpet in the total quiet that surrounded them.

A flash of light burst through the dense foliage, and Alyx lifted her arms in front of her face and squeezed her eyes shut. The glare pierced through her closed eyelids, its radiance causing her to squat in place and turn in on herself, hands held protectively over her eyes, body automatically shifting into defensive mode.

When the light faded, she slowly moved her hands away and squinted through the trees, pupils adjusting as she began moving forward almost immediately.

She approached camp and froze in place, eyes going wide.

Ursa was stooping to move a branch away from the hole Chase had dug in his quest for water. The black wolf and the brindle silently circled her on both sides, but she neither flinched nor acknowledged their presence in any way. A blur shot up out of the hole straight for Ursa, and Alyx took advantage of her distraction to attack.

From behind, the woman jerked as Alyx wound her arm around her neck in a headlock, wheezing breaths escaping as Alyx tightened her hold. Just then, her eyes looked down over the woman's shoulder to the thing she was clutching in her arms.

The wolf-pup, its tiny body trembling.

Its mother approached, eyes beseeching. It did not attack, but seemed to be trying to communicate with her once-ally that this was her offspring.

Alyx felt her grip loosen, and Ursa took the opportunity to speak in a strangled whisper. "Please. Don't hurt them. They're innocent, and he's just a baby."

"I'm not..." Alyx released her hold and took a step back. "I'm not going to hurt them. It's you I want."

"Fine. But I'm not leaving them. So if you want me, you'll just have to tag along."

"I don't ... What is going on here?"

"No time. They'll be on us in minutes." She gestured to the two wolves, pacing mere feet away.

"Why aren't they attacking us now?" Alyx wanted to know.

"I'll explain it all when we reach our destination. Come. I can't hold them long. I'm out of practice. And I can't do it again. That was the last time I'll tap into the power."

"Hold them? Power? What do you mean?"

"You'll see," she replied as she began walking.

Eyes ever watchful, Alyx retrieved both her own and Chase's backpacks, and followed.

CHAPTER 15
CHASE

Chase walked behind this dimension's version of his best friend. *This* Mason seemed ... different. Not just his appearance, no, but something else as well.

They continued walking through the woods, single-file.

At least I know I can trust someone here besides Alyx. Even if he doesn't know me in this world, he can't be that different from the Mason I grew up with. His DNA make-up remains the same anywhere ... I think.

"Hey, Mason? How much longer?"

His 'friend' ignored him.

"Would it kill you to answer a simple question?"

Silence. *His* Mason was rarely silent, at least with him. This was *weird*.

"Fine," Chase huffed, continuing to follow.

The foliage grew more dense making it necessary to focus all of his attention on tree branches and bushes. Mason did nothing to help, allowing twigs to swing back at him, nearly swatting him in the face, if not for blocking them with his arm. The path disappeared and each step became more treacherous.

At one point, his foot slid into a small gully and he twisted his ankle. His shoe was dripping when he pulled it out.

"Hey, water! Ha-ha-ha, found some water! Where we were, it was totally dry. Like, even when I dug down into the dirt, it stayed dry. Oh man, am I thirsty. Do you have any water?"

Mason stopped abruptly, turning to face him. "There's water all around you. All you have to do is look for it. It's weird that you don't know that. Where did you say you're from?"

"Um. I didn't."

"Well? Where did you come from?"

"I grew up in Dune Harbor," Chase stammered.

Mason shook his head. "Impossible. If you grew up here, then why are you so stupid?"

"Hey! Don't be a smart-ass. I'm not sure I even like you here." Chase glanced around.

"Well, ya know what? The feeling is mutual. You complain like a five-year-old. And you don't make any sense. Maybe I should just leave you behind." Mason squinted at Chase through his lashes.

"Nope. Lead on. I'll stop talking." Holding his hand over his heart, Chase smiled. "So, we *are* in Dune Harbor."

Mason turned and began walking again.

"But, wait! I really am thirsty..."

He halted when some kind of flask wrapped in leaves sailed above him. He leaped and snatched it out of the air. "Thanks!"

Clutching the precious flask like a well-received football, the extent of his thirst hit him like a defensive tackle, and his tongue stuck to the roof of his mouth like a slug. After a few moments of inspection he discovered the container had a flip-top. Once open, he threw his head back and gulped the entire contents in a few swigs like an after-game Gatorade, Adam's apple bobbing.

Sweat dripped down the bridge of his nose, and he swiped it away. The multitude of scrapes and cuts crisscrossing his torso and right shoulder, some bordering on serious, began to burn. The black wolf had done some damage, but he'd been too distracted until now to really pay attention to his body. Luckily, Enzo's saliva seemed to have healed his most serious injury, the shoulder wound caused by the black wolf's claws. Pushing back the pain, he trudged on. If he lost sight of Mason, he'd be truly lost. If that happened, he'd never find Alyx.

I wonder where she is? What if she needs me?

He studied his watch as he walked; the blocky, blue-framed hexagonal watch-face with intersecting cobalt lines connecting the blood-red numbers twelve and six, and another from three and nine. For the hundredth time, he searched the bronze-like metal perimeter for the tiny knob that had allowed him to turn back time and save Alyx on their last jump. The sides of the watch remained smooth—no mysterious knob protruding that could save him this time. Glancing up, he picked up his pace.

Can't think about that right now. Just keep moving.

Lost in thought, he failed to notice that Mason had stopped moving, until he plowed into his back.

"Umph!"

Chase apologized, backing away.

In response, Mason took a step back, gesturing Chase ahead of him.

"What, you want *me* to lead? Sure. But I have no idea where we're going."

Chase took first one step, and then another. On the third step, the world in front of him shifted. As with both the strange tree back at camp and the mysterious castle-like building in town, everything around him began to shimmer in and out of focus. His head began to spin, the evanescence of the forest in front of him had him blinking. Everything seemed to appear and disappear before his eyes, until the waves passed and he could *see*.

He reached his hand out, his feet moving forward. "What? What ... is this place?"

"Wow, you can see it already? It took me weeks of training to be able to. Why can you ... ? Doesn't matter, come on."

Chase blinked again, a slow smile turning his mouth up. "I gotta find Alyx. She's not gonna believe this place."

CHAPTER 16
ALYX

Alyx ran the scenario over and over in her mind, and she still couldn't make sense of any of it.

What was that blinding light, and why didn't the wolf-creatures attack us back at camp? What did Ursa mean 'hold them' with some kind of 'power'? Is my nemesis actually helping me, or is it all a trap? And where is Chase?

A sigh escaped her.

No choice. No choice but to follow. For now.

"Hey. Ursa? Where are we going?"

"It's better to just show you. And that's not what I'm called here. I don't choose to go by that name. My Other Selves do."

"You think changing your name will make me trust you? I'm here so we can finish what we started, *once* these guys are safe." She indicated the mother and pup.

"Fine. Follow. Or don't. It doesn't matter to me."

Alyx mumbled, "Like I have a choice."

Ursa gave her a sideways glance but said nothing.

They walked until Alyx's legs began to burn and shake. She grit her teeth and trekked on, not daring to show any sign of weakness to her foe. If the hunter could do it, then so could she. At one point, she thought she saw the strange beast that had taken Chase circling above the treetops, but each time she stopped to stare at the sky it seemed to vanish.

Are there more than one of them? Or just a hallucination?

This world is making me jumpy.

She shrugged, continuing on.

Her head jerked up when the hunter spoke. "We'll camp here."

"Is this our destination?"

"It's too far, and it's getting dark. And we need to rest. We'll continue in the morning."

"I don't need rest. I want answers. What if the wolves come back? Let's keep moving."

"No."

Alyx's fists clenched and she took a step toward Ursa. The low growl from the mother stopped her in her tracks. She relaxed her hands, the tension visibly leaving her shoulders.

"It's okay, Mama, I don't want to hurt you or your baby. Just her." She jerked her head in the other woman's direction.

The hunter shrugged. "She wouldn't be happy about that, I'm afraid. She's my friend."

"Friend?" Alyx said.

"We've known each other a long time, she and I. I call her Bea."

"Ha! Bea? Where did you come up with that?"

Ursa frowned. "It's short for Beatrice."

Alyx crossed her arms. "Is this some kind of joke?"

Ursa said nothing but looked at the mother-wolf-thing.

Alyx followed her gaze, sighing. Squatting with her hand held out. "Hi, Bea. I'm Alyx. Thanks for fighting with me back there."

The mother looked up at Ursa—or whoever she was known as here—then back down at her. The wolf took a cautious step forward, tickling her fingers with its whiskers as it sniffed. Apparently satisfied, the animal looked back up at the hunter.

"I think we can trust her, Bea. She won't hurt Bo," Ursa answered the animal's silent question.

Alyx frowned. "Bo?"

"The pup. He's important. A lot of people are looking for him. Well, one in particular." Ursa's eyes narrowed as she spoke.

"Ah. I guess that makes sense. Bea and Bo. Why not?" A hysterical laugh escaped, and she slapped a hand over her own mouth.

This isn't happening. Bea and Bo?

Her head tilted.

The animals seem to trust the hunter. What does it mean?

"I still think we should keep moving."

"It's too dangerous. We have to protect Bo, and we need our strength to do that. We'll continue in the morning."

"Fine. I'll look for firewood, in case we find something to eat."

Ursa shrugged. "Bea will bring us food." She nodded at the wolf. "Go, Bea. I've got Bo. He's safe." The two stared into each other's eyes for a beat, then Beatrice turned and bounded away.

Alyx turned to Ursa. "Hunter, if this is some trick..."

"No trick. May I call you Alyx?"

"It's my name."

"Okay. *Alyx*. Nice to meet you. I'm Liz." She held her hand outstretched, a slow shy smile beginning to spread.

Alyx looked at her outstretched hand, making no move to take it. "We've met, hunter. And I won't forget the things you've done." She turned on her heel and stomped away.

CHAPTER 17
CHASE

Chase scarcely breathed. His watch glowed bright neon blue, pulsating along with his beating heart. Cobalt eyes shone almost as brightly at the watch-face as they scanned what was in front of him, trying not to miss any detail of his surroundings.

He stood in a clearing deep in the forest; a wide swath filled with sparkling goldenrod that swayed gently in the breeze. When the wind blew, tiny flecks of gold released into the air, filling the air around them with glittering radiance. He held his hand out, and tiny pinpoints of light bounced off his skin and floated back into the air to swirl around him.

The ephemeral structure stood in the center of the clearing, surrounded by a moat. Like the two other mysterious things he had seen in this parallel world—the tree in the forest and the 'castle' building in town—this one seemed to shift in and out of reality, wavering on the edge of visual perception until it finally came into focus, morphing into a solid form. The structure appeared to be a one-story house with a picture window next to a jade green, oval-shaped door. Unfamiliar plants grew at its base in a riot of shades of green. Drawn toward it, Chase drifted closer without taking his eyes off the place for fear it would vanish again.

When he reached the water, clear as a diamond so that he could easily see to the smooth white rocks at the bottom, he bent and cupped some of the liquid in his hands, splashing it on his face and then taking a big gulp. It soothed his parched lips, tickling all the way down. When he stood, a walkway appeared over the water, and he looked at Mason. "What is this place?" he whispered.

"This place," he gestured, "is Dune Harbor's underground. Welcome to Dune Haven."

Chase's eyes flew to meet Mason's. "Dune Haven? Underground? What are you hiding from? And how does this place even exist? I don't understand."

"You'll see. Wait until the others arrive. Apparently, they think you're special. I guess they're right if you could see this place so quickly. Most townies can't see it. C'mon."

"Wait. If it's invisible to most people, why did you even bring me here?"

"Because Enzo wanted me to."

"Okay … who's Enzo?"

Mason's laughter shook his body. The sound echoed off the invisible walls of the circle, bouncing back at them as if a group was laughing instead of just one person.

Creepy.

"Don't you know? You've already met him."

Chase shrugged, looked back at the 'house', and tentatively placed his foot on the translucent bridge that had appeared over the crystal water. The bridge seemed real enough, he could feel the substance of it when he placed his weight on it. It held firm. He moved his other foot forward, and the bridge effortlessly took on all of his 170 pounds. It was like walking on water or floating on air. Or flying.

As he approached the door, he reached out to knock.

I want some answers.

Before his fist made contact with the wooden surface, it swung open on well-oiled hinges. With a glance over his shoulder, he turned and stepped into the house.

The door swung silently closed behind him.

CHAPTER 18
ALYX

Alyx sat with her back against a tree, legs bent and elbows resting on her knees. Her eyes were half-closed, shoulders slumped, giving the illusion that she was relaxed and on the verge of sleep. On the contrary, her eyes glowed with razor-sharp clarity. She may have to work with the hunter—*Liz* in this dimension—but that didn't mean she would let her guard down. This Liz might let her charade slip.

And when she does, I'll put an end to this.

She turned when Bo began slowly inching toward her, crawling low to the ground, pausing every few feet to stare into her eyes, as if searching her very soul for confirmation that he could trust her. When the pup came within a foot of her, it threw back its head and yipped three times. The playful sound was followed by the animal throwing itself onto its back, body wiggling as its bushy tail wagged back and forth on the ground. It curled into a U-shape, peering back at her with its head upside-down, gangly legs flailing impotently in the air, eyes beseeching. Another yip escaped.

Alyx reached a hand toward Bo, a smile spreading across her face.

"So, you want to be friends, then?"

Small mewling sounds filled the air, and the young creature's body wiggled as if it would burst.

Rubbing in small circles, she raked her fingernails lightly over its skin, eliciting an almost-purring sound from deep within its throat. Alyx cocked her head when her hands ran over two small bumps jutting from behind the pup's front legs. The fur was different here, almost a feather-like quality. A musky scent invaded her space, her nostrils first flared and then wrinkled at this new smell.

"Bo, you're awfully cute, but you need a bath."

"Yip." The pup inched even closer, the cold wetness of its snout nudging her hand.

"Oh, you like that, huh?" She threw both hands into the rubbing, and she could have sworn a sigh escaped the tiny creature. Alyx chuckled, a genuine smile lighting her face for just a moment before fading. Continuing to scratch, her eyes became distant as a memory flooded her brain.

Ten-year-old Alyx paused in her target practice, her eyes following a boy close to her age walking his dog in front of her house. Her head tilted as he stopped to ruffle the animal's fur, and it looked up at him with adoring eyes before its tongue flicked out to sweep across his chin. The boy laughed. A sound that made gooseflesh rise on her forearms and her heart pick up its pace. She sighed, her eyes following them until they disappeared. She turned toward her mother.

"Mom, can we get a pet?"

"Pets aren't necessary to your training, Alyx. Why would we get a pet?"

"I don't know. I just thought..."

"Focus on your training. That's what you'll need to survive your eighteenth year. A pet would be a hindrance. It's our job to prepare you for what's ahead. That silly boy?" She pointed toward the street. "He wouldn't survive a day of dimension travel. Most of them wouldn't. They live their lives in the here and now, completely oblivious to the battles being fought right under their noses. Remember that. I want you to stay alive to complete your year of jumping and come back home. That's my job. Keeping you safe means teaching you about the real worlds so you're not ignorant like that boy. A pet would be a distraction you don't need. Now, enough of this. Back to your training."

Alyx turned and stomped toward the target, ponytail bouncing with each step. She yanked the arrows out of the make-shift 'hunter' and moved back to shoot them again. Knowing her training wouldn't end until she hit the bullseye, she squinted, adrenaline guiding her arm. She released and hit the target dead-center. She did it again and again, each arrow striking home, directly into the heart of its mark.

Without a backward glance, she flounced into the house, careful to keep her eyes from straying to where the boy and his dog had disappeared around the corner. She knew better than to ask again. The answer was no. No always meant no in the Eris house.

Alyx shook her head, glancing down at Bo. He was now laying as close as possible, his fur tickling her leg.

When she looked up, she saw that Ursa—no, Liz— was gone.

Bo yipped when she jumped to her feet.

Turning in a slow circle, she scanned the area. Had it all been planned? The wolf-pup sent in to distract her?

Pets are distractions.

Her mother's long-ago words echoed in her mind, and her shoulders rose on a deep breath. She was right.

She looked down into the burnt-copper eyes of the animal staring up at her, and turned away, dismissing him.

It won't happen again.

She slinked forward, eyes laser-sharp.

No sign of the hunter, or the animal she called Bea.

The pup followed. That was fine, but she wouldn't be responsible for the thing. Follow, or not. It made no difference to her.

Should have killed the hunter when I had the chance. Stupid! I won't make that mistake again. Now, all I have to do is find her.

Protect my watch.

Find Chase.

Survive.

CHAPTER 19
CHASE

Awe filled Chase's heart.

He drank in the space—which seemed to go on and on—contradicting the expected size of the place from his first impression outside. There seemed to be no walls, and the furniture adopted that same air of luminescence he'd seen only in this dimension yet was beginning to take on a strange familiarity. Pillowy chairs invited sitting, and a cozy stained-wood table beckoned to come and enjoy a meal. Colors splashed and bled into each other like a rainbow born of a misty waterfall.

A smile began, his eyes twinkling.

I could stay here forever. This is home.

Wait, where did that come from?

Shaking his head, he turned back toward the door only to find that it was gone. Vanished, as if he hadn't just walked through it a moment before. An eerie calmness coursed through his limbs, and his watch dimmed, its blue light a faded glow on his wrist.

Chase was not alarmed by the missing doorway, instead he shrugged as if it made no difference. His inspection continued, body relaxed, a smile spreading.

Turning in a full-circle, the entire place just ... sparkled.

Though he hadn't seen his friend come through the door behind him, Mason stood with his hands in his pockets, eyes downcast. Chase noticed he was chewing on his bottom lip.

Mason only does that when he's worrying. A tiny alarm echoed through his consciousness and he stood straighter, cocking his head.

Is he nervous about something? Or is this Mason really that different from the Mason I grew up with?

The feeling passed, replaced by a flash of euphoria. He shrugged.

Who cares. What difference does it make? I feel more safe here than ... anywhere.

His eyes zeroed in on trays of food on the table resembling a royal feast awaiting its guests. His hand flew to his midsection when his stomach grumbled loudly. There was such a wide variety of food on this one table, it could feed a family of four.

Chase clutched a hand to his stomach as it once again gurgled, filling the quiet room like a trumpet blare. He turned toward the dining table.

Might as well eat. I mean, I don't want to be ungrateful and waste this perfectly good food.

"Humph," he grunted when he saw the bowl of clear berries identical to the ones Alyx had found near the strange tree in the forest.

Guess they're okay to eat.

He grabbed a handful and popped three of them into his mouth at once. Starbursts exploded in his head and behind his eyes, and as he looked around the room, everything was surrounded by a shimmering aura.

Whoa.

He grabbed another handful and sat down.

CHAPTER 20
ALYX

Alyx crouched low, eyes sharp, scanning the forest in a circle. Hunting the hunter.

Liz. Ha! I bet they don't even call her that here. All part of the ruse.

Her eyes narrowed.

Bo slinked beside her, hidden behind the feather-like leaves of a seedling ostrich fern, ears standing tall above the crown of green. He'd been following her since she'd begun her search. Alyx ignored him.

Her head tilted toward the sound of footsteps to her right. Bo backed against her leg, tiny body quivering against her. She rolled her eyes and continued her vigil.

A stick breaking had her back stiffening even more. Closer now.

A figure broke through the trees, so close she could have tripped him if she wanted to.

Barely breathing, she froze in her squatting position, hand clutched around the spark gun she'd taken from her backpack, glad she was reunited with her weapons. She remained still and unnoticed.

He passed by, and she began following, crouched low.

As she carefully placed her foot, she winced at the hot pain in her calf. Turning to find the source, she saw Bo, his tiny, razor-sharp baby-teeth nipping at her leg. When she turned, he sat back on his haunches and mewled. His eyes cut behind them, then swung back to meet hers. He mewled again.

"Is there someone else?" she whispered, her eyes searching behind them.

Another mewl.

She nodded, reached down to pick up the pup, and shrank back between two ancient pines, the branches closing around her mere seconds before another boy broke through the dense foliage just inches from where they'd been. She hugged Bo close.

"Thanks," she breathed into his musky fur.

The adolescent boy tripped over a tree branch, his arm flying up to rearrange his black-framed glasses. His eyes darted furtively around, red climbing his neck as he moved forward, stumbling again. He began mumbling to himself, reaching out to steady himself on a tree, before once again moving forward.

"Brian!" he hissed. "Hey, Brian! Wait up!"

A frown wrinkled Alyx's brow. "Hmm. Doesn't seem like much of a threat, does he?"

Bo wiggled closer, his tongue darted out to lick her chin.

Once again, she flashed back to the long-ago boy walking his dog. A sigh escaped. "What am I going to do with you?"

Stepping out from her cover, she never saw the first man until it was too late. While she'd been focusing on the younger boy, the first man must have circled back. Everything happened at once.

Her legs were swept from under her, and as she fell, she brought the Spark Gun around. Too late. It shot off four sparks of light at once, each one flying in a sporadic circular motion toward its target. Though she managed to fire, it missed, the sparks flying off into the trees. If the sparks had reached their intended target, the boy would have been incapacitated for hours. Instead, the man she judged to be about her own age, fell on top of her with a vise-grip around her shooting hand. The gun fell to the ground with a thud.

He called out, "Colin! Over here!"

Alyx tried to bring her knee up into his groin, as she'd been taught, but the one on top of her—she assumed this one was Brian—anticipated her move and dug his knees into her thighs, disabling her attack.

"Colin! I could use some help!" Brian yelled.

She bucked, nearly unseating him.

Once more and I'll get him off.

A loud rustling distracted them both as the boy, Colin, stumbled into view, glasses askew. He cleared his throat, reaching up to right his spectacles. He blinked, focusing on the boy on top of her.

"Uh. What should I do?" Colin asked.

Brian huffed. "I don't know, just..."

"Um." Colin jumped on top of Brian.

"Oommph! Not on me, you idiot!"

"Oh, sorry." He rolled and sat on Alyx's legs, all his body-weight trapping her there.

"Don't move, just keep her legs still."

There's no way I'm letting this child restrain me.

Alyx put all her effort into kicking him off, and almost succeeded when the other one—Brian—placed his hand almost gently down on her head. He mumbled a quick incantation under his breath. The words made no sense to her. A tiny light flashed under his hand, and she was powerless.

She vaguely heard a muffled "Sorry" before everything went black.

Bo ran off into the trees, tremors racking his body, his heart-breaking cries calling out for help that didn't come.

CHAPTER 21
CHASE

Chase pushed away from the table and leaned back in his chair.

"I can't eat another thing. Never thought I'd say that." He glanced at Mason, a satisfied smile spreading. "Sure you don't want anything?"

Mason stood, hands shoved into his pockets, giving one quick head shake.

"Fine. Then let's talk. First of all, what is this place used for? And where is everyone?"

"You should wait for … "

"I think I've waited long enough. If you know the answers, spill."

His friend stared at the floor, his pale complexion going crimson in a heartbeat as he gnawed on his lower lip.

"Look. I know you don't remember me, but we were best friends, once."

Mason's head jerked as his eyes found Chase's. "But, how can that be?"

"You'll just have to trust me. A lot of strange things are going on here, so it shouldn't be too hard for you to believe that we knew each other."

"I … guess it could be some kind of a forgetting spell making me lose my memory or something." He tilted his head. "Even if we did know each other, it really doesn't make any difference now."

"Nothing makes sense here. But I can tell you this. It *does* make a difference. I know you."

"Really?" He snorted. "What do you think you know about me?"

"I know you're a gamer, and you rock at it. Well, at least you always crush me. I know you suck at telling lies, and you chew your bottom lip when you're worried about something, like you've been doing since we got here. I know you're close to your parents. Like, really close. Their names are Jean and David Moore. Are they both okay? They always treated me like a son, too."

"You know my parents …?"

"That's what I've been trying to tell you."

"If you know my…" Mason lowered his voice to a whisper, eyes darting around the room. "They're in trouble."

"Trouble? What kind of trouble? Let's go. Right now. I'll help you."

"We can't. There's no door."

"What do you mean? There must be a way out." Chase got up and walked toward the wall, but no matter how many steps he took, the wall remained the same distance from him. "How is this possible?" Chase began running, but the perimeter of the room stretched with each step.

"I'm sorry," Mason whispered.

"What do you mean you're 'sorry'? What did you do?"

"My parents are in trouble, that's why I agreed to bring you here. I made a deal."

"Wait, I thought you said this place is a safe haven? Dune Haven, right?" Chase said.

"For some it is. Or at least it used to be. But not for you."

"What do you mean, not for me?"

"You're to be held here until he arrives. He's been waiting for you for a long time." Mason gestured toward the watch. Chase looked down at the glowing blue pulsations emanating from his watch.

"You mean this? What do you know about the watch?"

"Only that it's a magical watch, and it needs to remain here in Dune Harbor, the source of all magical energy."

"This place. It's really magical?" Chase asked. At Mason's nod, he continued, "Cool. So you know about the twelve dimensions?"

Mason's eyes widened. "Twelve dimensions? Are you telling me there are twelve other worlds?"

Chase's eyes dropped to the floor. "Um. No, I'm not telling you anything. You're supposed to filling me in, remember?"

Mason put a hand on his hip. "How about we trade information?"

Chase nodded. "Sounds like a plan. You first. How did this place become magical? Or has it always been that way?" His eyes followed Mason as he paced.

"It's always been magical, I guess. Don't you have witches and warlocks where you're from?"

The laugh escaped before he could stop it. "No. Not even close." He tilted his head. "I mean, I guess way back in the history of my world there were people accused of being witches, but the people at that time had trials and either decapitated or burned them at the stake. So, I mean even if they really were witches—and that seems unlikely—they've been gone for a long time. Most of us believe that they were killed because of mass panic, and that they were tried unjustly."

"Your people ... burned them alive? Wow, your home sounds even more dangerous than here."

"Well, we don't have giant fox-eagles that carry you off into the sky and drop you at weird magical houses that lure you in with free food only to trap you, so there's that."

Mason blinked. "You're saying there isn't any magic at all?"

"Not that I know of ... unless its hidden. But I've recently found out a lot of things aren't always what they seem."

"Well, our hometowns have that much in common, at least," Mason said.

"Everyone performs magic here?" Chase asked.

Mason shook his head. "We call witches and warlocks 'magicals', and non-magical people 'townies' because they believe whatever the town officials tell them. Original, right? A bear could fly down Main Street, and if the mayor told them it was a parade float, they'd believe him because they're afraid to accept the truth—that magic exists."

Chase chuckled. "What about the rest of the world?"

"Dune Harbor, U.S.A., is the base for all things magical, but there are other magicals spread out across the globe, yes."

"So, the townies—don't know *anything* about the magic?" Chase said.

Mason shrugged. "Mostly, no. They only see what's right in front of them, and if they don't believe, they'll never have the opportunity to know. They prefer their ignorance to the truth."

"Why don't you just show them? Make them see." Chase continued.

"Why would we do that? If everyone knew about magic, there would be chaos. That's why we're supposed to have someone who controls the magic-source in town. The Sovereign Warlock's job is to keep a magical balance, but..." Mason's eyes dropped to the floor, and he cleared his throat. "And besides, look what happened in your hometown. You said yourself, they decapitated the magicals, or even burned them." Mason paused, shuddering. "Imagine a world filled with people who had these powers, maybe 10-15-percent of the population, and the rest of humanity is left without even the ability to spark a flame in the dark. How long do you think before the mistrust sets in? The jealousy? They would hate us, fear us, and eventually kill us. People kill over lesser things than magic. No, if everyone knew of us magicals, there'd be a terrible war. We'd be hunted, forced to defend ourselves and our families, or worse—coerced into using our powers for evil." With those words, Mason broke eye contact and began gnawing on his bottom lip again.

Chase nodded, a troubled look in his eyes. He couldn't deny the truth of it. "Do you know a couple by the name of Ursa and Pavo O'Ryan?"

Mason shook his head.

Chase sighed. *This is gonna be harder than I thought.* "Okay. Tell me who it was that wanted me brought here. You said his name is Enzo?"

Mason's shoulders shook with laughter. "No. Enzo is the creature that brought you here. The fox-eagle."

"The creature's name is ... Enzo? Why on Earth would anyone name that thing Enzo, and what is he?"

"It's a nickname. He's an Enfield."

"Okay, I'll bite. What's an Enfield?"

"You really don't know anything, do you?"

Chase tilted his head, waiting.

"Fine. An Enfield is a chimera."

"Wait, I remember chimeras in books I read ... Are you telling me that creature, the fox with wings? That it's made up of different animals?" Chase flopped into a nearby chair, sinking low into the cushions.

Mason nodded again.

Chase's eyes glazed, he stared off into space. "I guess that actually makes sense. So, he has the head of a fox, right? And some kind of bird wings?"

"Yes. Head and chest of a fox. Front legs and wings of an eagle. Torso of a lion. Oh, and back end and tail of a wolf."

"I thought those kinds of things only existed in fiction."

Mason shook his head. "Enzo's the last of his kind."

"So, he could have killed me. Easily. Why did he bring me here?"

"Because his master told him to."

"And who's that?" Chase asked.

"The warlock who threatens my parents."

Chase blinked his eyes rapidly. A hazy fog seemed to settle over everything, and he held up his hand in front of him. His fingers blurred together, and he squinted and blinked again. "What's happening to me? I can't see."

"I told you, I'm sorry. You're going to forget everything I've told you soon. It's the berries. They're magical. And you're under his spell now. If you and the girl would have eaten them in the forest it would have made everything a whole lot easier."

"How can I stop it? I have to find Alyx and tell her ..." Chase stood on shaky legs, grasping the side of the chair for support. "Help me! What can we do?"

"I told you. I'm sorry. There's nothing I can do."

CHAPTER 22
ALYX

These two are idiots.

Alyx couldn't see anything through the black cloth bag they had placed on her head, but she could hear them well enough. She sighed.

All of my training, and I let these morons capture me?

They were brothers, that much was clear. Apparently the younger of the two—Colin—had followed the older one—Brian—without him knowing.

Brian spoke in hushed tones. "We just have to take her and drop her off at Dune Haven. Then we'll get what we came for, and we won't have to worry about a thing."

"Well, that should be easy, right?" said Colin.

"Should be. Let's keep moving. We're almost there."

When the spell—or whatever it was—had worn off, she'd found her hands tied behind her back and a bag over her head. She felt hands on her biceps pushing her forward, and staggered along.

I'll go peacefully. For now. Let them believe I'm helpless.

But when an opportunity presented itself, she was primed for it.

Pain shot up her toe when it jammed into a tree root, and she stumbled forward with an uncontrolled hop landing on yet another gnarly root. Her ankle twisted, sending pinpricks of heat up her calf. With her hands tied behind her back she had no way of bracing herself, and she fell sideways, landing on her shoulder with a thud. Upon impact the breath rushed out of her body, but she regained her bearings quickly and took advantage of the situation.

In the fall, the bag shifted up and she could now see Colin's feet as he bent over her, red high-top sneakers, laces untied and frayed at the ends of the string. Focusing solely on that pair of shoes, she kicked out, her feet connecting with the boy's knee in a sickening crack, and rolled to her side. Sitting on the ground, legs bent, just as she'd practiced in training hundreds of times, she pushed her arms down—still tied together at her back—around her bottom, squeezing her rump and thighs through the small circle her arms made until her hands were in front of her. Her arms burned with exertion and she panted, a feral glint in her eyes as she jumped up to face her captors. Boundless keeper energy coursed through her body.

Colin rolled on the ground in agony, clutching his bruised knee, a low moaning sound filling the forest, as he rolled side to side in the fetal position. "Aagghh! Oohhh, you-you broke my knee. I-I think she broke m-my knee." A single tear ran down his cheek.

Alyx didn't have time to feel sorry for the boy. She rolled her shoulders, bound hands in front of her.

If he hadn't tried to capture me, he wouldn't have a ruined knee.

She turned her attention to the other one. Brian. His eyes darted back and forth between her and his brother, the uncertainty plain on his face.

Alyx took advantage of his indecision.

She ran toward him, throwing her arms—still tied—up over his head so she held him in a bear-hug. They fell together in a huff of expelled of air. He rolled, taking her with him. She was bound to him as surely as the rope that held her hands. Wiggling around until she was on his back, she brought the rope around his neck from behind and pulled. His hands instinctively reached for the rope as his eyes bulged, red veins protruding.

Gasping for air, he wheezed out one word, "Please."

Alyx didn't relax her grip on the rope. Her biceps strained with the effort as she continued pulling.

When the hand clasped around her calf muscle, she flinched. Colin had dragged his battered leg across the ground, unrooting moss in clumps as he closed the distance to try to help his brother.

"Let him go. Please. We won't try to take you again, I promise. Please, don't kill my brother."

Her eyes locked with his over Brian's head, though she did not let up on the pressure around Brian's neck.

"Would *you* have let *me* go?" she spat.

"Yes. Yes. If it came down to killing you or letting you go, we would have let you go. I swear it." His eyes flicked to his brother, face beet red, blood vessels popping like crimson freckles on his cheeks. The desperate wheezing was slowing to small gasps. Brian didn't have much longer. "Please. Please. I'm begging you. We'll let you go, and we'll help you. I swear on my brother's life."

She snorted. "Only I have the power to swear on your brother's life." Her hands eased up slightly, and some of the redness receded from his cheeks. "Do you swear not to use your voodoo magic against me?"

"Yes! Yes, I swear it. We both do. Right, Bri?"

Still grasping the rope cutting off his oxygen supply, he managed to wheeze, "Y-Yesss."

"You better not double-cross me. I won't give you another chance."

"No problem. Please," Colin begged.

Alyx stood, holding her arms out in front of her. "First, you need to come cut this rope. I'm not letting go until I'm free."

"I don't have anything to cut it with, but I'm really good at knots. I'll untie it for you. No problem."

Though she had what was needed in her backpack that the boys had brought along with them, she didn't want to arm him with a weapon he might try to use against her.

"Hurry up."

He crawled, dragging his shattered knee, emitting small whimpers, and reached out to the knot. It took only a minute or two, and the rope fell away. Sweat dripped an uneven path down the side of Colin's face.

She sat back, rubbing her bruised wrists, and Brian rolled away into the fetal position, gasping for breath and coughing at the same time.

"Now, you'll tell me everything. I want to know who you are, where you were taking me, and why. Now."

"You got it. We keep our promises. We'll tell you everything we can."

"Not everything you can. *Everything*. Don't leave a thing out," Alyx said.

"Yeah, sure. Absolutely. We'll tell you everything. I mean, everything we can without getting ourselves killed."

"No, you'll tell me all of it, or I'll kill you both."

Colin sighed. "Fine. Everything. But you're not gonna like it."

"I haven't liked anything about this place yet. But I need to know what I'm dealing with. I came here with a friend. We got separated. You're going to help me find him."

"Oh, that part's easy. We were taking you to him anyway. Hey, Brian, if we take her to her friend, then, like, technically we've fulfilled our end of the bargain, right?"

Brian shakily pushed himself up, tremors running along his arms. The broken blood vessels stood out like chicken pox on his pale face, and violent purple bruises ringed his neck. His voice croaked out in a ragged whisper, "Maybe."

"Okay, c'mon. Heal yourself already and let's tell her what she needs to know so we can show her where her friend is and get out of here," said Colin.

Brian coughed. "I-I can't heal myself when I'm this weak. Healing takes energy. You try."

Colin shook his head. "Me? You know I don't have the magic in me like you do. I can't, Brian."

"Colin. You do have the magic in you. You can see Dune Haven, can't you? You just have to connect with the power inside of you. You can do it, Colin."

"I can't." Colin's head shook side to side.

"Try. For me," Brian whispered, lying back on the leaves and closing his eyes. "For *her*. You know why we're here. "

"O-okay. But you know I can't. *She* was the one who mastered magic, not me. I don't even know why you'd ask me to. If she was here..." Colin closed his eyes for a second, a faraway look crossing his features, then scooted on his bottom to Brian's side.

Alyx watched the siblings, and remembered her own brother back in her home dimension. A wave of nostalgia swept over her so suddenly her body shook with it.

"Hurry up," she hissed.

Colin placed his hands gently on his brother's throat, closed his eyes, and whispered, "Um. By ... Earth ... and Sea, By Wind and Flame, I ... call the sun's rays and light. Bring your ...healing forces forth, I ask with all my might. H-Heal these wounds, I implore of you, and through me your power rings true."

They waited in complete silence, not even the sound of their breathing breaking the quiet.

Colin's hands shook as he lifted them off his brothers neck. The purple bruises remained.

Crimson filled Colin's cheeks. "S-See, I told you I couldn't do it."

Brian placed a hand on his brother's arm. "You can. Try again. You have to believe it. If you can't do that, believe in *her*. "

Colin nodded, rounding his shoulders. "Okay."

Alyx said nothing as Colin took a deep breath and placed his hands on his brother's neck once again.

CHAPTER 23
CHASE

Chase whistled along with his favorite band as he moved through the house. He grabbed an apple out of the bowl, and sank his teeth in. Wiping the juice off his chin with the back of his hand, he closed his eyes in ecstasy.

I think this is the best apple I've ever tasted.

"Hey, Mason, you should try this." He tossed an apple to his friend. It fell with a thud and wobbled away when his friend missed the catch. "Your reflexes are slow." He smiled, taking another bite of his own apple. "What do you want to do today? The beach?"

"Uh, sure. Whatever." Mason stood stiffly, hands shoved into his front pockets.

"What's wrong with you? It's a good day to girl-watch."

"Nah. I'm staying here."

"Well, it's no fun alone. I guess you want to play Annihilation."

"Sure," Mason said.

"You okay, Mace? Got somethin' you want to talk about?" Chase tilted his head.

"I'm fine."

"Can't believe you lost all that weight. You look good, bro."

"Um, I guess."

"Want a beer? Uncle Charlie will never notice it's missing."

Mason shook his head. "No thanks."

Chase shrugged, popping off the top and tipping his head back to take a long swig. The liquid soothed his once-parched throat, and he closed his eyes.

"You know what? I feel good. Maybe we can go fishing or take a hike if you don't want to go to the beach."

"Whatever."

"Jeez, your a downer."

He spotted a shiny midnight-blue and black electric guitar propped in the corner, and his eyebrows raised. "Hey, where did that come from? You know, I always wanted to take lessons but never got around to it..." Walking over, he picked up the guitar and threw the strap around his neck. The weight of the instrument somehow felt familiar. He began strumming the chords, and it didn't sound half-bad.

He whooped, and his hands began flying over the strings along with the beat of the music suddenly playing in the house. His fingers kept a perfect rhythm, and a joyous laugh escaped. "You hear this? When did I learn to play?" Chase closed his eyes as the thrum of the music thumped in his chest, head nodding along with the beat. "I rock!"

An hour passed, and he continued to play.

Ha! I'm a natural. I should have done this years ago.

Pulling the strap up over his head, he rested the guitar gently back against the wall and glanced at Mason. A frown lined his friend's forehead, and he watched him draw his bottom lip between his teeth and nibble.

"Okay, spill. What's going on? I'm having the best day ever, and you're all depressed or something. Why?"

"No. Nothing's wrong, everything is how it needs to be."

"What the hell does that mean, 'everything's how it needs to be'?"

"All you need to know is everything is fine now. Or it will be."

"Man, you're talking in riddles. So weird. You're lying about something, I can tell. You might as well tell me now, 'cause you know you can't keep secrets from me."

Mason's eyes darted around the room, then he focused on Chase's shoes. He gave a negative shake without looking up.

"You're lying." He pointed to emphasize his point, his eyes landing on the watch glowing on his own wrist.

"No." His friend shook his head.

Still distracted by the watch, tiny fingers of apprehension danced up his spine. He stood up straighter.

"Why am I wearing this thing? Where did I get it? I never wear a watch. At least, I don't think I do. I don't remember..." A pressure began building behind his eyes, and he placed a finger on his temple, rubbing in a circle to alleviate the pain.

He looked questioningly up at his friend, whose eyes went wide as he silently shook his head.

"Is this yours? Here, I'll give it back to you." Chase reached for the watchband, frowning when he couldn't unfasten the strap. "Hey, it's stuck. What the ... ? Wait. This thing is attached to my wrist. Like, under my skin. What the ...? What did you do to me? Get it off!"

"Chase ..." Mason took a step forward, whispering, "Shhh. I can't tell you here. His eyes narrowed. "You have to trust me."

Chase sighed. "Of course I trust you."

"Good. I made a mistake. I thought I could do it, but ..."

"What? I'm sure we can fix it, whatever it is."

"I'm not sure we can," Mason whispered.

"You have to try. I'll help you. But you have to tell me what's going on," Chase said.

Mason stared intently into his eyes.

Chase saw the precise moment his friend made up his mind.

Mason nodded. "Okay. We have to get out of here."

He nodded in response. "Let's go, then."

Mason's breathing came in gasps, and red climbed his cheeks. "Don't question anything you see. I'll explain it later. When we're free."

"We aren't free now?"

"Not even close."

"Alright, lead on."

Mason's chest rose on a deep breath, and he clapped his hands together with a resounding *smack*. Bright light bloomed between his hands, growing to envelop both of them. Chase slammed his mouth closed, automatically jumping backward. He threw his arm up to block the beam of light from his squinting eyes. A rush of memories came flooding back with the glare. *Uncle Charlie falling sideways out of his chair, fork rattling to the floor even as his body flopped down next to it. The ambulance. The funeral.*

A gasp escaped as memories came barging back. He stumbled backward.

Alyx. The watch. His responsibility as a keeper.

He heard his friend yell, "Stay in the circle!"

As quickly as the light appeared, it was extinguished. He watched his friend desperately clap his hands together again, a look of panic on his face as nothing happened.

A voice filled the room.

"My dear Mason, I'm disappointed in you."

He saw Mason's quick intake of breath, wide eyes searching the room.

His friend stammered, "I-I'm sorry. It's not what it seems. I-I was only trying to keep him happy. Playing along. I swear..."

The voice boomed, "I'll deal with *you* later. For now, I want to get re-acquainted with my nephew."

"U-Uncle Charlie?"

"Hiya, boy-o. Nice to see you."

His uncle appeared in front of him, looking exactly as he always had. Robust, jolly, and full of vibrant energy.

Chase ran forward, embracing his uncle in a bear hug. He looked up, meeting Mason's look of distress. His friend began picking at his cuticles, and he took several slow steps backward, color draining from his face in a rush of paleness.

"Don't believe everything you see here, Chase," his friend whispered.

"What are you talking about, Mason? It's Uncle Charlie!" The smile wouldn't leave his face as his uncle's familiar chuckle filled the room.

CHAPTER 24
ALYX

Brian's chest rose and fell in sporadic bursts, his head pushed back into the pillow of moss surrounding him in an emerald halo, eyes squeezed shut. His brother's gentle hands covered the purple rope burns around his neck.

Alyx took a step backward. Eyes narrowed, she sat back on her haunches to observe as a dim spark of light bloomed under the younger boy's hands, followed by his whispers. She tilted her head, straining to hear his words.

"By Earth and Sea, By Wind and Flame, I call on Sun and Light. Bring your healing forces forth, I ask with all my might. Heal these wounds, I implore of you. Through me, your power rings true. From him to me. Let it be." Colin whispered the words with conviction, his own eyes squeezed closed. He inched backward, slowly lifting his hands away from his brother to clutch at his own throat. Brian opened his eyes, but Colin's remained closed as he fell backward, his breathing becoming labored. Purple bruises sprang up on Colin's neck even as they faded from his brother's. He gasped, falling backward.

"Breathe. It'll only last a minute or two. There's always a price to pay. Trade for trade. You're okay, bro," Brian whispered to his brother. Even as he spoke the words, the bruising began to fade.

Alyx opened her mouth and closed it. She jumped up and started pacing. "I don't … understand how this is possible."

Brian was sitting up, hands groping around his own uninjured neck, gaining strength by the second. His breathing was even and the broken blood vessels were fading from his cheeks. "Ha! You did it, Colin! I knew you had it in you!"

Colin fell back onto his elbows, chest heaving until the purple faded to a gray shadow-ring circling his neck, and he rasped, "I … do? Wow, I-I really do! Wait 'til I tell An…" His voice trailed off, leaving whatever he'd been about to say unspoken.

Brian reached out, grasping his forearm. "You will tell her. I promise. We both will."

Alyx stopped in front of them, hands on hips, and towered over the pair. "Tell who? You keep talking about some girl. Who is she? Start talking. Now."

"But my knee ..." Colin stammered, clutching his leg. "It still hurts. Bad," he squeaked.

Alyx looked at Brian, who seemed to be getting better by the minute. "Give me a few minutes to get my strength back, and then I'll heal you. Unless she wants to try." He jerked his head in her direction.

She jumped back, hands gesturing. "Me? Are you crazy? I can't do ... whatever he just did. And why would I want to, even if I could? You kidnapped me, remember? You're lucky I let you live to heal yourself." She tossed her hair.

"Yeah, Colin thought he couldn't do it either, and he was wrong. *Everyone* has magic inside of them, it's a natural energy that comes from the Elements. It's just a matter of whether or not you believe it. But it's okay, we'll take care of each other."

"Right." Shaking her head, she began pacing again. "Look, I'm not from around here, so I don't have it. Trust me. End of story."

"Believe what you want."

"I will." Her chin jutted out. "This place is crazy," she mumbled. "I can't wait to jump out of here." She raised her voice, "What is today's date? Do you know?"

"The date? It's the thirteenth. Of August," Brian said.

"Good. Still plenty of time."

"Time? Are you on some kind of a deadline or something?" Colin asked.

"You could say that. We're ... vacationing here until nine-nine. September ninth." She stared off into the trees, lost in her own thoughts. When she turned back, her voice was firm. "I need to find my friend. Now." She turned, looking at them over her shoulder. "After you tell me everything. Start talking."

Colin moaned. "My knee?"

She swung around, eyes narrowed. "You're stalling."

"No. I-I can't think. I'm weak from helping Bri, and my leg is throbbing."

She huffed. "Be quick about it. You have five minutes, and then I want answers."

"You got it." Brian turned toward his brother, then back at her. "We'll both be extremely weak for a while. Can we trust you?"

"I could have let you die. I didn't. That should be answer enough," Alyx said.

"Okay." Brian knelt by his brother's side. "Trade for trade."

"Are you sure you're strong enough? Maybe you need more time."

Brian glanced at Alyx. "I think we're out of time. She let me live. I owe her answers." He nodded. "Let's do this."

His hands were already glowing with sunbeams when they reached out for his brother's leg. His chant was louder than Colin's had been, and his confidence was obviously greater. After the words left his mouth, he fell backward clutching his own knee. "Damn, Colin. You weren't joking. That hurts."

Alyx shook her head.

Morons.

When the bone re-knit itself, Brian sat up, meeting her eyes. Black circles ringed his eyes, and the fatigue was obvious in the drooping lids. He sighed. "Okay. We'll tell you everything you want to know."

CHAPTER 25
CHASE

"Man, it's good to see you, Uncle Charlie!"

Coming out of the hug, Chase held onto his uncle's biceps and stepped back, not wanting to break contact. "You were dead. I saw you die. I thought keepers only existed in one dimension. How can you be here? Does that mean you weren't a keeper after all?"

"You want me to be alive, don't you, Chase?"

"Of course I do. You have no idea how much I've missed you." He yanked him in for another hug, taking one long, deep breath. His nose twitched. This man didn't smell like Uncle Charlie, who'd always smelled like an odd combination of Old Spice and sunscreen. After losing his uncle, he'd longed for the scent of him. It was one of those little things he hadn't really noticed when he saw him everyday, but had been so glaringly missing when it was gone. He clearly remembered holding his uncle's favorite battered gray sweatshirt to his face and breathing it in after the funeral. It was how he'd felt closest to him in his absence. Now, in this moment's embrace, the lack of any smell at all had him tilting his head.

Doesn't matter. There are bound to be some differences in parallel worlds. Doesn't Mason look different here? That doesn't mean he's not real.

"I have so much to tell you, and I don't even know where to start." Chase breathed. "I can't believe you're really here."

"No worries, boy-o. I'm not goin' anywhere. We have all the time the world to catch up." He winked. "Now, where's the food? I'm famished!"

"For once, I'm not hungry, believe it or not. The food bowls seem to be full no matter how much I eat. Wish we would have had these bowls at home." Chase sat at the table across from his uncle.

Charlie pushed the bowl of clear berries closer to his side. "Here, have some of these. I hear they're tasty."

Chase's eyes darted to Mason's. His friend cowered in the corner, pale face like a beacon against the dark wall. He gave a barely imperceptible negative shake of his head.

"Naw, thanks Uncle Charlie. I'm stuffed." He leaned back, patting his midsection.

His uncle's eyes narrowed in a way he'd never seen before, despite the smile plastered on his face. "Please. I insist. They're very tasty."

Chase shrugged, grabbing a handful of berries from the bowl. "Well, maybe just a few." Throwing his head back, he popped one into his mouth. Eyes roaming the room, the rainbow of auras surrounding everything in the space intensified, the blurred edges creating the illusion that every object was vibrating. His gaze landed on his uncle. The lack of any color surrounding his uncle should have been alarming. He shrugged again, popping another berry into his mouth.

"Uncle Charlie, how is it possible that you're here? Tell me everything. I have so much to tell you, too."

Charlie smiled, though Chase noticed again that it didn't reach his eyes. Strange. His uncle never did anything halfway. "Don't you worry about that right now, Chasey-boy. All that matters is we're together now."

A tiny alarm sounded in his brain, but he pushed it aside. Uncle Charlie was right. All that mattered was that they were together. In his peripheral vision, he saw Mason slinking further away and tilting his head.

"Hey, Mason! Come have lunch with me and Uncle Charlie."

The look of alarm that crossed his face was almost comical.

Chase gestured, waving him forward. "C'mon. I want to hear about your latest fishing trip. Catch anything?"

Mason froze, eyes wide. He slowly shook his head.

Uncle Charlie sat back in his chair, eyes landing on the boy. "Yes, Mason. Do come join us. I'd like to hear about your latest … fishing trip, too." With a wave of his hand, Mason began moving forward as if on an invisible string. He plopped into a chair at the far end of the table.

His face went crimson. "Um, I haven't gone fishing lately."

Charlie shook his head. "Tsk, tsk. That's not what I hear. Didn't you set out to catch a very big and important fish? And then instead of enjoying a tender filet you tried to set it free?"

"N-no. I didn't set it free. I was j-just toying with it. I would have …"

The older man's eyes narrowed. "Don't lie to me, Mason. You always were a bad liar. Even when you were three, you owned up to your wrong-doings."

"I-I'm not l-lying. I swear." Mason placed both hands flat on the surface of the table leaning forward, eyes intense.

"Why don't I believe you? It's a shame. Your mother will be disappointed that you failed her."

"Where is she? P-please. Let her go. I promise we won't interfere with ... anything. I miss her. And m-my dad, too."

"Ha! What a sense of humor you have! 'Let her go'." His barking laugh filled the facade of the room. "I'm afraid I can't do that. You know I can't. She'll come around, don't you worry. And so will you."

Chase was dizzy with trying to follow the conversation. A whisper of alarm continued in the back of his mind, but he shook it off.

What's there to worry about? Uncle Charlie's back...

He yawned, all the energy draining from his limbs. "I'm tired. Think I'll take a nap." He flopped onto the welcoming cushions of the sofa and fell into a deep sleep.

CHAPTER 26
ALYX

"Talk. Why did you kidnap me? Or *try* to." She scoffed, pacing back and forth in front of them, her toes kicking up moss.

Brian and Colin sat side-by-side following her progress, backs against a tree. Alyx noted the furtive glance the two boys shared before Brian began speaking in a low voice, as if someone might be listening, "Because the Sovereign Warlock sent out a message to all the magicals to bring them anyone who wears one of *those*." He pointed at her wristwatch.

Alyx glanced at her watch. "This thing is like a big purple target," she mumbled. "Go on."

"So it wasn't you in particular we were looking for. Just anyone who wears a timepiece on their wrist. There was a reward." Brian smiled.

As if I'm supposed to say 'Oh, well, if there was a reward then I guess it's okay.'

She stood directly in front of them and slammed her hands onto her hips. "A reward?"

"Bring him a watch—along with the wearer of course—and we'll gain access to more powerful spells."

"He holds the key to all of them," Colin interjected. "We need that to get our sis..." Alyx didn't miss the look his brother shot him.

Brian interrupted, "It doesn't matter why we need them."

"Wait. You kidnapped me to take me to some all-powerful sorcerer? So you two could become more like him?"

"Well ... sort-of." Brian glared at his brother. "And he's not just any warlock. He's the *Sovereign Warlock*. He guards the source of all magical power for the world, and it's located right here in Dune Harbor. Kinda like the king of all things magic. His job is to control the power so it doesn't fall into the wrong hands, and anyone who abuses the magic must answer to him. He's the judge and jury—the law in the magical community. The problem is, it's hard to harness all of that energy, and sometimes..."

Colin continued, interrupting his brother, "He wasn't always evil. And neither were his followers. The power got the better of him—of all of them—I guess. It's happened once before."

Alyx took a moment to contemplate. "He turned to dark magic?"

"Yes. It is rumored he still has the first Sovereign Warlock trapped in a magical prison. He used to serve under him, but he turned on his master and trapped him with his own magic," Brian said.

"Why doesn't some witch just come along and dethrone both of them?" She continued pacing, shaking her head. "Men."

Brian continued, "Oh, they've tried. Even his wife tried, but her heart was too pure to do what needed to be done, so she's locked in her own prison. I guess she still loves him or something. A tragic love-story. I've heard he still loves her, too, in the only way he's capable of loving anymore. He wants to turn her to dark magic so they can rule together, but she resists at every turn. She can't win. He'll wear her down eventually, or kill her. No one is more powerful than the Sovereign Warlock. He has a direct link to the Earth's energy, which as I said, is the source of all magic on this planet. He also has the power to cut-off that power source. But he'd lose his magic, too."

"I don't understand what all this has to do with me," Alyx said.

"There is a legend of lost worlds. Worlds that exist similar to our own, but unreachable. A multiverse unknown to most, magicals and townies alike. Only those closest to the Sovereign know about it, and we found out about it from... Well, it doesn't matter now. For some reason, the Sovereign Warlock thinks your timepiece is the answer he's searching for. He feels it would make him invincible to rule over all the lands instead of just this one. Some have a theory: It's possible the black energy is working through him to infiltrate the non-magical worlds." Brian shrugged.

"So, it *is* the hunter." She stared off into the trees for a beat. "I think I know who this Sovereign Warlock is. I'm here to stop him. If it's who I think it is, he's already tried to kill my friend and me, several times, in the past. He's a dangerous man."

"Whoa. You say you're not a magical, but you think you can stop the Sovereign Warlock?" The brothers made eye contact just before laughter filled the woods. "That's impossible. No one, even a magical, can stop him. He's almost invincible."

"Well, that may be true, but I have to try. First, I need to find my friend Chase. If I can't do it alone, maybe the two of us can do it together. He has one of these, too." She held up her left arm, the purple glow emanating from her watch drawing their eyes.

"Well, if he was captured as planned, then he's at Dune Haven. Soon as we feel strong enough, we'll show you. That's where we were supposed to take you, anyway."

Alyx rolled her eyes. "I have a feeling you feel strong enough now. Let's go."

"But ..."

"Now. Get up and lead the way."

"Yes, ma'am." Brian pushed to his feet on shaky arms, then reached down to help his brother up. The pair had the look of athletes who had just finished a triathlon. But they plodded along, leading the way nonetheless.

Just then, Bo burst through the trees, positioning himself in front of Alyx, tiny, squeaky growls directed at the two boys.

"Oh, snap! Do you see that, Bri? It's the hybrid puppy!" Colin jumped backward, stumbling and landing on his butt. He tore his eyes away from the small creature and looked at his brother. "The watch wearer *and* the hybrid? Oh, man, we'll be set for life."

"Bo. Come here, Bo. They're taking me to Chase. C'mon, they're okay," Alyx soothed.

The pup continued to stare at them, a low growl deep in its tiny chest. Alyx squatted, and he backed up until his trembling body was leaning against her leg. She tilted her head, a smile spreading. "My savior."

"He's not the only one." Liz stepped onto the trail, Bea by her side, gun pointing at Brian's chest. "These two are working for the Ruling Mage. The Sovereign Warlock himself. You don't want to follow them."

Alyx whirled, ready for battle. "Well, well. Look who's decided to return. I'd trust them before I trust another word from your mouth. Lying hunter. You left. Without telling me. Where, exactly, did you go, I wonder?"

CHAPTER 27
CHASE

A hammer was pounding on the inside of his skull. Clutching his head, Chase sat up on the sofa, squinty eyes darting warily around the room.

Alone.

The silence was a blessing. An electric blue light pulsed from his watch, and his squinted eyes were drawn to it. Slowly lowering his arm, he stared at it.

The berries. I remember... I didn't want to eat one. Something made me put it in my mouth, anyway. As if I wasn't in control of my own actions...

Placing his sneakers quietly on the floor, he glanced at the table. The bowl of berries was as full as before, even though he had a clear memory of having eaten half the bowl. He stood, stumbling forward in a stuporous state.

How long have I been asleep? And where is Uncle Charlie? And Mason?

As if in slow-motion, he drifted to the table.

It's the food. I'm not eating another thing here.

Regaining his senses little by little, he began moving more purposefully around the room.

I need to get out of here.

He glanced at his watch, which was now emitting a faint hum as well as a pulsing glow. Not urgently vibrating like when one of the hunters was near, more akin to a rumble that trembled along his arm. A languorous feeling settled into his limbs, followed by a shooting pain in the back of his skull. An unintelligible yell escaped, echoing off the illusion of walls surrounding him on all sides.

All at once, Chase could *feel* his uncle. Not in living, breathing form, but from within. That familiar presence was even now coursing through his veins, pumping through his own heart, flowing through the watch-face. A part of him, always. The very same blood that interspersed with his own and that of all the Walker-family keepers preceding them.

He panted the words through the pain, "Uncle Charlie."

The pain intensified. He flopped into the armchair, leaning forward with his head in his hands. Another yelp broke free. His watch thrummed its power through his left arm and into his chest, glowing intensely as it continued toward his head. The tingling power of the watch seemed to overtake the agony in his skull, to be replaced with a pleasant sort of numbness. He glanced at his wrist, eyes clearing minute by minute. His shoulders jumped when a voice boomed in his brain.

Chase.

"Uncle Charlie? Is it really you?"

Yes, it's me. You have to get out of there. You're not safe.

"How? I don't know how to get out of here. If I did, I'd be gone already."

Use magic.

"Uh, I don't have magic, remember?"

You do. It's in your blood. I'm tapping into it now, to talk to you. It's easier in this world. Not so simple in D-6. You have to believe you can do it. Wish yourself out of there.

Chase snorted. "Oh, okay. I'll just wish myself out of here, and poof?"

Trust me. Wish it, and it will be. Use the journal. It's in your blood. Take the pledge, and get out of there. The voice trailed off, fading into nothingness.

"Wait!" He jumped to his feet and began pacing. "I can't do whatever it is you want me to. The journal? Take the pledge? I don't know what you mean. I need your help." His right hand grasped the left just below the wrist, and he yelled at his watch. "Uncle Charlie? Uncle Charlie! I ..." Chase took a calming breath. "Okay. I wish I was out of here." The silence continued. Nothing changed. Leaping to his feet, he ran toward the wall. With each step he took, the wall backed up the same distance.

He flopped back down on the couch. "I need you," he whispered to his pulsing watch. "Uncle Charlie?"

When several seconds ticked by in silence, he let out an exasperated breath. Rounding his shoulders, he shouted, "I wish to get out of here!"

His legs buckled and he sank to the floor, elbows resting on his bent knees, head hanging.

I don't know what to do.

Eyes opening wide, he sat up straight.

Wait. He said 'the journal'. There's a journal in Uncle Charlie's box. The one we found hidden back home. Alyx has it. It's in my backpack.

Jumping to his feet, his eyes darted around the room.

I have to find Alyx. The answers are in the journal. Maybe it will explain what Charlie was talking about...

"I wish to be out of Dune Haven!" he shouted, hands cupped around his mouth. Seconds ticked by.

Nothing. The lines on his forehead stood out like scratches on a wooden floor as he paced circles around Dune Haven. Mason was right. He huffed out a frustrated breath.

This is no safe place for me.

Where are you, Alyx?

CHAPTER 28
ALYX

Alyx stood straight, eyes boring into the hunter.

"Bea and I were looking for food. Hunting, if you will." Liz answered, inclining her head, eyes remaining pinned on the two boys.

Alyx snorted. "Yeah. Right. And I'm here for a suntan. You expect me to believe that lame excuse?"

With the gun still trained on Brian, Liz reached with her other hand around to her pack. "We found fruit. It's in my pack. Go on, check it out. You'll see."

Grabbing the bag, she yanked the zipper and peered inside. The pack was filled with fruits of all kinds, some familiar and others not. Bananas—or at least some variation of them—half-moon-shaped, slightly larger than the average banana, and more orange than yellow. Next to those, what looked to be golfball-sized watermelons. And at the bottom the bag, small, clear berries. Grasping a handful, she pulled them out of the sack. They were similar to the ones she'd almost eaten at their camp in the woods. The ones Chase had smacked out of her hand. A smirk spread across her face.

"Huh. Guess these are safe to eat after all," she mused.

Brian and Colin started talking at once. "No! Those are enchanted by the Sovereign Warlock! He left them there for you to find."

"If you eat them you'll be under his spell, and compliant to his whims. Don't listen to her!" Colin shouted.

Her eyes flew to Liz, the hunter. "So, I was right all along. You're here to take me to him, aren't you?" Alyx demanded.

Liz shook her head. "They're trying to turn you against me. Don't go with them, they're the ones working for him. I want to help you. I promise, if you eat these berries, you'll be fine. The berries are safe. Give me one. I'll eat it right now."

Alyx bent over, laughter erupting in a bark of incredulity. "Trust you? Never." She stood, her eyes taking on a dangerous gleam. Taking a step in Liz's direction, Bea placed herself between them. Alyx halted. "I can't understand why she protects you.

Does she know you're working for the other side?"

"She knows I'd protect her with everything I have. She knows she can trust me, completely. She knows I would protect Bo the same way. Did they tell you The Sovereign is after *Bo*? Did they tell you that he's special, or even *what* he is?" Liz asked.

Alyx glanced at the brothers, both of whom suddenly found the dirt around their feet oddly fascinating. "Start talking. You mentioned a...hybrid-pup?"

Brian sighed. "The Sovereign wants the hybrid because it's possible the pup has special powers that could help him when he takes over all the worlds. It's rumored that the hybrid-pup has a power similar to that of your wrist-piece—something to do with his blood. It may carry the power to traverse from this world to another. Or so it is whispered within the magical community—at least those who know about it."

"What? But, why? Why would he have any power at all?"

"Because he's a hybrid chimera. She," he pointed in Bea's direction, "is its mother. And the Enfield is its father."

"A ... chimera? What's a chimera? I've never heard of this before."

Brian sighed. "Let me explain..."

. . .

"This is crazy. You're telling me he's part fox, eagle, lion, and what else? Wolf? That's not possible. I don't ..." Alyx retorted.

Liz interrupted her tirade, "But you've seen it. Remember?"

Alyx sighed, sinking to the ground. "I ... maybe. I saw the creature that carried Chase away, but I didn't get a real good look at it. Nothing in this place makes any kind of sense."

"You can't deny what you saw. They call him Enzo. A play on his name. Enzo the Enfield. He mated with Bea. Enzo used to be on our side, but when the new Sovereign Warlock took over, lines became blurred for everyone. We thought things would be better. That this man had a more pure heart than the last Sovereign. But we were wrong. Being in control of all that power... It does something to people. I don't know if its possible to stay on the side of light when holding that position. If there are two sides in this struggle, they're...foggy to say the least. And the townies— a nickname we local magicals use for non-magical people—know nothing. A war is waging right next to them, and they somehow remain oblivious to it all," Brian added.

Alyx frowned. "What war? I don't see a war raging."

"Not a war in the sense you're thinking. More of a silent war for control of the magic. The magical power source for Earth is located right here in Dune Harbor. There are magicals scattered across the globe, but this is the center of it all. We've always had a ruling mage to guard that power and make sure no one abuses it. Ironically, this Sovereign—and the last—are now the ones abusing the power. And there's no one to protect *us* from *them*," Brian said.

"I don't get it. Why don't the...what did you call them? Magicals? Why don't the magicals simply remove him from power?" Alyx asked.

Brian shook his head. "I wish it were that easy. Since The Sovereign Warlock alone has direct access to all the mystic power on the planet, no one is more powerful than he is, so no one wants to challenge him directly. That's why I said it's a silent war, fought mostly in the shadows. More of a power struggle."

Alyx looked away. "This war has nothing to do with me."

Bo snuggled up to her side, his rough little tongue darting out to lick the back of her hand. She automatically began scratching behind his ear, and he flopped on his side like a puppy. Running her hands over his flank, over the feathered bump nestled just behind its hip-joint she now knew was the beginnings of a juvenile wing forming, she sighed again. "My first priority is to find Chase. I guess if we protect Bo along the way, that's okay. But," she looked up, meeting the eyes of each of the three. "Let's be clear. I don't trust any of you."

Colin met her eyes and nodded. The serious look on his face causing chills to race up her arms. "That's good. You shouldn't. Trust anyone, I mean."

CHAPTER 29
CHASE

"I wish to leave this place."

Chase was losing his mind. He'd tried whispering the words. Chanting—singing—rapping—and shouting until hoarseness prevented it—all to no avail. He'd paced back and forth, back and forth, the room shifting with his every step, the wall moving in synchrony with his every move, like a school of fish anticipating the swimming pattern of its group.

I'll be trapped here forever. Wait. What if I'm still here on September ninth—the next jump time? Will I jump right from here, or will the magic in this world cause me to stay here, trapped in this dimension for the rest of my life?

At the moment, he couldn't think of anything worse than staying here for eternity. He truly would go mad.

What was it Uncle Charlie had communicated yesterday? He'd said make a wish. Chase flopped down on the floor, hanging his head. He snorted. Where's the genie when you need him? How many wishes will I be allotted? It all sounded so far-fetched—like a television series or children's novel. Things like this never happened in his home dimension. If only he could turn the page and see the conclusion, it would make this situation a whole lot easier. A frustrated breath whistled through his teeth, his brow furrowed. Next his uncle would tell him to use the Force. Or maybe find the One Ring and throw it into the fires of Mount Doom.

His stomach rumbled, and he jumped to his feet and resumed his pacing. "Oh, no. I'm never eating *that* food again." He gestured with his arm toward the table of never-ending sustenance. Another rumble escaped, and his hand flew to cover his midsection protectively. "I don't care if I starve to death. I'm not eating until September tenth," he grumbled to the empty space.

Just then, he was plunged into total darkness, the only light the soft glow of his watch creating a tiny blue haze. Not enough to clearly see anything. He'd been standing in front of the armchair, and he turned, reaching out blindly to find it. Though his arms swung in wide arcs in front of him, they encountered nothing but air. Turning his wrist to try to illuminate a small area, he squinted through the darkness and saw nothing. His breathing came in quick bursts, and he slowly moved around the inky blackness, walking in the direction where the table had been. Again, his arms flailed in front of him, and again he found nothing. Complete nothingness. As if the room had been empty all along.

Chase slowly sank to the floor, legs crumpling beneath him. The cold tile calmed his racing mind and the panic rising from within. At least the floor was there. He choked back the bitter taste of bile entering his throat. He wrapped his arms around his bent legs and clasped his hands.

Isn't this what they do to punish disobedient prisoners in jail? Solitary confinement. Or is that just in movies?

His forehead dropped to his knees, and he focused on his breathing. Closing his eyes, he searched his memory for something to distract him from his current predicament. His body rocked slowly back and forth as he turned within.

The beach...

. . .

Chase had no idea how long he sat there in the blackness. His butt hurt and pinpricks raced up his arms, but still he sat in the same spot. His stomach had long ago ceased its rumbling, so accustomed it had grown to being empty. He ran his tongue over cracks on his parched lips. Every now and then, he lifted his head to stare at his watch, willing Uncle Charlie to communicate. Each time he was disappointed. Either his uncle had lost the 'magical' ability to converse with him, or he wasn't allowed to help him. Whatever the reason, he was going to have to figure this out on his own.

The watch, with its sparse illumination, kept him sane. A beacon of glowing blue light in the all-encompassing darkness that crowded around him, enveloping him in its hopelessness. His head gave a desultory shake. He glanced again at the watch.

No. I can't give in to this madness.

Rounding his shoulders, he stood up. Swiping his hands back and forth like a zombie, he walked, searching for ... anything. He moved forward. When he encountered nothing, he drifted in the opposite direction. He walked to the left, then sidled to the right. Nothing.

He was totally alone here in this strange and powerful dimension. His head jerked up, his eyes probing the darkness.

Has this dimension always been this way? Powerful?

If it had, then the Walkers—his own ancestors—had been traveling here for many years.

My ancestors must have found a way to survive this place. If they could do it, then I can too. But I need a plan. Think. Think! Charlie said we have magic. 'It's in your blood'. Isn't that what Uncle Charlie said?

A small spark of an idea began to form, and a tiny smile raised the corners of his mouth in the darkness.

CHAPTER 30
ALYX

They walked in single-file. Liz with Bea close on her heels, followed by Brian, then Colin. Bo chose to stay back and walk with Alyx at the rear. She glanced down at him. He sensed her attention and looked up, meeting her eyes. Though his tongue lolled from the side of his mouth, with an air of regality he stood taller, walking in a near-trot like a proud toddler who'd just learned to walk without help. Alyx snorted, shaking her head then squinted ahead.

Don't trust anyone, Colin said. That's fine. I like it better that way anyway.

The hair on the back of her neck stuck in damp strands on her nape. The day's heat was climbing, and everyone could feel it in the stickiness that coated their skin. The backpack hung heavily on her shoulder blades, t-shirt sweated through underneath the bag. Everyone was holding their silence, the only sound that of their feet clomping through the brush and the harsh rasp of their erratic breathing. It took too much energy to talk. Swiping the back of her hand across her forehead, she wiped the wetness onto her shorts.

She'd lost track of how many hours they'd been walking through the heat of the day. Tracking the sun's movement, she was almost relieved to see its descent nearing the horizon.

Her voice made Colin, directly in front of her, jump and turn. "How much longer?"

"We're almost there. Just another mile or so," Colin answered on a wheeze.

Renewed energy fueled her limbs knowing they were so close to Chase. She picked up her pace. "Well, then, what are we waiting for? Let's move faster."

"Ugh. I don't think I can move faster. I'm hot, and tired of walking through the woods. I was just about to suggest a break..."

"No. No way am I taking a break if we're that close." To prove she meant what she said, she picked up her pace again, passing the whining Colin and coming up on Brian's left.

"Relax," Brian breathed. "We promised we'd get you there, and we will. But we don't have to kill ourselves along the way."

In answer, she brushed past him, Bo keeping up with her faster pace with little effort. When the pup reached Bea's side, he nudged playfully into her flank, and she turned, tongue darting out in a quick maternal lick. A small, involuntary smile turned up Alyx's lips. The little guy was actually very cute. She shook her head.

What would Mom say? I almost have a pet. Despite herself, the smile grew. Of its own accord, her hand reached down to ruffle the soft downy fur, and she could have sworn Bo smiled at her when he looked up, adoration gleaming from his eyes. She sighed again. *Oh, well. What can it hurt to make friends with the little guy while I'm here? I'll be jumping out of here, anyway. No big deal.*

When she'd almost caught up to Liz, she called out, "Hey. Colin says we're almost there. Is that true?"

"Yes," Liz answered curtly.

"So, what can you tell me about this place?"

The hunter hesitated. "You'll ... have to see for yourself."

"Why can't people around here ever give a simple answer?" Alyx wondered aloud.

Liz shrugged. "You'll just have to see. It's easier than explaining."

Alyx blew her hair out of her eyes. "Fine. Lead on."

"That's what I'm doing," Liz retorted.

Eyes narrowed, she followed. The quiet was shattered by a long, low howl, which set Bea into a flurry of movement. She began frantically herding Bo toward a copse of pine trees, and nudged him underneath. Once he was safely hidden, Bea returned to Liz, and guided her to the same tree.

Wow, the animal really does trust the hunter. I'll have to think about why later.

Alyx followed suit, finding shelter amongst the trees as she'd seen the others do.

"What's going on?" Alyx whispered.

"Shhh." Liz held up her hand.

The sound of wings flapping filled the space they had occupied only seconds before. Alyx held her breath as, through the pine boughs, she saw the Enfield up close for the first time as it landed gracefully on the ground, barely making a sound. If Bea hadn't warned them...

She had never been face-to-face with a fox, but knew that this animal was much larger than a typical genus Vulpes fox, which was much smaller in stature. If she were to step out and make eye contact with the beast, they would stand eye-to-eye, she was sure. Suddenly, its triangular head tilted, listening with its pointed, black-tipped ears standing straight up. Alyx studied the animal as its eyes scanned the area where they stood, noting the copper-colored eyes blended with the same color fur. Its chin and cheeks were snow white, nose coal-black, snout and whiskers twitching as it began sniffing furiously at the ground. The creature's massive body showed off its rippling muscles. Its flank was covered with a grayish-black coat that extended to its powerful hind-legs and tail. The front legs lacked the expected paws, instead the copper coat bled into feathers of the same color, ending in deadly yellow talons that had the look of spikes. Alyx had to admire them as the weapons they were. Then she remembered these very claws had carried Chase away...

It sniffed the ground they had covered, inch by inch, in no hurry as it sought out its prey. She refused to think of this beast as Enzo. The name gave a false sense of conviviality that this animal lacked.

In the space of two breaths, the Enfield charged the tree where Bo lay hidden. Bea howled as the chimera backed out of the tree with Bo in his mouth. Though it carried him gently as any canine parent would, by the scruff of its neck, Bo struggled and mewled, tiny paws clawing the air, making the hair on Alyx's arms stand on end. Bo's tiny unformed wings unfurled, uselessly flapping. Her mother's words echoed in her brain as she prepared to step out to defend the pup. *A pet is a distraction you don't need.*

Alyx took a deep breath and charged out of the tree directly toward the beast, ready for battle alongside Bea and Liz, a trio of enraged females ready to defend and protect. They made an intimidating and unlikely group, but stood together, fighting united with a common goal—for the moment.

It was not meant to be. With one more forlorn howl from Bo, he was gone, his father's hidden wings unfurled in one swift movement, and the beast took off in one giant leap. The group on the ground could do nothing but watch as the pup was taken higher and higher up into the air, farther and farther out of their reach.

Bea continued howling for long minutes. When Alyx looked at Liz, she was startled to see tears running wide tracks down the hunter's cheeks, dripping from her chin. Her hand brushed against her own cheek, the tears clinging to her fingers like crystals in the receding sunlight.

CHAPTER 31
CHASE

Chase had a plan. He had no idea what the odds of success were, but at this point he was desperate enough to try anything. In the darkness, he patted his pockets. Empty.

A knife. Had there been a knife on the table?

But the table's gone. How can I get the lights to come back on, the table to re-appear? Think, Chase! What was I doing when the lights went out? I was pacing ... thinking about the food. The food! I said something like: "I'm not eating until I leave this dimension." Did I say it out loud? Yes ... I did! That means ... maybe I'm being watched. So, I just have to ...

His voice echoed through the empty space, "Man, am I hungry." He patted his stomach. "I could eat just about anything right now. If the table was full of food like before, I'd eat everything on it."

Before he finished talking, the lights blinked on. His hands flew to cover his eyes. He squinted through the bright haze, eyes tearing. He brushed the tears away, blinking as his vision slowly adjusted to the light.

Everything had reappeared when the lights turned on. The table sat empty—except for one bowl in the middle of the table. The clear berries filled the bowl invitingly, tempting him—almost pulling him forward. Saliva pooled in his mouth, followed by a shooting stomach pain. Hunger was ripping his gut in two with fierce claws, and he doubled over against it.

Maybe just one...

He reached out toward the bowl, scooping up a handful and made a show of popping one into his mouth. "Ahh. Just what I needed. These berries are delicious." He opened his mouth, throwing one in the air and catching it in his mouth like he and Mason used to practice back home, only then it was with popcorn or salted peanuts, not cursed berries. Turning to the side, he spit the uneaten berries into his palm and made a fist to hide them.

"Now, what else is there to eat? I swear I could eat all day non-stop, that's how hungry I am." Scanning the table, a seven-layer chocolate cake appeared at the far end, one piece already cut invitingly. "Cake, yum!" He moved to the far side of the table, reaching for the knife. It was a butter knife, its edges just barely sharp, but he thought it would do. Placing the knife into his pocket, he began moving around the room, and a startled yell barked out when he bumped into something solid. A body.

He wasn't alone!

"Whoa. Sorry, man..." His eyes came up, and he jumped back. "Oh. Hi. Wait, I know you, don't I?"

"No. No we haven't met," the girl answered.

"Oh, yeah. Sorry. My mistake. I'm Chase." He held out his hand to the stranger he had once known only briefly, a memory of her body broken and bleeding on the floor of a battleship when she'd helped to rescue Alyx in the last dimension. D7. She'd taken a bullet for him. Died for him. Saved his life, and Alyx's too. But of course she wouldn't remember any of that. The person standing in front of him was the 'other self' of the girl he'd known. A different version of the same person. A carbon copy, just as Mason and everyone else here he'd known previously. Unless, of course, they were a keeper. Keepers alone can only exist in their home dimension—the reason he and Alyx never had to worry about bumping into their own other-selves in the parallel worlds they visited. He forced himself back to the present.

"Yeah. Hi. I'm Madison. You can call me Maddie." She firmly shook his hand, one quick shake.

"How are you ... here?" he asked.

She looked at him quizzically, tilting her head.

"I mean ... I've been alone here for a long time. At least I think it's been a long time. It sure seems that way." He drifted off. "Anyway, it's good to have someone to talk to again. Are you trapped here like me?"

"Trapped? No, I'm not trapped. And neither are you," Maddie said.

"Oh, great, then if you could just show me to the exit, I'd be happy to be on my way."

"Have you ... eaten anything today?"

Chase nodded. "Uh-huh. I've had a few things. Would you like something?"

"No. Um, no thank you. I've already eaten."

"Okay ... then what's up? I mean, what are you doing here?"

Maddie hesitated before answering. "I'm just here to make sure you have everything you need."

"Great. Like I said, just point me to the door ..."

She shook her head. "Well, I can't do that. You have to find it on your own."

"What, like some kind of test or something?"

"Well ... "

"So, clearly you're not here to help me. I guess I'm fine, then. You can go. Tell your boss I'm perfectly happy here."

Her brow furrowed. "Is that ... the truth?"

"Sure."

"Because he has a spell that sees through lies, so if it's not true he'd know it."

"No worries, it's the truth. Except, I do have one question."

"What is it?"

"Where's Mason? He was with me, and he just sort-of disappeared. I want to make sure he's okay," Chase said.

"Oh, he's at Dune Harbor Base. He's fine."

"Well, I'd kinda like to see him for myself."

"I don't think that's possible…"

"But you're here to check on me, right? To make sure I have everything I need? I need to talk to Mason."

She narrowed her eyes. "I'll see what I can do."

"You do that."

She walked to the far side of the room, and the wall didn't move away from her the same way it did every time he tried to approach it. A door appeared out of the air, shimmering on all sides. This one was different than the one he'd come through to get here. It was honey-gold, vertical wooden panels forming a rectangular entryway. She reached a hand out and grasped the gold filigreed knob, walked through the doorway, and disappeared along with the door. Chase blinked. He scrambled to the place the door had been, but the wall moved away with every step forward. His body physically could not reach the spot she had gone through. He put his hands on his hips and cocked his head, blowing out a breath through his teeth.

Okay, back to my plan.

He drew the butter knife out of his pocket, and placed it against his palm. *Why does everyone always cut into their palm?* You need your hands for *everything*. He shook his head, and moved the knife, replacing it on the backside of his forearm. He pushed the blunt edge into his arm, and slid it along the skin. The dull blade left a white mark on the surface, but did not break the skin. He sighed, trying again. Applying more pressure, he once again slid the knife along the tanned skin on his forearm. This time, blood seeped out along the narrow line. Chase smiled.

Uncle Charlie said it's in my blood. So, here's my blood.

Holding his arm over the bowl of berries, he squeezed until three drops of blood fell on top of the clear berries—*plop, plop, plop*—dripping down one berry onto another like a pinball until it fell to the bottom the bowl.

Chase stared at it, and waited.

CHAPTER 32
ALYX

Alyx took a hesitant step toward Bea. The creature seemed to have shrunk to half its size. Alyx reached her hand out, running it along the grieving Mother's flank, and felt her skin shrink away from the contact. A pitiful mewling filled the air. She spoke softly to the animal, "We'll find him."

"That may be next to impossible," Liz said, cursing.

"Why? Do you know where Bo's being taken?"

"Yes."

"Then we'll rescue him. After we find Chase, he'll help us."

"I don't think anyone can help us." Liz whispered.

Brian cleared his throat. "She can." He pointed toward Liz.

"If I could, I would. You know I would do anything to protect Bo."

"That's not true. You have almost as much power as the Sovereign Warlock. All you have to do is use it for good this time."

"I ... can't. I swore I wouldn't. When I used light magic to perform the simple shield spell to keep the wolf-beasts at bay back at your camp ... it took its toll. That was my first use of magic in a very long time. If I ever use the full balance of my powers again, I'll become what I once was. I swore I would never let that happen. I'll die first."

"But, you could save him," Colin blurted, face mottled red.

"It's not as simple as that. I said I'd protect him for as long as I could. I guess it was folly all along. I knew the odds of keeping Bo out of his hands were small, but I thought ... Well, it no longer matters. There's nothing we can do for him now."

Alyx grabbed her shoulders and shook. "Are you serious? You have the power to fix this, and you won't do it?"

"I don't know if I have that kind of power any more. I've changed. Believe me, you don't want to know that side of me. No one does."

"I have a pretty good idea what that side of you looks like—minus the fairy dust." Alyx stood inches from the other woman's face. "If you have the power to stop this, why wouldn't you? You just need to control the power if you're so afraid of it."

"Listen to you! 'Just control the power' ... coming from you. Someone who doesn't even believe in the power." As she spoke, her hands gestured frantically. "You've never felt the heat of the all-powerful energy pumping through your veins, taking control of your mind and kidnapping every thought, until that's all you care about. Only that, and gaining more power. Despite that, I found the will to fight against it. I turned away from it. Do you know how hard it was to do that? But you're so ready to believe the worst in me." She blew out a breath. "Everyone is. Though I've tried everything I can since my self-imposed exile to prove that I will never harm another living thing. Harm none. I don't know what else I can do to ..." Her words trailed off. She was talking to a retreating back.

Alyx was stomping in the direction they'd been heading. "Fine. Help—or don't. But I'm going to find Chase, and then we'll try to help Bea and Bo the best we can while we're here." She heard the hunter's words behind her.

"That's right. While you're here." Liz picked up her pace to catch up, then stopped, calling after her, "You'll be here for three more weeks thinking you can fix everything, and then you'll leave, and we all have to deal with your time distortions. Hypocrite."

Alyx heard the last words, and clenched her fists. She bit her tongue until the taste of copper filled her mouth. She walked faster. Brian and Colin kept surprisingly silent as they trudged along behind the her. Bea remained behind. Alyx looked back over her shoulder and saw the hunter squatting next to Bea, head down. Good. At least the animal wasn't left on her own.

She replayed the hunter's words in her head. *I've tried everything I can since my exile to prove that I will never harm another living thing again. Harm none.'*

Could it be true? Is the hunter—Liz—changed? Broken the mold forged by her 'other self'? Fighting against her fellow hunter, the Sovereign Warlock? And what does it mean if she has? I don't have time to solve these riddles now.

Squinting up ahead, she asked, "Are we heading in the right direction?"

"Yes." Her eyes tracked Brian's pointing finger. "See those goldenrod flowers up ahead? It's just beyond those. Dune Haven. That's where your friend is, and it's also where we were supposed to bring you when we, ah, kidnapped you."

Alyx snorted, keeping up her brisk pace, leaving the boys ten feet behind. Though they were panting, she was not. Her keeper's blood kept her pace steady along with her heartbeat. She reached the yellow flowers, and raised her hand to shade her eyes from the setting sun. "Okay. Where now?"

"It's right there." Colin gestured. "See it?"

"Is this some kind of a joke? I don't see anything."

The brothers looked at each other, brows raised. "Does that mean she can't see it?"

"Can't see what? All I see is a clearing in the middle of the forest."

"But …"

"Dune Haven is right there, in front of you. Are you telling me you can't see it?"

"Yes. That's what I'm telling you. I don't see anything. What does this mean?"

Her head swiveled as the brothers argued.

"She thinks like a townie. That's why she can't see it."

"But she has the watch, and she came with the one we've been waiting for. I thought…"

"None of that matters if she can't see what's right in front of her."

"We'll camp here for the night. See if anything changes."

Alyx walked through the clearing, and though she tried, still saw nothing except moss, grass, trees, and wildflowers growing sporadically.

Cupping her hands against her mouth, she shouted, "Chase! Chase! Can you hear me? I'm here!"

CHAPTER 33
CHASE

The silence boomed in his ears. Staring intently at the bowl, he willed something to happen. But the berries remained unchanged, the drops of blood already coagulating on the skin of the fruit. The room stayed the same as always. He was still trapped here in this prison alone.

He growled, "C'mon! I want to …" He paced. "This should have worked. Why didn't it work?" His voice rose an octave with each word.

If his blood was the key, then he was determined to use it to unlock the door. With two fingers, he pinched his wound until more blood oozed out. Dabbing his fingers in it, he bent and wiped a crimson streak on the floor, the chair, the table. Nothing happened.

Why is nothing happening? I feel like I'm so close to the answer. I need you, Uncle Charlie. Can you help me one more time?

The watch on his wrist remained impassive. He tapped at it with his pointer finger. "Charlie?" He ran his fingers through his sun-streaked blond hair until it stood on end. "How can I do anything if I'm trapped in this box?" Standing, he grabbed the dining chair and flipped it over, the sound of it thumping to the floor echoing in the quiet room. He paced away, put his hands on his hips, sighed, and returned, reaching down to set the chair right.

As if through a tunnel he heard a voice. He strained to hear more, walking and then running closer to the sound. As usual, the wall moved with him.

"Alyx? Alyx!" He froze in place, willing her to hear him. He cupped his hands to his mouth and screamed her name again and again, "Alyx!"

Is it really her, or is this some kind of magic? Like Uncle Charlie? I have to find out, one way or the other.

"Chase? Chase! Can you hear me? I'm here!"

"Alyx! I hear you! Yes! Can you hear me?"

"Chase? Can you hear me?"

"Yes! I hear you! Alyx!" Other voices filtered through the haze. She wasn't alone.

"Alyx! Can you open the door?"

Chase lowered himself into the armchair, sinking into the downy cushions. He sat without moving, leaning forward, ears straining to pick up any minuscule sound. *She'll open the door any minute, and we'll be together again.*

He waited until the voices drifted off and all he heard was silence. "Alyx! Alyx!"

Hours passed without a sound. Chase barely moved from his current position for fear that he would miss it. Miss her. She was so close, and yet they couldn't find each other. There had to be a way. There had to be. He jumped to his feet and began running around the room, calling out as he went, "Alyx! Can you hear me? Alyx!" He dumped the blood-coated berries and they scattered, wobbling away in various directions. Grasping the bowl, he brought it down on the table repeatedly, the banging echoing in the small space. *She has to hear me. She has to.*

Is she still there? Or did she leave because she couldn't hear me? It sounded like she was just beyond the wall. So close...

Chase dropped into the chair, head hanging.

Magic sucks.

Every few minutes, he jumped up, repeating the noise-making process so Alyx would know he was here.

Eventually, he slept.

• • •

His eyes flew open with one quick movement.

Did I hear...?

He could just barely make out the words. "Chase? Can you hear me? I'm here."

His laugh burst out of him, and he jumped to his feet. "Yes! Alyx, I'm here!"

"Chase!"

Not knowing how much time they had before she disappeared again, his shout became urgent, "Alyx! The journal! Look in the journal!"

"What? I can't make out ..."

"Journal! Find the answers in the journal!"

"Urinal? You need a bathroom?"

"No! No! Journal, get the journal!"

"Internal? Are you ... having stomach problems?"

"No, journal! The journal."

"The journal? Your—uncle's notebook?"

"Yes! Yes! Get it!"

"I'll check it later. Right now..."

"No! Get it now! The journal has the answers."

"But we already looked for ..." He heard some mumbling, then, "Okay. Be right back."

He waited. "Alyx?"

Silence.

"Alyx!"

Silence.

"Alyx! Alyx, please answer me!"

Why can't I hear her? What happened?

CHAPTER 34
ALYX

With the sun's first rays sending warm tingles racing from the part of her hair down her scalp, Alyx shook the inverted backpack, the contents scattering around her feet. Squatting, she mumbled to herself as she snatched up the box.

We already checked the stupid book before the jump. There wasn't anything helpful there before, so why is it so important now?

The hinges protested as she opened the lid. She pushed aside several envelopes filled with inter-dimensional currency, a vial of blood, an always warm-to-the-touch canary-yellow jewel, and a lock of hair, grabbing the journal from underneath.

"Chase? I got it!"

Tilting her head to the side, she listened. No answer. She sat, backside gently cradled in the cushiony moss, her bent legs holding the book up. Carefully, she pushed back the cover. Taking special care not to tear the time-worn pages, she flipped through the book past the list of names to the page simply labeled '7'. Carefully, she turned to the next page—the page that should have the number '8' scrawled across the top like the others, but instead it was blank. Nothing. More frantically, she flipped to the next page. '9.' Then back again. Still blank. Between the pages of dimensions seven and nine were bare, as they had always been.

It doesn't matter. Nothing in this journal makes sense anyway. It's all just gibberish...

Rolling her eyes, she flipped the leather-bound book closed with a *snap*, making Colin's shoulders jump.

"This is no help to us at all." Jumping to her feet, she called again. "Chase!" Nothing, no response. "I wish he would answer. Why won't he answer?"

"Well, maybe he's not there anymore. Or, maybe, like, he's under some kind of dark spell." Colin's eyes widened. "Or maybe the Sovereign Warlock took him to his secret lair to, like, eat his heart or..."

Brian rolled his eyes. "Colin. Knock it off. He's probably just sleeping." He looked at Alyx. "So, you still can't see anything?" He gestured to the grassy area.

She glanced in the direction he indicated. "No. And I can't see anything in this book, either."

Brian shook his head. "Well, you're no help. Guess we'll have to do this alone. You wait here."

"What? Wait? I'm coming with you."

"That's stupid. If you can't even see the place, how are you coming with us?" Colin interjected.

"Well...isn't there some kind of spell you could use to help me see?"

"Um. I don't think so. Or if there is, I haven't learned that yet."

Heat traveled up Alyx's neck. "Well, I'm coming, and that's the end of it. I'll just hold onto the two of you, and maybe you'll—I don't know—take me with you or something?"

Brian nodded. "That might work. No promises, but it just might work. C'mon, Col. Let's go in."

Alyx walked in the middle grasping both of their hands in a vise-grip, Colin on the right and Brian on the left. They walked together toward the middle of the grassy clearing, determination evident in the set of her shoulders and her marching feet.

"You sure you don't see the house? A bridge over water?"

Alyx stared ahead, as if willing these things to appear. But still, nothing. Just meadow. She stood up even straighter.

Brian stopped abruptly and she nearly plowed into him. "Okay, here's the door. Are you ready?"

"Yes." She nodded.

Brian took a step, and his body disappeared right before her. One minute he was there, and the next he was not. Her wide eyes turned to Colin. She clutched his hand more tightly than before. "Don't go without me."

Colin glanced at their entwined hands, color creeping into his cheeks. "Um. I'll try. C'mon." He looked at their hands again.

Alyx stepped forward in sync with Colin's step. He disappeared just as quickly as his brother had. She stared around the clearing. She was alone. "Hey! Where did you guys go? Colin! Brian! Chase!" she screamed. Adrenaline pumped through her body. She was primed for action. A fight. Anything would be preferable to ... this.

Finally, she sat in the exact spot the boys had vanished. *I'm not moving until they come back with Chase...*

Barely paying attention to the sun's slow arc across the sky, or the shadows growing and receding once again, she sat.

• • •

Snap.

Alyx jerked her head to the left. *Someone approaching? Or something?*

Snap-crack-snap.

She slowly rose to her feet, backpack in her hands, eyes darting around the clearing. No sign of movement. She rounded her shoulders when her hand closed around a weapon. The Inferno Ray—a deadly weapon that implodes a target on contact. A gleam lit her eyes.

Come on.

"Quit cowering in the trees. Come out and face me," she called.

Three sets of eyes glowed orange in the darkening light of dusk as the wolf-beasts slinked through the trees and stood shoulder to shoulder, creating a line.

"I wondered where you went. Well, I'm not in the mood for a fight, so …"

She placed her hand around the weapon until her fingers fit perfectly into each grooved trigger and squeezed without hesitation. The laser shot out with a sharp *boom* until it reached an invisible force that circled the area like a dome. The weapon's beam seemed to absorb into some kind of clear wall. For the first time she saw the circle that surrounded her, the tiny flecks of gold flitting in the air as if in slow motion as they rose from the goldenrod plants that bordered the circular space. The creatures seemed to be frozen outside the sphere, as if they couldn't enter this area, and the same midnight black leader with a beige streak on its side from before threw back its head and howled. That solitary long, high-pitched ululation reached her ears as if from a great distance. Within seconds, more wolves appeared just on the outskirts of the circle slinking through the brush to stand side-by-side in a line on one side around the perimeter of the dome. Alyx drew in a quick breath and whistled through her teeth. With great effort she forced her eyes to break away from the beasts enclosing her and focused on what was in front of her.

Everything within the circle was suddenly surrounded by dizzying waves of color. She held one hand to her temple and the other up in front of her, and focused on the gold flecks that danced around her fingers. Eyes wide, the bridge appeared almost nonchalantly as if it had always been in front of her, the surrounding ripple of crystalline water reflected the sun so that she had to shield her eyes from the blinding light. *How could I have not seen this before?* Slowly, she turned to look behind her.

The cottage stood majestically, rising up in the center. She was standing on the edge of the bridge, multi-colored cobblestone path leading invitingly to the cozy front door. It looked like an enchanted cabin in the woods.

Her feet began moving, faster, faster, until she was standing directly in front of the hand-made wooden entryway. She reached out a hand, and her mouth dropped open as the door swung inward.

With a brief hesitation, she moved forward to step through the doorway, and just as she placed her foot through the opening it all disappeared. She blinked. In a heartbeat it was gone. All of it. As if it had been a figment of her imagination taunting her all along.

"No! It was *here*. I saw it!" Eyes frantically darting, she blinked, reaching up to rub her eyes, then looking around again. A green, mossy field. No cottage with a green front door. No dome. No water, bridge, or golden dust. Just the clearing in the forest.

She looked over toward the trees where the wolf-creatures had stood, but they had vanished as well. Slumping to the ground, her breath hitched. "I'm not leaving here until I see that again."

CHAPTER 35
CHASE

"Alyx!" Chase ran toward her, only to have her disappear right in front of him. He turned toward Brian, arms gesturing. "What happened? Where did she go?"

Brian shrugged his shoulders. "Don't know. I've never seen *that* happen before."

"Maybe, like, the Sovereign Warlock took her, and now he's using her as bait to lure you in. And he's drinking her blood from a wine glass to help his powers grow. I bet he's wearing her watch now, too! Or something even worse," Colin whispered.

"Stop being so dramatic, Colin. We just saw her a minute ago. She's probably just struggling with believing in the magic that is right in front of her. She couldn't see it remember? Just like the townies who don't see. She's just like them."

"Well, she must have seen it, or we wouldn't have seen her at the door just now. Right?" Chase paced.

"I-I guess. This is all new. I didn't learn about any of this in my training." Brian's eyebrows furrowed. "I'm not even sure which side we're on anymore."

Chase took a step toward this world's version of a friend he'd once known well, and placed a reassuring hand on his arm. Turning to the younger boy, he raised a brow. "And why would he use her as bait when I'm already his prisoner?" His eyes bored into Colin's eyes.

Chase turned back toward Brian, his urgent warning was barely a whisper, "Don't say too much here. I think we're being watched."

Brian's eyes widened, and he searched the room before coming back to Chase. He gave a slight nod. "I still don't understand how you knew my name."

"Long story. I don't have time to fill you in now. All I'll say is it has to do with this." He held up his arm indicating his watch.

"Alyx has one, too, and *she* didn't know me." Brian's eyes narrowed.

"We ... aren't from the same place. I only met her recently, and she never met you. You can trust me, I swear," Chase answered.

"Ha. You're stupid if you think I'd believe that. Don't you know you can't trust anyone anymore?" Brian said.

"I'm starting to. This place is ... different from anyplace I've been." Chase's eyes briefly took on a far-away look, then refocused on Brian. "So, why are you here?"

"Okay, now don't get upset. Some of this you probably won't like…"

Chase crossed his arms. "Spill."

"So, the Sovereign Warlock put out a reward for anyone who delivers the watch-bearers to Dune Haven. He knew you were coming. Someone already brought you here, so we captured Alyx to bring her here, too."

"You two? Captured Alyx? Guess you didn't do such a great job of it since you're in here," he pointed to the floor, "and she's out there." He pointed out. "I'm just surprised she didn't take you down."

Brian cleared his throat, blotchy patches of crimson crept up his neck. "We did capture her, but she … um … got away. Turns out, she wanted to come here to find you anyway, so we came together. Willingly. She came willingly." He held up his hands, palms out in a show of surrender.

"So, if you were supposed to bring her here, why can't she come in?" Chase tilted his head.

"I don't know for sure, but my best guess is that because this is a place of magic, she can't enter unless she believes and has some magic inside her."

"Magic insider her? No. We don't have magic. We aren't from here."

"You don't understand. *Everyone* has magic in them."

"Everyone from *here*. How many times do I need to tell you? We're not *from* here. We come from a non-magic place, where magic doesn't even exist."

"Do you hear what you're saying, man? You say you come from a place where magic doesn't exist … even as you wear that magical watch. You're not making any sense. I can *feel* the power in it." Brian pointed at the watch.

Chase glanced at the timepiece on his wrist, the electric blue glow pulsing with his heartbeat. "I …" he stammered. "I guess you're right. I hadn't thought about it that way." He slumped into the nearest chair. "Look, none of that matters. I need to get to Alyx. That's all I care about. Before you arrived, I was trying to use my blood…"

"Oh, man. Blood magic? You were trying to use blood magic, and you've never even done magic before?" Colin's eerie whisper caused goosebumps to crawl up Chase's arm.

"No, I wasn't trying to do magic…"

Brian interrupted, "What were you using blood for, then?"

"I don't … really know. Doesn't matter. It didn't work anyway."

"Tell me exactly what you did. Don't leave anything out. If I'm gonna help you, I need to know everything. Blood magic is serious." Brian frowned.

Colin's eyes were huge in his pale face. "Yeah. Blood magic is Gates-of-Hell scary."

Chase looked from one to the other. "Okay. I didn't realize … So, I cut my arm here." He held up his arm. "And then I let it drip on the berries. They were in the bowl, but I dumped them..." Pointing to the scattered berries. "And, um, then when that didn't work, I, um, wiped my blood in different places in the room."

"Did you say anything while you were doing it?"

"I-I don't remember. Maybe. I was kinda ... talking to myself, I guess."

The brothers huddled together, their voices hushed, hands gesturing. Chase leaned closer but could only pick out a word here or there.

"Hey? What's going on?"

"Your blood could have changed everything. We want to try some things and see if what you did had any affect on this place. Sort of like a test."

"Okay. So ... what do we need to do?"

"Not what *we* need to do. It's what *you* need to do."

"Fine. What do I need to do?"

"A spell."

Chase sighed. "I keep telling you that I can't do magic. Why won't you believe me?"

"Well, if you really can't, then nothing will happen. What do you have to lose?"

"Okay, I guess. It'll prove to you that I don't know magic. Tell me what to do."

"First test: You need to eat one of those berries."

"Yeah, right. I'll just eat one of the berries just because you told me to." He humphed. "No, thanks. I think I've had enough of those berries. You said it yourself, 'Don't trust anyone here'. You're crazy if you think I'll eat one of those enchanted berries. You eat one, if it's so important."

"If you won't try it, then we'll never know," Brian said.

Chase sighed. "Know what, exactly?"

"Whether you've taken the power of this place away from the ruling Sovereign Warlock. You could have the power here now. And if that's true, then the Sovereign will come after you in a challenge as soon as he knows. And that could be any time."

"I just want to find Alyx and get out of here. I don't want a challenge."

"It may be too late. You used the blood magic. Along with that watch, it may be all that was needed to shift the power."

"Wait, I thought the Sovereign Wizard guy was all-powerful."

"Yes. He is. But maybe not here at Dune Haven. Not anymore. He himself created this place before he defeated the last Sovereign Warlock. Before *he* took power. This place," Brian gestured, "was intended as a safe haven from the ruling mage at the time. The first Sovereign. To protect us from his evil. A place his power couldn't touch. But when he took over, he slowly started to change. Began to act like his predecessor more and more. Put simply, he started to turn to the darker side of magic. So it's possible that this place could be turned against *him* now. A safe haven from *him*. No one has been brave enough to try it. You may be the one to turn the power. But be warned. The power is all-consuming. If it could change a man like that into what he is today—you might not like what you become if you take the power for yourself. You may have honorable intentions, but all that can change in the face of total control of all things magic."

"I don't want to be that person. I'm not here to take over power or for some kind of a war. I won't be here much longer anyway…"

"You won't have a choice."

"There's always a choice. Just because the new guy in charge went all Anakin Skywalker on the town doesn't mean I can do anything about it. It has nothing to do with me," Chase said.

Colin tilted his head, asking, "Who's Anakin Sky-runner? Is he coming, too? Does he wear a watch like you and Alyx?"

"Skywalker." Chase waved a dismissing hand, rolling his eyes. "Never-mind."

Brian took a step forward, his eyes boring into his. "But, Chase, you could be the one we've been waiting for."

"I don't care. I just want to get out of here."

"I'm telling you, if you eat one of your blood berries, that could very well happen. Because if you're in charge of this place now, you won't be trapped anymore."

Chase paced. His eyes were drawn to one berry in particular, the streak of blood that had dried in a stripe down the middle of the fruit reminded him of a holiday candy cane. Cheery and inviting, even.

As he stared at it, he could have sworn he saw it move. Just a slight back and forth roll. He blinked, his hand slowly reaching out for the berry.

CHAPTER 36
ALYX

Alyx did not sleep. She replayed the moment everything had come clearly into focus over and over, trying to decide what to do next.

It was the Inferno Ray. Had to be. It—forced me to see, somehow. What if I fire at the invisible dome wall again?

The weight of the cool metal against her palm settled her mind and calmed the humming in her brain. She was more comfortable around firearms than most things—she'd been around them for as far back as she could remember. It was like greeting an old friend, or savoring a favorite flavor. Cradling the piece against her she stood, scanning the pitch-black clearing.

This weapon had saved them once in the last dimension. Firing the gun required fitting her whole hand around the weapon, four fingers and thumb nestled firmly into each specific notch and squeezing each trigger at the exact same time. A memory of Chase learning to fire the Inferno Ray flashed through her mind. The picture of him doubled over, laughing at the accidentally-incinerated tree made her lips twitch. It seemed a very long time ago, but in reality it had only been weeks. With newfound determination, she stood, rounding her shoulders.

Should I wait until dawn? What if everything appears again, but it's too dark to see it?

Absently, she chewed on her bottom lip. Though her fingers itched to fire the weapon, her mind stilled her hand. She relaxed, finger by finger, and sank back to the ground still clutching the Inferno Ray. As she'd been taught all her life, she knew that acting on adrenaline would always lose to a well-thought-out plan. The Eris family were planners, always prepared with a plan—or two.

Occasionally, her ears perked at a rustling in the woods outside the circle, though whatever was out there did not show itself again. At least, not that she could see. She hugged the weapon closer to her body as a sudden shiver shook her frame. Squinting through the black night, she scanned the shadows of the treetops that surrounded the clearing in a perfect ring, but her nighttime eyes could not detect anything. This must be what it's like to be an animal caged in a zoo, your every move tracked by watchful eyes. Something was out there, she knew for certain. She focused on the tranquil, dim glow of her watch, her long sigh breaking the silence.

I'll wait for the first rays of light. Then I'm going in.

· · ·

She jerked awake and jumped to her feet, body tense, muscles protesting at her body's sudden change of position. Gently massaging her own neck, she looked around. Nothing had changed.

There goes my hope that the cottage would magically appear in the morning.

Releasing her death-grip on the weapon, she gently placed the Inferno Ray at her feet and flexed her stiff fingers. The sun was waking for the day, just beginning its slow climb in the horizon, casting long shadows through the trees that spread across the clearing, needles pointing upward saluting the new day. A shiver racked her body, despite the cheery light of dawn. Her damp shirt clung to her. She pulled it away from her skin, reaching up to push back her sweat-soaked hair, readjusting her ponytail.

She'd dreamt.

Foggy dreams of wolves and chimeras, wizards and witches. And woven through all of it: magic. Spells and curses. Good versus evil. And blood. So much blood.

Wrapping her arms around herself, she fought another shiver of premonition. *Something bad will happen here. Something we didn't prepare for. Couldn't prepare for.*

It was only a dream, screamed the logical part of her brain. Nonetheless, gooseflesh spread up her arm. *Then why does it feel so real?*

Mentally shaking herself, she reached for the gun again, and then was ripped from her reverie at the sudden appearance of the brindle wolf. It burst out of the trees at full-speed, running straight toward her, eyes glowing through the morning shadows. When it reached the edge of the circle lined by golden flowers, it slammed face-first into the invisible wall of the dome. Next to it another wolf appeared and repeated the action only to slam its whole body into the wall right next to its comrade.

Alyx adjusted the weapon as one after another of the wolf-creatures followed suit, and with each slam into the barrier, tiny white lightning bolts raced up branching off in zig-zag patterns, exposing the dome's concealed protection until it fizzled and faded. A dozen or more wolf-creatures picked themselves up and repeated the process over and over again, slamming again and again as they slowly moved around the circumference of the circle. The coal-black leader stood off to the side, eyes glued to Alyx the entire time. She stared back.

They're testing the perimeter! What will happen if they ...?

She took one deep breath and squeezed the trigger. Her target: the black.

BOOM!

Fissures of yellow lightning raced around the sphere set off by the laser, intermingling with the tiny electrical bursts of the creatures ramming their bodies at the dome. Her eyes made contact with the black leader once again, her smile fading at the look of triumph on the animal's face. As close to a grin as a creature with a canine snout can achieve.

I'm doing exactly what it wants.

The Inferno Ray clattered to the ground at her feet.

She looked up just in time to see the cottage disappear right before her eyes once again.

I can't believe I forgot to look for the house after I fired! The wolves distracted me from my purpose...

An enraged snarl escaped her own lips.

How are these animals so smart? And why can't they come inside?

Her head jerked up.

Magic. It's been magic all along.

CHAPTER 37
CHASE

Eyes wide, he focused entirely on the berry. The connection between Chase and this tiny piece of fruit made no sense. And yet, he couldn't break his eyes away.

Did the berry move, or is it my imagination? Is this whole thing a trap? Just part of the plan?

Chase didn't blink as he stared solely at the crimson-striped berry. Everything else disappeared. The berry began rolling toward him. He jumped back. It wobbled as it rolled, until it settled right at his feet.

Weird.

"You did it!" Colin clapped once.

He ripped his eyes from the berry. "Huh?"

"You called the berry to you and it came."

"No, I didn't..."

"Look." Brian pointed.

Chase followed Brian's finger, and saw that, unbeknownst to him, his own hand was reaching out in front of him with fingers splayed. He cocked his head. "Uh, I don't know..."

"You called to the berry with your magic. It's one of the simplest spells. If you eat it and you don't fall under the Sovereign's will, then the power has probably already shifted."

"Probably?"

"Well, we have a few more tests after this one, but you still need to eat the berry first. That's the simplest way to find out."

Chase reached for the berry, and without another thought, popped it into his mouth. It *felt* right, and what did he have to lose. He'd been eating the berries since his arrival at Dune Haven anyway. How could one more hurt?

As he ground the berry between his teeth, starbursts exploded behind his eyes. A tingling began to spread from his tongue, down his throat, to his gut, and throughout his limbs. Little pinpricks tingled on his scalp, as if the hair stood on end. His shoulders raised with a deep sigh, and he looked around the room with new eyes. His watch amped up, its usually faint glow turned up a few notches. Another kind of warmth spread up his arm.

"How do you feel?"

"Um …"

"Do you feel under his control?"

"No."

"Ha! It worked! Right, Brian?"

"Well, maybe. Let's try something else. Can you go out the door, Chase?"

Chase cocked his head, and took a step toward the wall. As before, the wall moved away from him. He looked at Brian, eyebrows raised.

"Wait. Let me think. You're clearly not under his control anymore, but…" Brian began pacing. "There must be another step. Like, a spell you need to do, or something, to make it take hold. We just have to figure out what that is."

"How will we do that?" Chase asked.

"I don't know," Brian answered.

"Great."

"Hey, I don't know everything about magic. I got you this far, didn't I?"

"Yes, but if we're still trapped here, I don't understand what that means."

Just then, the door appeared, and outside they heard Alyx shout. The door remained just long enough for the sounds of an electric battle to reach them, and then the door disappeared just a quickly.

"Alyx!" Chase turned to the others. "She's in trouble! We need to get to her. Now. What do I need to do to get control of this place?"

"I have an idea. Maybe you just need to say it. Like in a spell. Just say the words out loud."

"Okay. What should I say?"

"I don't know … maybe just say 'I take control of this place,' or something. Words make the spell more powerful. You didn't need it for the berry because that was simple magic. This is harder. Give it a try."

Chase called out in his strongest voice, "I, Chase Walker, take control of this place. Dune Haven. I take control of Dune Haven."

They all waited a beat, searching the room for some kind of change that never came.

"Well, that clearly didn't work."

"Okay. Maybe it needs to be more elaborate. Try calling on the elements. Like this: By Earth and Sea, By Wind and Flame, I call on Sun and Light. My pledge is to protect all those seeking refuge from the fight. Within the boundaries of this circle, the darkness has no say. I will seek no harm to others, this I vow on this very day."

"Wait. I told you, I'm not gonna be here long. I have to leave on September ninth. I won't have a choice. If this works, what will happen to the people after I leave?"

"I don't know. But you'd be giving them a safe place for a few weeks, at least. What do you care?"

"I have to think…"

All heads jerked at the sound of an eerie howling outside the walls.

Chase blew out a breath. "Okay. I have to get to Alyx. I'll worry about the rest later. I'll do what you ask." He rounded his shoulders and stood up straighter. With prompts from Brian, he repeated each word, his voice raised so it echoed in the space. "… this I vow on this very day."

The room immediately started to shake. Chase grabbed onto the back of a chair, his eyes darting around the room. The lights blinked off and then on, and all three boys looked on as the walls became solid and the door appeared. Chase took a step toward the door, and it remained stationary. He began running.

"Alyx!"

CHAPTER 38
ALYX

Magic.

How hard can it be?

Alyx paced back and forth, mumbling to herself. She'd watched Brian and Colin heal each other...and there had been that flash of white light when she'd been chasing the hunter—Liz—in the woods.

So, it has to do with words and light.

Or some combination of the two. She chewed her nail until it was down to the skin, ignoring the wolves surrounding her, continuing to hurl themselves into the invisible wall. The Enfield had licked Chase's wound and he had healed. That had to be magic, too. *Maybe saliva, or just bodily fluids of any kind, play a part?*

I'll stick to words, for now. But how will I know what to say? I think Brian said something about the Earth and its dirt, or something. Or was it the ocean water? Why didn't I pay closer attention?

She moved to the next fingernail and began gnawing at it. Taking her hand away from her mouth, she shouted, "The Earth and Sea, um, give me power. So, I guess, let me see the house." A jagged hangnail stuck out, and she pulled the nail off past the quick, drawing blood. Raising her injured finger to her mouth, she licked the blood away. "Damn it." She began pacing again. Throwing her head back, she screamed, "I want to go inside!"

The wolves froze. One last lone creature crashed into the clear barrier, and they all stopped, their heads turning toward her as one. "Okay. I must be on the right track," she breathed.

She angled her body so she could look the black directly in the eyes, and yelled again, "I want to go inside! Let me in!"

The animal tossed its head back and howled. All of the wolves sprang into immediate action, turning to run through the trees. Within seconds, they were gone as if they'd never been there at all.

Alyx blinked. What was all that about? And then the golden flecks floating in front of her caught her attention. She spun around. It was there. The cottage. Right in front of her.

Yes!

Without wasting another minute, she ran at the door, shoulders down, ready to run through it with force if necessary. Nothing would stop her from getting to Chase this time. Nothing.

Her feet pounded on the cobblestone path, her watch amped up as her blood pumped through the watch-face. She was ready. She closed her eyes as she prepared to ram the door, just as the door opened on its own. The momentum carried her through the frame and she stumbled, her eyes flying open as someone caught her fall.

"Brian? Thanks." Her eyes searched behind him even as she spoke. "Chase?"

"Alyx!" He held out his arms and she dove into them. The feel of his arms around her was pure heaven. She knocked her forehead on his chin and barely noticed, tucking her face into his neck and breathing deeply. She felt the rumble of his laughter through his chest and into her own. "Missed me, did ya?"

She leaned back, searching his eyes, her own serious. "Yes." Going on instinct, she reached up, cupping his face in her hands, and pulled his lips to her own. His eyes widened in surprise for a second, but he caught on quickly, leaning down to meet her. The searing heat of lip against lip was addictive, and she tilted her head to get closer.

Colin whispered, "Eww, gross. Get a room, you two."

Brian cleared his throat. Loudly.

Alyx jumped back, missing the warmth of his body against hers immediately, but feeling the heat climbing into her cheeks until she thought she'd internally combust. Suddenly embarrassed, she looked everywhere but at Chase, Brian, or Colin. She cleared her throat. "So, um. Hi."

"Alyx." Chase breathed her name, and her eyes slowly rose to look into his. "I missed you, too."

She nodded as he reached for her hand. She met him halfway, their fingers intertwined, and her head dropped to stare at their combined hands, eyes rolling when they landed on her own jagged nails.

"So, what is this place?" she asked.

"This place? Oh, it's mine now. I'm in charge. It's called Dune Haven, but I'm thinking about calling it Walker's Haven, or something like that."

Alyx snorted. "Right. That's why you've been trapped here and I couldn't get in." She smiled. So like him. Always arrogant.

Chase shook his head. "No. I'm serious. I did blood magic to take over the leadership here."

"You did magic?" She pulled her hand back. "What are you saying?"

"So, apparently there's been this feud over the power of the source of all magic, which resides somewhere in town. One guy was in charge, and another guy created this place to keep people safe from his evil power. But then he went Darth Vader on the town and turned bad himself, but he could still control this place since he created it, so no one had a place to hide from him. I did blood magic without even knowing it, and when I put it with the words, this place became mine."

"None of that makes sense at all."

"Let these guys explain it to you, they tell it better than me."

She looked at Brian, who seemed to be having trouble meeting her eyes. "He's right. I'll tell you everything. But be warned, we may not have much time once the Sovereign Warlock finds out he's lost Dune Haven."

CHAPTER 39
CHASE

Chase scratched his head.

This is more complicated than I realized.

He sighed. Sitting cross-legged on the floor, he repeated the words for what seemed like the thousandth time, his words rushed, "By Earth and Sea, by Wind and Flame, I create this portal to end the game. The light will lead, the dark will fall. The powers of light to save us all. From them to me. Let it be." Silence followed. His shoulders lifted on yet another sigh. He looked up. "I don't get it. Why does it always have to rhyme? Why can't I just say 'let's go'?"

Brian paced. "What? I don't know. Never thought about it. It's just the way it has always been." Hands on his hips, he turned. "I thought we could make a portal to transport us to town to save some time, but I guess we'll just have to go by foot. Let's go."

Chase turned toward Alyx when she spoke, "Wait. The wolves are still out there. They might be just waiting for us to leave this place."

"The wolves' loyalties lie with the first Sovereign. They will do anything to help him break free and regain his power. He created them, you see. They probably left when they sensed the power shift. They'll need to work out a new plan," Brian said.

"Created them? What do you mean he 'created them'?" Alyx demanded. "How do you create a species?"

Brian's hands gestured. "What does it matter? None of that matters anymore. If you're going to try to help the people here, we have to go into town to confront the Ruling Mage. There's no other way to do it."

Alyx faced Chase. "Why do we have to help the people here? We don't even know them. We're leaving, anyway. I don't understand why we have to get involved. Again."

Chase reached for her hand, looking into her eyes until she blushed. "Because it's the right thing to do. And because I believe that the Sovereign Warlock is the watch-hunter. Isn't that part of our mission here? Find the hunters and stop them from causing the exctinction of the remaining watches and their keepers?"

Alyx looked away. With one curt nod, she mumbled, "Yes."

Brian interrupted, "He won't have a choice, anyway. Once Chase took the power of this place, his fate was sealed. The Sovereign Warlock will not back down to the challenge. And that's exactly how he'll view this shift in power. A challenge to his authority."

"Okay. You said he created the wolves. What did you mean by that?" Chase asked.

"Not him. The first Sovereign. Let's get out of here and I'll tell you on the way. We have a long way to go to get to town," Brian answered.

Chase held up a hand. "Wait, let's try creating a portal one more time."

"Fine. Once more." Brian grumbled, "It didn't work before, I don't know why it would be different now."

"I have an idea. Alyx, do you have the journal?" Chase asked.

"It's useless, Chase. The pages are blank for this world, just like they were when we looked before the jump." She went to get it.

"But, maybe they're not blank. I was thinking, since this is a place of magic, maybe, I don't know, magic can open the pages or something."

Brian cleared his throat. "That might be true. But I don't see how that will help with a portal, and we need to go. Either make the portal, or let's walk. But one way or another, we need to get to town. I don't think a book with blank pages is the answer."

Chase reached out and took the journal. He ran his palm over the leather cover, and as always, his family history tugged at him. This book had been written long, long ago by his ancestor, Elias Walker, to share information about each of the twelve dimensions with each new generation of keepers. Elias was the creator who made it possible to travel to parallel worlds by creating the twelve watches. Now, there were only three watches left in existence because the watch-hunters had destroyed the rest, along with their keepers. Red filled his eyes as he thought of them. His enemies. Shaking off the hatred, he focused on the book. Slowly turning back the pages, he found the blank, yellowed paper he'd been looking for. "Okay. Show me." Waiting, he met Alyx's eyes. "Oh, yeah. It's supposed to rhyme or something. Okay. By Earth and Wind, by Flame and Sea, show the secrets of this world to me."

Silence. He tried, over and over, using different words each time, and still nothing happened. He slammed the book closed. "I guess I was wrong."

He felt a hand grasp his forearm and turned to find Alyx looking into his eyes intently. "It's okay. We'll find our way without it. We didn't have help last time and we managed okay. We'll do the same here. Let's try the portal one more time. If that doesn't work, we'll walk."

Chase took a deep breath and nodded. Searching out Brian, he said, "Let's try again."

"Sounds good."

Colin lay sprawled on the couch, one leg up on the arm, the other bent with his foot on the floor. Eyes closed, his sporadic snores filled the room as if he didn't have a care in the world. Just then he shifted, grumbling as he smacked his lips, then resumed his snoring. Brian walked over and slapped his other foot so it fell off the sofa arm. Colin sputtered, "What? Hey! Why'd you do that? I was having a dream about..."

"Don't care, Col. Time to go. Chase is going to try one more time to make a portal, and if he fails we're hiking."

"Wha-? Aw, c'mon, Brian. I don't want to walk anymore. Why don't we just help him? Like, combine our magic or something?"

Brian hesitated, his words picking up speed as he spoke, "Ha! Good idea, little bro! Get over here and let's try it."

Chase's mouth dropped open. "You mean, all this time, you've just been standing there watching me when you could have been helping all along?"

"Hey, it wasn't so long ago I was like you ... just getting introduced to magic. I was thinking that you needed to do it since you hold the power here now. But it can't hurt to give your power a boost with ours. Everybody, let's cast a circle. Chase, you start and we'll follow your lead."

Chase's eyes followed Brian as he sat next to him on the floor. "How do I do that?"

"Oh. Yeah. I keep forgetting you're so new to this." Brian sighed. "Okay. Everybody sit in a circle."

"C'mon Alyx." Chase held out his hand to her.

She gave a quick negative shake and backed up a step. "What, me? No, I don't..."

Chase turned toward her, eyes beseeching. "We need all the help we can get. *I* need you here. What if we open a portal and you're not with us? We'd be separated again, and I'm not willing to risk that. Please, Alyx. I need you here if I'm doing this."

She ran her hand through her hair. "Fine. But I need to tell you all this hocus-pocus creeps me out. It's just not right. Not to mention that I might hinder the magic, since I ..."

"You'll do fine. If I can do this, so can you." He squeezed her hand when she sat on his other side, and Colin flopped to the floor between Alyx and Brian. The four sat with legs crossed on the floor facing each other, hands resting on their knees, Chase's and Alyx's fingers loosely linked where their knees touched.

Brian began talking, "Okay that's north and south." He pointed forward and back, then left to right. "And there's east and west." He cleared his throat and began,

"I call on the elements. Earth. Air. Water. Fire. We thank you for your energy." He paused, meeting each of their eyes. "Say it with me. By Earth and Sea, by Wind and Flame, I—we—create this portal to end the game. The light will lead, the dark will fall. The powers of light to save us all. Four call on that energy today. We need your help to be on our way. Through them to me. Let it be."

The air became eerily still, and then a sudden wind whipped through the room, ruffling their hair. Alyx swiped hers back from her face. The front door banged open just as a pinprick of light appeared directly in front of them. A person, silhouette framed by rays of sunlight, filled the doorway. Eyes widening, Chase broke the circle as he lunged to his feet, and the tiny point of light signaling the beginning of a portal sputtered and died out. Fingers grabbed at him in an attempt to hold him back, and he shrugged them off, intent on running toward the person who had entered his sanctuary.

"You!" he screamed as he ran into the person with his head down, shoulders first, and the two fell in a heap on the floor with a muffled *oomph*. The rumble of a low growl filled the space, and pandemonium broke loose as the others jumped to their feet, everyone shouting at once.

CHAPTER 40
ALYX

"Chase, no!" Alyx was only one step behind him.

Brian reached out. "Wait!"

"Don't...!" Colin wailed.

Alyx dove into the pile of people and grabbed Chase's arm, his muscles bunched as if on a spring ready to launch. "Chase! Get up!"

Her eyes pleaded as Chase looked back at her, fist cocked and ready to take another swing. "Huh?"

"Get up. That's Liz. It's ... complicated. Just let her up and we'll explain." Alyx watched him slowly ease up, brows furrowed, sitting back on his haunches.

"What are you talking about?" Chase demanded.

"Just let her up. She's ... trying to change ... here," Alyx mumbled.

"And you believe that, Alyx?" He stood, looking down at the hunter, then back up at Alyx in disbelief. "I don't understand. She's the hunter, right?"

The way he was looking at her made her pause before continuing. Alyx sighed. "Yes. She hasn't denied that. But we were trying to work together before I got here. She says she's trying to change, Chase. I don't know if I believe her, I really don't. But I haven't seen her go back on her word. Bea seems to trust her, and so did Bo, so ..."

"Bea and Bo? What are you talking about?"

Nodding, she squatted next to Bea, running her hand down her flank. "Friends. This is Bea, short for Beatrice. The hunter goes by Liz in this world. She used to harness the power of dark magic, but she says she has been trying to change. I think I might ... believe her. She was sort of helping me find you, until Bo was taken."

Chase's eyes narrowed, head tilted. "I can't believe I'm hearing this. You're actually taking the side of the hunter?"

"I ... guess so. At least for now." She studied Chase as he let her words sink in. He nodded, but made no attempt to mask his feelings as he continued to glare at Liz..

"For now," Alyx repeated.

Liz stepped forward, offering a hand-shake, but Chase stood with arms crossed squinting down at her. With one quick nod, Liz's hand dropped to her side. Turning away, her raven ponytail bobbed, giving her a youthful appearance despite her age. The hunters had been around since the watches' invention, boasting an almost immortal quality that allowed them to age at a very slow rate through the passage of time. *Almost* immortal. They *could* die, as they all knew well.

Chase turned to the animal, pointing. "You say she's called Bea?"

"Yes."

He squatted, the low growl reduced to a low grumble, she backed up when he reached out a hand to her. "It's okay, girl. Bea. I'm Chase. I shared my beef jerky with you back in the woods a while back, remember?"

Bea tilted her head back, her eyes locking with Liz. "It's okay, Bea. He's Alyx's friend," she soothed.

The animal stood still, allowing his touch with just a small flinch. She obviously wasn't sure about him yet, either.

"So, where's her pup?" Chase wanted to know.

"Bo. His name is Bo. The Enfield took him. We think he's been taken to the Sovereign Warlock," Liz answered.

"Enzo took the pup? But why would they want him?" Chase asked.

"Same reason they want *us*. They call him the hybrid. Bea is his mother. Enzo is his father. They think his blood has similar properties to our watches. He wants to use the blood to travel to other worlds so he can rule them all," Alyx said.

"I knew the pup looked strange. Sounds like we got here just in time," Chase added.

"I was thinking it was bad timing ... but either way, I'd like to try to take Bo out of there if we're headed that way anyway. He's innocent, and doesn't deserve to be used this way," Alyx said.

Chase shrugged. "Sure. No promises, but we can try to save the pup—hybrid— whatever you want to call him."

Liz chimed in, "Bo. We call him Bo. He's just a pup, and he's never been away from his mama before. That's why we came back. Bea and I want to help save Bo. I'll do whatever I can to help ... except call on the dark magic. I won't. I can't." Liz placed a hand on Bea's flank as she spoke. "I'm not strong enough to fight against it again, and I won't be able to help anyone if it takes control of me like before."

Bea whimpered, and Alyx swallowed and looked away. She could almost respect this woman standing in front of her. She was trying to make a better life. Trying to help them and these creatures she called her friends.

A week ago, I would never have believed I'd be sharing breathing space with a hunter, let alone working with her.

She cleared her throat and walked to stand in front of Liz. "Okay. So when you arrived, we were working together to create a portal into town."

"Good idea. That would be a faster way to travel." Liz nodded. "I can talk you through it, if you need me to. Even though I'm not harnessing the power, I know just about everything there is to know about it. I think I can help that way, if not magically."

Alyx smiled. "Thanks, though I think we were about to succeed just before you came in." She paused, head tilted as an idea occurred to her. "Wait. *How* did you come in?"

"I ... sensed a shift in power here. And even though I won't use the power, I do still know of its existence. As long as you believe in the power and can see Dune Haven, you can enter for refuge," Liz said.

"You sensed it?" Alyx asked.

"Yes. I guess you could say I know how to work my way around magic. I've had lots of practice."

Brian spoke for the first time, "Well, you're right about the power shift. Chase used blood magic to take control of this place."

Liz whipped her head up. "You used blood magic?"

"I guess so. I didn't know it at the time, but I did use my blood."

"And you used a spell with it?" She tilted her head.

Chase nodded. "Brian helped me with that."

"We need to get out of here. Now. I can't believe he hasn't come for you yet. Move! Get in the circle. Quickly!"

Without another word, the four sat back in the same spots as before, then looked to Liz, awaiting her next instructions. "I can't come with you. That would be tempting fate. I'll meet you there. Bea, get inside the circle. You go with them. I travel fast alone."

Bea whimpered. Alyx agreed. "Come with us. It's better if we stick together." She reached her hand out.

"I ... can't. Now, go. Begin the spell. I'll meet you there. I promise. Hold hands to close the circle." Liz disappeared out the door. Clasping hands, Chase immediately began chanting the now-familiar words, and the others joined in.

A lone howl erupted from Bea as the wind picked up, tossing bowls of food off the table with a crash as their hair whipped in front of their eyes. A drinking glass shattered on the floor, but none of them stopped or even noticed. A pinprick of light appeared in front of them as before, only this time it stretched and grew until it was the size of an 8-inch by 10-inch picture frame. Through the rectangular opening, they could make out people walking along white concrete sidewalks, some with heads bent toward their phones, others walking along with arms loaded with beach-gear, young children trailing behind in tears. Small, quaint, touristy buildings with an 'old-time' feel lined the street.

No one seemed to notice them through the tiny portal.

Alyx held her breath, waiting for the opening to continue growing, but its size seemed frozen. Pushing back her hair again, she yelled, "It's not working! We'll never fit through that!"

"Keep repeating the spell..."

Four voices continued chanting until suddenly, Colin was lifted off his feet as if he were floating, and his body turned to sunbeams as he was sucked into the portal. Brian followed his brother, and then Bea, Chase, and finally Alyx.

The fluttering in Alyx's stomach pulled her along, and she could hear someone screaming.

She squeezed her eyes shut when she realized it was her own voice she was hearing.

CHAPTER 41
CHASE

Sitting on the sidewalk looking back, Chase could still see through the portal into the living room at Dune Haven as if through a tunnel. He watched Alyx disappear from the center of the circle they had cast on the hardwood floor into bursts of sunbeams and shoot through the rectangular opening like a cheap back-yard firework. Once through the passageway, the light swirled until she regained her solid form. His mouth dropped open. The air around her shimmered in visible waves, like heat coming off the blacktop on a mid-summer day. Once everyone was through, the portal dissolved into vapor as if it had never been there at all.

Butterflies continued to flit around in his gut, reminding him of the tickling sensation he'd gotten just before plunging downhill on the roller coaster at Dune Harbor's annual 'Christmas in July' Fair. One quick bark of laughter broke free, and his head swiveled to see if anyone had heard. He pushed himself off the cement to stand, the heated concrete burning his palms. Chase blinked as his eyes adjusted to the sunlight directly overhead. One hand up, he blocked the sun and squinted.

At least traveling through portals isn't like jumping dimensions.

"Hey! Watch it!" A man pulling a cart with large, gray, rubber wheels overstuffed with beach buckets, towels, boogie boards, and an assortment of other beach-gear, swerved to avoid a collision. A can of spray sunscreen fell from the top with a metallic *clang* and rolled down the block. "Hey Dawn, can you get that?"

A woman, hair askew, bent to pick it up in one hand, a squirming toddler held against her side with the other. "Bray, I told you to put the sunscreen *in* the beach bag." The young boy yawned as he peeked out from behind her, tear streaks drying on his sandy cheeks, whatever event caused his recent crying jag was now forgotten. The woman, after placing the suntan lotion precariously back on top of the heap, reached for the boy's hand. "Come on, Ty. Let's get you home for a late lunch." Ty turned, flicked a finger toward the beach cart, and the sunscreen wobbled and began to fall once again. Suddenly, the bottle froze in midair, and then moved backward, gently settling back on top of the pile of towels once again as if a hand had reached out and placed it there. The boy's mother bent to whisper in his ear, and Chase couldn't make out the words.

The haggard family, obviously just leaving a fun-filled morning at the beach, continued on their way. Chase's eyes followed them, mouth agape. He watched them until they turned a corner and disappeared from sight, and even then continued staring. Taking one quick step in their direction, he paused. Flinching at a gentle touch on his arm, he turned to see Alyx's concerned eyes boring into his.

"Alyx. Did you see that family?"

"What? Oh, I guess so. They turned at that corner, right?" She pointed. "Why?"

"That was Bray, Dawn, and Ty. They seem so ... different. And in this world, Ty has magic. And a baby sister."

"Everyone's different here, Chase."

"I know that. I do. It's just so—I don't know—*real* when you see people you know who don't know you anymore." He sighed. "And I guess I'm disappointed to see Ty here. I guess I sorta hoped he might be the last keeper we've been searching for. But if he's here in this dimension, he can't be a keeper since we don't have other selves and we only exist in our home dimension." His eyes drifted up the street once again, and a sigh escaped.

Brian's voice broke through his reverie. "We have other things to worry about." He raised his eyebrows and jerked his head toward Bea. "It won't take long for people to notice *her* here."

Chase shrugged. "She could easily be mistaken for a pet dog."

Brian turned. "A what? Did you say *pet* dog?"

"Yes."

"Why would anyone try to turn a wild animal into a pet?" Brian asked.

"Wait. You're saying dogs aren't pets here?" Chase said.

"That would be crazy, wouldn't it? You could get attacked in your sleep."

"Wow." Chase raised his eyebrows at Alyx, then addressed Brian. "Were dogs ever pets?"

Brian nodded. "Long ago, we had two brutal attacks—one in Dune Harbor and another about a hundred-miles from here that took out an entire family—and after that the government declared it illegal to own a dog as a pet."

Alyx leaned in, whispering, "Just add that on to all the other differences here."

He nodded. "This is weird."

Colin spoke for the first time since traveling through the portal, "Hey, why are you whispering? My teacher told me it's rude to whisper right in front of people."

Chase stepped back. "You're right." He looked up and down the street, busy with locals and tourists enjoying the beautiful summer day. This was the hub of Dune Harbor town, aptly named Main Street, and he recognized some of the buildings, though not all of them. The post office, the American flag flapping against the flagpole creating a metallic clanging at windy intervals, the municipal building, a gift shop and a realtor's office. "What do we do now?"

"We need to get out of here. See, right there?" Brian pointed across the street at an angle. "That's Dune Harbor base. You know, the Sovereign Warlock's evil magic lair."

"What? You mean that realtor's office?" He read the sign aloud, *"Dune Harbor Realty ~ Owning Your Own Home Is Not An Illusion."* His eyes met Brian's, head tilting. "Really?"

"Oh, that's more than a simple realty office. That's just a front for what's underneath. In the basement. The Illusion spell obscures it from the townies. Even us magicals can't easily see through the powerful concealment spell."

Chase took a step back. Right now, all he could see was the storefront illusion the same as everyone else. He squinted, concentrating all his energy on *seeing*. Nothing. He'd seen before, from above when the chimera—Enzo—had been carrying him. This had to be the place that had looked like a castle and courtyard from his bird's eye view.

If I saw it then, why can't I see it now?

He blew air through his teeth, shoulders slumping. "I can't see it. Can you?"

"No," Brian and Colin chorused.

"What about you, Alyx?"

She was so intent on the building she seemed to be oblivious to him.

"Alyx? Can you see it?"

She jerked out of her trance. "I ... don't know. It ... sort of ... shimmered a second ago, but now it just looks like it did before."

"Okay. So what do we do now?"

He looked back at the building, just missing the man who had exited. The man was walking the opposite direction, and Chase did a double-take. He looked very familiar... "Hey, is that ... ?"

Brian grabbed his arm, "Get down!"

"Wha-?"

"Down!"

They all squatted behind a parked midnight black GMC Acadia, meter blinking red. Chase's heart pounded in time with the watch against his ribcage.

"Why are we hiding behind a car?"

"That was the Sovereign Warlock. And you're not ready for a confrontation just yet."

"That was the Big Guy? But, I could have sworn he looked like someone I know..." He peeked around the car, but the man had disappeared around a corner. "Huh. Guess I was wrong."

CHAPTER 42
ALYX

They walked briskly, eyes darting as they moved, following Brian and Colin until they reached the boys' house. Their family lived in a one-story single home on 12th Street, the lawn mowed in perfect diagonal lines, walkway lined with a pattern of red and yellow gerbera daisies symmetrically spaced in visual invitation to proceed to the cherrywood-stained front door. The small cement porch was lined with multiple potted plants in a riot of colors placed with intentional abandon, and the large doormat declared: 'Everything's Better At The Beach'.

As they sneaked around the side of the house and into the backyard, Alyx cleared her throat. "Uh, if you live here, why can't we go in the front door?"

"Shh. Because we don't want our parents to know we're helping you. You'll stay in here." Brian pointed toward a small shed, painted in the same shades as the front and looking every bit as neat as the main house. "You'll be safe, and we won't get in trouble." He opened the double door outward and gestured. "It's not so bad. A win-win, really."

Alyx peeked inside, then back at Brian. "What are we supposed to do in there?"

"Practice." He nodded once as he answered.

Her eyes were incredulous. "What do you mean, practice? All I see is a bunch of lawn-care supplies. Should we practice mowing the lawn? Or pruning the bushes?" She glanced at Chase and rolled her eyes. "This is ridiculous. We don't have to stay here."

Chase stepped forward, and she hesitated. "Wait," he said. Turning to Brian he asked, "We need to know why we're here and how you're going to help us. We don't know what you want us to do. Tell us the plan."

Alyx moved when she saw Colin grab hold of Chase's arm. Colin pleaded in rushed tones, "You're gonna defeat the Sovereign Warlock and help us save our..."

"Colin." Brian interrupted his brother with a hand on his arm, then addressed Chase and Alyx. "You need to train and become stronger to defeat the Sovereign to save yourselves. That's all you need to know."

Alyx moved to stand between them, looking into Chase's eyes. "We don't have to do this. It isn't why we're here." She took his hand. With one squeeze, she continued, "Let's just find our own way until the jump. Why do we always have to get involved in things that don't pertain to us?"

Conflict was evident in Chase's eyes, and for a moment she thought he would capitulate. Then he broke eye contact and looked from Colin to Brian to Bea. "But it *does* pertain to us. We don't really have a choice, do we?"

"There's always a choice," Alyx retorted.

Chase shook his head. "Don't forget the hunter *is* our problem, and he's the one they're asking us to challenge. Isn't that why we're here?"

"Not the only reason. Things seem ... different here. There's Liz, and the magic. Nothing is as it seems. Flying chimeras and intelligent animals. And even the page in the journal is blank. What do you think that means, Chase?" She glanced away and back again. "I'll tell you what I think. It means we shouldn't get involved. This place needs to be left on its own to figure this out. Past keepers obviously haven't been able to make a difference here. Why should we be any different?" Alyx asked.

Chase paced away, then back, hands gesturing. "We *are* different. We're the first keepers ever to jump together. Think about it. I don't think you really mean what you're saying."

"Don't tell me how I feel or don't feel. You don't even know me that well," she retorted. Her breath caught when he took a step closer, bringing them nose to nose. She held her ground, not moving away. His whispered words sent sparks through her limbs. His breath tickled her upper lip, and she breathed in the dizzying scent of him.

"Oh, I know you." If possible, he leaned even closer. "I know you, Alyx."

His eyes stared so intensely into hers, and his gaze alone sent tingles down her arms. Her head felt light, and her eyes glanced quickly at his lips, then away. She heard the smile when he whispered against her cheek, "Why do you constantly fight it, Alyx?"

Their lips touched, and Alyx felt her body lean forward. The kiss was as gentle as a butterfly's wings, and yet it set her entire body on fire. His indrawn breath had her tilting her head to get closer ... until Colin grunted.

"Oh great, here they go again. Hey, can you two wait until you're in the shed to do that? It's disgusting to watch you drooling all over each other."

Alyx turned her head, breaking the contact with a step away. She saw Brian's retreating back as he disappeared inside the house. Looking back at Colin she whispered, "Sorry. I-I forgot you were here."

"Me too. Sorry." Chase blinked.

"Just get in. We'll bring you food when we can. And when our parents are sleeping, we'll come teach you what we know about magic. Well, Brian will, I guess. He knows more than me."

She nodded absently. A small smile turned up the corners of Alyx's lips at the bemused expression on Chase's face. And was that a blush? She stood up straighter, a purely female power-surge filling her body with a magic of its own. "What were you saying, Chase?"

"I think I was, um, saying that we don't have a choice here. What about Bea and Bo? Who will help them if not us?"

The smile dropped from her face when she looked at Bea's head tilted up, her golden eyes conveying a silent plea. Alyx's shoulders drooped. "Fine." She stomped into the shed and sat in the corner.

Bea walked inside, laying close enough to Alyx that she could feel her fur tickling along her calf-muscle without actually touching her. Alyx looked up when Chase stepped in, eyes now clear and boring into her with a new kind of intensity. The door closed behind him, the only light coming through the small windows just beneath the roof. His eyes glowed despite the shadows that hid his face.

He began walking determinedly toward her, and if her keeper's heart had the ability, she knew it would be racing against her ribcage right now. Instead, she drew in a sharp breath.

CHAPTER 43
CHASE

Chase's easy smile spread slowly. He halted directly in front of her, raising an eyebrow.

"Alyx?"

"Chase, I..." she stammered.

"I'd really like to kiss you right now. But I won't if you don't want me to."

Bea's chest rumbled, back arched and blocking his access to Alyx. The animal clearly sensed Alyx's mood shift, and was protecting her.

Chase backed up a step. "It's always your choice." His eyes glowed in the shadowy shed, and he watched Alyx ease to her feet, her eyes never leaving his.

She blew out a long breath. "Bea. It's okay. Chase isn't going to hurt me."

Bea's head whipped back and forth between the two humans, and she sat down. The growl faded away and she cocked her head.

He watched Alyx reach down to run her fingers gently over the animal's head, and his heart swelled. "Alyx?" He asked, unsure of her response now that nothing stood between them. He would not make the first move. Her head jerked up, and she took one tentative step toward him. Reaching out, his fingers brushed gently against her cheek. His hand continued on, gently cupping the back of her neck, pulling her slowly toward him, his eyes asking for permission. "Are you sure?" he choked.

In response, she leaned in. Their lips met as if they'd never parted, resuming where they'd left off and setting off fireworks across in his vision. He closed his eyes and sank into the kiss, the little noise she made in the back of her throat nearly his undoing. His mind went blank, and all he could do was feel.

Alyx.

She lifted her arms, wrapping them around the back of his neck, and stood on her tiptoes fitting herself against him.

A low, intense rumble shook the small shed, and they broke apart. Alyx touched a finger over her own lips before running to the tiny window. Chase followed, eyes wide. Lightning streaked through the sky, striking the roof of the house. Flames sprang up as Brian and Colin ran out of the house toward the shed.

"Come on! We have to go!" Brian shouted, arms gesturing as he sprinted.

Chase tore open the door and stepped outside. "What's going on?"

"It's the Sovereign Warlock. He must know we're helping you. We're not safe here."

"What about your parents?"

"They're okay. Colin's talking to them now." He pointed.

Sure enough, Colin had a cell phone to his ear. "Brian, it's happening there, too! We have to help Mom and Dad!"

Alyx bent and placed her hand on Bea's back. "Where should we go?"

"I don't know." Brian grabbed her arm, pushing her toward the back of the yard. "Just away from here."

Chase turned thoughtful. "I think maybe I have an idea."

"Wait. I thought you weren't from here?"

"I-I'm not. It's hard to explain. I know this place even though I've never been here. You'll just have to trust me."

"Fine. Colin and I have to go help our parents. It's probably best if we don't know where you are, anyway, in case he interrogates us. We've been found out. The game plan has changed. Find a place to hide. When you can, find a man named Carson. Carson Murphy. He runs a souvenir shop on Atlantic Avenue. He'll help you. Good luck." With that, the brothers took off running the other direction.

Finding Alyx's wide eyes, Chase started moving. "Let's go."

• • •

Chase's legs pumped up and down, up and down. Occasionally, he stopped to look back over his shoulder. Alyx was right behind him, keeping up without much effort thanks to her watch and the powers it transferred to her. He picked up his pace.

Movement from above caught his attention.

The Enfield.

Enzo was following them.

How will we ever hide from the Sovereign if he can follow us from the sky?

Stopping under the cover of a tree in someone's backyard, he waited until she stopped next to him. "Will he come down here?"

Alyx shook her head. "I don't think so. Wouldn't townies notice a magical creature if he lands? I think he's just following to report our whereabouts to the man in charge."

"Okay ... so we just have to lose him."

She nodded. "Yeah. That's all." Chase glanced up, then started moving again. "I hope."

CHAPTER 44
THE SOVEREIGN WARLOCK

The man known by the Magical community as the currently ruling Sovereign Warlock paced back and forth. To the townies, he was known by a different name. His appearance was nothing short of typical. Thinning chestnut hair speckled with gray, deep blue eyes highlighted by laugh-lines, casually dressed in a green polo shirt displaying the logo for Dune Harbor Realty, and khaki pants. He had the misleading appearance of a quintessential small-town 'guy next-door.'

"I'm disappointed in both of you. You know I'm only trying to protect everyone in this town the best way I can. The townies have no idea of the power that is centered here, and what I'm doing is for their own good. For all of us. Why are you fighting me on this? And why are you sitting on the cold floor when I've provided you with all the comforts of home?"

Mason Moore and his mom, Jean, huddled on the floor ignoring the homey furniture, arms wrapped around each other. Mason's head tilted up a notch. "You're not doing this for them. You're doing it for you. For the power. You're right. This all started with you trying to save the town. But somewhere along the way, you changed."

Jean spat on the floor and glared at the man towering over them. Her hair hung in strings around her face, black circles giving her eyes a sunken look. "You murdered my husband."

He chuckled. "Now, you know that's not true, Jean, and it hurts that you can't see the bigger picture here. But I won't give up on you. I know you'll come around. Both of you. Until then, you'll need to remain here."

"In prison."

"You can look at it that way, if you want to. I prefer to think of it as a sanctuary from all the evil that lurks just around the corner. You know I created Dune Haven as a refuge from the last ruling mage. A safe place away from town. Now that I'm ruling, the entire town of Dune Harbor is a safe haven, so I have no use for that little cottage anymore, anyway. But you," he nodded at Mason, "you helped someone take back the power of my shelter in the woods. And that is unforgivable merely because you plotted against me. *You* put yourself here. It's not so bad. For a jail, it's very comfortable."

"This cell is no different from the one that holds the last Sovereign Warlock. And the town is a prison, too."

"Funny you should mention him. The last wizard. I saved all of us from his black magic, remember? You do remember how dark this town was then? You seem to forget, I'm the good guy here."

"Yes. I do remember. You were the good guy. But you changed once you took power. I only wish you could see that the magic you wield is dark magic, too. It seems to be part of the job description. You're power hungry. It's all you care about now. Why is it so important to rule over other lands no one even knows about?"

The Sovereign's eyes narrowed, the smile he'd worn dropping from his face, and a feral gleam shone out from his pupils. "If I don't do it, someone else will," he snapped. "You can rot down here until you to see things my way."

He waved his hand as he marched from the room, and a surge of magically charged electricity filled the space followed immediately by low moans from its two occupants. When the magical surge faded, they clutched hands. A tiny, broken voice filled the room, just before Mason's mother hung her head, her sob echoing in the small room that thrummed with dark power.

"I miss my husband."

"I know. I miss Dad, too."

•   •   •

The Sovereign Warlock stomped from the room, down another hallway and into another, wider room. He paced in front of his worktable lined with potions and ingredients, a scowl marring his average features. His lair, located in the basement of Dune Harbor Realty, was a front for his true calling: to protect the people of Dune Harbor from the magic on which the very foundation of the town had been built.

Sometimes, as he was now, he was torn. There were times when his old self would fight back, and he became muddled and confused about his scheme to take control of all twelve worlds.

He sank into a chair, bent forward, hands grasping his head. A moan broke free, and his body rocked back and forth, back and forth.

What if the boy is right? What if I'm just as bad as the warlock I replaced?

Lurching to his feet, he swiped madly at the table, vials and bottles clanging and scattering across the cement floor.

No! I'm doing this for the greater good. He's just like his father was. Weak and narrow-minded. David Moore couldn't see the bigger picture, and neither can his son.

But I can.

A small, mewling sound interrupted his introspection, and he slowly stood. Walking to a small cage in the corner, he bent and peered inside.

"Hello, little hybrid."

Bo flinched, and huddled into the far corner of his prison. Its tiny cry echoed in the cell.

"It's okay. I'm not going to hurt you. Yet. You're the key to all of this. At the next full-moon, you'll help me to save not only the people in this world, but the people of all the twelve dimensions. You're the key, little hybrid."

He stood, straightened his shirt, and sailed from the room, confidence restored.

I know what my purpose is, and nothing will stop me from achieving it.

A flick of his hand turned off the light, and he marched up the unfinished cement stairs into the Realty office just as a townie pushed through the front door, little bell jingling to announce a customer. On his way by, he glanced out the large picture window displaying a view of the small grassy courtyard that sat in the center of the building square, his eyes sweeping over the eight Adirondack chairs placed invitingly around a what appeared to be a large fire pit. The sun beat down cheerily onto the multi-colored chairs in painted lime-green, lemon-yellow, raspberry-red, and mandarin-orange that bordered the homey garden filled with a scattering of herbs and flowering annuals and arranged in a circle around the pit with a cement border. The courtyard served as a showcase for backyard staging in homes for sale. He continued past the window, pasting a smile on his face.

"Ah, hello, Mrs. Ruiz. I have some leads on selling your house. Come. Sit down and we can talk more about it."

The elderly woman smiled and sank into the cushioned metal chair on the other side of his desk, patting her white bun. It was wound so tight not a hair escaped its strict confinement.

"Thanks. The sooner I can move into the retirement community, the better. I just can't stay in that house another minute now that Mr. Ruiz is gone." She leaned precariously forward, wobbling on the edge of her seat, and held up a hand to cup her mouth as she continued in a whisper, "And I think my neighbor's house might be haunted."

"Now, now, Mrs. Ruiz. I'm sure it's nothing of the sort. You let me worry about the selling. That's what I'm here for, to help the people of this great town."

"You can call me Mariana."

"Wonderful, Mariana. It's such a lovely name. Now, let's get your house sold, shall we?"

CHAPTER 45
ALYX

Alyx blindly followed Chase, Enzo always within view. They stayed to the shadows and trees as much as possible, but still the chimera seemed to know their whereabouts, always circling above.

"We have to lose him, before we reach our destination," she whispered.

Chase frowned. "I agree. I'm just not sure how."

She followed Chase, Bea keeping pace, staying as close to him as possible until they reached the next house. The midday heat had chased most people inside, allowing them to remain inconspicuous, but she couldn't stop the feeling that they were doing something wrong. Like criminals. Slinking along the side of the house, bricks scraping through the thin fabric of her shirt, Alyx leaned forward to scan the sky.

"Wait, I don't see him anymore," she frantically whispered.

Chase took two steps away from the house then back again, pressing his back against the bricks under the roof's overhang so close to her she could feel the heat emanating off his arm along her own.

"No, he's still there," he cursed. "If he follows us, we won't have a chance of hiding." He kept moving, and she followed. They stopped under a canvas tent-style canopy set up next to a pool in someone's back yard.

"There has to be a way..." Alyx growled. She clenched her fists and would have paced if she had the space—and if they weren't on the run from a flying multi-specied beast.

Suddenly her head whipped up. "Why don't we create a portal to go ... wherever you're taking us."

Chase turned toward her, grasped her forearms, and planted his lips on hers in one quick kiss. "Why didn't I think of that?"

She returned his smile. "Because you need me, that's why. To tell the truth, I don't know what you'd do without me," she teased.

Chase's eyes pinned her in her place. "I don't either. We make a good team, you and I. In more ways than one." He winked, and her earlobes burned with embarrassment.

I'll never get used to his candidness.

The flush spread to her cheeks. "I-I guess so. O-okay. Let's try it. Where should we go to do it?"

"How about right here?"

"Don't you think we should find more cover first? I mean, these people may not even know about the magic. If we …"

"Yeah, you're probably right." His eyes moved, scanning the area. "I know where we are. The houses are pretty much the same as home. We're really close to Mason's house, let's head there. Maybe we'll find Mason home, but if not we can use his house anyway. I wonder if they still keep their spare key in the bottom of the mailbox? I know that house as well as my own. It's one block over. Follow me."

"But Enzo …?"

"Let's just make a run for it. He knows where we are anyway, and besides, if we can create a portal it won't matter if he knows because we won't be there anymore. It's actually a brilliant plan. They'll think they have us trapped, and we'll already be gone."

Alyx nodded. "Okay. Let's go."

In the air above them, Enzo let loose an interminable and desolate baying that caused a shiver to run down her back despite the heat of the day.

Bea, body pressed up against her leg, threw her head back and sent up a return howl. Alyx bent and wrapped her arms around the animal. Bea backed out of her arms, her small body shaking uncontrollably as she leaped away to the cement patio. She glanced once at Alyx, and then ran around the side of the house and disappeared from view.

Alyx's feet thumped in the grass as she chased after Bea without hesitation.

"Alyx! Let her go. If she doesn't want to stay with us, there's nothing we can do about it. Alyx!"

Though she heard him, she didn't look back. Her eyes darted, searching for Bea. In a whisper-yell, she called, "Bea! Bea, come back!" Her mother's words weaseled into her mind yet again: *Pets are distractions.* She was currently living the truth of those words but found that she just didn't care anymore. Sometimes, she was learning, distractions could lead to a more fulfilling path. *Sure, if I never make connections and bonds, I won't have as much to lose. But what kind of lonely existence would I be leading?* Throwing a glance over her shoulder, she met Chase's eyes before continuing on. Distractions are the things that make life worth fighting for. She wondered if her mother would ever understand that. She mentally pushed her musings aside to focus on the task at hand. Locating her friend, Bea.

Catching sight of a bushy tail, she saw Bea lope across the street, disappearing between two more houses.

Chase caught up and ran beside her. "I hope you know what you're doing."

"No. I just need to keep her safe."

She ignored his long-drawn-out sigh and moved faster. "Bea!"

"Bea!"

She flinched when another howl erupted from above but kept moving.

"Bea!"

CHAPTER 46
CHASE

Chase followed, if grudgingly. He'd stopped trying to talk sense into Alyx. She wasn't listening anyway and seemed to feel some kind of misguided responsibility toward Bea and Bo. Maybe even a bit of guilt that the pup had been taken. Who knew she had a soft spot for hybrid beasts and wolf-creatures?

What's next—adopting a family of stray cats? He snorted as he ran alongside her.

At the sound, she barely glanced his way, so focused was she on her target. Bea.

Shading his eyes, he glanced upward. Yep, the chimera—*still can't think of the beast as Enzo*—remained up there. Every now and then it would disappear from view only to swoop back into his line of vision again. Almost taunting them.

His feet slapped the brick patio in the current yard they were sneaking through. Bea had squeezed herself under a small tunnel at the bottom of a line of boxwood bushes, and they stopped and looked at each other. Without a word, Chase raced into the bordering yard and around the bushes, Alyx following closely on his heels.

Did we lose her?

"Chase, I don't..."

"There!"

He took off running toward the gray blur, disappearing into yet another yard just as a yell broke through his concentration bringing him to an abrupt halt, Alyx nearly plowing into his back.

"Hey! Why are you sneaking around in my yard?" A frail woman screeched with a hint of Latin accent, white hair streaked with mere remnants of the ebony it had once been pulled up into a tight bun that only served to accentuate her sagging wrinkled skin. She squinted in their general direction, creating even more crevices on her face. In her right hand, she struggled to hold a metal baseball bat off the ground. Meager protection if they *had* been there out of malice. Recognition dawned immediately.

I know her. Mrs. Ruiz. My next-door neighbor at home in Dimension 6. Cowering in the underground beach shelter in Dimension 7. Still living in the same house here in Dimension 8. But she won't remember any of it.

Holding his hands in the air, he smiled his most engaging smile. "Hi. Sorry to trespass. We're just ... um ... chasing after our pet. It ran through your yard and went that way." He pointed. "We don't mean to cause you any trouble."

"Pet, you say? I could have sworn I saw one of those wild wolf-dog inbreeds run through, but I wasn't wearing my glasses, so I can't be sure. I hope that's not your pet, because that would be breaking the law, young man, wouldn't it? Well, don't come back, or I'll be forced to use this." She hefted the bat with effort, her bony arms shaking, skin hanging loosely and wobbling back and forth with each tremor. "And I called the police, so if I were you I'd be on my way. Especially if you have a *dog*." Her brittle voice and hunched posture were probably the least threatening thing he'd ever seen. He fought a smile, instead nodding.

"Have a good day, ma'am."

Her eyes followed them. They didn't waste any time leaving the yard. He looked back once. Behind them, the bat made a heavy *clang* as the old woman lowered it to the ground, leaning on it like a cane. *How had she remained standing without it*, he wondered. Putting her out of his mind, he continued walking.

Alyx ran up the block, then back again, eyes wide and lost. "Do you see Bea?"

"No. But don't you think it's strange that she led us here?" He nodded toward the house in front of them. Observing her moment of realization, he watched her mouth drop open.

She whispered, "Yours and Uncle Charlie's house? I mean, Bray, Dawn and Ty's house?"

"I wonder if they live here now? In this dimension."

"Should we knock on the door?" She took one step toward the walkway and stopped, unsure. "Maybe not. They don't know us here. How would we explain...?"

Chase stood up straighter, adjusting his backpack. "Wait. We may not have to explain as much as you think. I saw them, and Ty used magic. If Ty is a magical, then his parents must be, too, right? So they know all about the Sovereign Warlock. Maybe they can help us." He studied the house. "What do you think?"

"Right now, we don't have many choices. If the old lady really did call the police, they'll be here soon. We don't want to have to answer questions, right? We don't even know if the police know about magic. Or if they do, which side they're on."

"You're right." He took a deep breath. "Okay. Let's go."

Just then, the front door opened and Dawn stood there, wildly gesturing them forward. Chase glanced at Alyx, nodded, and they both ran toward the house. Dawn stood back, and they entered the foyer and halted just inside.

A flying object whizzed past his head, and he ducked just in time.

"What the ...?"

CHAPTER 47
ALYX

Alyx watched the book sail past Chase's head, and immediately reached for her blade disc, shoulders back, eyes alert.

Dawn scrambled across the floor, shielding Ty from their view. She stood facing them, but looked back over her shoulder and scolded, "Ty! Stop! We don't throw books at visiting guests. I invited them in, baby. It's okay."

"We come in peace?" Alyx shook her head at Chase as he held both hands up in front of him. "Why did he attack us?" she asked.

Dawn's eyes went round. "Attack you? No! I'm sorry. He's just a boy. It was an accident, I promise. Practice, that's all."

Chase tilted his head. "Practice? Practicing what, exactly?"

"Well, magic, of course. You should know that," Dawn answered.

"At the risk of sounding stupid, why on Earth we should know that?" Alyx asked.

"Well, you traveled through a portal, didn't you? Back on the street. I saw you."

"Yes. Yes we did. Why didn't you say anything?" said Chase.

"Oh, I couldn't. My husband doesn't believe in magic, even though I've tried to show him. He'd rather believe in ghosts than in something he sees with his own eyes." She rolled her own. "He thinks our house is haunted. That's why I have to train Ty in secret. We only do magic when Bray—that's my husband—is at work. He wouldn't approve."

Alyx glanced toward the baby in a playpen in the corner of the living room. "Is your daughter a magical, too?"

Dawn shook her head. "No. At least, not yet. I think Samantha takes after her father."

"Have you seen a dog-like animal around here? She's our … pet … and we can't find her. She came this way," Chase said.

"Oh, you mean Beatrice? Yes, she's out back. Follow me." Dawn walked toward the back of the house.

"You know her?" Alyx searched out Chase with wide eyes. He shrugged and moved to the back door. She followed as if in a daze.

Dawn held open the painted white metal screen door and gestured. Alyx ran past her, going to her knees on the soft grass. "Bea! Why did you run? I was worried that Enzo would ..."

Bea crept forward and pushed her snout into Alyx's neck, the cold moisture reassuring her that her friend was okay. Her breath hitched. She cleared her throat. "Why did she bring us here?" Alyx directed her question at Dawn.

"I perform a nightly shield ritual on the house. To protect us—myself, my children, my husband. Since he doesn't believe, it's the only thing I can do to protect us. Don't worry, even the chimera can't see you here. Shields are my strongest spells. It's my specialty. You really don't have to worry."

"Are ... you saying that we can hide here?" Alyx asked.

Dawn shook her head. "That wouldn't work because of Bray. How would I explain your presence to him? All I can offer you a safe place during his working hours. I'll do that much for a fellow magical. But you can't stay here when he's home."

"Do you know Bea's friend Liz?"

A shadow crossed her eyes. "Yes."

"Did you know her when she was...dark?"

"Dark? That's an understatement if ever I heard one. You have no idea ..." She paused, took a deep breath. "I did know her then. She and the last Sovereign ruled together, equals in their hunger for power. But she redeemed herself when she saved Ty from the last Sovereign Warlock and helped to lock him up. I owe her a debt of gratitude." She blew her bangs out of her face, obviously conflicted. "Look, I don't know how long she can fight the dark power that she's holding back. Make no mistake, it's still inside her. She's merely controlling it now. I've seen what it did to her before, and like a power switch, she could go from light to dark in an instant. You shouldn't trust her." She hung her head, and her voice trembled, "I saw what it did to the wonderful man who is now known as the ruling mage. Dark magic can break a person. Believe me."

"You knew him? Before?"

"Yes, I knew him very well. The man I knew is gone. I fear he's lost forever. But that's all for another day." Her eyes took on a faraway look, then refocused. "You can hide here from 8:00 am to 3:00 pm on work days. No weekends. If you abide by my rules."

Chase stepped forward. "That's fair. We'll be happy to follow your rules. And thanks for the safe place. So, you say you're training Ty? Every day?"

"Yes. He's so smart, and such a fast learner! He's already mastered fire! I'm so proud of him." She leaned down to place a gentle peck the top of his head.

"Can we join in the training? We're beginners, too, and we have a lot to learn."

"Beginners, you say? But I saw you travel through a portal. How can you be beginners?"

Alyx's eyes followed Chase sat as he spoke, "We had others helping us, but we've been separated. I can't explain everything, but here's the short version: The two of us just arrived here, and though we are magicals, we didn't know that until we got here, and were never given the opportunity to properly train. We traveled through the portal from Dune Haven with our friend Brian and his brother Colin, who were going to train us, but the Sovereign found out and we became separated before they could teach us anything."

"Brian and Colin Heck? Yes, I know them," she interrupted.

"Yes. They seemed to think I could challenge the ruling mage since I took over the power of Dune Haven with blood magic ... sort of by accident. I'll be leaving this place one way or the other on September 9th—whether I want to or not. I won't have a choice. So, If I'm going to help this town, then I need to practice before that time arrives. Oh, and the chimera stole Bea's pup—the hybrid—and it's searching for us, too." He nodded at Alyx. "I think that covers everything, right?"

Dawn's hand shook as she held it to her mouth. "You're the ones he's looking for. The ones that have come to save us?" She reached out, grasping his left arm to study the watch. The timepiece must have sensed there was no threat, and did not release a deadly stream of electricity as it had been known to do as a defense mechanism. "And you performed blood magic to challenge the Sovereign Warlock? Are you crazy?" She stumbled backward, pushing Ty into her leg. "I ... don't know what to do. I have to protect my family. That comes above all else. But I also have to protect the town. I'll help you in any way I can, as long as it doesn't harm my family, or anyone else. Harm none."

"Yes. Harm none."

"According to magical lore, your people have been here before, and have failed. Please tell me you won't fail us this time."

Alyx grasped Chase's hand. They both nodded. "We'll do the best we can, Dawn. We promise."

"Well, I hope your best is good enough. Do you have a plan?"

"A plan? No, we don't. We were hoping you could give us some direction. Starting with training. There's no way we'd stand a chance fighting him with magic now. We barely know the basics."

"That, I can help you with. Bray has to work a half-day today. We spent the morning at the beach and he went into the office late, so that means he'll be home later than usual. Let's start now. With fire." She gestured to Ty. "Ty can help. Show them what you can do, baby."

Ty stepped forward without a sound, cupped his hand palm-up, and a small spark appeared and grew until it reached the size of a baseball. Eyes wide, orange flames dancing in their center, the small group watched as the fire grew into the size of a basketball.

"That's enough, Ty." At his mother's direction, he closed his hand and the fire instantly disappeared as if it had never existed. If not for the lingering fumes that flared her nostrils, Alyx would have doubted her own vision.

Dawn smiled. "Now let's show them how to do it."

CHAPTER 48
CHASE

Practicing magic is not as easy as they make it seem in books and movies.

It was grueling, tedious work, and when it was time for them to go, Chase's arms hung slack at his sides. They'd broken both a lamp and a mug during their first training, but overall it had been a successful session. The windows were still intact and the television was still standing, so he was looking at it as a win. Dark circles lined his eyes, and pain gripped his midsection as his stomach rumbled. He was famished. Despite his lethargy, his eyes glowed, and he smiled at Alyx.

I created fire from thin air. We both did. And I made a lamp move with my mind. Well, okay, it was a spell, but it was definitely a Pyro and Jean Grey moment.

He glanced at his palms, but no evidence remained of the fire that had existed there just moments ago.

Amazing. Mason would never believe it. Well, my Mason from home, anyway.

His smile disappeared as he thought of his friend.

Dawn carried out a plate of peanut butter and jelly sandwiches, and Chase grabbed one and ate it in four bites while sitting on the floor with his legs crossed. "Thanks," he mumbled while still chewing, a smudge of peanut butter on his lip. He swiped it with the back of his hand, then his tongue darted out to lick it off. Ty sat next to him, copying every move he made.

"Eww. Chase, you're disgusting," Alyx chided, then she turned and smiled at Ty who responded with a giggle.

Chase swallowed with one big gulp, his Adam's apple bobbing. "You didn't think so in the shed." His eyes twinkled.

"Food wasn't smeared all over your face then, or I never would have kissed you." She turned up her nose.

Dawn looked from one to the other. "Oh, so you're a couple, then?"

"Yes," Chase said.

Alyx said, "No."

"Sorry I asked." Dawn cleared the paper plates and cups and carried them to the kitchen, leaving them alone.

"Chase, we don't have time for a romance …"

"That's where you're wrong, Alyx. There's always time for a romance. Stop making excuses. Feel the magic that surrounds you." He winked, pointing to the half of a sandwich she held in her hand. "You gonna finish that?"

"I'm holding it, aren't I?" She took two more dainty bites, and then held it out to him. "I'm actually full. Here."

He ate it in one bite. "I don't know how you survive on the little you eat, but it's more for me, so I'm cool with it."

"Okay, so we have to figure out where we're going to spend the night, until we can come back here tomorrow."

"Why don't we stick with the original plan and head over to Mason's house. If we can't stay here, it's the next best thing to home. And it's only five and a half blocks away."

"Okay."

Chase leaned back and felt a sharp stab of pain. "Ouch." He brought his hand around, and a triangular shard of ceramic lamp base was imbedded in his palm. "Whoops. Guess we missed a piece when we cleaned up." Grasping it with his pointer finger and thumb, he pulled it out, then sucked on the immediate surge of blood that appeared.

Dawn entered with a filled plastic grocery bag and handed it to Chase. "Here, this should hold you over until tomorrow when I can get to the grocery store. It's just more of the same: sandwiches and some cookies. And bottled water. I'll go get a bandaid for that. You should come wash it with soap in the sink. Healing isn't my strong point."

"Naw, I'm fine. Just a scratch. Thanks. For everything, I mean. Really, we can't thank you enough. Hold on, I think we have some money we can give you to put toward the food since you'll be buying extra for us. I wouldn't want to put you out if you're gonna feed us every day. And I really hope you're gonna feed us every day." Chase laughed.

"That's not necessary. You don't need to give me anything …"

"Yes, it is. It's the least we can do to repay you for your kindness and help. Alyx, do you have the box?"

She nodded, walking to where she'd left it in her backpack by the front door. Tugging the zipper, she once again removed the box and handed it to Chase. They all flinched as the hinges protested like fingernails on a chalkboard. Reaching out, he picked up the journal to move it out of the way, forgetting his injured hand. The cut oozed blood—just a drop—onto the journal causing an immediate reaction. A powerful electrical current filled the room, reminiscent of the day he'd first discovered the watch in his uncle's belongings—when he'd still been ignorant of the twelve parallel dimensions. The hair on his arms and legs stood on end, and electricity permeated his entire being and through the watch on his wrist. His exhaustion completely forgotten, his limbs tingled with the need to move. Slowly he stood, clasping the journal to his chest. The room seemed to come to life, a power surge of energy vibrating the entire house and bouncing off the walls and every piece of furniture in the place. His body thrummed with it, and he stared at the journal in his hands. It seemed to be back-lit with pure light, as he imagined an angel might be if it came down from heaven to show itself.

Dawn froze in the doorway, shock all over her face. She grabbed Ty and picked him up, just as the baby's cries traveled down the stairs. For a moment, Dawn ignored the cries. "What's happening?"

"I-I don't know." Talking was an effort as his tongue seemed swollen with electricity. "It was the blood, I guess."

"More blood magic. Oh no ..." Regaining her mobility, she raced up the steps with Ty in her arms. "I have to do some research. He may be able to track the blood magic!" she called back over her shoulder as she disappeared.

"Chase," Alyx whispered.

At first he didn't react.

"Chase," she repeated calmly. "Open the journal."

Reverently, he flipped open the cover, and the pages flipped of their own accord to a page labeled simply: 8. Where before it had been nothing but an empty page, now appeared hand-written, scribbled words that filled every corner.

CHAPTER 49
ALYX

Alyx stepped forward, peering over the top of the journal Chase held in his hand. Now that the journal was open, the room had stopped pulsing and returned to normal. All traces of electrical—or more accurately, magical—energy drained from the house leaving them with an eerie silence that was almost more disturbing than the sudden power surge had been.

"Of course this page in the book would need magic to open it up. Why didn't we think of that?" Alyx asked.

Chase said, "Yeah. Blood magic. Remind me next time we're in a tight spot to open up my veins and bleed myself. That seems to be the answer around here."

Alyx rolled her eyes, moving to stand next to Chase, whose own eyes never left the journal page with an 8 scrawled in calligraphic style on top. "What does it say?" she said.

"Not sure. It looks like it was written in a hurry." He squinted at the paper, trying to decipher the ancient flowery handwriting. "There are some sketches, looks like maybe it's a portal?" He pointed at one in the upper left corner, his watch glowing so bright it cast an iridescent blue illumination over the yellowed page in the journal. The small drawing depicted a swirling oval coming out from the Earth just over the spot where Dune Harbor would be. "What do you think?"

"Yes. Maybe our portal out of here?"

"But why would we need a portal out of here when we already have a one-way ticket out? I think the portals only work within the current world, anyway." He continued scanning. "Wait. This is a spell. It's a little smudged, but I think I can make out most of it."

"*The Destruction Spell. *To be used only as a last resort.*" Their eyes met. "Uh, I don't think we'll need that one." Alyx cocked her head. "I wonder why your ancestor put that in here? Did he think the magic would make the whole town evil and we would need to destroy the town?"

"I don't care why it's in here. I'm not gonna destroy anything," Chase said.

"What if we don't have a choice? I mean, things are *bad* here."

"What are you saying, Alyx? That you're willing to destroy the town and all the people in it? Dawn? Ty? Samantha? Mason? Brian? Colin? And what about Bea and Bo? That's not for us to decide."

"I agree. But if there's no other choice, isn't it better to destroy one town than to let someone rule over all the worlds? Can you imagine what would happen if they figure out how to control the twelve dimensions? It wouldn't just affect this place, but all of the multiverse. Think about it," Alyx said.

He shook his head. "I don't know what we're supposed to do. I'm starting to wish I'd never chosen any of this. The watch. Being a keeper. Traveling the twelve dimensions. All of it." He shoved the journal at Alyx and paced.

She placed a hand on his arm. "Sometimes I feel that way, too." His head jerked up, eyes searching hers. She could tell she had surprised him. "It's true. Sometimes I wish I hadn't been born a keeper. But then I realize, there's nothing I can do about it. Everything happens for a deeper purpose. It's my destiny. *Your* destiny. For whatever reason, we were chosen to traverse the worlds that most people never even know exist. For their sake, and ours, we have to do what we were meant to do, no matter how hard that might be."

"I know. I know you're right. Sorry."

"No apology necessary." She stepped into his open arms, and they stood just holding each other. Her head rested on his chest, and she could feel the steady beat of his heart in perfect unison with her own. Their combined warmth created a cocoon of solace where only the two of them existed. She sighed, closing her eyes and breathing in the dizzying scent of him. *Home.* A smile curved her lips.

Dawn's urgent voice shattered the moment. "Can you two come up here?" she called down the stairs.

They broke apart, but continued to hold hands as they took the stairs. Dawn and the children were in a small bedroom lined with bookshelves. Scattered books littered the floor, and she sat with the baby on one leg, an open book on the other. "Sometimes, blood magic can be tracked. It leaves a mark in the atmosphere, so I wasn't sure if he could track it back to the house. My house." She looked up and back down. "If that was the case, none of us would be safe here. But I think I can give my shielding spell a boost with this." She pointed at the page. "We should be okay. I think."

Her frantic eyes looked them over. "Watch Ty and Samantha while I perform the spell. And then you have to leave. I don't have much time before Bray gets home. We have to hurry." She thrust Samantha into Alyx's hands and ran from the room with the book in her hands.

Alyx held the baby at arm's length. Drool leaked from the corner of the child's mouth, and a bubble formed on her lips as she babbled the gibberish of toddlers. "Gross. Here." She pushed Samantha toward Chase, but he shook his head.

"Uh-uh."

"Well, what am I supposed to do with her?"

"I don't know, cuddle her or something?"

"But she's all ... wet."

Chase laughed. "Figure it out."

Ty looked from one to the other. "Don't you know anything about babies?"

Alyx shook her head. "Not really. It wasn't part of my training."

"Jeez. Just put her on the floor and play with her."

"Oh. Okay. I guess I can do that." She placed the child on her back on the floor, and the toddler immediately started wailing, legs and arms flailing in the air, mottled face scrunched in anger. Alyx looked up. "Now what?"

Ty instructed, "Put her on her butt. She can sit up, you know. She doesn't like to lay down 'cause she can't see anyone."

Alyx gingerly picked up the child and sat her on her bottom on the shaggy carpet. Samantha, slobber still flowing, smiled, tears forgotten—though the wetness on her face showed the proof of her unhappiness mere seconds before. Clear snot ran out of one nostril, pooling on her upper lip.

This child leaks more fluid than a car.

Alyx stared, a slow answering smile spreading. "She's actually kinda ... cute."

"Yes, she is, isn't she?" Chase looked at the baby. Her fine, light-brown hair curled in ringlets framing her chubby face. "Hi Sammie-girl. Aren't you the prettiest baby ever? What a cute girl you are!"

The baby smiled and cooed in response to his chattering, staring at him with those clear, blue eyes. A mini, female version of her mother. "She likes me! What a cutie. Yes, you're a cutie, aren't you?"

Suddenly, a rattle flew past Alyx, hovering right in front of Samantha. The giggle erupted out of her, rising up from her gut and shaking her whole body in the way only babies can laugh. She reached out in an uncoordinated way, eventually grasping the toy and bringing it to her mouth to gnaw on it with her toothless gums.

"Wait! Did she do that? Move the rattle?"

Ty laughed. "No. It was ... uh ... me." He looked up through his lashes sheepishly.

Dawn burst back into the room, snatching up Sammie and replacing books on the shelf. "I think I've done it. I amped up the shield spell. We should be safe here. For now. You have to go. Bray will be home any minute."

"Okay. Thanks, Dawn. The last thing we want to do is put your family in any danger. Where's Bea?"

"Just living in this town is dangerous. Bea can stay here, in the yard. She'll be safe there, she knows how to stay hidden. That way, she won't draw attention to the two of you. Go, now. I'll see you tomorrow." She stopped and grasped first Chase's hand, then Alyx's. "Be safe."

CHAPTER 50
CHASE

A strong sense of *deja vu* swept over Chase as he exited the house of his youth, and he looked back over his shoulder as they hurried down the walkway, eyes sweeping over the familiar house. Taking one deep, steadying breath, he missed no small detail of the single brick structure in that one glance. It was apparent in subtle variances that this wasn't his home. Not really. The once black shutters were missing, and the towering rhododendron bush that was so old it reached the bottom ledge of his bedroom window was replaced here with climbing white and pink roses. And of course, the decorative style throughout the house, inside and out, was completely wrong. But the bones of the two-story structure remained the same. He looked up and down the street, eyes landing on Mrs. Ruiz's house and the blocky sign on her front lawn declaring 'For Sale.'

"Looks like Mrs. Ruiz is moving. I wonder if Mr. Ruiz is still alive in this world? At home, he'd passed away. She relied on us for a lot of things. I wonder if she has anyone to help her here?"

While they watched, the curtain in the front window rustled, swinging back and forth.

"She's watching us. Let's get out of here." Alyx shrugged. "You lead, I'll follow. Are you sure going to Mason's house is the best place to hide?"

"No. I mean, at home it would be. But here? I have no idea. We just have to go by instinct, and my gut is saying go there. After we're settled, maybe we can visit the souvenir shop and search for the guy, Carson Murphy. You know, the one Brian told us might help us? I didn't know his last name then, but I'm assuming it's the same Carson from our last jump. We did find him hiding in the run-down souvenir shop in Dimension 7, after all, and how many Carsons can there be in one small town? Then, he was a retired military weapons specialist. Who knows what he is here. Anyway, we'll start at the Moore's and go from there."

"Okay." She reached for his hand, and he gave hers a squeeze. "Lead on."

"Yes, ma'am." He smiled, moving at a leisurely pace. "This time, we don't have to trespass on anyone's property to get there. Just a young couple out for a stroll on a breezy evening, enjoying each other's company."

"I-I guess we don't need to hurry. And we should make more effort to blend in. We won't continue our practice until tomorrow, anyway…"

"Hey. You're right. Tonight is for us. Let's stop by Mason's house and see if anyone's there, then stop by the Souvenir Shop, and then we can head to the beach to have a picnic with our sandwiches. Might as well take my girl on our second date while we're here. The least we can manage is one date in each world we visit." He bumped her shoulder with his, eyes sparkling.

She smiled, bumping him back with a bit too much force. "Do you always take girls on dates to the beach?"

Rubbing his arm, he flinched. "Ouch. No. Just the special ones." His grin was incorrigible.

It felt so good to do normal things like flirting with the girl he loved.

Lighthearted for the first time in the two weeks since they arrived here, there was a bounce to his step as they strolled along.

• • •

MRS. RUIZ

The boldly flowered curtain at Mariana Ruiz's house fluttered. The old woman lurched at her realtor's voice. She'd forgotten he was here, inspecting the house. "You have a lovely home. Would you be opposed to packing some of this stuff up before the showing? Your collections are impressive, but in selling, less is more, Mrs. Ruiz. Less *sells* more." He chuckled at his own joke.

Distracted, she pulled back the curtain once again, straining her head at an angle until her cheek bumped the cold glass.

"Mrs. Ruiz? Mariana? Is something wrong?" Leaning down, he peered out the window next to her but saw nothing but the empty sidewalk and a lone sedan pulling into a driveway down the block.

"What? Oh, no. Just a bunch of teenagers running wild, if you ask me. I caught them sneaking around in my yard. I took care of it with the threat of Mr. Ruiz's baseball bat. I doubt they'll be back." She nodded solemnly.

The Sovereign Warlock tilted his head, a calculating gleam in his eyes. "Have you seen them before?"

"Never."

"Were they … wearing anything on their wrists? A watch, perhaps?"

"A watch, you say? No. I don't remember seeing any watch. Well, maybe. I can't be sure. I wasn't wearing my glasses, and I wasn't exactly looking at their wrists while they were trespassing on my property. Why do you ask?"

He smiled, but it didn't reach his eyes. "Oh, no reason. Just being neighborly. I like to introduce myself to the neighbors of the houses I'm selling. A courtesy, really. If the neighbors are on our side, it makes the sale that much easier."

"Well, they were no neighbors of mine. And thank goodness for that, especially since they're keeping company with one of those dirty wolf-dog inbreeds. I don't want anything to do with any of that. No sir."

"Wolf-dog inbreed? You saw one here in town?"

"Yes. It ran through my yard just before they did. As if they were chasing it, or something. But again, I didn't have my glasses on…"

Turning, he made quick time to the door, stopping just long enough to call over his shoulder, "I'm afraid we'll have to reschedule, Mariana. I forgot I have … an appointment. I'll be in touch."

The door slammed behind him, and Mariana Ruiz huffed. "Well, how rude."

CHAPTER 51
CHASE

They walked along, fingers intertwined and swinging gently back and forth with each step. Chase rubbed his thumb gently in circles across her palm, and her pupils dilated. Every now and then their eyes would meet, communicating their thoughts more clearly than mere words could express. He smiled and her lips curved in response, followed by the familiar pink tint that crawled up her cheeks as if she could read his thoughts. His chest puffed.

I can't imagine being anywhere else but here, even in the midst of magical chaos.

At an intersection, Chase glanced up, nodding his head toward the street sign. His pace quickened, pulling her along.

"Here it is, Seacrest Boulevard. This is Mason's street. Three houses up." Chase pointed at a Cape Cod style house, grayed wooden siding with a matching aged-wood fence. The two large picture windows that sat on either side of the large stained-wood door were framed by black-painted shutters that were chipping and in disrepair. The front lawn had been replaced by once-white stones yellowed by the elements. A frown turned his lips down as they walked up to the barren porch. "This seems wrong. Mr. Moore—David—was so proud of his lawn back home. Some of his neighbors had turned to lawns replaced by rocks for easier upkeep, but he wouldn't hear of it." His pace slowed. "I'm getting a bad feeling about this."

Relief was evident in her stance. "Me too. Maybe we shouldn't ..."

His nose wrinkled. "Do you smell that?"

Alyx nodded. "What is it?"

A shiver worked its way from his lower back upward until the base of his skull tingled. "Yeah. Let's..." Turning, his grip on Alyx's hand tightening, he took two steps away from the house and then halted, shoulders slumping. His eyes pleaded. "Wait. I have to know if Mason is here. What if he needs our help?" Breaking away from her, he strode to the front door and rapped three times before she could change his mind. He saw Alyx cover her nose with her hand. The stench was stronger on the porch. It definitely originated from this house.

"Chase…"

"I know what you're gonna say. You think I don't know him here. But I do. I know him. He's my best friend, and if he thought I was in trouble, he'd be there for me. I know he would. And remember I did meet him here, in this world. Before you arrived at Dune Haven. He tried to help me."

He knocked again.

"Let's check out the back door. I know where they used to hide the key." He jumped down the two porch steps in one leap, and headed around the house.

"Chase, let's get out of here."

"Can't. Sorry. Stay there, guard the front. Be right back."

He heard her grunt and the sound of her footsteps and didn't have to look back to know she was behind him. A smile spread. *I knew she wouldn't listen.*

Rounding the back of the house, he halted once again. The odor intensified, and Chase breathed through his mouth to try to mask the scent. The backyard was worse off than the front. Weeds grew knee-high, and the shed that had once been Mr. Moore's pride and joy because he and Mason had built it together looked as if a strong wind might bring it down. The shed door, attached by only one hinge, hung precariously at an angle and panels of wood were missing so that you could see inside. A sapling maple tree appeared to be growing out of the floor, it's branches reaching for the sunlight through the broken walls.

"What the…?" Chase turned to look at Alyx.

"Chase, this can't be Mason's house. It looks like no one has lived here in years. And it smells like there's something dead in there."

"I know. You're right. But I still have to go in and make sure. Can you understand?"

"No. Your best friend isn't here. He lives back in your home world, D-6. These people, no matter how familiar they seem, are strangers." She placed her hand on her hip and blew at her bangs. "We don't have to go in there. There's nothing there."

"If it was me in there, would you go in?" His eyes searched hers.

She looked away, back again, and huffed. "Fine. In and out. I don't like this."

"Agreed. In and out. For the record, I don't like it any more than you do." He turned to the back door, not surprised that it was locked when he turned the knob. Bending, he lifted the edge of the rotted doormat. "Well, the key's not here. Let's search for another place someone might hide a key."

After searching what seemed like the entire yard, Chase sighed. "Guess it's not gonna be that easy."

"It never is," she snickered.

"I'll kick it down. Stand back."

"Wait. What if, you know, we can open the door … magically?"

"Even if there's a way to do that, I don't know how. Do you?"

"Dawn would know how. Let's ask her to teach us tomorrow. And we can also ask her if she knows anything about this house."

Chase paused, head tilted. A minute passed. "Okay. You're right." He glanced back at the house. "But I'm going in tomorrow, one way or another."

"Agreed."

"Alright, then let's go meet Carson."

The tingle in his spine lessened with each step away from the house. When they were up the block, three houses away from the Moore's house, he glanced back over his shoulder. The little home shimmered, a light fog surrounding just that one residence. He picked up his pace. An icy coldness turned his fingers frigid, and he reached for Alyx's hand only to find hers were just as chilled as his own.

CHAPTER 52
LIZ

As Liz neared the town, the pain in her head intensified. Falling to her knees, she clutched her head, hands fisted in her hair. Eyes squeezed tightly shut, she fought back the darkness that threatened to consume her. It pumped through her arteries and permeated her body like a cancer, and she pushed it back for the thousandth time. Her body thrummed with the heady intoxication of black magic warring with the overpowering agony of resistance. She knew how to make the pain go away. It would be easy. So deliciously easy to let the dark have its way. This kind of power was as persuasive as it was addicting, she knew. But still, she resisted the overbearing urge to just give in. Though she swayed in that direction for just a millisecond and the torture momentarily eased, again she turned back to the light, pain doubling its intensity for her efforts. Lightning bolts seared behind her eyelids, branding her retinas. So great was this inner battle that the air around her swirled as if it had taken a life of its own, whipping the strands frantically around her face in a supernatural dance.

I-cannot-let-it-take-me. Not yet.

Another wave swept over her, and she couldn't breathe. Her skin, pale and clammy, stood out like a beacon against her tousled raven hair, and anyone looking on might assume she was in her death throes, so obvious was her distress.

Luckily, she was alone.

A low, torturous moan escaped her cracked, dry lips, white foam bubbling at the corners of her mouth.

Beatrice. Bo.

Her friends when no one else wanted her. Her first adult experience with love. They trusted her. Believed in her in a way no one had since she was a child. None of this was their fault.

I can't let them have you.

And still, the black side of magic swirled around her, beckoning for release. Sinking its evil claws into her skull until she thought it might crack open like an egg if she didn't let its force in. The smell of lilacs—her favorite scent—accompanied all of the other enticements in this arsenal of persuasion in a battle for her soul. It would be so easy...

No!

With her last thread of energy, she pushed back using the picture of Bea's sweet muzzle lying trustingly on her lap; Bea standing protectively in front of her; Bo cuddled by her side—and lost consciousness.

Slumping on the ground, limbs slack by her side facedown on the earth, she sprawled alone at the edge of town and dreamed of bygone memories best left forgotten. Memories that she had locked away in the nether regions of her medial temporal lobe now burst free in her vulnerable state. Memories the darkness wanted her to remember. They replayed like a movie behind her eyes, begging her to give in to her past.

In sleep, she remembered...

• • •

Eight years old. Young Liz lay in bed, a lone tear trailing down her cheek to land in the wet spot already pooling on her pillow. Clutching the stuffed teddy bear she had stolen from her friend's bedroom that afternoon, her breath hitched as she desperately tried to fight the tears. She swiped the salty drop with the back of her hand, sniffling as snot ran out of her nose. She wiped that, too, rubbing it on the side of her mattress.

Her friend James was dead. Dead, never to return. She and Stuart had witnessed it. Their trio was down to two. This teddy bear was the only physical thing she had left of him, and she squeezed it closer to her chest. Despite her valiant effort, another tear broke through the barrier and before long her shoulders were wracked with sobs as she replayed the events of that fateful day—each small movement was followed by a searing heat that radiated from the welts on her back.

The day had started as any other.

She'd gotten up as she always did and foraged for any small amount of food she could find, and ate—or didn't depending on her findings—before searching out her mother. She wasn't sure if the woman who raised her had actually given birth to her, though she had called her by that name for all eight years of her life. Mother wasn't a loving soul, though she did take care of all of Liz's needs and keep her safe, which is all anyone can truly ask for. In Mother's words: Be grateful for what you have. You never know when even that will be gone.

On that particular day, the sun was shining bright, and a hot breeze blew in through the open window. Liz pulled her damp hair up and tied it into a ponytail. It was oppressively hot already, and the day had just begun.

Her mother worked long days at the factory and cleaned houses at night, so she was left to fend for herself most days. It was hard for a single mother in those days. After school, Liz was expected to work. She kept the house clean and did all the cooking so when Mother returned home to sleep before the next day's work, she didn't have to mop the floor or prepare a meal. Liz did all of that for her and was happy to help. Most days.

But this day was so beautiful, and she could picture in her mind how the ocean water would cool her sticky skin, so she decided it wouldn't hurt to seek out her only friends, James and Stuart. Sometimes, the three of them would ditch school to have a dip at the public beach.

Despite their differences, they all got along. Liz was the planner, always in charge despite being the only female in the group. Stuart grudgingly followed her lead, even though she was a girl. He was the calculating one. And James was the people-pleaser. Always ready with a smile, he kept the group running smoothly, knowing just what it took to keep each one happy, putting out any fires along the way. The politician, she supposed. Liz smiled as she meandered along behind him. She could so easily imagine him as president of the United States of America someday. And she would rule by his side, since a woman didn't have the opportunity to run for office back in those days. But no mistake, they would rule together.

She skipped, giggling as she grabbed his hand. Pushing him behind her, she yelled, "Race you!" just before she took off running, the boys loping along behind. Throwing a glance over her shoulder, she noted James's booming laugh as he picked up his pace, and Stuart's frown, eyes glaring in determination.

While she took her time entering the water slowly, the boys took off running into the surf. That was the last time she saw James alive. No one could have known how strong the undercurrent was that day, or that James would be ripped out to sea.

Mother had punished her that night. The snap of the belt slapping her bare back made her flinch and cringe, but she knew that mother wouldn't stop until she lay still. She tried. She really did. But couldn't stop the wince that she knew would prolong this flaying. "It's your fault the boy is dead, you know." *Slap.* "If it wasn't for you..." *Slap.* "...he would never have skipped school." *Slap.* "And he'd still be alive." *Slap.* "His parents blame you." *Slap.* "And so do I." *Slap.* "You and that Stuart." *Slap.* "You're both no good." *Slap.* "Evil." *Slap.* "I have to purge you of this evil." *Slap.*

Liz's prone body twitched as she relived the memories of her youth. That day had been only the beginning.

CHAPTER 53
ALYX

Alyx hurried along beside Chase, a frown curving her lips. She was neither prone to worrying, nor was she a follower. No, she was a get-it-done kind of girl, and there was a certain amount of pride that came along with that. If one plan didn't work, well then, try the back-up plan. And if *that* didn't work, go to plan C. A leader role was her preference, and she rarely had the inclination to change her mind once a decision was made. She'd been trained to make the most practical decisions. Her number one priority was to protect the watches and their keepers.

But that had all shifted after she'd met Chase. He'd changed her, and she didn't know if admitting that to herself was a good thing or a bad one. Whether it would help or hinder their mission.

She was worried now. About him. Would he do what was needed if it meant hurting the other self of someone he knew from home? Added to that, would he be able to forgive her if *she* made the most beneficial choice for everyone—even if he didn't agree with her? The furrows in her brow deepened. Realizing she'd been nibbling on her fingernail—again—she spit out the nail and glanced at Chase's profile. She had to make him see. Shaking her head, she pushed it aside.

"So, when we get there, how do you think this Carson can help us?"

His shoulders rose. "He helped us last time, in Dimension 7, remember? He created the diversion we needed to take control of the town. Without Carson's expertise in explosives, we'd have been stuck. He proved there that we could trust him."

"Yes, but you have to remember that was then. In a different place. A different time. A different version of Carson—his other self."

"Not so different, I think. Seems to me the people are the same. Their DNA hasn't changed, just their circumstance. But what's at the heart of them? I believe that remains the same, no matter which dimension we jump to."

"You're being naive, Chase. We can't trust anyone except each other."

"That's what Mason said back at Dune Haven. Don't trust anyone. But even though he knew the Sovereign Warlock was watching us and he knew there would be consequences if he was caught, he still tried to help me. He tried to help me escape before fake Uncle Charlie stopped him."

"How do you know that wasn't part of the plan all along? Maybe everything he told you was a lie. I mean, your uncle was a lie, right? I never asked you: How did you see through it? How did you know he wasn't your uncle's other self?"

"He felt wrong. I was duped at first, I think because I wanted so much for it to be him, but after a while it just clicked. Maybe the real Charlie helped, with the aide of this." Chase held up his left arm, the watch seeming to pulse in agreement.

"I guess it's logical that you could sense it, especially if your uncle was a keeper as we suspect. That would mean he's one-of-a-kind like us, since keepers only exist in their home dimension, which is why we don't have to worry about bumping into ourselves in our travels. And if your uncle was a keeper, his spirit lives on in the blood pumping through the watch, even though his body passed on." She sighed. "So promise me one thing."

His response was immediate, "Anything."

"We come first. You, and me. We'll try our best to keep everyone here safe, but we watch each other's backs first. Deal?"

"We don't even need to make that deal. It's a given." He winked.

"Okay. So, let's make a plan. What should we say to Carson if we find him?"

"Who needs a plan? I'll just improvise."

She rolled her eyes, her feet slamming just a bit harder on the cement with each step when his bark of laughter burst forth.

Idiot.

• • •

North Main Street was the heartbeat of Dune Harbor town. Quaint shops lined the street parallel to the beach, and pedestrians strolled along eating double-scoops of ice-cream that dripped down the side of waffle-cones and onto their palms in the humidity of early evening. Mothers pushed strollers, fathers carried toddlers on their shoulders, and people smiled and nodded, an occasional "Hi, how ya doin'?" or "Where ya from?" could be heard amidst the cries of exhausted toddlers. Black-painted light posts with bowling ball sized circular lights lined the street, and a center median that separated the two-way traffic boasted dogwood and elm trees, their bases circled with a spatter of colorful and well-tended wildflowers. At the end of the town square, a huge rectangular sign announced: Welcome to Main Street, Dune Harbor USA. Town hall stood proudly next to the U.S. Post Office, and live reggae music filled the air from the Harbor Bar & Grill, tables filled with people and spilling out onto the seashell-filled cement sidewalk, more still stood in line waiting for their chance at one of those tables.

Wafting through the air was a myriad of scents that are most often associated with vacation trips. Caramel-coated popcorn, a variety of pizza—from plain cheese to white broccoli topped garlic, cotton candy, and funnel cakes beckoned passersby to follow their noses.

Alyx couldn't get enough. She had never been on a vacation, and her eyes darted back and forth trying to take it all in. She gave an answering squeeze when Chase grasped her hand, and her eyes went huge when a boy walked by carrying the biggest stuffed shark she'd ever seen.

"Where is he going to put that thing?" Her wide eyes followed him until he disappeared around the corner.

"Doesn't matter where he puts it. It's the thrill of winning the game that matters."

"Game?"

"Yes. There's an arcade over there," he pointed and continued, "and he won the stuffed shark by playing a game. We'll have to try it sometime. Maybe later."

"Um. Okay."

"But first, let's visit the souvenir shop and see if we can find Carson, okay?"

"Yes. Carson. Right."

"Hey." When he didn't continue, she tore her eyes away from the street-show and met his eyes, brows raised. "I have an idea. We don't have to go to the beach later. Let's stay here—right here on Main Street—for our date. I'll win you something at the arcade. Sound good?"

"Hmm? Yes. Yes, let's stay here. Okay," Alyx's voiced trailed off.

His laughter barely registered through her wonderment. She couldn't decide if she liked the jubilant chaos that made the air vibrate all around her, or feared it.

Chase pointed toward the street. "Have you noticed the cars?"

Alyx nodded. "Do you think they're solar powered?" Each vehicle's roof was covered in some kind of paneling, with a spinning fan-like antennae jutting up from one side.

"Probably," Chase answered. "We knew there'd be differences world-to-world."

Alyx shrugged, continuing to peruse her surroundings.

Chase picked up the pace, pulling her with him. She clasped his hand tighter, smiling as warmth spread out from their entwined fingers.

"Look, Harbor Souvenirs is just around the corner on Second Street, just as I remember. Much of Main Street is the same as D-6. Just a few subtle changes." He tugged her hand and she followed, distracted by all the new sights and sounds. The window displayed swim suits and beach chairs, and words painted across the glass boasted in flowery script: *Last Stop, Harbor Souvenirs. We've Got a Touch of Everything You Need to Make Your Vacation Magical.*

"I think we're in the right place."

A tiny bell jingled as they entered the store. Surf boards, boogie boards, and water skimmers hung on the back wall next to flip-flops and beach towels. Jimmy Buffet played in the background, singing about eating in paradise. A shelf displaying various levels of sunscreen and sunburn remedies stood next to that. Food and snacks were off to the left, toys and t-shirts to the right. In the back of the store stood the cashier's desk.

"Okay, I guess we should..." she began, her words halted by Chase boldly marching right up to the counter. She cringed at his bluntness.

"Hi. I'm Chase Walker. I'm looking for Carson. Carson Murphy. Is he around? My friend Brian told me to come talk to him."

The man behind the counter reached up to scratch his sun-tinted brown hair and paused. "Hi. I'm Aidan. You're looking for Carson, you say? Show me a sign."

"A sign?"

"If you don't know what I mean, then maybe you'd be interested in our new line of t-shirts? They're on sale until tomorrow."

Chase glanced around the shop, then held his palms out and whispered the words Dawn had taught him. The spark sputtered at first and then grew in intensity until the flames leaped and danced. The door jingled, and he doused the flames as quickly as they appeared. "How's that for a sign?"

"That will do. Come." Aidan looked toward the customer at the far side of the shop, calling, "I'll be right with you." He turned and began walking, assuming they would follow. Which, of course, they did.

Alyx was dumbfounded that Chase had flubbed his way through that greeting so easily. He never ceased to amaze her. As they approached, the back wall shimmered out of focus for just a split-second, and the man—Aidan—walked right through it and disappeared from view. Chase glanced at her over his shoulder, shrugged, and followed. A portal of sorts?

She stood straighter and put her foot forward, right through the wall itself. A pulling sensation began in her toes and moved to her heel and ankle and continued rising up her leg until the rest of her was sucked through the opening to the hidden room on the other side.

A man with pale skin covered in copper freckles and red-tinted hair with matching beard stepped forward, offering his hand in a firm shake. "I'm Carson. What can I get for you?"

Behind him stood shelf after shelf of vials and boxes, each labeled meticulously. Familiar things like sugar, sage, rosemary, garlic and mint. An entire row of various types of candles. Another filled with ancient-looking leather-bound books. Oils, herbs, crystals, stones. And things they had never heard of.

Chase looked at her over his shoulder, and wiggled his eyebrows up and down.

His next words made her draw in a sharp breath.

"Do you have what we need to defeat the Sovereign Warlock?"

Carson took an involuntary step backward. He reached a shaky hand up to scratch his beard, and stuttered, "I-I'm afraid you'll have to l-leave. I can't help you."

CHAPTER 54
LIZ

Still asleep, Liz moaned as the memories flowed like water toward the sea, suppressed for so long—but now set free by her subconscious mind—they burst forth in a rush...

Age twelve. She and Stuart skipped school again.

Knowing she would pay the price later, she could almost feel the sting of the strap's edge against her bare skin, but shrugged. The scar tissue was so thick now, she barely felt it anymore. Since she'd stopped flinching, the beatings didn't last nearly as long as they used to. Mother lost interest the moment Liz stopped caring. When she'd stopped fearing the beatings. Ceased feeling the pain.

The duo stayed hidden all day and well into the night, lying on their backs in the grass, staring up at the stars.

"We've been looking at the same stars for years. Why should we keep looking up there? What's the point? It'll be the same tomorrow, and the next day. And the day after that. This is a waste of time, Liz." Stuart whined.

"Don't you think it's fascinating? I'm sick of my life. I wish I could go up there and just disappear. I've been studying at school, and Mr. Smith said he'd teach me anything I want to know about the stars ..."

"You're so naive, Liz. He probably wants to get close to you, if you know what I mean. You're a girl. And pretty, too. Why do you have to know about such things, anyhow?"

"What does being a girl have to do with it? I'm looking for knowledge. Knowledge is power, Stuart. And power is what I want more than anything. If I'm powerful, then no one can ever ..."

"Can ever, what, Liz? Can ever hurt you? You'd better get over that or life's going to be rough for you."

"Life already is rough, for people like us. Don't you wish sometimes that you could be someone else? Like, pick a name out of the stars and change who you are? Start again?"

"No."

"Oh, c'mon, play along. I'll be Ursa, and you be ... let me think ... oh, I know! You're Pavo. Names plucked from the constellations. From now on that's who we are." She smirked, not telling him that his new name meant peacock in Latin, while she'd given herself a more dignified name. Ursa ... the bear.

"We can't just change our names, Liz. It's not that easy."

"Sure it is. Don't call me Liz. From now on, I'm Ursa. We could even change our last name. Look," she pointed up at the sky and continued, "see those three stars lined up, right there?"

He sighed, reluctantly nodding.

"That's Orion's belt. He's a hunter, strong and powerful. He'd never let anyone beat him. I'll be Ursa O'Ryan, and you be Pavo O'Ryan. That sounds much more sophisticated—more intimidating—than Liz and Stuart, don't you think?"

"Whatever. We should head home." Stuart—now Pavo—stood, reaching for her hand. "Don't let your mother beat you tonight. You're almost as big as her now. You could fight her."

"You know, maybe you're right. Liz didn't have the strength to fight back, but maybe Ursa does."

That night for the first time she wrestled the belt away, and gave her mother a dose of her own medicine. And Ursa confirmed something Liz had suspected for a long time.

She *liked* the power.

•   •   •

Age eighteen is usually an exciting time in a young girl's life. Not for Ursa. The opportunities presented to most graduating students weren't extended to the likes of her. Pavo was all she had.

She didn't love him, not in the way her youthful-self had innocently loved poor James who was nothing more than a decaying skeleton by now. But Pavo was the only one who cared about her—even though she'd embraced the evil side her mother had always assured her lurked inside her heart—so she must try to love him. Or at least tolerate him. When Mother had died last week, she knew marriage was the only option for a young woman alone. She turned, her veil raised, leaning up to accept his kiss.

"I now pronounce you husband and wife. You may kiss the bride," The reverend finished in the same monotone he'd used throughout the short ceremony, then yawned. A lone stranger stood as witness.

As they walked out of the building, she looked at him. He did not make her heart race, but they did have common goals in life. Common beliefs. They knew that their kind weren't given a thing. That meant they had to take it for themselves. And she knew just how to do it. Theirs would be a marriage of convenience and alliance. She was confident it would work out splendidly.

. . .

Age twenty-five was when the real magic happened. A miracle happened.

They were going to have a baby.

She and Pavo had been planning a robbery at the lab for weeks, and if things went as they hoped, this would be their last heist. Over the years, they'd puttered around with thievery, always careful to steal small things that wouldn't cause a big commotion. Just enough to keep them living a comfortable life without getting caught. When the money from one gig ran out, they searched out the next mark. But that was all about to change.

Liz laid a loving hand over her midsection. She had to build a better life for the child she now carried inside her. A baby that she never knew she wanted but now inexplicably loved beyond reason. It had been instantaneous, this love that filled her heart the moment she learned of the tiny child growing in her womb. She hadn't known she was capable of such strong emotions. Not since she was a young child herself, and James ...

This child would be good, decent, and loved beyond measure. All the things she wasn't. She swore on the life of her unborn child that she would do everything in her power to give it the kind of life she had always dreamed about.

But for that, they needed money. Lots of it. The kind of money the laboratory gig could provide. For them, and for the child.

They made a pact that this was the 'big one.' The job that would set them up for the rest of their lives. The laboratory was built by a wealthy scientist to conduct his research—no questions asked. They'd watched as four large men hauled in the large safe, faces straining and muscles bulging. Watching from the shadows, they had seen the wad of bills the man had extracted from his pocket to pay the movers, and dollar signs danced in their eyes. Apparently, the scientist had something valuable to hide. Valuable enough to keep locked in a large metal safe.

If everything went according to plan, it would be perfect. The three of them would be set for life. Hadn't they endured enough hardship in their lives? Wasn't it their turn to come out on top? This was their chance.

If all went as expected. But Ursa had learned long ago that in most cases, things don't always go the way they're supposed to, and she wasn't wrong to worry this time.

The scientist—Elias Walker—rarely left the building. So on this particular night, when he walked out, turning back to lock up at precisely 6:02 pm, and strolled down the block jangling his keys, she knew what she had to do. They would break in, pick the lock on the safe—her specialty—and get out before he even knew what hit him.

Easy.

"Let's go," her urgent whisper traveled to his ears alone.

"You're sure we're ready?" he asked.

"Now's as good a time as any. Let's go," she repeated more emphatically, a challenging gleam lighting her eyes.

Walking up to the door as if they belonged there, Ursa stooped to pick the lock. It was well-constructed, but then again she had lots of practice. In exactly nine minutes eleven seconds, the door was open, and they disappeared inside. Producing a candle from her pocket, she struck a match to light the wick and held it out in front of her to illuminate the darkened rooms. Her head jerked when she heard a squeaky drawer opening off to her left.

Only Pavo, ransacking the desk drawer.

"Leave it. We need to find the safe. He wouldn't keep anything of value in the front room."

"How do you know?"

"I said leave it. We came for what's in the safe. You know how dangerous it is to veer from the plan."

They walked deeper into the bowels of the laboratory.

CHAPTER 55
CHASE

"You can't help us? Or you won't?" Chase cocked his head, studying Carson's already fair complexion as it turned an even paler shade of white making his freckles seem to jump off his face.

"Chase." Alyx placed a hand on his bicep and tugged. "Let's just go."

In a low but bold voice, Carson regained his composure and spoke, "Won't. That would be a stupid thing to do. And I'm not a stupid mage."

"Look, Carson. I'm here because Brian and Colin Heck sent me. They were helping us, and they seemed to think that maybe, just maybe, I could help this town by defeating the Sovereign Warlock. There was a power-shift at Dune Haven, and, well, I'm in control there now. We have a spell. Will you look at it? I'm not sure what it will do or if it can help, but I'd like to try before I leave here." As he spoke, he pulled the journal out of the sack. "Please. All I'm asking is that you look at it." He held the book out, already open to the page labeled: 8.

Reluctantly, Carson grasped the book in his hands, and the air went eerily still. Suddenly everything seemed exaggerated. The sound of their breathing echoed in the dead silence, and when Chase blinked he could have sworn that small movement made a sound like the hammer of a gun. And could the gooseflesh that suddenly sprang up on his arms have made a series of popping sounds?

Though the air remained comfortably warm, each breath he took was visible in the air. The same was true of all of them.

Carson's whispered response resonated like a scream in the small room. "Whoa. What is this thing?"

"It's a … spell book that has been passed down from my ancestors. I'm fairly new to magic, so I need your help to decipher the spell. If you'll help us."

"The Destruction Spell? Never heard of it. What exactly are you looking to destroy?"

"Nothing, unless I have to. Look, I don't want to hurt anyone. You want the Sovereign Warlock gone as much as I do. So help me."

"I don't know how you think you're gonna perform something like this

Destruction Spell without hurting anyone. I mean, the name itself implies devastation."

"Will you look at it? Just look. Please. If you think we can't use it, then we won't. But I have to believe my ancestors thought they could help me by adding this spell to the family book. All I'm asking is for you to look at it," Chase said.

"The Hecks sent you, you say? Why didn't they come with you?"

"Because the Sovereign Warlock found them and destroyed their house. Last we saw them, they were headed to find their parents. I assume they're in hiding somewhere. We have no idea where—we haven't seen them since we split up."

"The Sovereign attacked them, you say? Why would he do that?" His hand absently combed his beard in a downward motion. "You'll have to prove it." He stood straighter. "What about Annabelle?"

"Prove it? I told you, I don't know where they are. And I don't know anyone named Annabelle."

Alyx stepped up to the counter, placing her hands on the steel counter. "All you have to do is go see their house. It was on fire when we left, so there has to be visible damage. Some kind of electrical energy caused lightning bolts to strike the house on a perfectly sunny day."

Carson sucked in a breath and whispered, "The Firebolt Spell."

"That sounds about right," Chase said.

"But why? Why would he attack them? They're a nice, magical family. They don't bother anyone, and always follow the Ruling Mage's decree." Carson shook his head. "It doesn't make any sense. Unless ... it was Annabelle."

Chase chose his words carefully, "Brian was trying to do something to help the Sovereign Warlock. He wanted to earn some kind of reward, and I guess he failed to complete his mission. Colin was helping him." He tilted his head. "Who is Annabelle?"

Carson dismissed the question with scowl and a hand wave. "Doesn't matter." He paced back and forth once. "I'm going to take a walk to the Heck residence and see if I can corroborate your story. Leave the book here. If what you say is true, I'll study your Destruction Spell and share my findings with you. But I have to know you're telling the truth first."

"Fine."

"Chase, we can't leave the book here," Alyx interrupted. "Maybe you could make a copy? Do you have a copy machine?"

Carson stared at her with intense eyes for a moment, then nodded. "Fine. I'll make a copy, then."

Chase held out his hand. "Thank you. We'll come back in a couple of hours. Should we come in the same way as before?"

He gave one curt nod. "It's the only way in." Disappearing around the corner with journal in hand, Chase captured Alyx's eyes until Carson reappeared and held it out, saying "Feels like old magic."

"It is, I guess." Grasping it in his hands, he pushed it deep into his backpack. "Can I ask for one more favor?"

"What?" Carson's eyes narrowed.

"We just went by the house at five-one-three Seacrest Boulevard, and it looks abandoned. I ... got a bad feeling when we were there. Do you know it?"

"Yes. I know it. And you're right, it's empty. No one lives there. Not anymore. You should stay away from that house."

"Can you ...?"

"No. I'm not going near that house. I'm heading to the Heck's, and then I have one more stop to make before I meet you back here, so if you want me back here in two, I need to go. No promises."

"Thanks."

"Don't thank me yet. You don't know what you're getting into."

"You're right, I don't. But I really don't have a choice either. I'll see you back here in two hours." Chase reached out for Alyx's hand, and they were pulled through the wall together.

CHAPTER 56
LIZ

Ursa followed the hallway, each step taking her deeper into the laboratory, her vision hampered by the windowless structure, her only guide the erratic glow of the candle. She ran her hand along the unadorned, smooth wall and walked as quickly as she dared, Pavo following behind her.

At the end of the hallway was another locked door constructed of a thick metal and protected by two keyholes and a padlock. Something valuable must be behind that door, she guessed. Why else would it be so heavily guarded?

"Here." Shoving the candle at Pavo, she took out her toolkit, splaying her hand over her small baby-bump for good luck, and squatted in front of the keyhole. *This is for you, little one,* she thought.

This would require patience. Extracting what she needed, she got to work expertly maneuvering her two picks inside the tiny lock mechanism. Picking locks required the use of all her senses. Touching the tips of her tools with her tongue, she inserted them into the small opening. She felt for the tiny clicks that would indicate success, and listened intently to the inner gears as she shifted the pins ever-so-gently, coaxing them into position to release the lock. There was even a faint but distinct smell when all pins aligned and clicked into place. Sweat beaded her face, but she ignored it even when a drop of perspiration tickled its way down her nose to dangle precariously from the tip.

When the final barely-audible click reached her ear, she slowly turned the pick and listened to the victorious sound of the lock opening. A gleam entered her eyes, and she moved to the next lock. Twenty-two minutes passed before she had released both locks. She stood, triumphant. Reaching for the candle, she stepped back and gestured to Pavo. He'd already extracted his metal-cutter and made fast work of dispensing the padlock. With a slight shake in her hand, Ursa reached for the doorknob and turned.

Excitement stormed through her veins, and her heart pumped in victory. Turning, she reached for Pavo, giving him one fast kiss that promised more later before marching boldly through the doorway that led to a steep set of stairs going down. Practically running now, she descended into the level below the lab.

Another door. This one with only one lock to foil. Elias Walker must be confident that no one would get beyond his first door. She smirked.

Taking a deep breath, she got to work.

When that door swung inward on its well-oiled hinges, she took a steadying pull of oxygen and stepped through the opening. Her nose wrinkled. The stale basement air combined with the scent of victory, and she savored it with a smile. Her eyes combed the room.

A worktable, meticulously cared for gleaming with polish. A box constructed of glass sat alone in the center. Closing the distance in just three steps, she stared down at the box. With her steady thief's hands, she picked up the shoe-box sized container and peered inside. Her breath created a fog of steam which she impatiently brushed off the surface.

"A watch?" Her eyes met Pavo's over the box, a frown marring her face. "What makes this watch so valuable it has to be hidden away?"

"Who cares?" He shrugged. "The safe is in the corner."

Replacing the watch and box, her eyes glowed as she approached the safe that stood level with her shoulders. "Yes. The good stuff is in here." It took nearly as long as all the other locks combined, but finally the door of the safe opened.

"What the...?"

"More watches? Is this some kind of a joke?"

"They must be worth money...." She paced. "But what good are they to us? We can't sell them. There has to be more!"

"I told you this wasn't worth it. Let's just get out of here."

"It can't be for nothing. There must be something here we can use."

She began rummaging throughout the room, despair segueing into furious rage. Digging her fingernails into her palm until it broke the skin, she clenched her fists until they shook.

Pavo's words only infuriated her more. "Let's go. We'll find a new mark. I'll pick this time."

She turned, slapping him across the face. He grabbed her arm by the wrist and squeezed, the pain making things more clear. "You're right, of course." She nodded, rubbing her wrist even as he rubbed the handprint on his cheek.

As they turned toward the stairs and failure, the sound of movement from above snapped them both into action. They moved as quickly as only thieves can to hide behind the massive safe. Squatting down, they sat almost on top of each other they were so close, barely breathing.

Footsteps echoed and gained volume as they got closer. "What the...? Who's there?" A man's voice—no doubt the scientist—boomed into the silence, causing her shoulders to flinch.

We're caught. We'll surely rot in jail for the rest of our days. Her hand flew to her midsection, and her breath hitched.

Their only defense was to stay hidden and hope he didn't conduct a thorough search.

More words reached her ears. Was someone with him? Or was he really a mad scientist conversing only with himself?

"Someone knows. I'll have to. Have to do it now. I need more time. But no, I have to. I'd hoped to wait, but now I have no choice." The echo of his loafers on the barren cement floor were like drumbeats in her ears. "No choice."

She heard him run to the safe, removing the timepieces and their boxes, and dared not peek around the side to see what the man was up to. He wasn't looking for them, that's all that mattered. Maybe they'd survive this, after all. Patience. Wait him out. She focused on keeping her breathing as slow and quiet as possible. Breath in, breath out. No sound.

Elias Walker was now mumbling and chanting incoherent words, and the air seemed to be sucked out of the room. The entire lab seemed to sizzle and shake, the odor of electricity sucked into her lungs made her want to gag but she managed to suppress it. A pressure built in her ears until they popped, and she cupped her hands over them to block it out. The chanting continued, causing an eerie shiver to race up her limbs. What is he saying? The urge to peek was unbearable.

Slowly, she inched her head around the side of the safe. She needn't have worried, the scientist, white hair framing his face, only had eyes for the watches that lined the worktable. Lightning seemed to strike from above, followed by the appearance of twelve silvery blobs that seemed to float over the table. If there had been windows in the place, she was sure they would have shattered so great was the force of the energy building here. A shooting pain ruptured in her right ear, and when she reached up her hand came away with blood. And still, her eyes were drawn to the table. One by one, the watches seemed to be sucked up into the mercury-like masses, eleven in all, until all that remained was the one watch and the man himself. He reached out to fasten that watch around his own wrist. He turned toward the safe.

"I'm going home. I'm sorry. Remember through time that it was you who chose this path. Your fate is your own." His hands shot upward, and the lightning engulfed both of them, vibrating through their bodies and beyond. She crawled out from behind the safe, no need for cover now. He'd obviously known they were there all along. Flinching when something on the floor dug into the tender skin on the palm of her hand already torn by her nail, she clasped the yellow rock and reached for Pavo's hand. A bit of uncut golden chrysoberyl stone broke off, embedding under her skin.

Sudden cramps gripped her midsection, and she doubled over, cradling her womb as blood flowed, pooling between her legs on the floor. Her broken wail echoed off the walls, and she could have sworn she heard a baby's cry mingling with her own anguished voice as she mourned a child she would never hold. Her arms ached with the desperate need to cradle the baby that was forever lost to her.

The next memory she had was of waking up on the floor in the bowels of the lab. The scientist; gone. The baby; lost. Watches, never to be seen again. The hatred? All-consuming.

As time passed living in this world as magic became more and more apparent each passing day, she and Pavo discovered the truth about the watches and the twelve dimensions. Their only goal in life became to hunt down the madman who had made them into the monsters they'd been turned into that fateful night. He'd robbed her of her only child, and from that day on she would never be able to carry a child in her now-barren womb.

The enemy? Elias Walker—and his family of keepers. She and Pavo would never have a family. Why should the Walkers, and the eleven other chosen men, have all the power? Power over the twelve dimensions. They didn't deserve it. It should belong to her. Her and Pavo.

• • •

Lying on the ground on the edge of town, Liz opened her eyes. The memories usually suppressed deep in the wells of her subconsciousness replayed—as if they happened yesterday and not over one hundred years ago—in her unconscious mind. The old familiar anger and bitterness crawled through her body like a living thing, it struggled to take root and desperately maneuvered for control. She ran her finger gently over the lump forever on her palm. The stone remained a part of her. Laying her hand on her flat stomach, a tear fell in mourning for the child that was stolen from her so long ago; for the mother she would never become.

She'd given up Pavo to turn to a lighter way of living, finally letting go of the hatred that had controlled her for so long. He would never forgive her if he ever escaped the prison where he currently existed. He'd been the original Sovereign Warlock, and she had ruled by his side. In truth, she'd been in charge, allowing him to take on the public leadership role while she ran the show in the shadows. Good thing, or she might be the one in prison right now. Best not to let the keepers know that the new Ruling Mage and the hunter they sought were two different men.

Clenching her teeth, she pushed it back. All of it. She was aware that the boy, Chase Walker, was an ancestor of the man who had changed her. The man who had created this monster she had become. He had given her near-immortally and knowledge, but also had taken so much, leaving nothing but this burning need for revenge and destruction. Made her life—already a miserable existence—extend into the unknown for possibly centuries of torture. When she'd shifted, so too had all of her other selves in all of the known dimensions. They all carried on Elias Walker's curse, cast on her that long-ago night. She wasn't only doomed in this world, but in all worlds. The same was true of Pavo and his 'others'.

The blood of Elias Walker himself pumped through the boy's body, and the watch he wore on his wrist. He was here right now, and she had the power to destroy him. She could squash him like a bug with a tiny flick of her wrist.

But she wouldn't.

For now.

Pushing herself to her feet, she impatiently swiped at the hair in front of her eyes and began moving briskly toward town. She had to save Bea and Bo and make sure Pavo stayed where he was. Wouldn't he laugh to find out that an animal had wormed its way into her cold heart, causing her to work against him?

Get to town, save Bea and Bo. That's all I care about now.

After that? Well, after that she'd have to decide on which side of magic her loyalties fell.

CHAPTER 57
ALYX

Alyx sat in the 1960s themed ice-cream parlor, small round tables surrounded by hot-pink chairs, with Chase across from her. Black vinyl records lined the walls, an Elvis Presley statue stood proudly by the door—a plastic triple-scoop ice-cream cone forever held in his frozen hand—greeting customers as they entered the air-conditioned, bustling shop. The waitress sauntered over to their table wearing a white throw-back dress that swirled around her shapely, tanned legs, blond hair up in a messy bun, and stood waiting for their order, pen in hand. Alyx recognized her immediately, though the other girl regarded them as complete strangers.

"Um ..." Alyx perused the menu yet again.

Chase laughed. "Here, let me help. Can we order the waffle sundae for two? Do you want hot fudge or salted caramel topping?" He glanced at Alyx. Another chuckle broke free when she shrugged. "We'll have both, please."

"You got it." The waitress—Ava— scribbled on her pad and marched to the counter. She turned and winked at Chase over her shoulder.

A surge of heat filled Alyx's cheeks. "Well, I see some things don't change world to world. She's still flirting with you. Am I doomed to watch this play out in every dimension? I think I might be sick." She mimed gagging.

"She doesn't know us here. Absolutely nothing to be jealous of."

"Jealous? In your dreams, pal."

"I'm serious. There's nothing to be upset about." His eyes seemed to see straight to her very heart, and she broke eye-contact.

"I-I wasn't. Upset, I mean."

"Good to hear." Chase winked. "Okay, so after ice-cream, where do you want to go first? The arcade? Or shopping? Maybe catch the sunset at the beach?"

"Chase, we don't have time for all of that. We have to get back to the souvenir shop in less than two hours. And why would we go shopping? Is there something we need?"

"C'mon, Alyx. We have plenty of time. Have a little faith in me, okay?" He smiled.

Just then, Ava placed a large oval platter in between them with two bright-pink plastic long-handled spoons. Only looking at Chase, she boldly said, "Let me know if you need anything else. I'll be right over there." She pointed to the counter with another wink before strutting away, hips swaying.

"You would think I'm not sitting right here, the way she acts. It's embarrassing." Thrusting her spoon into the sundae, she tasted the frozen dessert and her eyes went wide. She forgot about Ava as she and Chase enjoyed a cool treat on a hot August evening pretending they were just two normal teenagers out on a date.

• • •

The arcade was in-your-face, blinking lights and laser sounds. Screeching tires and shooting guns. The disco beat of catchy music underlaid everything else. Air from mega-fans attached to the ceiling and angled downward blew the odd combination of perspiration and popcorn around them. The rectangular room had no door as if one wall was purposely missing from construction so that everyone could walk in and out all along the storefront. A string of multi-colored lights flashed from the walls. People of all ages stood in aisles between side-by-side game systems, either waiting for their turn to play or watching a game in progress. Haggard mothers and fathers stood holding tickets, coins, and a myriad of stuffed prizes.

Chase broke her out of her reverie. "I wonder if they have Annihilation in this world."

"What's ....? Oh wait, that's the game you played with Mason before your first jump, right?"

"Good memory." He smiled, gently squeezing her hand in his. "There it is! C'mon." Pulling her along, he stopped in front of a large black console. The person currently playing stood holding an orange plastic gun aimed at the screen and was shooting aliens that were dropping from the sky faster than he could pull the trigger. "Looks the same. Man, I rocked at this game back home."

"Good for you. I bet you're so proud." She smirked.

He crossed his arms in front of his chest. "Want a challenge?"

"Oh, yeah. That's fair. I've never played before."

"I'll teach you first. Then we'll play."

"Maybe we should try another game. One neither of us has ever played. In the name of fairness."

"You're on. After I play one round of Annihilation."

She rolled her eyes, but when he stepped up to play couldn't help but be impressed by his skill with a weapon. Remembering a not-so-long-ago day when they'd been target shooting and he'd shot a heart-shape into a tree from across the clearing with a pistol. A smile turned the corners of her mouth upward.

"Okay, your turn." She grasped the weapon, calculated its weight and compensated for the lightness. Squeezing off some practice rounds, she blew away everything on both the beginner and intermediate screens. When the game ended, Chase blew out a breath. "Not bad. I should have known you'd excel at this game. It is weapons, after all. Your specialty." He chuckled. "Okay, now it's your choice."

Slowly walking the length of the arcade, she occasionally stopped to watch a game. Her eyes lit up. "That one." Pointing at a game system, she practically smirked.

"Boomerang? You want to play Boomerang?"

"Yes."

"Okay. Let's do it." He dug out a coin and placed it in the slot. It took her ten minutes to blow him away.

End Game.

Her eyes twinkled up and him, and a rare giggle broke free. She won by a landslide. "It's just like throwing a blade disc, except it returns to you."

He smiled back. "Of course. I should have realized you'd be good at this one. You won fair and square. I want a rematch." Glancing at his watch, he sighed. "We don't have much time. Let's cash in our tickets and head back to see Carson. We've been here longer than I realized. Time flies when you're gaming."

She followed him to the desk, the flashing words 'Prize Desk' above with a gigantic arrow pointing down at the counter. Were people so dumb here they couldn't find the desk without an arrow to guide them? She wondered.

The teen working behind the counter looked at them with a bored expression. "You got, like, two thousand six hundred-three points. Choose from any shelf. Whadaya want?"

Alyx studied the prize options as if she was making a life-altering decision. Finally decided, she pointed to what she wanted.

When she finished, Chase already held a small brown paper bag in his hand. "Ready?"

"Yes." Her arm wrapped around a large stuffed shark and her other hand clutched a tiny pink teddy bear.

"Let's sit on this bench for a minute or two."

"Okay." She lugged her winnings. "I feel slightly ridiculous now that we're not in the arcade anymore."

"I got you something." He sat on the cherry-stained bench and handed her the bag. The sun had set while they'd been inside, and the street was illuminated by the circular street lamps and lights from the businesses that would still be open hours from now. So much artificial light that it was almost as bright as daytime.

Alyx placed the stuffed menagerie on the bench beside her, then slowly opened the bag. Her family hadn't been big on parties or gifts, so she did not rush. Peering inside, she reached a hand to the bottom of the bag and pulled out a necklace. On a black string, a dainty silver heart caught the light from the street light next to the bench. She blinked back the burning that sprang behind her eyes, and blinked again. Raising her eyes, she looked at him. Really looked at him. His hair with a slight curl, those blue eyes that could see *everything*. Those dimples.

She felt him reach out and take the necklace, and as he fastened it around her neck his touch sent delicious tremors down her nape. "Chase, I ..." She got lost in his eyes.

"I love you, Alyx."

Rounding her shoulders, she answered him. "I love you too, Chase." He kissed her then. Just a little peck, but it got her blood boiling. Then she remembered. "I got something for you, too."

She pulled out a keychain with a tiny silver dolphin dangling from the end. "It made me think of you swimming with the dolphins."

He cupped her face gently in his hands and kissed her again. "It's perfect." He attached the keychain to the strap on his backpack, and they stood. Heading back toward the souvenir shop hand in hand, tiny dolphin swaying back and forth with each step.

Alyx reached up a hand and ran it over the heart she now wore around her neck and smiled.

CHAPTER 58
CHASE

Blending in with all the other tourists as they approached the souvenir shop, Alyx wearing her purple backpack and clutching her winnings under her arms; Chase, backpack slung over one shoulder, his arm casually slung around Alyx, whistling random notes as they meandered along. To anyone looking, they were just two kids enjoying each other's company, out on a vacation-date during their planned annual escape-from-reality. An elderly couple meandered by holding hands, the woman smiled and nodded as they passed. Alyx smiled back.

Until the air went still.

Chase froze in place. "Wait. Something doesn't ... feel right. Do you sense it?"

"No, I ..." She tilted her head. Activity around them continued as if no one was aware of a change. "Yes. Yes, I do. A sort of ... staleness to the air."

"Exactly." He scanned their immediate surroundings. "The souvenir shop looks dark. Like it's closed. Something happened."

"What if Carson betrayed us? He could have gone straight to the Sovereign Warlock and told him all about us. It could be a trap."

"It's possible, but I really hope that's not the case. I sensed that we could trust Carson ... he could be hurt."

"You trust *everybody*."

"Stay here." He walked up to the door and tugged. Definitely locked. He hurried back to Alyx. "I'm not sure what we should do. Carson has a copy of the destruction spell. What if he gave it to the Sovereign?"

"I can't believe we just fell into his deception so easily. I know better. We need to get out of here."

Chase held up a hand. "Wait. Let me see if there's a back door."

"Carson said the front was the only way in." Alyx put her hands on her hips.

He raised a brow. "Who's being too trusting now?"

Since the building was set in a row connected to other shops along the street, they had to walk up the block and around a t-shirt shop and a bakery to reach the alley behind the stores. The rear of the building was unadorned, plain multi-colored brick with a flat back door—no doorknob—at each shop, the business' name painted in white lettering across the scratched gray metal doors. He marched right up to the one labeled 'Harbor Souvenirs' and rapped three times.

"This isn't a good idea, Chase." Alyx frantically whispered, eyes darting.

Chase chanted the now-familiar words of the fire spell he'd learned just this afternoon, and a flame appeared in his cupped hands. Noting that it sparked faster each time he performed the spell, he held the flame up to the door. "Here's my sign."

A sudden electrical energy charged through their bodies, and magically-guided letters began appearing on the door as if an invisible hand was scratching them into the paint—except no one was there but the two of them.

Appearing one by one in a sloppy hand, when complete it read: *Something came up. Had to leave town. I'll find you when I return. I'll have what you need. —C*

After they read the message, the words faded away leaving no trace they'd been there at all. "What do you think?"

"I don't think we really have much choice, do you? I mean, he has the copy of our spell and we have to at least get that back. Maybe we're wrong and he hasn't betrayed us. We have to give him a chance. He's the only one who can give us the ingredients we need. If, in fact, we ever really need the spell."

Alyx blew out a breath. "I guess so." She frowned. "We can talk to Dawn about it tomorrow."

"For now, let's get out of here."

"Where are we going? We don't have a place to stay."

"I've been thinking about that. Couldn't we just hide out in Dawn's backyard? I mean, that's where Bea is. We can hide if Bray comes outside. I think it's the safest place since Dawn protected the house." He looked at her for confirmation.

"We really don't have many choices unless we sleep out in the open somewhere. But then we'd run the risk of drawing unwanted attention. And we're absolutely *not* going back to Mason's house now." She paused, then nodded. "Let's go to Dawn's."

Despite heading back in the same direction he'd traveled countless times back home, a tremor of apprehension wiggled its way into his neck and he reached up to rub the sore muscle with his thumb. As they left the highly illuminated, bustling Main Street behind, the eerie glow coming from the now-sparse street lamps gave off little light making him wonder what lurked just out of the lightbulb's gleam—like a child certain of the existence of an under-the-bed monster. Reaching for Alyx's hand, he picked up his pace.

Rounding a corner, Chase stopped. Claws of fear clasped around his spine, and his back stiffened. "Did you hear something?"

Alyx dropped his hand, reaching for one of her blade discs she carried in the holster under her shirt. "No." She slowly moved until her back was up against Chase's. He drew some comfort from the wave of heat emanating from her body to his.

Standing halfway between two street lamps, the glow did not reach them as they squinted into the darkness. Her pupils grew to accommodate the shadows of night as she scanned. "I still don't ..."

"There," Chase pointed between two rental houses. "Eyes. Do you see them?"

A pair of luminescent eyes were the only thing visible, the creature's body obscured by the all-encompassing blackness that surrounded them.

Alyx drew in a sharp breath, nodding. "What should we do?"

"I think we should keep walking and see if it follows."

She nodded again. "Agreed. Let's move."

"It could be somebody's pet cat and we're freaking out."

"Or it could be something sent to attack us. Seems too tall to be a cat."

The two began moving, slowly putting distance between them and whatever lurked in the shadows, its glowing eyes following their every move.

"I don't like this." Chase walked faster, grabbing Alyx's arm and pulling her along. He turned another corner, and a neon red blinking sign flashed into view. *Vacancy.* "There. Let's go."

They ran, occasionally looking back over their shoulders. Whatever had been watching them had not followed.

A bell jangled on their way in. Alyx stood on the inside of the door squinting out into the night, as Chase approached the counter. A middle-aged man with thinning hair appeared through another door yawning, his bleary eyes blinking and unfocused. Chase recognized him. Nick Wentz. The same Nick who had built an underground sand fortress in D-7. Of course, as with all the others-selves here, in this reality they were strangers to him. Still, Chase was relieved to see a familiar face.

"Can I help you?" asked Nick.

"We'd like a room."

"You're in luck. We have one available. Fill this out." Nick slid a paper and pen across the vinyl surface.

Retrieving cash from his backpack he handed over the exact amount along with the form, thankful his uncle—or whoever had gathered currency from each dimension—had left the box for him to find.

Once inside the rented room, Chase leaned back against the door, locks firmly in place. He took one deep breath. "Guess we're safe, for now."

His body flinched as in the distance a lone howl broke the silence of night, echoing through the streets and into their tiny hotel room as if the animal was lurking right there next to them.

CHAPTER 59
ALYX

"I think the floor would be more comfortable," Alyx grumbled, rubbing her back. She yawned, eyelids remaining at half-mast. The combination of rock-hard hotel mattress and worry about their current situation had kept her up most of the night. There were too many variables surrounding them, making it impossible to form a reliable plan.

"The couch isn't bad. I slept like the dead." He chuckled at her expression of annoyance.

"Say that again if you want to make it permanent," she snapped.

His laughter was like fingernails on a chalkboard. "Let's go. It's 7:50. Dawn said we could arrive at 8:00, remember? I want to start practice as soon as possible."

"Fine. Can I at least brush my teeth first?" She stormed into the bathroom, his muffled laughter only making her mood surlier.

I hate morning people. Always so chipper and bright when there should be nothing but silence.

When she emerged, a styrofoam cup of steaming coffee was thrust into her hand. She breathed in the lifesaving scent of brewed coffee beans, and studied him over the rim as she took a tentative sip. "Thanks," she mumbled, feeling silly now that she was more awake.

"No problem." He held up a bulging brown paper bag. "I got bagels too. I already had one."

"Mmm-hmm." She continued sipping.

"So, now that I've had all night to ponder it, I'm convinced it was just a cat or raccoon or something. We're just being paranoid."

She grunted. "We have every reason to be careful, Chase. This is a strange world we're in, and crazy things have been happening since we arrived. We *should* be paranoid. It's how we'll survive."

"Well, at least you're awake now. Let's go. You can drink that on the way."

"Fine." She marched out of the room. "How many nights did you book us here?"

"Two. I figured we could extend it if we need to." He locked the door and followed behind her.

They walked in silence, arriving at Dawn and Bray's house at 8:20. Once again, the door opened when they were half-way up the walkway.

"Mornin'," Dawn said, smiling as they entered. She glanced up and down the street once before closing the door, aware of the curtain fluttering in the window next door. "That Mrs. Ruiz. So nosey. I swear she knows I have to sneeze before I do." She shook her head. "The kids are in the kitchen eating breakfast."

"I brought bagels."

"Oh, thanks. You didn't need to bring anything, but I do appreciate it. Bagels will be a special treat."

He held out the bag as if it were an offering. "We're in your debt for helping us."

"Nonsense," she answered with a smile, taking the bag and heading toward the back of the house. "We magicals have to stick together."

Ty sat at the table, a glass of orange juice and bowl of colorful cereal with toast in front of him. He smiled, a smudge of grape jelly on his upper lip. "Hi!" he said, his tongue darting out to lick the sticky sweetness off first his lips then his fingers. "Ready for practice?"

Alyx smiled, nodding. The kid was cute. He reminded her of what Chase must have looked like at that age.

Samantha was buckled into a highchair, pureed baby food smeared all over her cheeks. Her chubby little fingers pushed the food around the white tray, and she reached up and smashed it into her own hair, which stood on end coated in the sticky orange substance. A giggle burst out of her, and she slammed her hands flat onto the tray, causing the food to splash upward off the messy plastic surface. More giggles interspersed with baby-babble followed, and she repeated the trick over and over again. "Baga-gabba-bab-ma-ma!"

Dawn laughed. "I swear she's ten times messier than Ty ever was." She wiped the baby's mouth with the bib that hung around her neck and then moved to clean the tray. "I think you're done here, princess." She smiled and the baby held her arms in the air toward her mother. Dawn unstrapped the child and held her on her hip, dropping a peck on Sammie's wet hair as she wiped her daughter's hands.

The smile dropped from Alyx's face. "Oh no! I just remembered that I have something for the kids, but I left it back in the hotel room."

"Well, I wanted to work on portal spells anyway. It's not usually a beginner lesson, but since you've already performed one, I thought it would be easier for you. Why don't we practice making a portal to your hotel room, and you can retrieve your gifts? It'll serve two purposes."

"Okay. That sounds like ... fun, actually."

Chase interjected, "Yes, it does. But we have to update you on some things that happened last night first. And maybe learn a spell to unlock a door. Is there such a spell?"

"Yes. But ... why do you need that? You're not planning something illegal, are you?" Dawn frowned.

"No. Nothing like that. Well, at least I don't think it is. We went to visit an old friend's house, but it's trashed. I want to make sure no one's in there, but all the doors are locked."

"Where is this house?"

"Not far from here. It's the Moore house on Seacrest Boulevard."

Dawn's face drained of color, and she hugged Samantha to her chest so hard the baby whimpered. Finally, she managed to stammer, "Your friend lives ... there?"

Chase nodded. "My friend Mason used to live there."

"Mason's your friend?" Dawn asked.

"Yes. So, can you help us?"

Her head was already shaking. "No."

"No?"

"No. I can't help you break into that house. It's the heart of black magic in this town."

"What do you mean?"

"I told you I knew the man who is now known as the ruling Sovereign Warlock? That he used to be a good man, until the black magic took him?"

He nodded.

Dawn took a deep breath and whispered, "That's his house. When good magic goes dark, it creates a sort-of vacuum of evil. It takes the energy—sort-of hijacks it—from the existing light magic and when it turns, it's even more powerful than black magic alone. That house is unstable. Even the townies keep their distance, they can sense the bad vibes even though its true form is concealed from them."

Chase took a slow step forward, grasping her arm. "What do you mean it's his house? Isn't that house the Moore's house?"

"Yes," Dawn answered, a pained look on her face.

"What are you saying?"

"David Moore is the man you're preparing to fight. Mason's dad is the currently ruling Sovereign Warlock."

"I don't believe it!" Chase stumbled backward shaking his head, and Alyx grabbed his arm. For once she didn't have a plan. She had no idea how to help Chase deal with this.

CHAPTER 60
MRS. RUIZ

David Moore watched the pair enter the house next door, a calculating gleam in his eyes. "So, Dawn is helping them. You know, Mrs. Ruiz ... Mariana. This could have been easier for both of us if you just would have cooperated." He looked at the old woman, sitting in the armchair restrained by invisible chains. She glared up at him, testing her bonds. Her meager strength was no match for the magical ties.

"Who are you? What's going on around here? Untie me this instant, young man."

"Oh, no worries, Mariana. Just shut up, and you'll be fine. If you annoy me too much, I may have to dispatch you to Heaven—or Hell—just a little bit ahead of schedule. I'm hoping that won't be necessary, but it's entirely your choice. Don't test my limits. You may not like what you discover."

Though her chin trembled, she lifted it up a notch anyway. "But you're just a-a real estate broker. A father. A husband. I've known you all your life."

"There are things going on in this town you have no knowledge of."

"What kinds of things?"

"Magical things."

"Ha-magic! You sound just like my grandmother. She used to babble about magic, too. *La Magia.* She lost her mind before she died, you know. That's what'll happen to you if you're not careful."

"Enough! I only need your house. I have no need of you, so shut your mouth and leave me to my work, and you may live through this."

Wisely, she did as she was told, but she couldn't stop the defiant gleam that lit her milky eyes as she stared at the man she thought she knew.

She looked down at her invisible restraints.

Maybe her grandmother hadn't been *loca.* Maybe magic is real, after all. A small respite from her current plight, true. But a tiny spark is all that is needed to ignite a flame.

• • •

ALYX

Alyx held on as Chase stood, his hand trembling as he leaned on the wooden chair for support. "It can't be true." His eyes pleaded with Dawn to retract her words. The expression on his face broke Alyx's heart, and she felt helpless.

Dawn's words didn't help. "I'm sorry. It was a shock to everyone when he kept things running the same as the last Sovereign. We thought it would be different..." She broke eye contact and stared at the floor. "We thought he was our savior. But I'm beginning to believe the power is too much for any man to control. The dark magic guides him now. I fear he's lost forever."

Chase said, "No. I can't believe that. I won't. We have to bring him back. The David Moore I know would never hurt the people he loves ... or anyone else for that matter."

"He would and he does, every day. I'm sorry," Dawn answered.

Chase shook his head. "Then I have to grow stronger so I can help him fight it. The honorable man I know is still in there. I know it." He reached up and placed a hand on top of Alyx's as it rested on his shoulder, and met her eyes. "Our mission hasn't changed, only shifted. We have to get Mr. Moore out of power and return him to his family."

"What about the hunter? He's imprisoned by magic. If Mr. Moore loses power, he'll regain control and things won't change here. And you have to consider that David Moore may not want to turn back."

"We'll figure it out. All of it." He stood straighter, rounding his shoulders. "We have to train twice as hard. Let's go."

"Okay, let's refine your knowledge of portal spells. They are easier in a group because combining power is always stronger, but they can be done alone with lots of focus." Dawn clapped her hands. "This will be new for Ty. Pay attention, baby." She cast the circle, and they all entered and sat. "Let's start with the hotel room. You have to picture where you want to go, so both of you picture your room. You don't have to completely enter the space. It's like creating a mystical pathway to a place without actually leaving your current location. Alyx, you should be able to retrieve your items without staying in that place. I want you to concentrate and only part of you will enter the room. Grab what you need and force yourself back."

It took several attempts, but finally Alyx was able to lean her upper body into the room and grab what she needed. She paused to look around, a triumphant gleam in her eyes. The hotel room, flowered quilt balled up on the unmade bed as they'd left it. Seashell curtains drawn over windows in need of a good cleaning. A pile of coins leftover from the arcade haphazardly thrown onto the table next to the small black television set. She turned. Behind her, she saw Chase, Dawn, Ty, and Samantha sitting in the circle as if through a telescope. Looking down at herself, only the upper half of her body—no legs—hung in the air. A laugh bubbled up from her center, shattering the complete silence of the room.

I'm in two places at once. Kinda creepy, with a splash of miraculous! Good thing the maid isn't here right now.

With disappointment, she pulled herself—like a shift in molecules—back into Dawn's living room. Standing, she bowed at Ty as she handed him the stuffed shark she'd won at the arcade, and then turned and handed Samantha the pink teddy bear.

"Wow! A shark? That's lit! Thanks, Alyx." Ty clutched the blue shark to his chest, jumped up and hugged her leg.

Alyx swallowed. Reaching down, she awkwardly patted the top of his head. Why did her eyes suddenly fill with moisture? She blinked it back and looked at the baby, who was happily gumming the teddy bear, drool leaking from both sides of her mouth. A laugh broke through her emotional episode.

"Thanks for thinking of my kids, Alyx." Dawn smiled at her. "You've taken to the portal spell rather easily. I think this may be your strong point."

A blush crept up Alyx's cheeks. "Thanks."

"Now we need to find Chase's strengths. Let's try some new things."

They worked until 2:45, and then dragged themselves from the house with leaden feet.

For the next week, they continued the same grueling schedule without rest. Each day, their powers were growing along with their confidence and magical knowledge base. Despite their progress, a dark cloud hung over them as they trained. They were on a deadline.

September 3rd dawned with rolling gray clouds and sheets of pouring rain that pounded the crushed-seashell embedded sidewalks. They had six days left in this world. Six days to complete their mission. Six days before they jumped to the next dimension, leaving this world behind.

CHAPTER 61
CHASE

That night, a strangely familiar man with white hair visited Chase's dreams. They'd had no communication with him since the previous world, D-7. He'd appeared to them randomly there, and had helped Chase utilize his watch's powers to turn back time. The tiny, round knob that had allowed the time-shift to happen had not shown itself again after he'd gone backward through time to save Alyx in Dimension 7.

Though Chase remained in deep REM sleep—his eyes darting behind his lids—somehow, despite his sleep-state, he was aware that this visit was set more firmly in reality than in dream. As if to prove it, the air in the hotel room crackled with electrically charged energy surrounding the two sleeping in the room—one in the bed and one on the small couch. Inside Chase's head, the scene played out:

"I can't help you here, boy." The man paced, his body strong, though at first glance he had the brittle look of the elderly. *"I'm afraid you're on your own. Your watch cannot move time here as it did in your last quest. You have to get it right the first time. There won't be a second chance."*

"Who are you?"

"We share blood. I created that watch you wear—and all the others. But there's only so much I can do here, where magic already rules."

"Elias Walker? Are you my great-great-great grandfather Elias Walker? Oh, man, I have so many questions..."

"And I've no time to answer them. Your blood has strong ties to magic. It's inside of you. Use the magic. Use what's in you."

"But how? How do I use it? What am I supposed to do?"

"That's for you to discover on your own."

"Then why did you come to me at all?"

"So you would know. You've already discovered our blood is the key. It can give power, and it can take it away. You have a choice to make."

"But..."

"I trust you'll make the right choice."

"Wait!" Chase sprang off the couch, sweat beading his forehead and soaking through his t-shirt. He felt Alyx's hand reaching out to soothe, but shook it off as he paced. Striding to the door, he flung it open to breathe the fresh air. A person stood on the threshold as if knowing the door would open in that instant.

His hand flew to his throat and he took one involuntary step backward before regaining his composure. "Oh. Liz." He scowled.

Alyx made it to the door in four strides. "Liz. You're here."

"May I come in?"

Chase stepped back, gesturing with his arm. Liz stepped slowly into the room, closing the door behind her. "Where's Bea?" Her eyes searched the small room and returned to his questioningly.

"She's safe." Chase studied her. Something was off.

Alyx asked, "What took you so long? I thought you were right behind us? Where have you been?"

"Fighting my inner demons. Where did you say Bea is?"

"I didn't. So, who won? You, or your demons?" Chase said.

Liz avoided eye contact. "Hard to say. I'm sworn to protect Bea and Bo, that's all I can promise."

"Guess that puts us on the same side," Chase said, crossing his arms.

"I suppose it does." She looked down her nose at Chase, a feral glint flashing for an instant behind her eyes before it was extinguished. She spoke directly to Alyx from then on, "So Bea. Where is she?"

"A friend's house. We'll take you there in the morning. For now, let's all try to get some rest. You can have the bed, I'll sleep on the floor," Alyx said," Alyx said.

"I prefer to sleep alone. I'll return in the morning," Liz replied.

Chase shrugged. "Suit yourself."

"I always do." She turned to leave. "By the way, you're being watched." She sauntered out of the room.

"Liz?" Alyx called. When the other woman turned to look over her shoulder with her eyebrow raised, she continued, "Thanks. For your help."

Liz gave one curt nod, then disappeared from view.

"She's creepy," Chase whispered. "And everyone's talking in riddles."

"She's on our side, and that's how I'd like it to stay. Even the odds a bit, if you know what I mean."

"I guess. Just remember, she could turn on us at any time," he warned.

"So could the rest of them. *You* should remember *that*." She grabbed two bottled waters and tossed one to Chase. "Now, tell me about your dream."

"It was a night for visitors, it seems." He frowned and began recounting his dream-visit.

After he filled her in, she frowned. "You think the man with white hair is the creator—your ancestor—Elias Walker?"

"He didn't deny it."

"He didn't admit it, either. That would make him impossibly old, and even though he was only in your dream tonight, we did see him alive only weeks ago."

He shrugged. "The hunters are as old as the watches. What makes you think the creator couldn't still be alive?"

She paced to the window, parted the curtain, and gazed out into the coal-black night. "I think we should find a new place to stay. Liz said we're being watched."

"I have a feeling anywhere we go in this town, we'll be under surveillance. Let's talk to Dawn about it in the morning."

• • •

DAWN

Dawn's eyes traveled from Liz's head to her toes. "Are you on the side of light?" She blocked the doorway, not allowing her to pass into her house.

"I am on the side of light. I can't promise that's where I'll stay," Liz answered, eyeing her back.

"Then I can't allow you entrance to my home. I won't let you near my family unless you can make the pledge." She crossed her arms protectively over her chest.

"You're so sure I can't come in without the pledge?" Liz cocked her head.

"I'm really good at shielding the people I love. You won't get near them without the pledge. Take it or leave it."

"Well, since I am on the side of light right now, I'll do it. But only because I'm choosing to, not because you intimidate me in any way."

"Oh, I don't care why you do it, as long as you do." She held her hand up, palm out in front of her, and Liz raised her hand so they stood palm-to-palm. "I'll do the spell."

"As you should, since I'm not practicing magic of any kind right now," Liz huffed.

The wind picked up as Dawn called on the elements, particles of light swirling around the two women, bursts of air whipping their hair in a wild dance around their faces. Neither paid attention as they stared into each other's eyes. They were bound. Bound by light magic.

Liz breathed the words almost impatiently, "I pledge to do no harm to the occupants of this house and any who enter within these walls." The specks of light moved in circles around their hands, spinning so fast they gave the illusion of golden ribbons swirling around them.

When it was done, Dawn brushed her hair back with her fingertips, smiling. "Come in."

Liz nodded once before striding confidently into the house, eyes searching. "Bea?" she called. In a silver streak of fur, the animal ran from the back of the house, leaning its body up against Liz's legs. She reached down and ran her hands over the canine body, closing her eyes. "Hi girl," She whispered.

A happy yip filled the air, Bea's body trembling in excitement. The animal threw its head back and its tongue flicked across Liz's chin.

Ty entered the room just then. "Who are you?"

"I'm Bea's friend. Who are you?" Liz answered.

"I'm Ty. Do you know magic?"

She inclined her head. "I used to."

"Don't you miss it?" Ty asked.

"Yes." A darkness flashed in her eyes for just a moment before disappearing once again. She turned, ignoring the boy.

Dawn reached for her son's arm. "Ty, baby. Liz used to be on the dark side of magic, but she's changed."

"Oh, that's good. Welcome to the light side, Liz. I'm glad you're not dark anymore."

"You can call me Ursa."

Dawn interrupted, "Her name is Liz, so that's what we'll be calling her."

Dawn observed Chase and Alyx making eye contact over Ty's head, brows furrowed as a flood of doubt fogged their vision. She didn't disagree with their misgivings.

Throughout that day's training, she kept a close watch over Liz. Dawn didn't sense another glimpse of the blackness in her eyes as Liz gave tips on how to improve their magical abilities.

Dawn sighed. *We have to trust her.*

And besides, the pledge wouldn't allow her to work against them now, anyway, so what did they have to worry about?

CHAPTER 62
CHASE

In the early afternoon on September 6th with the sun beating down from a nearly cloudless blue sky, heat so thick each step was like wading through a pool of molten lava, Chase discovered his strength in magic.

They'd moved to the backyard to avoid unnecessary breakage inside, and had been practicing hard all day. Fatigue cloaked his entire body like a shroud. Despite the weariness, his limbs practically thrummed with the power of his last spell. He wanted to sleep for days and run a marathon at the same time.

"Wow," he breathed.

"Yeah. Just, wow," Alyx echoed. "Think you could do that again?"

Liz interjected, "If he could do it once, he can do it again—now that he knows how."

"That's incredible. I've never seen anything like that before," Alyx whispered.

Dawn stood, wide-eyed. "Me neither."

Alyx considered her words. "Why couldn't I do it? We both said the same words, but it worked differently for him than for me. Why?"

Liz titled her head. "Each person has unique abilities. I understand you excel at portal spells? That's your strength. Dawn's strong point is shield spells. Ty's is fire. This spell is Chase's strength. It sort of chooses you, I guess. I'm not sure how else to describe it. It's something in your genetic make-up that allows you to connect more completely with some spells over others."

Chase cocked his head, staring intently at Liz. "What was your strength? When you were practicing magic, I mean."

Ignoring the question as if she hadn't heard his words, she continued, "Now you just need to hone these skills. Keep practicing. We still have 40 minutes before we have to leave."

"I'm okay with that." The smile flashed as he raised his arms. "And after practice, I'm gonna need about twenty burgers and a gallon of Gatorade. And a nap. I'm hungry, hot, and tired. In that order."

His dimples only deepened when Alyx rolled her eyes. She turned to the other woman. "Let's meet up again in a few hours to continue practicing. We can practice on our own now that you're here, Liz."

"We'll need a place to practice where the townies won't see," she answered, a thoughtful look in her eyes.

Alyx smiled. "I'll portal us to the woods from our hotel room. No one will see us there. Then, we'll portal back when we're finished. It'll be good practice."

Chase agreed. "Good thinking. But first, let's eat."

• • •

BRAY

Just after Alyx, Chase, and Liz turned a corner, Bray started up the walkway to his house. There were shadows under his eyes as he trudged up the two low porch steps, and his shoulders drooped giving him the appearance of a hunchback.

"Daddy!" Ty bellowed, running to the door to greet him. Straightening, Bray forced a smile and scooped his son into his arms. He breathed in the scent of his child, and to some small degree it calmed him. He needed all the strength within him to do what he needed to do. To ask the questions he knew he had to ask of her, and yet at the same time wanting to cast away the knowledge those answers would bring.

"Hey Squirt, have a good day?" His grin didn't reach his drooping eyes as he spoke to his son.

Dawn appeared in the doorway. "Hey! I didn't have time to cook dinner, so how about we order a pizza tonight?" Distracted, she stretched up on her toes to peck his cheek, and continued straightening the house, not really looking at him.

His eyes traveled the length of her, and his heart throbbed painfully in his chest. He looked at the floor. "Hey."

Maybe I could ask her tomorrow? If I never ask, my suspicions will never be confirmed.

The beginning of a tension headache was marching its way up his neck and into the back of his skull. Tiny hammers pounded on his temples. He felt like a stranger in his own home. Walking past Dawn, he picked up Sammie and put his forehead against her cheek. The smell of baby food and soap enveloped him. A unique baby smell that made tears spring up in his eyes.

Dawn bent to pick up more toys off the floor, her arms already loaded down with playthings. "So, what do you think? Pizza?"

"Pizza's fine," he croaked.

At the strained sound of his voice, she turned. "Bray? Bray. Is everything okay? Did you have a bad day at work?"

"No. Work was fine," he mumbled.

"Something's wrong. What's wrong, hon?"

"Can we ... talk in private?" He did not meet her eyes, looking past her at the wall. The dreaded moment was here. He'd been tortured by this inevitable confrontation since the day before and could see no way around it. Hopelessness coursed through his blood, pumping through his somehow still-beating heart.

"Um, sure. We'll put Sammie in her playpen, and Ty can go out back to toss his ball around. Give me a minute." He watched her retreating back as she left the room, her curly hair bouncing in just the way he liked.

God, how I love her. I can't bear it.

Eyes burning, he blinked repeatedly to hold back the flow of tears just waiting to burst free. Dawn returned, her eyes searching his, a worry line appearing on her forehead. She gently took the baby from his arms and walked her over to the playpen, expertly arranging Sammie's favorite toys around her. Taking his hand, she pulled him into the kitchen.

"What's happened?"

"I-I ..." One lone tear broke through the dam and leaked from the outer corner of his eye to roll a lazy path over his cheek, its progress halted by the stubble of evening scruff. Dawn reached up to wipe the salty drop, her eyes filling with tears of their own though she had no idea what was coming.

"You're scaring me, Bray. Tell me."

His breath hitched. "I need to know. Are you having an affair?" The words tore out of him in a rush, as if he had to get them out quickly or he wouldn't have the courage to say them at all.

"What?" Dawn's hand dropped from his face. "What? Why would you even ask me that question, Bray? I love you. You know I love you. Why would you ever think that? Don't you trust me?"

He looked deep into her eyes, and wanted to believe her with every molecule in his body. But he knew he had to move forward. "It was something Ty said last night. When I was tucking him in."

"Okay. What did he say?"

"He wanted to be tucked in with a shark stuffed animal I had never seen before. I asked him where he got it." He paused, noticing how her eyes changed at the mention of the shark. It was true, then. The pain in his chest as his heart shattered into a million small shards was worse than he'd ever imagined, and another tear broke lose.

She was shaking her head, and her voice broke as she whispered, "It's not what you think, hon. I promise you."

"Ty said someone named Alex had given it to him, but that you'd told him not to tell me about it. Did you really do that, Dawn? Did you tell our son to keep secrets from me?"

Her eyes dropped to the floor, but he didn't miss the look of pure panic before she hid them from his view.

Yes, it was worse. This confrontation, as he'd played it out in his head thousands of times throughout this long day, was somehow even worse than his imagination could have conjured. It was all true. The look in his wife's eyes damned her in a way her words couldn't contradict.

"Please. Let me explain."

"I don't see how you can explain this away. How can I ever forgive you for this? And do you know what makes it worse? What rubs salt in the wound?" He began pacing, letting the rage of the reality of it all fill him up as his words gained volume. "You involved our children. Not only did you betray me, after all these years, but you let some other man into our children's lives. That's not playing fair, Dawn." Like a deflated balloon, he hung his head. "I don't know you at all." Without lifting his head, the last words poured out in a broken whisper, "Do you love him?"

"Alyx isn't a man. She's a girl."

"Oh ... well ... great. So you're having an affair with another woman? It makes no difference. The point is that you're having an affair and have made our son an accomplice in the whole thing."

"No. I'm not having an affair. Sit down. Listen to me. I'll tell you everything. I promise. I love you, Bray. I'd never betray you that way. Never." She reached up, cupping his cheeks in her palms. Leaning in, she kissed his lips, alarmed when he did not kiss her back. "I love you. I have kept secrets, but not the kind you think. I tried to show you once, and you didn't believe me. Let me get Ty. We'll show you together. Stay here."

She jumped up, calling Ty from the yard. "Ty! I need you, baby. We're going to do a little demonstration for Daddy. No more secrets. Understand?"

A beautiful smile lit his son's face. "Daddy? You're gonna love the magic. It's totally lit, I promise! Watch what I can do."

"The magic?" he managed, before speechlessness gripped his tongue and he groped for the chair.

Flames grew into a fireball in his son's hands as naturally as breathing. It was clear that Ty was controlling the fire, and had done this many times.

Bray's eyes cleared and he sat up straighter as he watched the magic unfold around him.

CHAPTER 63
CHASE

From his vantage point sitting on the floor of the hotel room, shabby carpet worn through in patches rubbing against his palms, Chase leaned back on his arms and blinked as Alyx followed him through the portal. Sunbeams streaked through her temporarily porous body pierced with daggers of light. As she gained substance the holes seemed to close up, shutting the rays out until she was standing above him in solid form wearing a smile like the cheshire cat. The last of the tiny portal suspended in air behind her disappeared with a *snap*.

I'll never get used to that.

They'd been practicing for hours, the only witnesses the woodland creatures that lived in the town's surrounding forest. Their ability to perform magic with confidence was growing by the hour.

"Man, I'm exhausted." Pushing himself up, he headed toward the bathroom, stopping in the doorway to look back over his shoulder. "You're getting really good at that. Portals, I mean."

"Thanks. I can ... I don't know ... feel the wormhole now, and it's malleable. Like I'm molding it into what I want it to be. Shape, size, location. It's a rush knowing I'm controlling all of that." Her eyes gleamed. "You're good, too. Really good. It blows me away to see you controlling magic so easily. Like you've been doing it all your life."

He laughed. "I guess you could say it's in my blood. Don't let the power go to your head. You know what happens to power-hungry people around here."

"Right. You don't have to worry about me, Chase."

"I'm not." He winked, and turned, closing the bathroom door behind him. He called out, "Hey, maybe we should both come back here to live when our year of jumping is over." What he didn't say out loud was: *If we survive.* He knew that was an impossibility, anyway.

When keepers turn nineteen-years-old, they could choose in which dimension to live out the rest of their lives. The watch always returns to its home dimension, and the keeper's ability to travel the twelve dimensions ends. If a keeper chose to stay in a world other than his own, he—or she—would have to leave his home dimension for good, along with all the people there, and that just wasn't going to happen. Knowing that didn't make the thought of being separated from Alyx any easier, and a bubble formed in his throat. *I'm not thinking about that now. We still have time…*

While running the toothbrush across his teeth, he went over the plan for their current predicament. They hadn't heard from Carson since the mystical words had scrawled themselves across the rear door at the souvenir shop, and they didn't have time to wait any longer.

A frown turned his lips down. *I hope Carson's okay.*

It would be awful if he'd gotten involved in something dangerous because of them. Since they didn't have the ingredients they needed for the Destruction spell, their original plan that had involved rescuing Mason, his parents, and Bo, and then destroying the realty shop with the destruction spell would no longer work. They had also planned to take out the residence on Seacrest Boulevard using the same spell. The Moore's house. If it truly was the source of black magic in Dune Harbor, then they needed to eradicate it from the town forever to move forward. Two places to deal with. The Moore house and the Realty shop.

Without Carson and the ingredients needed to implement his ancestor's spell, they needed to come up with a different plan. Liz had an idea, but her only concern was getting in to grab Bo. She didn't care about the townspeople or the Sovereign Warlock, as long as she saved Bo from his clutches.

She doesn't care about the two of us, either, he reminded himself.

He spit into the tan porcelain pedestal sink, and watched the bubbles circle the drain before disappearing.

His wide eyes shot up to the mirror. Slamming out of the bathroom, he exclaimed, "I think I have an idea."

. . .

September 7th. Forty-nine hours until the jump that would forever remove them from this world. Two thousand, nine hundred forty minutes to save Bo, Mason, Mr. Moore, and the town from black magic.

"It's risky. We could blow our cover before we even begin." Alyx paced the small room along the same path on the carpet that possibly hundreds of feet had traveled before her. "And I don't know if Liz will go for it."

"Yeah. I agree, she's a wild card. But we can't do this without help."

"So, just like in D-7, we use a distraction. And then we swoop in and save the others. Saving the Sovereign—I mean David Moore—will be up to you."

"I know I can save him. I have to. You'll portal into the realty shop, and I'll head over to the house on Seacrest Boulevard and wait for Mr. Moore. If I can lure him there, then you can get in with Liz and rescue Bo, Mason ... and anyone else that might be trapped down there. They won't want to alert the townies that anything is happening, so we know they'll keep this ... battle for lack of a better word ... out of sight to keep the town's magic a secret."

"I just don't like us splitting up, Chase."

"It's the only way. We'll be fine. I have a good feeling about this. What could go wrong?" His eyes crinkled at the corners, and he winked.

Alyx shook her head, and started for the door. "Don't get too confident. Even the best-laid plans have loopholes. There's something we're not thinking of..." Swinging the door open, she jumped back, slamming it so hard that it shook the cheaply built door frame. Reaching up, she quickly engaged the chain-lock. Eyes wide, she turned back to Chase.

"We're not alone. They found us."

"What? Who found us? The Sovereign? Let me see." He reached for the doorknob, but Alyx blocked the door with her body.

"Don't open that door."

"Come on Alyx, let me go. Whatever it is, we'll take care of it."

Alyx shook her head, pointing to the window. Cautiously—her nervous energy was beginning to transfer to him—he approached the seashell curtain. Grasping the edge between his fingers, he slowly pulled the thick cloth back, then let it drop where it swung forlornly back and forth for a second before settling back into place.

"Okay. So we aren't leaving through the front door, I guess."

"No."

"Well, we're not safe staying here. We can't just wait for them to come in through the window." His head tilted toward the glass.

Reaching out, he pulled the curtain back creating an opening just big enough for him to see out. Wolf-creatures stalked and paced right outside their room. At least a dozen of them surrounded the hotel. He heard a scream, followed by running feet, and a door slammed a few doors down. An eerie ululation pierced the early morning silence creating more sounds of commotion all along the hotel front.

Sitting sentinel right next to the door—their only exit—was the black wolf. The leader of the pack. The same one he'd had a run-in with in the forest. The very same one he'd shot, apparently not fatally. The one who had torn up his shoulder that Enzo had healed with his saliva in mid-air.

Just then the beast turned, as if sensing him looking. As if it had a debt to settle. When its golden eyes made contact with his own, a shiver raced up his neck, and he let the curtain drop once again.

"Okay. So, secrecy is no longer an option, I guess."

"No. And we don't have the luxury of choosing when this confrontation begins. The Sovereign Warlock is on to us. I guess he has been all along. We've been mere pawns in his magical game since our arrival."

"Well, I'm good at games. First move, let's get out of here. Are you too weak to create a portal to transport us?"

"Too weak? Ha! Stand back, buddy." Her eyes narrowed as she chanted the words to the portal spell so quietly he had to strain to hear it. "Where do you want to go?"

CHAPTER 64
CHASE

Mrs. Ruiz's yard was well-tended. Chase stood, dusting off his pants. Grabbing his backpack, he threw it over one shoulder.

"Good idea, portaling here. As soon as Bray leaves for work, we'll head over to fill Dawn in."

Alyx scanned the yard, drawn to the myriad of colorful round bush-like chrysanthemums—with an overabundance of buds in various stages of growth stretching toward the sun—evenly lining the house in a multitude of shades and planted with no clear pattern, the false cheeriness they conveyed in contrast to their current situation. Chase followed her gaze.

She nodded, turning to meet his eyes. "Just be quiet. We don't want to draw the old lady's attention, right?"

"Yeah. Right." He glanced at his watch, walking toward the plants. "7:45. He'll be leaving soon." Plucking a purple flower from one of the plants, he walked to her side. Reaching up he gently pushed her violet-tipped mocha-colored hair behind her ear, positioning the blossom on top. He felt her shiver when his finger brushed the tender skin at her nape, and his body answered with tremors of its own that traveled all the way to his toes. They were standing so close she had to tilt her head to see his eyes, bringing their lips dangerously close together.

A blush slowly crept up her neck spreading to her cheeks, and her breathing quickened. "Let's focus. What would Mrs. Ruiz say if she caught you helping yourself to her flowers?"

"She'd say I'm stealing her property." Shrugging, he said, "I couldn't help myself. It's your color. It suits you."

Her eyes darted away. "W-what are we going to do about the beasts roaming town?"

"What are we going to do? I'll tell you." He stepped back, widening the space between them so he could breathe again. "Nothing. They think we're in the hotel room, so they'll stay there guarding the door. We follow the plan. Keep focused. I have a feeling when we sort out the rest, the wolf-creature issue will resolve itself."

"You're not worried at all?"

"Not about that."

"Interesting. I would have thought you'd be tortured with images of innocent townspeople being torn into bloody pieces by those razor-sharp teeth." She tilted her head.

"I don't think that's a possibility. We take care of the ruling dark mage, and they'll leave."

"So, what if they find us?"

"We just have to make sure they don't."

"Yeah. Okay. Easy. We'll make sure they don't." She rolled her eyes. "Good plan. What could go wrong when you've thought out all the possibilities?"

"Exactly." He nodded once, glancing at his watch again. "8:00. Isn't Bray usually on his way to work by now?"

Her eyes cut to the house next door. "Yes." She cocked her head. "He must be running late today."

"Yeah. I'm sure that's all." His eyes narrowed, and he began pacing. "8:05."

"Something's wrong."

"Let's give it five more minutes, and if he hasn't gone, we can go knock on the door. We'll think of some cover-story if he's there and everything is normal."

"Agreed. Five minutes."

His eyes flew to the curtain in the window as it fluttered. "Uh-oh."

"What is it?"

"She found us. Mrs. Ruiz knows we're here. She's watching out the window."

"Great. Last time it was a baseball bat. What do you think it will be this time?"

"A frying pan?"

"A broom?"

They both chuckled, continuing the game.

"A wooden spoon?"

"A cane?"

The sparkle fled their eyes at the male voice that boomed behind them. "A magical counterpart?"

Both spun around to confront this new threat. It couldn't have been worse. It was the Big Man himself. Chase stepped forward. "Mr. Moore! It's so good to see you, Mr. Moore. Do you remember me?"

"Remember you? No. No, I'm afraid not. My other self is the one you speak of. But I do know *of* you. It must be wonderful to be able to travel all twelve dimensions at will. I didn't know of them until I took power here. But now that I know, I have so many questions for you! Won't you come in and sit down with me? Let me pick your brain a bit?" He was every bit as charming and easy-going as the man he'd known.

"What do you want to know?"

"What do I want to know? Why, everything, my boy. Everything. From both of you." Chase gestured behind his back to Alyx. When he glanced her way, she gave one slight negative head shake. He desperately tried to communicate with her using only facial expressions. He flicked his eyes to the neighboring house while keeping up the conversation with Mr. Moore.

He didn't need to create a distraction. The distraction had come to him. He walked toward the Sovereign Warlock. "I'd be happy to sit down and talk to you. Let's go." He gestured again behind his back so only Alyx could see it. Knowing she would think through all possible outcomes, he knew she would choose the smartest course of action. She had to go get Dawn and rescue the others while he occupied—and tried to save—the ruler of darkness.

They entered the kitchen through the back door, and he relaxed a bit when Alyx did not follow him in.

I knew I could count on her to be practical.

"So, why are you in Mrs. Ruiz's house? Is she here?"

"Yes, she's ... occupied in the living room. Let's sit down here to have our chat." He gestured to the small kitchenette. "Where's the girl?"

"Girl?"

"Yes. The girl that was with you. The keeper." He strode to the door, flinging it open with so much force it banged against the wall and then back again, a small gouge in the wallpaper appeared behind it, tiny pieces of drywall rained down on the floor. "Where is she?" he demanded, spinning back around.

"I don't know. But you don't need her. Ask me anything you want to know. I'll tell you."

David Moore sneered, and flinging his hand in front of him, he threw Chase back with a magical force he hadn't been prepared for. Chase's eyes widened as he realized just how outmatched he was before a shooting pain exploded in his back and head as he slammed into the wall. Sliding to the floor, he struggled to his feet.

"I wanted to do this in a civilized way, but I can see that you are scheming behind my back." Visibly reigning in his emotions, he continued, "Move." He pointed to the archway leading to the living room.

Chase walked through the doorway chanting under his breath, and vanished.

CHAPTER 65
ALYX

The second Alyx's fist connected with the door to knock, it swung open. Bray stood in the entryway, eyeing her from head to toe.

She stammered, "Um. Hi. Is Dawn home?"

"Yes. You must be Alyx."

Her eyes widened. "Yes. Yes, I am."

"I've heard a lot about you in the last fourteen hours."

"You have?"

"Yes. I'm still...getting used to the idea of all this... It seems I'm married to Hermione Granger." He smiled crookedly.

"Bray, invite them in."

"Oh. Yes. Sorry." He stepped back, gesturing her in.

Dawn stepped forward, took one look at Alyx's face, and clasped her by the forearm. "Where's Chase? What happened?"

Her eyes flicked to Bray once, and then back to Dawn, eyebrow raised. A smile spread across Dawn's face. "It's okay. I told him everything. No more secrets." She reached for her husband's hand. "Right, hon?"

"That's right." He stood straighter, wrapping his arm around her shoulders.

The words poured out of Alyx in a rush, "Chase is next door with the Sovereign Warlock. I don't know if Mrs. Ruiz is working with him or not, we never saw her. Chase went inside with David Moore. He didn't want me to come with him. I think he wants us to go on with the plan now."

"Plan? What plan? Did Carson come back with the ingredients? We haven't ..."

"Chase and I came up with a new plan. He'll distract David Moore, and we go rescue Bo and Mason. I know, I know, it's risky, but we may not get a better chance. I don't know how much time he'll be able to stall him. We portaled out of our hotel room to Mrs. Ruiz's backyard."

"Why didn't you come straight here?"

Alyx's eyes flicked to Bray again. "Um. We didn't want to come over until we were sure he," she tilted her head in Bray's direction, "left for work. Sorry. We didn't know you were telling him about ... us."

"That makes sense. I'm sorry, I should have let you know it was okay to come. Bray took the day off to meet you." She clasped her hands in front of her, fidgeting. "This is my fault."

Bray reached out. "Hon, I don't see how this is your fault."

Alyx nodded. "I agree. It's no one's fault, but we have a job to do."

"Why did you portal in the first place? You've always walked here before, right?"

"Oh. The wolf-beasts were guarding our hotel."

Dawn gasped. "What? They were in town?"

"Yes. And people could see them, too. They were causing a big commotion."

"Oh my." She wrung her hands until they turned white. "That's not good. Not good at all. They've never shown themselves to the Townies before. Why now?"

"I think it's my turn to say it's my fault. It's all happening because Chase and I are here."

"Well, that may be, but this just confirms that things are way worse than we thought here. Something must be done."

"Chase is distracting the Sovereign Warlock now. Let's get this done. If I portal us into the base, we can rescue Bo, Mason, and anyone else who needs help. But there's not much time, and Chase may need our help when we're finished. Let's get in, get out, and find Chase. Are you ready?"

"Dawn. I told you I don't want you to get involved in all this." Bray's eyes held a silent plea for his wife alone.

"And Bray, I told you that we don't have a choice. If things go bad and the Magicals are willing to show themselves, then it's only going to get worse around here. I have to go. You stay here with the kids. No one will get through my shield spell. Don't leave the house. If you do, you'll be unprotected."

Bea appeared, leaning her body up against Alyx's legs. Squatting down, she ran her hands over the smooth fur along the animal's flank. "Let's go get Bo." Bea threw back her head and an excited howl escaped, the sound bouncing off the wall of the great room.

Alyx began casting a quick circle, and the chanted words poured out in a rush. An opening appeared almost immediately, hovering in the air.

Bray clasped his wife's arms, his worried eyes boring into hers. "Be careful. I love you." He leaned down and lay his lips on hers.

She reached up on tiptoe to meet him, throwing her heart into the kiss. "Be right back."

Her chant combined with Alyx's and she was sucked through the portal, followed quickly by Bea. Just as Alyx was about to go through, Ty ran into the room from the kitchen and leaped through the wormhole before anyone could stop him.

"No! Ty, no!" Bray stepped forward, hands outstretched. His desperate expression rocked her when his eyes met hers. "Get him back. Please."

She shook her head. "I can't. I'll do my best to keep him safe. Both of them. I'm sorry," she whispered, just before disappearing from the living room.

CHAPTER 66
CHASE

The moment Chase vanished, he dove for cover.

He can't see me. I have the advantage. Now, what to do with it ...

"I see you've been practicing your spells. Shame, I really didn't want it to go this way."

Chase felt himself flung backward once again, he stumbled and fell but maintained the cloaking spell with effort. Lurching to his feet, he sprang out of the way just as another magical blast hit where he'd been standing only moments before.

David Moore's chuckle raised goosebumps along his arms. "It only takes one misstep, one crack in your concentration to hold onto the spell, and, well ... I think you can figure out the rest. I can keep this up all day, you know."

Though he knew silence was a better path—he *knew* it—he was still powerless to stop the taunting words that fell from his own lips, "So can I."

He moved fast to dodge the force of the next attack.

Stupid.

He'd given away his location with his jibe.

I'll have to be smarter if I hope to come out of this in one piece. If there was any chance of prolonging this to keep the Sovereign Warlock occupied for his friends to do what they needed to without risk of confrontation.

Though this spell—the one he'd been practicing since he'd discovered it was his magical strength—made him invisible to those around him, any sound he made could still be heard by anyone listening. Treading as lightly as possible, thankful for his rubber-soled sneakers and the carpeted floor, he moved around the room, dodging energy blasts at every turn. A low, strangled moan distracted him. His head whipped around, and for the first time he noticed Mrs. Ruiz sitting on the chair. Not sitting of her own free will but restrained somehow. Though there were no visible bindings, her hands lay one on top of the other on her lap, and she struggled against unseen shackles. Her mouth was closed as if it was held that way with glue. Possibly some kind of gag spell? She made eye contact, hers going wide in recognition.

No, it couldn't be. How could she...?

Her eyes desperately pleaded with him...*as if she could see him.* He looked down at himself patting his own chest, relieved to see he was still transparent. How could *she* see him, but the most powerful man in town couldn't?

He held his finger up to his lips in a gesture of quiet, moving slowly toward her. She understood, purposely averting her eyes. When he reached the sofa, he held his finger up again, and squatted slowly, reaching out toward her invisible handcuffs. They were bound as surely as if they were tied with rope, and in fact the skin around her wrists was chaffed from her struggles.

"Where are you, boy? You've no chance of escaping me, you know. Might as well just give it up now, and I'll be in a much better mood than if we keep up with this farce. You're only wasting time."

That's the plan, thought Chase.

After several attempts to physically break the restraints, he began chanting so low even Mrs. Ruiz had to strain to hear his words. *"Earth, wind, fire, sea. Break these bonds and set her free."*

He repeated the chant several times, and saw the moment the spell worked. The old woman's gnarled hands separated only slightly, but it was enough to know she was free. Leaning close to her ear, he whispered, "You're free. Don't move yet."

With a barely imperceptible nod, she indicated her understanding. He stood, slowly moving away from her. *Creak.* A loose floorboard moved under his weight, and he dove to the carpet just as a blast whizzed above him.

"Only a matter of time. You're trapped here. Come on, I'll make some coffee and we can sit and chat. Like we used to in your home world."

He knew the words were a trap, and he needed to buy more time. *The stairs. I'll lure him upstairs away from Mrs. Ruiz so she can escape.*

Leaning on the wall for support, he stood creeping toward the steps. He reached out for the railing, placing his foot gently on the first rise. When he was half-way up the staircase, he froze. An erratic wind whipped around him inside the small living room, followed by a quick flash of light. The next voice he heard was familiar. So familiar it made his heart swell and tears of joy spring to his eyes.

"Chase, boy-o, where are ya?"

He turned, and Uncle Charlie was standing larger than life next to an end table adorned with a ceramic vase of dust-covered artificial flowers, right there in the Ruiz's house. Struggling to quiet the words that were on the tip of his tongue, he closed his eyes for a second to think.

It's not my uncle. Uncle Charlie is dead.

A surge of anger shook his limbs, and he turned away to block out the beloved image of the robust man who had loved and raised him. Swallowing back the mix of emotion, he replaced it with an image of Alyx. Then Mason. Dawn, Ty, Bea and Bo. He thought of Liz, who was fighting every day to beat back the darkness that had once consumed her. If she could do that, he could resist this one thing. Taking deep, purposeful breaths, he continued moving cautiously upward, ignoring the abomination impersonating his uncle below.

When the Sovereign Warlock recognized that he could not play on Chase's emotions in that way a second time, he cursed amid another flash of wind and light, transforming back to his true form.

"Ah, I see you're too smart to be fooled this time. Clever. We'll have to try another way, then. Remember, whatever happens now is your fault." The sound of footsteps followed his taunt, and Chase had to lean backward to see the man was now standing right in front of Mrs. Ruiz. "My dear Mariana. The boy has left me with no other choice." He held up his hand, releasing her vocal cords just before an unseen force gripped her by the neck. Speaking to the room in general, he raised his voice, "I won't let up until you show yourself, boy."

Suddenly able to talk, Mrs. Ruiz managed just a few strangled sentences before the tightness in her throat made it impossible to talk. "Not ... his ... fault. Yours. Grandma ... right. She ... had ... the ... sight. Don't show ... yourself ... boy. Not ... for ... me. It's okay. Mr. Ruiz ... is ... waiting." The gurgling and choking sounds that filled the silence stopped him once again. *No.* He slowly eased back down two steps, and could see her eyes bulging out of their sockets, the red veins standing out like amateur Halloween zombie make-up. Her hands flailed in the air trying to grope for something that wasn't really there.

The Sovereign Warlock hissed through his teeth, "I'm not bluffing, boy. Don't tempt me."

A war waged inside Chase. He did not want to make this decision. In the end, it came down to human decency. He could not stand by and watch someone else suffer on his behalf.

"Wait. I'm here." Letting the spell fade away, his body flickered in and out for a moment, then regained its solidity. "Let her go." When he reached the bottom step, he heard it—though his mind refused to acknowledge it for what it was. A snapping, like the cracking of a dozen eggshells, as the old woman's head flew to the side at an unnatural angle, before she slumped to the side and slid like gelatin to the floor. Unmoving.

"No!" Chase charged toward the Ruling Mage.

CHAPTER 67
ALYX

They crept through the front offices of the realty shop, past the inviting courtyard and colorful chairs, Dawn clutching Ty's hand in a vise-grip. "I'm not happy with you, young man," she whispered.

Ty hung his head. "Sorry, Mommy."

Her eyes filled with tears. "It's okay, baby. We'll talk about it tonight. At home. Just don't leave my side, okay?"

His tiny nod had her breath catching in her throat. "Maybe I can help."

She was shaking her head before he finished speaking. "You just stay by my side. That's what I want you to do. Understand?"

"Yes, Mommy." Ty's shoulders slumped.

Alyx led the way down the stairs. At the bottom, the space opened into a large room with a tall, rectangular metal worktable in the center. Bottles and vials littered the ground, their contents scattered across the floor as if someone had flung them there in a fit of rage. Spices and what were once liquid substances now dried onto the cement. Furniture was arranged in a makeshift sitting room in the far left corner, and the plain white curtains were tied back with sashes to let in natural light. A small hallway led off to the right, and Alyx nodded toward it. "This way. Hurry."

Bea ran ahead, nose to the ground, tail straight out. A whimper burst from her chest, and her body began trembling. She raced the other direction, toward the couch. Then they all heard it. Happy little yips interspersed with a high-pitched mewling.

"Bo!"

Rushing to the crate, Dawn's arm shot out to unlatch the door. The moment he was free, Bo ran to Bea, nuzzling his head against her neck. She sniffed every inch of his body, checking for injuries as any mother would. Bo made the rounds stopping to greet each of them, the bouncy playfulness of a young pup making everyone smile when he licked their cheek or head-butted their legs. His tiny, unformed wings opened once before curling back in against his sides. During the reunion, his fluffy little tail never stopped moving, and with each wave it lifted the spirits of everyone in the room.

Sitting back on her haunches, Alyx spoke, "Okay. That's one big checkmark. Now, let's find Mason and get out of here."

A murmur of agreement spread throughout the room, and they headed in the direction of the doors. She smiled at the sound of a familiar, muffled voice from the other side. "Back for more, are you?"

"It's him." She raised her voice, studying the door as she spoke, "Mason. It's Alyx. I'm Chase's friend. He sent me here to rescue you. Tell me what to do to get you out of here." There was no visible doorknob, lock, or chains. Clearly he was held by magical means.

Dawn held her hands flat against the metal door and closed her eyes. "It's sort-of like a shield spell. Give me minute. Watch Ty for me." She began chanting, running her hands over the entire door and frame. "I think I can break it, but it'll take some time." Sweat beaded on her forehead as her whispered words continued to flow.

"Can I help?" Alyx asked.

The flow of words remained constant, and she did not stop to answer. Instead, Alyx called out to Mason, "Mason? We're trying to get you out of here. Can you do anything to help?"

"If I could get out of here on my own, don't you think I would have done that already?" he answered.

Alyx bristled. "Yes. I'm sure you would have. But now that you have help, is there anything you can tell us that would speed up this rescue mission?"

"Not that I can think of."

"Fine. Stay back from the door. I'm coming in." Alyx created a portal—easy because it was such a short distance—and appeared inside the room. It was decorated much the same as she imagined their home might be. Cozy. Cheerful. At complete variance from anyone's idea of jail. Mason was huddled on the floor, his arm around a feeble-looking woman. "Mrs. Moore?"

The woman's eyes stared straight ahead, and the sheer emptiness in them made her take a step back. "Do you think I can portal all of us out of here?"

"I doubt it. My dad ... I mean the Sovereign Warlock ... is very powerful. It can't be that easy. We tried when we first got here, but our magic seems to be stifled here. Not gone. I can still feel the power of the elements. Just, like, frozen or something."

"Well, let's give it a try." She turned and spoke the familiar words and the portal appeared. "You go first."

Mason spoke, "No. My mom goes first." He reached for her. "Come on, Mom. Let's get out of here."

The woman followed the motions and did as she was told, but showed no indication of a spark behind her dead eyes. Mason pushed her toward the portal, but it would not pull her through as it usually did. Alyx faltered. "You try," she said to Mason.

"No. I'm not going if Mom can't come."

"Fine. I'll be back." She jumped into the portal, reappearing on the other side of the door. Dawn was still chanting, her eyes closed. Bea and Bo huddled off to one side.

"Where's Ty?"

Dawn ceased her magical incantation, eyes clearing instantly. "What do you mean, where's Ty? Ty! Ty, baby, where are you?" she turned her furious eyes on Alyx. "I told you to watch him. How did he get away?"

"I-I ... portaled into the room. I thought ... maybe ... I could get them out without opening the door. He was right here ... I was only gone a minute."

"He's just a boy. I have to find him. Now." She took off, a mother's worst fear written all over her face. "Ty!"

"I'm here, Mom."

"Oh, thank God!" She ran to him, yanking his body against hers. Leaning back, she admonished, "Don't wander off like that. I told you to stay with me."

"I know, Mom. But I can feel the fire burning. Down there." He pointed to the floor under the worktable. Dawn got down on hands and knees, running her hand over the floor.

"I don't feel it baby. It's cool to the touch. No fire."

"No, Mommy. It's there. I can feel it. It's calling me."

Alyx and Dawn looked at each other over his head.

"L-let's get back to opening the door, and we can get out of here." Dawn returned to the door to resume her work. Turning once to call over her shoulder, "Stay with Ty."

"You have my word."

"Good."

Alyx looked down at the cold, smooth floor, wondering why a shiver raced up her spine.

CHAPTER 68
CHASE

Chase started toward the man but veered off, approaching the crumbled body that lay at an unnatural angle, broken. No human neck could maintain that angle and still function.

"You have blood on your hands, boy."

His voice broke on a shout, "Why? Why did you do it? I was coming down. Giving myself up. You didn't have to…"

Falling to his knees by the old woman he'd known—albeit in another place—all his life, Chase gently felt for a pulse knowing, and yet hoping despite the knowledge, that it was futile. She was gone. He'd seen her light fade even before he'd reached her side. She was indeed reunited with her husband in another place. Gently reaching out to lay a trembling hand on her wrinkled cheek, his head jerked up at the callousness evident in the next words that reached his ears.

"No. I didn't have to. I wanted to." The Sovereign's jeering visage had all the blood running to Chase's face in a rush of fire that burned his retinas. Clenching his fists, he slowly stood, facing the man. He wanted to tear this man limb from limb. Snuff out his light the way he'd so casually extinguished another. Tremors raced through his body in a struggle to control this all-consuming rage, making his muscles bulge in restraint, his veins stand out like magenta spiderwebs along his inner arms. Even knowing that the match would be uneven and he would most likely lose in any kind of confrontation, it didn't stop the burning desire to attack. Somehow—he would later look back and wonder how he had managed it—he kept his feelings in check, though not without tremendous effort. He shook his head and squeezed his eyes closed for just a moment.

It's the darkness talking. Mr. Moore is still in there.

"Why do you care? She was a nuisance. A nosey busy-body townie. An old lady who would likely have passed away on her own soon, anyway. I'm curious. What does her life matter to you?" David Moore jeered.

"Everyone matters. All life—in any world or form—adds a tiny piece of humanity to us all. Every beating pulse is an artery carrying essential energy to the Earth. When it fades out, it's like a large puzzle with a missing piece. You may find another piece that you can mold to fill the space, but it will never be a perfect fit—the picture will not match up. Everyone is unique and adds their own essential vibe to the multiverse. It's not for any man to decide when that light will burn out."

"She's not worth your pain, boy."

Chase shook his head. "You don't understand. Everyone is worth the pain. I feel sorry for you if you can't see it. You could once, you know."

"That man—the man I used to be—is gone. I'm much more powerful than he ever could have been."

"More powerful, maybe. But what about Mason? And your wife Jean? What about them?"

"They'll come around. You'll see. They'll all come around to my way of thinking, maybe even travel the twelve dimensions with by my side."

"What if they don't? Why do they have to be bullied into your way? Don't you care about them at all anymore?" Chase asked.

The Sovereign Warlock frowned. "Of course I do. They're still breathing, aren't they?"

A feeling of relief so intense swept over Chase that he couldn't breathe for a moment. "That's good to know."

"You thought I killed my own family?"

Chase's eyes cut to the body at his feet. "I hoped not. The man I knew was the gentlest soul alive. He treated me like a son."

"I'm not that man. I never was."

"I know."

"I can see that you think you can bring out the good in me, but it's not going to work, you know. I'm too far gone to save. And you and I have never even actually met." He sneered.

Chase shook his head. "No one is too far gone to save."

David Moore shrugged. "That's where we disagree. Now, let's go."

"Go? Go where?" Chase asked.

"To base. Tonight's the full moon, and now that I have you and the hybrid, there's nothing more I need to perform the dimension spell. Tonight, I travel the twelve dimensions."

"I'm sorry, but that's not going to happen." Chase had been slowly inching toward the front door, and quickly chanted the words to the cloaking spell. He vanished a split second before he ran out the door, catching the Sovereign Warlock completely by surprise. Thankful for both his sneakers and his stamina, he broke into an all-out sprint with one clear destination in mind.

. . .

There was only one place to go. It was inevitable.

As he rounded the corner onto Seacrest Boulevard with the sounds of David Moore in fast pursuit behind him, a ululant howl broke the silence sending recurrent chills of foreboding swarming through his body. His head jerked upward, and he saw the Enfield circling above, gracefully landing on the roof of the house as it folded its wings into itself. A gargoyle guarding its territory. He froze in place halfway between the two, thankful for the cloaking spell that protected him from their vision. His one saving grace.

The Sovereign Warlock threw his hands in the air, calling on the Earth's water in a furious chant. Rain began pelting his head and shoulders from a clear, blue sky.

Oh no!

Suddenly, the Sovereign was looking directly into his eyes. Glancing down at his own body, he saw why instantly. The cascading rain water made his outline clearly visible to both Enzo and the Ruling Mage. Shoulders slumping, he let the cloaking spell go, regaining his solid form.

There was nowhere to hide. He was trapped.

CHAPTER 69
ALYX

When the last chant fell from Dawn's lips she drifted back from the door, immediately reaching out for Ty's hand and grasping it between both of her own. Her face glowed with an aura of ghostly paleness, the only exception the purple half-circles framing the underside of her eyes. "It's done." She stumbled, collapsing into the nearest chair.

Alyx lay her hand on her friend's back. "Thank you." She gently squeezed Dawn's shoulder, then looked up, calling out, "Mason? Try the door. I think we've broken through the magic."

All eyes—both human and canine—focused on the door. Seconds that seemed to drag on into eternity ticked by, and Alyx took a tentative step forward just as the door burst from its hinges. The force of it flung the group backward, and they scattered in every direction as the odor of sulfur filled the room. The door clattered and clanged before settling in the center of the cement floor. Mason, one arm slung around his mother's shoulders with the other supporting her waist, walked slowly through the doorway.

"Sorry. It feels so good to have my power back, it took a minute to reign it in. Everybody okay?"

Amongst nods and affirmative murmurs, everyone gathered next to the worktable. A frown slanted Alyx's eyebrows, and she said what everyone was thinking. "Does anyone else think maybe that was just a little too easy?"

Dawn tilted her head. "Easy? Speak for yourself." Using the table to heave herself up, she wobbled on her feet.

"I guess. Okay. We've accomplished both things we set out to do, so what do you say we get out of here? Let's find Chase."

No one had been paying Jean Moore the slightest bit of attention. When her arms flailed in the air in a trail of sparks, it took them a moment to catch up. The door leading up the stairs slammed so hard it shook the hinges and for the first time she stood tall and straight, a foreboding light shining from her pupils. "I'll not let you harm my husband."

Dawn took a shaky step forward, almost crumbling when she let go of the table. "Jean. It's not him..."

"Shut up! It's him," screamed Jean. "It is. He's in there, we only have to make him see. Help him remember who he really is. Save him."

Alyx nodded, holding her hands out palms up. "Yes. That's exactly what Chase said. That's what he wants to do. We're on the same side, here. We are not your enemy."

Jean was shaking her head before the words were out of her mouth. "No. You'll do anything to save your friend. I can't let you hurt my David. We'll stay here and wait for him to come back."

"Mom ..." Mason held a hand out toward her. "We aren't doing him any good locked up down here. Let's get out of here, and we'll figure out a way to help him once we're free."

Jean was shaking her head before he finished speaking. "No. I'd rather be locked up down here for eternity, as long as we're with him." She spoke to her son without taking her eyes off Alyx.

"Mom..."

"No, Mason. You won't persuade me. We have to stay true to your father."

Mason pleaded. "Mom, I miss him as much as you do, but he hasn't stayed true to us. We have to..."

"You won't change my mind. He *has* stayed true to us, in his way. He didn't kill us like he did the others, did he?" Jean said.

"Mom. Listen to what you're saying. He killed them. All those people who resisted his rule after he defeated the last Dark Ruler. He killed them, Mom. Slaughtered them with magic. My dad wouldn't..."

"No! Those people—Pavo's people—were no good anyway. They were bad people that did even worse things, and they got what they deserved."

Mason's eyes went round. "Harm none. No one deserves that, Mom. It wasn't for Dad to decide their fate. And for what? Power? The power has changed him. He's changed, Mom. You know he has. You've seen it. He's ... different." His hand trembled when he held it out toward her. "Please. Come with us. Please."

"I'm not going anywhere. And neither are you." Jean gestured, indicating everyone in the room.

Mason pleaded, "But Mom..."

"Enough!" More sparks flew sporadically from Jean's fingers as she tried to control her emotions along with the return of her magical abilities, little firecrackers glinting off Dawn's forearm. When the flare landed on her bare arm, it burrowed under her skin, traveling inside her like a firefly just under the epidermis in a zig-zag flight up her arm. Dawn swatted at it, a low, keening moan escaped as she tried to stop the thing's movement inside her body.

"Mommy!" Ty ran to his mother and threw his arms around her neck. He glared in Jean's direction. "Make it stop."

"I can't. Once the power is released I can't control it anymore. I never was good at controlling the magic."

A tear leaked from Ty's eyes. "Yes, you can. You can do it. Make it stop."

"I can't," Jean whispered.

"Try. Please."

"No. I-I can't."

The tiny spark continued its serpentine journey upward. Over the bump of her bicep, around her shoulder, sidling up her neck. It traveled up her cheek heading toward her eye ... or her brain.

Alyx gripped Jean by the shoulders, demanding, "What will it do to her?"

"It's a domination spell. When it bores into her brain she'll either answer to me, or she'll die," Jean said.

Mason gasped. "Mom! You'll be just like him if you do this! Please!"

"I'm sorry. It's too late to stop it."

Ty cried, "No! Mommy! Mommy, don't let it. Fight it, Mama. Use your shield. Shield your brain. You can do it."

Dawn reached a hand up to cup her son's face. "I'm too weak to fight it. I've been trying, baby. I won't yield to her. I love you, Ty." She slumped to the floor.

"No." Ty stood, turning slowly to face Jean, tears streaming unchecked now. "No!"

CHAPTER 70
CHASE

Chase took off running toward Seacrest Boulevard and the house he once knew so well. In another time. Another place. Now a hub of dark power. Throwing his hand out in front of him, he didn't slow down as he chanted the lock-release spell Dawn had taught him. The door flung immediately outward amid the high-pitched squeal of unused hinges, and he burst through the doorway without pause. Once inside, he turned.

In no hurry, the Sovereign Warlock sauntered toward the house, a small smile plastered on his face. He glanced up at the Enfield, chuckling, before turning back to him. "My dear boy. Running into this house is not going to save you."

Backing up slowly, Chase turned and ran for the staircase. When he was halfway up, the rotted wood gave out and his feet fell through, the needle-sharp splinters of broken wood jutting outward stabbing into his flesh effectively trapping him in place. Suddenly the floor boards shifted creating a smooth downward ramp, and he slid to the bottom of the stairs. On the way down, he chanted the vanishing spell and disappeared again. David Moore loomed over him, making a *tsk-tsk-tsk-ing* sound, the smile still intact. "Oh, you might as well give up, boy. You're no match for me. You caught me off-guard the first time. It won't happen again."

Chase kicked out—and being invisible the older man didn't see it coming— swiping the legs out from under him until he thumped to the hardwood floor. The smile finally fell from his face. "I'm losing my patience." He stood slowly and turned. "Enzo!" he called.

The chimera stalked, powerful muscles bunching with each step in the leonine way of all large mammals, into the house with nose twitching. Chase crab-walked backward through debris and who-knew-what else, the smell of decay intensifying with each movement. The whispered words of the vanishing spell fell off his tongue as he moved. His hand landed in a wet, sticky substance setting an involuntary shiver free inside his body. Not daring to breathe, he dropped and rolled in the mess until it coated his body in the hope that it would mask his scent from the animal and help him stay hidden in plain sight. The goo coated him as truly as sap on a tree. Despite the smell permeating his nostrils causing an involuntary gagging in his throat, he rubbed the black grease over his face and into his hair. It had the reverse effect. Instead of aiding in his inconspicuousness, it made his outline clearly visible despite using his strength in magic. Too late to correct his mistake, Chase lurched to his feet, intending to run further into the house.

Enzo loomed in front of him, blocking his every movement. The Sovereign stood in front of one exit, the chimera guarded the other.

Nowhere to go. Trapped.

David 'The Sovereign Warlock' Moore laughed deep in his throat. "You're only drawing out the inevitable. Come, keeper. Let's do this in a civilized way. I'd rather you go with us peaceably. Or you can go by force. Either way, we're going back to base. Your choice." He stood straight, foot tapping.

Chase clenched his fists, staring at the disgusting floor. A crossroads. He could go with them and hope that he'd given Alyx and Dawn enough time to have achieved their goal. Or he could continue to fight, despite the knowledge that he couldn't win in any kind of battle against the magician standing across the room from him. At least not alone. Sometimes it's best to cut your losses.

He nodded, coming fully back into focus as he let go of the last remnants of the vanishing spell. "Okay. Let's go."

"Ah, he has some sense left in his brain after all, Enzo." Mr. Moore turned back to Chase. "Good choice, boy." Gesturing with his hand toward the front door, he smiled. "Shall we?"

The Enfield backed up, allowing space to pass. He looked into the creature's eyes as he brushed by. "What kind of father gives up his offspring to evil? Do you know what he—" he tossed his head in David's direction, "—plans to do with Bo? Even Liz wouldn't give up her only child to the darkness." He sighed, shaking his head as he continued out the door. "Can you even understand me?"

The chimera blinked, returning his stare. Was that a flicker of emotion he saw before the animal turned away? He couldn't be sure. He wasn't sure of anything right now.

"Ha! Liz? You obviously don't know her very well if you think that's true, boy. You have no idea what she's capable of."

Dismissing Chase, the Sovereign Warlock stalked out the door and froze in his tracks.

The street was teeming with wolf-creatures—some pacing, some sitting, one even lying on the blacktop panting as if it hadn't a care in the world. When the trio exited the house they snapped to attention, the beast's menacing stare bringing them to a halt. Enzo tilted his head back, a chilling howl lending a horror-movie-like quality to the moment.

At the center, Liz stood, hands on her hips in a challenging stance. "That's right. And neither do you," she said.

David Moore faced her. "So, you're working with the pack now?"

"They were loyal to me and Pavo once. I only had to strike a bargain with them to form a new agreement."

"What bargain?" David asked.

"Don't worry about that. All I want is the hybrid. Then we'll leave peaceably."

"Never. I'll never agree to that. The hybrid is essential."

"Fine. Then I'll have to take him," she said.

"You can try, but without the use of magic that won't be possible." He smiled.

"Suit yourself, but I implore you to think long and hard. I'll make the sacrifice if need be in order to do this one good thing. I think maybe it's what I've been meant to do all along. He's innocent. I'll ask you again. Give the hybrid to me," Liz demanded.

David shook his head. "As I said, I'll never agree to that."

Liz turned to look at Chase, her intense stare boring through him. He wasn't sure what she was thinking until she gestured by tilting her head to the side. He didn't need more of an invitation. His legs started moving, and he sprinted toward Dawn's house. Toward Alyx. The wolves did not follow.

An alarm bell blared in his brain when he heard Liz's muffled chanting as he put more and more distance between them. The air around him became thick, and though a coughing fit overtook him, it did not slow his progress despite looking back over his shoulder as sparks flew from what seemed like every direction.

She said she couldn't use magic anymore... She's giving herself over to the darkness to save Bo. Making the ultimate sacrifice knowing she won't be able to resist the dark...

Picking up the pace, his desperate feet barely hit the sidewalk in his haste.

CHAPTER 71
ALYX

Alyx held out her arms, palms out. "Ty. Ty, we can't help her like this," she soothed, "you just need to stay in control. Control it."

Two fireballs sprang from each of Ty's palms, growing so rapidly that within seconds they were the size of basketballs. His pupils—aimed only at Jean Moore—flickered with tiny flames as the wind picked up, tossing his hair and feeding the flames in his hands with precious oxygen. They continued to pulse, expanding with each surge and casting an angry orange glow on the walls and ceiling of the room. Alyx inched toward the boy, watching the scene play out in front of her.

Mason stepped in front of his mother, blocking Ty's view of her. "Please, don't hurt her. It's my mom."

Ty's gaze flew to the older boy, an intense look on his young face. His words, spoken so quietly as to be barely audible, tore out of him, "She hurt my mom."

Eyes wild, Mason pointed toward Dawn. "Yes. She did. But her chest is still moving. See? She's alive. We can help her. But you hurting someone else isn't going to help. Please. I'm begging you. Don't hurt my mother."

The flames flickered and ceased to increase in size, though they did not sputter out. Ty blinked, searching his own mother for signs of life. He saw that her chest was indeed rising and falling. "Tell your mom to release my mom from the spell."

Mason went to Jean, grasping her forearms he turned her toward him. She refused to look him in the eyes, instead staring at but not really seeing the wall over his shoulder. He gave a gentle shake. "Mom, please. Look at me. These people are here to help us. We won't hurt Dad. I won't let that happen. But we're not helping him by remaining locked up in a basement. Please. Release her. Or at least try. She has children, too. Ty, and his baby sister. They need her, just like I need you."

"I told you, I can't." Her eyes dropped to the floor, shoulders slumping once again causing her to shrink in size more similar to the woman who had been in the prison with him.

Mason shook her again. "Mom. Don't go back inside yourself. I need you."

"I'm sorry. I can't." Jean's knees gave out, and she melted to the floor, sobs wracking her body.

Ty's growl shook the room. His flames grew to the size of inner tubes—like the ones they used to float on the lazy river at the water park—and the floor under them began to shake. Ty's eyes burned with magical energy fueled by desperation. The worktable began to vibrate and shake, and the floor seemed to pulse like blood pumping through arteries.

Alyx dropped to her knees in front of the boy getting as close as she dared to the dancing fires. "Ty. Ty! This is not the answer. Let's see if we can help your mama. Maybe if she hears your voice she'll be able to fight it."

"No. If she fights it, she'll die. That's what *his* mom said. Now that the domination spell has reached her brain, she answers to her or she dies. If she fights it now, she'll die. And then I'll burn his mother, too." He jerked his head in Mason's direction and his flames twirled in a mad dance, jumping and lashing forward and back as if they had a mind of their own.

Mason stood looking down at his own crumbled mother, a hint of fear emanating from his eyes. "He's right. Dawn's better off unconscious until we can figure out what to do. I'll keep working on my mom, but I think we may need to figure this out on our own. I've seen Mom like this before, and there's nothing I can do to snap her out of it. When we were trapped in that prison, I tried everything to reach her but nothing worked. In this state, she's harmless."

Alyx retorted, "Not harmless. We made the mistake of believing that before. We won't do it again. Let's tie her up in case she decides to snap out of her trance again. We can't trust her." She set about restraining Jean with some packing tape she found on the floor near the workbench.

A frown wrinkled Mason's brow, but he agreed with one crisp nod. "Okay."

Bea, who huddled in the corner of the room farthest from the flames with Bo, slinked around the edges of the room toward the stairs. When she reached the bottom, she bounded up two steps at a time until she reached the door and began furiously sniffing the base and up around the edges. When she couldn't reach she went up on hind legs and continued her inspection. The creature looked back over its shoulder from a standing position leaning on the door, and whined. Alyx tilted her head. "What is it, Bea?" The animal whined again. "Can we break the spell?" She hurried up the steps to join Bea and began feeling all around the edges of the doorframe. "If only we had Dawn's abilities to break through this shield."

Mason slowly shook his head. "No. Not entirely a shield. It's a locking spell, sort of the reverse of a shield. One is meant to keep things in, the other to keep things out. If we can break the magical lock holding the door we could get through." He joined them at the top of the stairs.

"What about a portal? Why can't we just use my portal to get out of here."

"You could portal through most locking spells, but this one feels ... different."

"I have to try." Alyx lifted her arms and the now-familiar words fell easily off her lips. Not one to give up easily, she repeated the words over and over, each time with no results. Finally, her arms fell limply to her sides, shoulders slumped. She looked up, meeting his eyes with despair.

Mason was shaking his head. "He would have used every power he had to protect this room. And combined with Mom's power, I don't think there's much chance of ..."

Alyx interrupted, lifting her head a notch, a determined gleam in her eye. "But I got you out, didn't I?"

"Yes, but he would have assumed that the lock on this door would be enough. Although you did get in with little effort ... I don't know. It doesn't make sense."

"Maybe it was meant to trap whoever came down here. Easy entrance, but once you're in you can't get out."

"I think you're right. It's useless. We're trapped here until Dad gets back."

Alyx's head whipped around. "Wait! Dawn taught us a lock-release spell. I think maybe I can do this. Stand back." She held her hands flat on the surface of the door, chanting the words she'd been instructed to say. Over and over, she repeated the words until sweat beaded on her forehead. A wave of dizziness overtook her, and she grasped the railing for support. "I'm starting to see why Dawn was so tired after breaking you out. I don't think I'm strong enough to do this on my own."

Mason nodded. "It's the combination of my Mom and Dad's magic that makes it hard to get through. Maybe if we combine our energy we can do it together."

"Yes. Let's try."

Once again, she placed her hands on the cool surface of the door, and Mason did the same next to her. Bea kept her paws on the door as well. Several minutes passed with only the sound of their combined voices to break the silence.

Mason panted, "I can feel the lock. It's so close, but it won't give."

"I feel it, too." She turned. "Ty. We need your help."

The boy was staring intently from his mother to Mason's, the fireballs still flickering with life in his hands. He gave no indication that he'd heard the request.

"Ty. Please. We need you. Come help us. It's the only way to help your mother."

He didn't even blink as if her words could not break through the agony and hatred that swirled around his body like a living thing. So young to be bombarded with such powerful emotions. Such tremendous decisions for a child.

"Ty! We need you!"

Bo crept closer to Ty, despite the burning flames that jumped sporadically nearby. In a surge of bravery, the pup jumped up on the boy's leg and whimpered. He began licking his leg under the hem of his shorts. Ty slowly lowered his eyes to the canine. He blinked and turned to the others on the landing at the top of the stairs.

Blinked again. For a minute or two, his head swiveled back and forth between his mother, Jean and his friends. Blink.

The fire began to slowly fade away until there was nothing left of it but a smell of burning that remained in the air. Reaching down, he held his hand out to Bo. The puppy's tongue flicked out to lick his fingers causing just the hint of a smile turning the corners of his lips, though his eyes remained haunted.

"Okay. Okay. Let's do this," Ty said.

He raced up the stairs along with Bo, aligning his powers with theirs in a furious chant, their combined voices rising united. The air in the room began moving in a circular motion forming a swirling cone that danced uncontrollably around the space.

From below, Jean Moore groaned and rolled to her side into a fetal position as their words rose on the wind.

CHAPTER 72
CHASE

Bray gripped Chase's shoulders as soon as he burst through the door. "Where's Dawn? Is she okay?"

"I don't know. I was hoping they'd be back already. That's why I'm checking in." Chase turned to look back out the door. Neither man nor beast had followed him. At least not yet. He slammed the door closed and threw the locks into place.

"What's happening? We need to go get them. Maybe they need our help."

"We have to trust them. Give them more time."

Arms gesturing wildly, his words bursting out in a rush, "More time? They've been gone for hours! I don't know about you, but I'm not okay with my wife and son in danger. I need to do something." Pacing the floor, his hands fidgeted in front of him until the baby's cry broke through his agitation. Striding to the other room in a few quick paces, he returned with Sammie held close against his chest. She peeked at Chase, her pixie-like cheeks moving up in a smile.

"What can we do?" Bray asked.

Chase walked to the back door to look for signs they were being watched. Nothing stirred except a flash of red as a robin flitting from tree to bush and back again in the light of pre-twilight as the sun began its descent. To his eye, everything seemed as it should be. He turned back. "I've been thinking. I'm going to the souvenir shop. I need to find Carson. I just came from the Moore's house on Seacrest, and after feeling the strength of the power inside it I really need that destruction curse. It's our only chance at eradicating the blackness that exists on that plot of land." He began pacing, shoving his hands deep into his pockets.

"Fine. I'll come with you."

"No. Dawn said you needed to stay here. You won't be safe anywhere but here, and besides, you need to watch after Samantha. I promise I'll check in when I can."

"I'll bring her with us," Bray said.

"I don't think that's a good idea. Neither one of you will be safe out there." He pointed out the window. "There are wolf-creatures roaming the streets of town. No one's safe. Except here. Dawn made sure you had a safe haven here at the house. I think it's best if you stay here with your daughter. You're not a magical. How will you fight magic without magic?"

"I don't care what you think is best. This is my family, and I need to do something. I'll figure something out. We'll take the car." He disappeared into the kitchen, then returned with keys jingling. "Wait. Here. I need something from the safe." He shoved Sammie into Chase's hands and launched himself up the stairs. Chase could hear him rooting around on the floor above.

When he returned, he had a gun in one hand and a diaper bag in the other. "I brought my Glock 9mm and extra ammo. That should work, even against a magical, right? Let's go." He scooped Samantha out of Chase's arms, and marched toward the door, baby bag flung over his shoulder with a bottle sticking out of one outer pocket, and his gun peeking out of the other. "I'm ready."

"Do you think it's legal to carry a weapon in a child's bag? What if you give her the gun instead of the bottle?" Bray stared him down. Chase sighed. "Okay. It's about to get dark. Are you sure you want to risk it?"

Ignoring the question, he walked out the door calling back over his shoulder, "Let's go."

• • • •

This car, like the others Chase had seen in town, was equipped with its own personal vertical spinning wind turbine where the antennae should be. The roof was covered in solar panels, slightly different from those he might see at home but still recognizable. Chase clutched the safety handle while Bray maneuvered the velvet red Jeep Lightning right up to the caution-yellow painted curb directly in front of the souvenir shop, ignoring the sign declaring 'no parking'. They immediately piled out of the car and hurried to the front door.

"This thing really runs on solar power?" Chase asked.

Bray nodded. "A combo of sun and wind power."

"So, no gas at all?"

"Gas?" Bray frowned absently as they halted directly in front of the souvenir shop.

Chase shrugged. "Never mind." Holding a hand over his eyes, he squinted through the glass door. "If we can't go in this way, we'll try around the back."

Samantha, strapped facing out with her back against her father's chest into a papoose, kicked her legs and babbled with tiny spit bubbles forming on her lips. Chase smiled down at her, and she cooed. "Buh-ba-ba-gaba." More saliva bubbled out, and she giggled. "Da-da. Ma-ma. Ta-ta."

Laying a hand on her shoulder, Bray hugged his daughter and dropped a kiss on the top of her head. "Dada's here, baby. We're gonna get Mama and Ty back, don't worry."

Chase tested the door, rattling it back and forth. Locked. The words of the now-familiar lock-release spell sprang from his lips, and the resulting click was more satisfying than learning his first magic spell. "Hurry."

They entered the building quickly, closing the door behind them, and worked together to close the blinds.

"Seems deserted. I don't think Carson is here." Bray walked the aisles, brushing against a rack of colorful plastic beach buckets, not stopping to pick them up when two pails rattled onto the floor, spinning until the motion was stopped by contact with the shelf-bottom.

"He could be in the back."

"The back? I didn't know there was a back area."

"You wouldn't know about it. It requires magic to see it. I wonder if you'll be able to see it now that you know about all of it."

"Lead the way and we'll see."

Chase walked beyond the counter and right up to the wall. "It's through here." He pointed.

"Through the wall?"

"Yes, you just, sort of, step right through it. Watch." Once his foot broke the barrier, he was pulled through as before. He turned, calling from the other side, "Come on. Just sort of … walk through."

He could hear Bray tapping the wall on the other side, obviously blocked from passing through. As he stared at the flat surface, a chubby little foot suddenly appeared suspended like an ornamental decoration. A delighted giggle echoed through the plaster, arms appearing next through the drywall. Her hands clapped on this side while her body remained on the other, and her incessant babbling had a jubilant air.

Bray's voice raised, a note of hysteria overlay his next words, "Uh. Chase? Sammie can come through but I can't."

"Yes. Yes, I see her." His wide eyes were staring at a foot and two hands still sticking through the wall before all at once disappearing as if they'd never been there. Seconds ticked by. "Bray?"

Just then, Bray—Sammie in tow—came through and stood next to him. "Wha-?"

"It was Samantha. She pulled me through with her." He looked at his daughter with wonder. "Good girl, Sammie. Just like your mommy." He kissed her tousled hair again. "M-m-mwa." She leaned back, looking at him upside down, and giggled. Her pudgy, dimpled hands grabbed onto the stubble on his cheeks and she stretched up to loudly kiss him, leaving a trail of wetness on his chin. Bray didn't even seem to notice the slobber, but returned her smile.

"Okay. Carson's not here, but let's hang out a bit and see if he comes back. And if not, maybe we can find the ingredients we need for the destruction spell in his supplies."

Lying the journal he'd removed from the backpack on the counter, he began searching the aisles for the supplies he needed.

CHAPTER 73
ALYX

There was no sound to accompany the release of the locking spell, more a feeling from deep within. The small group gathered at the top of the stairs in the realty shop fell silent. Alyx raised a brow at Mason, and rested her hand on Ty's shoulder.

"Is it ... unlocked?"

"Only one way to find out." Mason pushed—not physically but telepathically—and the door swung quietly outward on well-oiled hinges.

Alyx let out the breath she'd hadn't known she was holding, and a wave of relief so strong she was dizzy with it overwhelmed her. "Okay. Let's get out of here." She took a step through the doorway and halted at Mason's words.

"Wait. We can't leave them here," Mason whispered, detaining her with a hand on her arm.

Ty ran back down the stairs. "My mom. I'm not leaving Mommy."

Alyx rolled her eyes. Strands of hair had long ago escaped her ponytail and framed her face in loose, unkempt curls. Her sigh was accompanied by a frustrated growl. "Fine. I guess we'll have to carry them. Hurry, we need to get out of here." Descending the stairs quickly, she squatted next to Dawn and shoved one arm under the older woman's shoulders, the other under her knees. Rising slowly, she stood on shaky legs. Dawn's head hung back, her arms flung out at her sides. Dead weight. After taking just a few steps, Alyx slowly lowered her back to the ground. "We're not going to get far this way. I won't even make it up the steps carrying her this way."

Ty ran to his mother's side, placing a hand on her forehead. "I'm staying with Mommy."

"Ty..."

"No. Go get Daddy. He'll come save us."

"I'm not leaving you here, Ty."

"Then we have to figure out a way to take Mommy with us."

Another sigh escaped. She looked at Mason. "Is there a magical way to move them?"

Mason paced. "I'm thinking." Back and forth. Back and forth.

"Think faster. We've been here too long."

"There has to be something here we can use. Be right back." He disappeared through the doorway into the realty offices upstairs.

Ty moved back to the floor beneath the worktable. Slowly he squatted, lying his hands flat against the cement floor. A rumble began under their feet, almost imperceptible at first, then growing to a crescendo until there was no mistaking the shaking of the floor under them.

Alyx jumped back, holding out an arm to Ty, bracing herself against the wall with the other. "Ty, what are you doing?"

"I'm calling on the power."

"The power?"

"Down there. I can feel it."

"Ty..."

The entire room shook and swayed. Alyx approached the boy, intent on breaking whatever magical connection he seemed to have with the energy underneath them.

She couldn't let him bond with the magic down there. He had to resist it—he was just a boy. She could feel the darkness and the power in that place.

Black magic.

• • •

Mason raced down the stairs dragging a rectangular coffee table with him. "We can use this. If we turn it upside down, we can put them on top and carry them out of here." He stopped short when he felt the floor bucking under his feet. "What?"

"It's Ty. He's calling on the darkness. We have to stop him."

Mason raised a brow. "How do you know he isn't calling on light magic?"

Alyx's head swiveled toward Mason. "I guess I ... don't."

"All magic comes from the elements. Light and dark."

"I guess I don't understand it fully yet."

"Okay, let's load them on here, and give it a try." Together they lifted Dawn and placed her as gently as possible onto the table. "Will both of them fit?"

"They'll have to. We don't have a choice."

Placing Jean halfway on top of Dawn, they each grabbed two of the upright table legs and lifted. "It won't be easy, but we have to try."

"If we can just lift them up the steps, then we can drag the table and once we're outside you can use your portal. We don't have to get them far, just out of the building."

Alyx nodded, rounding her shoulders. "We can do that."

Muscles burning, they lifted the table with women in tow, and hefted them up one step at a time. She called back, "Ty, we have your mom. Let's go."

His head snapped up, tiny flames burning in place of his pupils, and blinked.

"Mama?"

"Yes. We have her. Let's go!"

As he stood, the floor ceased shaking, though a crack had formed in a jagged line across the cement, and the worktable now lay on its side by the far wall.

Ty ran to the stairs to follow them up.

Painstakingly, they reached the top of the stairs, their combined labored breathing echoing in the quiet building. Once at the top Alyx lay her end on the carpet and raced to the other side to grasp the table leg, adding her weight to pull it across the floor. The unconscious women's feet dragged on the floor as they hung off the end, the berber rug cushioning them from injury. Dawn lost a shoe, and they ignored it. Bea gave one quick bark as if to say *'hurry!'*

Mason glanced over at Alyx, a smile forming on his face when they reached the glass front door. She smiled in return, reaching up to push through the door. When she turned, her gasp was swallowed by the sound of masculine laughter coming from outside.

"Well, well. Look who's here. I lost one keeper, only to have another fall right into my hands. This is splendid! Now I have the hybrid baby and a watch keeper's blood to use after all." The chuckle made gooseflesh run across her arms.

She raised her eyes, first making eye contact with the Sovereign Warlock, then past him. The cry that escaped her lips was filled with defeat. Wolf-creatures stalked through the street all heading toward the Realty Store. *Where's Liz?* The black led the way, confidently strolling up front, its feet silently hitting the blacktop as it approached. Another glance showed her the pack of at least two dozen more of the beasts. *We're trapped inside this building.* Her head whipped up.

A portal! We broke through the spell on the door, maybe I can...

Alyx raised her hands and began the chant. The tiny portal flickered and began to form. She could feel the Sovereign's eyes fly to her, and he chuckled again. "Enzo?"

The chimera crashed through the glass, shards scattering in every direction, one embedded in her cheek. She had no time to remove it as the Enzo knocked her backward, further into the bowels of the realty shop, past desks and computers, photos of cheery houses on the market. She backed up again and again, past the all-glass door leading to the courtyard, until the stairs were at her back. The chimera nudged her through the opening and she lost her footing, falling backward in a flailing of legs and arms as she desperately tried to grasp onto something in her long fall to the bottom. She landed with a sickening *thud* on the cement floor below.

CHAPTER 74
CHASE

Chase raced up and down the aisles, grabbing this and that off shelves and returning to place them on the counter next to the journal. "Okay, clear glass container, sage, white candles, white rice, lavender. Check. I have the vial of my ancestor's blood right here." He patted his pocket, then ran his finger down the list of ingredients on the age-browned paper, stopping at the next ingredient listed. "Chimera feather. Great. How are we supposed to get a feather from Enzo?"

"Enzo? Who's he?" Bray looked up from playing with Sammie.

"Um, he's an animal. Have you ever heard of a chimera?"

"Are you kidding? I read all kinds of fantasy books when I was a kid. I know what a ... wait a minute. Are you saying what I think you're saying?" He raised his hand—the tremble clearly visible—then lowered it quickly.

"Yes. Chimera's are real, and there's one here in Dune Harbor. His name is Enzo. An Enfield. He's the last of his kind."

"An Enfield? I don't think I ever heard of that one..."

"It's got the body of a fox, wings of an eagle, tail end of a wolf. Pretty impressive."

"Please tell me this—Enzo, you called him?—is on our side."

Chase was shaking his head before all the words left his tongue. "I'm sorry. No."

"Oh, great." Bray's shoulders sagged. "This gets better and better."

"Yes, and it's even worse than that. The spell says we need one of his feathers."

"Well, how are we supposed to get one?"

Chase sighed. "I have no idea."

"Then we need to go. I have to find Dawn. She needs me, I can feel it," Bray said.

"Ma-ma-ma-ma!" Sammie, suddenly serious, seemed to agree.

"Let's just get all the ingredients we can from here, and then we'll head out."

"Okay, hurry. What else do we need? I'll help search. Everything seems well-labeled here, it shouldn't be that hard."

They worked together until the countertop was filled with all the ingredients for the destruction spell except for the chimera feather and one other ingredient.

"Goldenrod warmed by the summer sun. I know where we can find that, but it will take time we don't have."

"Where is it? Can't you just, like, beam us there? Like they did when they jumped through that hole at the house? The one Ty went through." His eyes clouded at the thought of his son.

"Yes! Good thinking!" He slapped him on the back. "We could use a portal to go to Dune Haven. That place was surrounded by this kind of flower. And there's plenty of summer sun. I'm not as good at portaling as Alyx, but I think I can do it…" He began casting a circle. "By Earth and Sea, by Wind and Flame, I create this portal to end the game. The light will lead, the dark will fall. The powers of light to save us all. Take me to the place I need, the root of summer's goldenrod seed. From the Earth to me. Let it be." A portal appeared, flickering in front of him in and out of clarity like a flame dancing on the wind. He barely heard Sammie clapping her hands and babbling as if highly entertained.

Just as he was about to attempt to move through the unsteady wormhole, his head jerked as he heard a shout. As soon as his concentration broke, so too did the portal.

"Wait!" Carson appeared with another man in tow. "Don't go!"

"Carson?" Chase let the portal flicker and disappear. "Where have you been?"

"I was seeking a friend. Someone I think you'd like to meet. He lives alone in the mountains, the next state over. Not an easy man to find, let me tell you."

His eyes swept over the older man. He had a grandfatherly look about him in his jolly round cheeks and wide girth, though his deep blue eyes held an air of wariness that didn't quite fit that picture. Chase looked to Carson. "Are you going to tell me who he is?"

"Oh. Yes. This is George. George Apollo."

"Hi George." Chase reached out a hand and gave one brisk shake.

The other man held on, staring at his watch. He slowly turned Chase's arm to have a better view of the watch-face. "I haven't seen one of these in years," he breathed in awe. The man had salt-and-pepper hair and a receding hairline which was clearly visible as he bent to study the timepiece.

Chase pulled his arm back. "You know about the watches? Apollo? Wait, Apollo! I've seen that name before. In the journal. Your family was the chosen bloodline in Dimension 8! You're a keeper?"

"Yes, some of my ancestors were keepers. But not me. My birthday is February 11th. I wasn't born on one of the chosen dates that would allow me to travel the worlds. But I do have the bloodline, which comes along with the knowledge of the twelve worlds. My family's watch disappeared along with my grandfather many years ago. We never did find out what happened to him, or to the watch. He just ... never returned. Neither did the watch."

Chase rested his hand on George's shoulder. "I'm sorry. It's just so exciting for me to meet someone else that knows of the existence of the watches and their dimension travel abilities. I have so many questions..."

"*You* have questions? I've never traveled the dimensions. I'd love to hear about it..."

"Yes. After. After we finish this we can talk. Right now, we have to find the ingredients for the destruction spell. That's where I was going. To get the goldenrod plant from the forest. Then we have to figure out how to get a chimera feather."

Carson interrupted. "No need. That's why I went to see George. He has more magical supplies than I could even dream about. When I have a difficult order, he always has just what I need. That's why I was gone for so long."

"And when he filled me in on why he needed those particular items, I came along to see for myself. And damn if it isn't true. Carson says there's a girl with you?"

"Yes. She's trying to free my friend and the hybrid baby from the Sovereign Warlock. I need to destroy the house and find her. She may need my help." Chase gestured behind him. "This is Bray. His wife and son are with her. They're magical, too. Do you have the goldenrod *and* a chimera feather?"

"Of course. It's my job."

"How did you acquire a chimera feather? If you don't mind me asking?"

"Oh, I have my ways."

"What, did Enzo let you pluck it right out of his wing?" Chase smirked.

"Oh, I didn't get it from Enzo. He's not the only chimera that lives in this dimension. He's only the last Enfield."

Chase's mouth formed an 'oh,' but Bray froze in place. "Are you saying I've been living amongst all of these creatures, as well as witches and wizards, all this time, and knew nothing about it?"

Carson, Chase, and George answered in unison, "Yes."

Bray shook his head and sank into a wooden chair. "Nothing is as it seems. Everything, even the people, are forever altered for me."

Chase thumped his back. "That's a good thing. You're seeing clearly for the first time. I didn't know about any of this until recently, either. I know how you feel, though there is no magic in my home world. At least ... I don't think there is." He tilted his head, eyes squinting. "Okay. Let's take care of some of the black magic by destroying the Moore's house."

Carson nodded. "I'll help you with the spell, the rest is up to you."

"Deal."

George took a step forward. "I'm coming with you."

Outside, the sun had completed its daily arc while the full moon shed its light on the little town of Dune Harbor. The next sunrise would bring September 8. They were running out of time.

CHAPTER 75
ALYX

Time passed in a swirling fog of pitch-black and shades of gray. There were drumsticks pounding on her cranium in a steady beat. Alyx thought she could make out a familiar tune, but trying to form a coherent thought only made the thumping in her skull increase tenfold in a crescendo. She stopped trying. Sinking further into herself was so much easier, so she gladly entered the fog once more.

She was oblivious to the passage of time as it flowed around her. The only thing that mattered was escaping the pulsing that enveloped her entire body. Diving back into the pain-free black pool, she backstroked further away from consciousness.

A high-pitched howl broke through the mental barrier bringing her thoughts into semi-clarity once again, and she squeezed her eyes as tightly as she could trying desperately to deny any semblance of a reality that brought with it only pain. A throbbing in her wrist beat its drum in time with her headache and she clutched it close to her body, but that was nothing compared to the searing agony raging like fire in her left leg. Turning her head to the side, her lids wrinkled in her quest to paste them shut.

If I could only go back to sleep...

"Alyx! Alyx, wake up!"

Ty?

She heard a low, keening, moan as if through a tunnel, and didn't at first realize it was coming from her own throat.

"Alyx!"

Another whimper, this one longer than the last, escaped her lips. *Can't hide in the darkness. Ty needs me.*

She cracked one eyelid only to snap it shut, shying from the blinding light of the full moon. *Wait ... the moon? How long have I been out?*

Fighting past the wave of nausea that came with the light, she forced her eyelids apart, her whole body flinching. Another round of nausea overwhelmed her, but she swallowed it down, taking in her new surroundings, ignoring the ever-present pain that ravaged her entire being from inside-out.

She was in some kind of a courtyard. *Where am I? Where did they take me? I remember... Enzo. And ... falling. Then blackness. How did I get here, and how much time has passed?*

Forgetting for a moment her injuries, she tried to push herself up but fell backward when she applied weight to her wrist. Clutching her arm to her chest, she tried again using her good arm. When she was sitting, she looked down at her own leg and gasped. Her left leg sat at an unnatural angle, the fibula clearly broken and needing medical attention. Voices broke through the panic sitting on her chest making it hard to breathe.

Forcing her eyes away from her own broken leg, she looked up. David Moore—the Sovereign Warlock—stood next to a circular cement pit, probably five feet in diameter, in the ground. A large fire pit, maybe? He was staring at whatever was down there and didn't at first notice that she was awake. Enzo stood off to one side, a sentinel guarding its master. The creature made eye contact across the courtyard and took one protective step closer to the man. She let her eyes roam, confusion wrinkling her brow. They were surrounded on all sides by tall buildings—or was it just one building that opened in the middle? Behind the Realty shop? And the wolves, or whatever breed of canine they were, surrounded them all. Several brightly-colored Adirondack-style chairs lay haphazardly scattered on their sides, illuminated by the light of the full moon. She read the words *Harbor Realty* painted on the back of one. *So, we* are *in the courtyard at the center of the Realty shop.*

The creatures sat submissively around the pit in a semi-circle, an air of expectancy making the air thick, an unnatural intelligent gleam in their eyes. Jean Moore, awake and alert, held her husband's hand, and Dawn lay—still unconscious—a few yards away. Ty returned to crouch by her side after Alyx sat up.

Mason. Where's Mason?

Suddenly, she felt eyes boring down on her. *His* eyes.

"Ah, you're awake. Splendid. You won't miss the show. Of course, it doesn't matter if you're awake or not. I only need your blood, but still, it'll be more fun if you're awake." The Sovereign Warlock smiled a friendly smile, a grandfatherly air about him. A face that inspired trust and compassion.

Alyx knew better. It's ironic that often in that moment when you reach your lowest low, in times when hopelessness burrows its roots deep into your very soul, when you've reached just beyond your breaking point—that's when you see things more clearly than at any other point in your life.

People, she'd learned in this world in particular, were not always what they seemed. The man across the plaza was capable of all kinds of evil, despite his proven trustworthiness and common DNA with his 'others' in the last two worlds.

Everyone, everywhere, truly does have a price. This man, with initial honorable motivation, had succumbed so easily to the need for power.

On the seesaw of life, desperation could cause even the most honorable of men and women to teeter-totter in the direction of immorality. Oh, not everyone made the full leap, but rather just tiptoed on the edge only crossing the line temporarily before pulling back. Others crossed completely over never to return.

She could feel it churning within herself at this very moment, and recognized it for what it was. The potential to blur the lines of right and wrong. She would do practically anything to get her and Chase out of here in one piece. She glanced at Ty, who would stop at nothing to protect his mother. The power within him burned in his eyes, ready to be unleashed. As the pain ran free throughout her body, Alyx thought of Liz, who was guilty of horrible deeds in her past but had still fought hard to push back and choose a better life. She could only hope she was still fighting. And she turned back to David Moore. He'd started this quest for power with good intentions—and now would do anything to achieve his goal of power. It was all a matter of perspective, really.

Not one to let despair have its way, pushing the aches along with her deep thoughts into the background, she fought for a way out of this situation. *Think!* She blinked, searching with all that was in her for the one answer, the easy solution to this problem she was faced with. It continued to elude her.

How could this end well, when everyone around her had the potential to go dark at the slightest sign that things wouldn't go their way? There could only be one winning side, but is there really ever a winner when someone else has to lose? Two sides to every story, both believing their way was the right one.

Clutching her arm closer, she answered, "Where are we? What is this place?"

"Where? I'll tell you." David Moore glanced at the moon, slowly arcing across the sky. "We still have time yet. This," he pointed into the pit, "is the hub of all magical energy. A magical base of sorts. The realty shop was built around it. I plan on tapping into this power so I can do what you do. Travel all the worlds. Keep everyone, everywhere safe from harm by ruling all dimensions. Save the worlds. And I need you to achieve that goal." He frowned, his hands balling into fists. "I wanted it to be the ancestor of the creator, Elias Walker, himself, but he got away from me. So I'll have to settle for you. It should be enough, combined with the blood of the hybrid." He held up a small crimson vial, began pacing. "It has to be enough."

Jean placed a hand on her husband's arm. "It will be." She smiled into his eyes.

"My love, I'm so glad you're here by my side at last." He reached down, placing his hand on top of hers. They smiled into each other's eyes like a happily married couple celebrating years of love and admiration—in direct contradiction to the current situation. If not for the pit surrounded by magically created wolf-creatures with power swirling all around them, it would have been a heart-warming scene to behold.

He glanced up at the moon once again. "It's almost time. Let's begin."

Alyx desperately fought through her still-foggy brain for a solution, but all she could seem to focus on were more questions.

Is Chase okay?

Where are Mason and Liz?

She turned toward Dawn's still-sleeping form, the other woman's chest steadily rising and falling. Glancing around, her eyes searched.

Where did Ty go?

CHAPTER 76
CHASE

Chase, along with his new companion George, approached the house on Seacrest Boulevard with bold steps. He patted his front pocket, which contained a vial holding the combined ingredients of the destruction spell. After preparing the concoction, Carson and Bray had chosen to stay behind at the Souvenir Shop with the baby. At sunrise they planned to head back to Bray and Dawn's house to hunker down under the protection of Dawn's shield spell—apparently it was well-known in the magical community that Dawn's shields could withstand just about anything you could throw at them. Bray had been easily persuaded since he wanted to see if Dawn had returned home in his absence.

It was up to Chase—and George who'd insisted on tagging along—to execute the plan.

His family's ancient spell gave his confidence a boost, and it carried him right up to the front door.

George surveyed the house, and whispered, "Wow. You weren't joking 'bout the power here. I can feel it in my bones."

"Last time I was here, the stairs took on a life of their own, and the house itself fought against me. We'll need to stay sharp."

"Oh, I'm well-versed in magic, son. I may not be a keeper, but I excel at what I do. I live alone in the mountains so I can practice my craft freely. I won't be a burden, I promise. You may even find me useful."

"Great. Okay, let's go." The door—still ajar from his last visit—allowed him to stride right in without hesitation, George close behind him. To all appearances, the house looked run-down but otherwise like any other house might. The stairs had repaired themselves, and the carpet was no longer covered in whatever sticky substance had coated him before. "It looks ... normal."

"Don't let that deceive you," George whispered in reply. "Let's head to the basement, like we discussed."

"This way." Chase walked toward the kitchen entryway, only to slam headfirst into an invisible barrier. Stepping back, he rubbed his forehead.

George shouted—all semblance of quietly sneaking in now gone—sparks flying from his fingertips, "Stand back!" An electrical arc, similar to those emitted from the watch, flew from George's hands to clash with the magical wall, his deep voice chanting words Chase could barely make out. He stood meekly by feeling more helpless with each second that ticked by. "Tell me how to help." The older man ignored him, eyes completely focused on his task. A spark leapt out of the stream of contained lightning, striking Chase's left arm. He swatted at it, jumping backward. The tiny spark traveled down his arm and into his watch, which began vibrating and humming. Staring down into the watch face, his eyes widened when the electrical stream erupted from the watch to combine with George's magic. Heat engulfed his wrist as the watch took on a life of its own.

Holding his arm straight out toward the doorway, the electricity seemed to absorb directly into it, creating a rippling in the air. "It's not working."

"Yes. It is. Keep it up," George hissed between his teeth, sweat beading on his forehead.

Chase lost track of how long they remained there, a volley of electrical bursts combining in a mystical battle of wills. Suddenly the sound of glass shattering filled the small room and Chase jumped back, ducking to avoid any contact. His blank eyes searched the floor for signs of destruction that didn't appear, and he patted his chest. "What ...?" There was no evidence of the victory—if in fact they'd won the battle— or any broken pieces of the transparent wall that had been blocking them moments before. George turned to face him and gestured, "You first."

"O-okay. You're sure it's ....?"

"Yes. It's safe." George gave one curt nod.

Chase glided forward, and walked straight through the doorway as if there had never been a blockage. He breathed a sigh of relief, just as the floor—as the stairs had done earlier—shifted, his feet falling through holes that had not been there seconds earlier. "Look out!" he called over his shoulder. The walls began to pulse and an inky black substance crawled like onyx lava down the walls toward the floor.

"It's the house. It's trying to prevent us from reaching the source in the basement." He held his hands in front of him, and tiny electrical currents raced under his skin. "No worries."

"No worries? I don't see how we ..."

"Did I mention that controlling electricity has always been my strength?"

"No. No, you didn't. But I still don't see how that can help."

"Just give me a minute."

"Wait. What are you doing?"

"Why, I'm calling all the electricity from the town. Directing it here. Stop talking. I need to concentrate."

Chase looked down. He couldn't see his feet underneath the linoleum flooring, and the black blobs continued further down the wall. His eyes tracked the slow progress as it slimed past the base of the wall onto the floor, heading directly toward him. "Hurry!"

Outside, the neighborhood went suddenly black. At the same time, the house on Seacrest lit up like the annual Fourth of July firework display set off on the Sunset Beach.

CHAPTER 77
ALYX

"Bring the hybrid to me," the Sovereign bellowed.

A form appeared from behind him in the moon-cast shadows, and recognition did not at first click with Alyx. As he approached the ring, his features came more clearly into focus, and she gasped, "Brian!" She hadn't seen him since her first day in town when she and Chase hid in his parent's shed.

His eyes widened when he saw her. The sheepish look on his face was enough: He was working for the Sovereign Warlock.

Stupid. He'd tried to kidnap her for this man, and still she'd believed she could trust him. Her face heated and a grunt escaped. "You're still working for him? Even after everything? He destroyed your house."

He did not answer, though his shoulders slumped even more.

"How are your parents?" she spat.

His head whipped up, and though he again refused to answer, something in his eyes gave her pause. *I bet the Sovereign has his parents. Either that or they're dead. That makes Brian dangerous. But to whom?*

He turned to the Sovereign. "Where is the hybrid, sir?"

"What do you mean, where is he? He's right over there in the cage, where I put him after defeating Ursa—*Liz*—whatever it is she's calling herself these days." He flung his arm to the far side, and all eyes followed to the cage.

Defeating Liz? What is he talking about?

Brian turned toward the small crate, and sighed, shrinking back. "It's empty."

The Sovereign raised his arms and fire snapped out of the pit, rising in tandem into the air with a *crack* before receding back into the Earth. "Impossible." The cage flew through the air, landing at the man's feet. "Where's Liz?" he bellowed. "I thought we'd taken care of her. I left her bleeding in the street. She can't be ..." He stormed away, disappearing into a doorway that led inside, Jean right behind him. Alyx assumed it led to the realty shop, but did not know for sure.

As soon as he was gone, Brian raced to her side. "You're hurt. Where?"

She scowled at him. "I'm okay. I'll be fine."

"I said where?"

She huffed. "My wrist, my leg, and there's a bump on the back of my head."

He squatted down next to her, placing his hands first over her wrist, then her skull. Taking the pain into himself as she'd seen him do once before, he grimaced as he healed her head and wrist. When he reached her mangled leg, he fell backward with the pain, eyes closed, breathing labored. His chest heaved as he felt what she'd been feeling.

She ran a hand over her leg, amazed at her perfectly re-knitted bone. It was pain-free. She reached out to Brian, feeling a touch of remorse that he'd taken on her pain, then reminded herself that he was working with David Moore. When the pain left his body, she cocked her head. "Why?"

"It's my sister, Annabelle. Colin's twin. She follows the Sovereign. Not by force. It was her choice. My family is trying to get her back, though she doesn't seem to care about us anymore. In a way, she reminds me of Liz, only reversed. It was my sister that destroyed our house, not the Sovereign Warlock as we assumed. She didn't even know if we were inside when she did it. Every time we think we're getting close to her, she punishes us in some way. That day, it was the house. Next time, who knows?" His eyes looked through her. "I'm the only one willing to admit that maybe she's too far gone to ever come back to us. But we have to try."

"So, where is she?" Alyx asked.

"I don't know. We haven't seen her in weeks. Since before you came here. We fear she's lost to us forever. When I kidnapped you, I thought it was a way to earn his trust so we could get close to my sister. I was hoping to find her here. My parents are waiting outside. And Colin is searching inside."

"Okay, you'll have to fill me in on the rest after we get out of here. Can you heal Dawn?" She pointed.

Brian turned toward the unconscious woman. "What's wrong with her?"

"She's under some kind of spell ... a dominion spell?"

He was already shaking his head. "No. The healing spell only works for medical problems, not magical ones."

Alyx nodded. "Okay. We have to ..."

The Sovereign returned in a clap of thunder, storming to stand in front of them. "Where is the hybrid?"

Alyx and Brian made eye contact, confusion evident. "How would we know?"

"Don't take me for a fool! I want the hybrid, and I want it now! We don't have much time!" He paced, pointing at the moon already beginning its descent in the night sky.

Alyx, aiming to soothe, answered calmly, "I don't even remember how I got here. The last thing I remember was falling down the stairs. Then I woke up out here."

"And I've been with you, sir." Brian stammered. "I saw you put the hybrid in there myself."

David Moore's voice echoed in the silence. "Then where, do you suppose, is it?"

A young girl, hair a riot of chocolate curls, came through the entryway, Colin dragging his feet meekly behind her as if being pulled along with an unseen force. In her arms, Bo shook, his wild eyes emanating fear.

"I have him." Annabelle spoke in a high-pitched voice.

Brian lurched forward. "Anna ... thank God you're okay. Wait until Mom and Dad see you ..."

"They already have. I have them restrained inside so they can't stop what's about to happen."

"What do you mean ...?"

David Moore's laughter rose on the wind. "Good girl, Anna. Now, let's get started."

"I didn't do this for you. I did it for me." Annabelle smiled.

"What?" demanded the Sovereign Warlock.

"You didn't think I'd just sit back and let you have all the fun, did you?" she said.

"Be careful, girl..." he warned.

Just then, Jean Moore stepped out of her husband's shadow, a magically controlled arrow flying toward the girl. At the same time, Bea lurched out of the shadows and bit down on Anna's arm causing her to lose her hold on Bo. The pup dropped to the ground and ran straight for Alyx, leaping into her arms. The arrow struck true, piercing first Bea's body and continued through her into the heart of the girl, who gasped and clutched at the animal and the arrow sticking from her chest.

Alyx, Bo in tow, began edging toward the door even as Brian and Colin ran to their sister. Bo whimpered and tried to run to its mother, but Alyx held tight. Bea couldn't be saved, she could see that from here.

Anna managed one final burst of magic as her eyes zeroed in on Jean. Jean's body suddenly levitated into the air moving slowly, in a flailing of arms and legs, until she hovered over the ring of power. When Anna took her final breath, her hold was broken and Jean plummeted with one small scream into the pit below. Her screams echoed in the courtyard, then suddenly cut-off. The silence that followed announced Jean's fate.

"No!" David Moore fell to his knees in anguish, his burning eyes taking on an even harder edge. Rising to his feet, he threw his head back and roared. "Your family will pay for this!" he screeched at Brian. He raised his hands, all of his power directed toward Brian and his brother, who cowered, tears streaming from his eyes in mourning for his lost sister. A black cloud—the Death Mist spell—erupted from the Sovereign's fingertips heading toward the boys. The haze got to within inches of them—they stood bravely awaiting their fate—and then stopped, hovering.

Another bellow escaped, and the Ruling Mage concentrated all his energy into the deadly mist. No matter how much power he pushed into it, it would not go beyond the barrier. "What the ...?" His eyes traveled the courtyard, searching for the reason his power was failing.

Dawn stood—released from the dominion spell at the moment of Jean's death—aiming her shield at Brian and Colin.

"You'll pay. All of you will pay for this!" The mist spread until it filled every shadowed corner of the yard, turning the brightly colored Adirondack chairs coal black as the moon continued its downward trek across the night sky.

CHAPTER 78
CHASE

Chase used his arm to shield the blinding light. It was brighter than the mid-day sun reflecting off the ocean in July, and George's voice rose as the voltage doubled. He felt rather than saw the shift in the floor, and yanked his feet free of the linoleum. The skin around his ankles scraped and tore on the jagged edges and he felt the warm, sticky, wetness of blood. Once free he balanced on the still-shaky surface, groping for the wall, slowly making his way toward the basement door. Grasping the doorknob, his hand was scorched by heat, but still he turned the knob before releasing his hold. The door banged open, causing him to jump back as it slammed into the wall so hard the doorknob embedded into the drywall.

A living black haze of ever-changing shapes swirled erratically from the lower floor up into the kitchen invading the space like a dark fog, but when confronted with the blinding electrical light it quickly retreated back downward. Chase approached the top step, reaching into his pocket to extract the vial containing the destruction spell. He glanced at George, whose eyes had gone opaque, arms raised as he controlled the electricity now contained inside this one house.

"Do I need to go down, or can I do it from here?" Chase wondered. When no answer was forthcoming, he placed his foot on the next step, carefully descending into the belly of the beast. When he got to the fourth step he felt the wood give out, and his foot fell through the board. His body lurched forward, and he clutched the handrail just barely managing to hold on rather than plunging headfirst down the rest of the stairs. Misty black fingers reached for his legs, and he could swear that he felt them grip his ankles and pull.

Lurching away, he desperately searched for the vial. "Oh no! I think the spell fell down there!" Panic took hold of his body, his limbs going weak and trembly before he mentally shook himself.

George hissed through gritted teeth, "That's where we wanted it. Say the words. It'll have to be enough."

The house itself rebelled, walls pulsing as if alive, and Chase tightened his grip. For a moment, he feared he had forgotten the words he'd committed to memory before their arrival as his mind went temporarily blank. Then suddenly the words were there, and he could hear himself chanting them as if from a distance. He repeated the words over and over, so many times he lost count. Shaking his head, he turned toward George. "I don't think it ..."

A groaning, like the sound a wooden ship might make just as it's about to be swallowed underwater, made his body flinch as he covered his ear with his one free hand. An earthquake shook the entire house, creaking and moaning as the foundation cracked and the structure tilted amidst unnatural screams from below. In the chaos, Chase hung on and closed his eyes, breathing the words of the spell one last time. The wind sucked at his center, pulling him toward the blackness below. As the wind continued to roar through the tiny kitchen, the roof was ripped from the house in one quick burst—one minute it was there and the next it was gone. The night stars twinkled down at them almost mockingly in their serene beauty. Tipping his head back he spotted the line of three stars that created Orion the hunter's belt directly above, the taunting glow reminding him that there was work yet to be done—if he even survived.

George raised his hand and a bolt of lightning lashed out and wrapped around Chase's forearm. He pulled back, instinct telling him to fight against this new threat when his eyes followed it to its origin, and as soon as he realized it came from George, he grasped it like a rope. Little tingles raced around the skin of his palm and anywhere the thing touched his skin, but he held on knowing he wouldn't survive if he gave in to the force that was pulling him toward the basement.

"We have to get out of here!" Chase called above the cacophony, inching his feet ever closer to his new friend.

"Agreed. We need reinforcements." George threw his head back, bellowing into the night, "Apollo!" The one word seemed to echo, rising up out the top of the house like a megaphone blast.

The stars suddenly winked out, blocked by the body of an enormous beast that was coming at them from the opening created by the absent roof. Four huge padded paws came closer and closer. Chase scrambled backward, away from the creature. It hovered, unable to land on the shaky floor, looking expectantly at George. Chase studied the thing—white feathered eagle head, body of a much more powerful land animal with four legs. A large cat, maybe?

Just then it turned toward him and snapped its enormous golden beak in a *clack-clack-clack*, black-ringed yellow eyes boring into his. When it opened its mouth, Chase could see the lean, pink, triangular tongue that writhed inside, and when it turned the two nostril holes at the base of the beak that were the size of gambling tokens.

George threw out two more lightning ropes that lassoed the animal around its bright-white feathered neck. It barely flinched as the older man leaped onto its back, or when George yanked the lightning rope that still circled his wrist, yanking him up behind him. Clearly this was not the pair's first ride together, even though this was a huge first for Chase.

As they ascended, rising up and out of the house, they looked down in time to see the house blown to bits. One more minute and they surely wouldn't have survived the blast. Oddly enough, the thing he noticed as they flew away was that the explosion made no sound at all. A silent bomb—an oxymoron if there ever was one. Shouldn't the destruction of a physical structure go out with a thundering bang? The house was there, and then it was just … gone. Nearly invisible rings of light circled the remains of the house, and then winked out into blackness.

Chase blinked, taking one deep, long breath. It was done. They'd destroyed the source of black magic in his hometown. Now, all they had to do was bring David Moore around to the man he should be, and things would go back to normal in this little coastal town. If Alyx hadn't succeeded in doing just that already.

Power was restored to the rest of the neighborhood as lights re-lit all over Dune Harbor at once. Mothers lit night-lights as they tucked their babies in for the night, and young children—no longer afraid as lightbulbs hummed back to life—brushed their teeth and dreamed of another day of jumping the waves and digging in the sand. The electric company workers shook their heads, unsure what had caused the initial power outage … or what had eventually fixed it. They were only happy to go back to their own homes and snuggle back into bed pressed against their slumbering spouses.

CHAPTER 79
ALYX

As Alyx looked on with chest heaving in shallow bursts, Dawn shielded their small band from the Death Mist spell. Though the spell held for now, Dawn wouldn't last much longer, it was clear in her stance and trembling arms. She'd been through a lot in the last few hours.

Alyx's eyes shifted to survey the area. The wolf-creatures were still compliant, not reacting to any of the events that had recently transpired. The death mist was not directed at them, so they remained unaffected. One even licked its paws as if bored. Another lay on its side, stretching its limbs in an utterly relaxed pose. As if there was not a worry to be had in this world. *Why are they here?*

She hugged Bo closer to her chest and could feel his rapid heartbeat and erratic breathing. Tiny whimpers rumbled in his throat accompanied by tiny tremors that shook his whole body. She leaned down to hug him closer. *Poor guy.* Its father gave him over to the Sovereign Warlock, and its mother died protecting him.

I have to keep him safe. Make sure she didn't sacrifice herself for nothing. But who will protect him when I leave this place?

With frantic eyes, she searched for a way out of there. Tentatively sending out magical feelers, she began focusing on creating a portal. Maybe while he's distracted, I can create a wormhole to get us out of here. At least temporarily stop this so they could re-group. The whispered words dripped from her lips and she could feel the spark begin to ignite. *This just might work!*

And then the words froze on her tongue, and she let them sputter and die along with the glint of magic.

Where is Ty? We can't leave without him.

Edging closer to Brian and Colin, she reached them just as Dawn let out a cry. "Ty!" Alyx's head whipped around.

"Mama!" Ty ran toward his mother.

Tears streamed down Dawn's face, and a renewed energy pulsed out of her. "Get behind me, baby."

"No, Mommy. I can help."

"No!"

"I'm not just a kid. I called for help from the flames under the floor. Help is coming, Mama."

Dawn tried to guide him behind her. "Just get behind me, Ty. I can hold the shield better if I know you're safe."

"You hold the shield, and I'll use my fire to fight him." Ty wiggled out of her arms.

"No, baby, don't."

Ty ignored her, fire growing from his palms. The young boy faced the enemy, his eyes glowing with pupils of dancing candlelight. His fireballs grew and he reared back, flinging them forward to roll in midair like a tornado of flames that rolled through the death mist like a bowling ball. David Moore stopped to deflect the attack, causing him to lose focus on the Death Mist as it dissipated. The ground around them rumbled and shook, and Alyx tripped and fell once, feeling arms pulling her back up she glanced and nodded at Brian, then began running. Suddenly, the pack of wolf-beasts stood at attention.

Alyx, Bo, Dawn, Ty, Brian and Colin burst through the back door into the realty shop just as Liz limped through the street-facing doorway looking like she needed a hospital bed.

"Liz! Hurry, we have to get out of here! Come with us," Alyx yelled.

"No," Liz replied.

Dawn said, "But, David is releasing a Death Mist, and we have to..."

Liz shook her head, causing a blood-streaked strand of ebony hair to stick to her face. "I can't."

"Yes, you can. We need to get out of here and make a new plan. We don't have time. Let's go!" Alyx pleaded.

"I can't. I need to be here for what's about to happen. I think this is what I was meant to do all along."

"What are you talking about? Just—please—come with us now. We can figure out the rest later," Alyx said.

Liz shook her head again. "I struck a bargain with the wolf-creatures. It is done. But you're right, you do need to get out of here. You won't survive if you're here when he is released."

"When ... who ... is released?" Alyx asked.

Liz swung her eyes around to meet Alyx's stare. Dead eyes. "Pavo."

"The first Sovereign Warlock? Why? Why would you release him?"

"I was coming to do that, but the boy has already begun the process. I can feel him." She inclined her head toward Ty. Her eyes traveled to Bo, and she reached a hand out to him. Her head whipped up, and a small flicker of life re-entered those dull eyes. "Where's Bea?"

Alyx dropped her gaze. "She's gone."

Liz's shrank in on herself. "No," she whispered. "I should have been here for her. I'm sorry. So sorry, Bo." She placed her hand on Bo's trembling back and leaned in. The pup licked her face, lapping at the fat teardrops that dripped slowly down her cheeks. She stood taller, a dangerous glint shining out from her eyes. "Go. Get out of here. Keep him safe. This isn't your battle, but I have to finish it."

The small group started toward the door, only to be flung backward. They hit the wall all at once, crumbling to the floor like bricks. Turning, expecting to see that David Moore had caught up to them, Alyx gasped as recognition dawned.

The Hunter. She'd grown accustomed to ignoring the mad vibrations of her watch, assuming it was Liz that set off the built-in alarm. Now she knew that this time, it had been the hunter's counterpart who had set off the watch's warning bells.

Liz spoke first, "Pavo. So good to see you after all this time."

"I'll deal with you and your treachery later, Ursa. Where is he?"

Liz-Ursa pointed, indicating the back way out. "Let them go. This isn't their fight." She spoke calmly.

"No. No one leaves until I sort out this mess. I've been gone too long, and I have a lot of catching up to do."

"Your wolf-beasts are out there."

"Good." He gestured with his arm, "After you."

Re-entering the courtyard, Bo still grasped in her arms, Alyx began to despair. Now they were fighting not one, but two Sovereign Warlocks. The wolf-creatures immediately moved as one, throwing back their heads and howling into the night. They flanked Pavo as soon as they saw him. No longer relaxed, they were now in full-on guard mode, protecting their master.

How are we ever going to get out of this?

The minute David Moore locked eyes with Pavo, the fight began. There was no hesitation or any need of words. Black lightning bolts—jagged lines of shiny raven-colored electric streams—flew out of each of the battling warlock's fingers, darkening the early morning sky with a static energy. The magically inspired lightning clashed, creating an arc of dark power and purple-black sparks to shower down upon them.

No one but Alyx noticed the glint of light on the horizon indicating morning was near as the men each fought for control of the power that pulsed around them.

September 8th dawned as the two men fought in the small courtyard of a respectable business on Dune Harbor's Main Street. Alyx frowned. One more day.

They had one more day here in Dimension 8. At exactly 9:09 AM on September 9th, she and Chase would forever leave this place, whether they were ready to go or not. They would move forward, pulled by a power not their own.

She couldn't help but wonder just what they would be leaving behind. If they even survived.

Where are you, Chase?

CHAPTER 80
CHASE

The cool pre-dawn air slapped against his face, his short hair parting unevenly down the middle as it was blown forcefully back. Chase was glad for it. After what he'd just experienced, the night breeze, like a splash of cold water against his skin, seemed to prove that he was still alive. He held onto George's back, squinting into the wind, his legs wrapped around a beast that shouldn't exist—the mythical chimera—but somehow did. Feeling the power of that muscular body beneath him, his yell competed with the breeze whistling past his ears. "What is this thing?"

"What?" George called over his shoulder.

Leaning closer, Chase shouted, "What is this thing?"

"A Griffin."

"He's on our side?"

George gave an affirmative nod. "He's been with my family for years."

"Apollo. You gave him your family name. Makes sense."

Another nod.

"Hey, thanks. For ... back there," Chase said.

"Glad to help."

"Where are we headed?"

George paused before answering. "To the woods, away from town. People will be waking soon."

"No! We can't! We need to help the others at the realty shop. The source of all magical energy is there. The Hub. We destroyed the black magic source, but the Sovereign can still tap into the hub and turn it black."

"Sorry." George shook his head emphatically.

"Please. You're from a keeper family. There's a keeper there, and she needs our help. She needs us."

"I told you, I can't..."

"But she needs us! And ... and I love her. Please!" He felt rather than saw the older man's sigh. With one last desperate plea, he tried once more. "If you can't, then drop me off. Please. I have to go back."

In answer, George leaned down, speaking unheard words to Apollo. Its avian head swiveled around once, its glowing yellow eyes boring into Chase so long it made him fidget. Pupils contracting, shining with an awareness no bird of prey should possess. Chase met the Griffin's eyes and mouthed again, "Please, help me."

The animal broke eye contact to look at George. Chase thought it might have performed an eye-roll before whipping its head back around and flying in a wide arc, an airborne U-turn. Maybe just a trick of the light, he didn't care as long as this creature was headed back toward Alyx and his friends.

They glided over dark houses, the inhabitants still sleeping peacefully in their houses and hotel rooms before the blare of their alarm clocks would signal the start of a new day, blissfully unaware of the turmoil squirming to break free beneath the ground under their beach homes. Even the vacation partiers had already headed home in search of the escape of slumber, more than happy to waste away the day sleeping off the effects of a wild night until the Earth completed its rotation once again.

Up ahead, he spotted it. The first time he'd seen it had also been from the air, when he had been clutched in the claws of Enzo's grasp. Back then, he thought he was crazy, thinking he'd seen a castle with a courtyard at the center. Now, he knew better, and because of that could see it more clearly than before. The walls no longer shimmered in and out of focus as they'd done that not-so-long-ago day, but instead seemed as solid as the buildings that surrounded it. Knowing that the townies could only see the facade that was the realty shop gave him pause. What else did the non-magical people drift by and accept as normal when, in fact, it was anything but? Just a few months ago, he was one of them, completely ignorant to the truth of who and what he was. Would those people, too, wake up one day and gain enlightenment? Or would they live their entire lives never knowing? The latter was the more probable of the two.

The Griffin circled the buildings in a wide arc landing on the flat roof of a structure across the street, its four wide padded paws absorbing any sound. Chase and George jumped off, landing with a *thump* on the roof's tar coating. Chase turned to look more closely at the creature, who was in turn studying him with a tilt of its avian head just as thoroughly. Its short tawny hair and long tail with a tuft of russet fur at the end, accompanied with four enormous clawed paws gave away what had been eluding him until now. "A lion's body, eagle's head?"

"Yes." George gave a curt answer. "Look, we have to get Apollo out of sight. I know you don't care, but I've followed the rules of magic all my life, and I'm not going to change that now. It's imperative that the townies never see him."

"I understand. But I don't think you're aware that the rules are bending as we speak. The wolf-beasts are here. In town. And non-magical people saw them marching through the streets. They even reported it on the news."

"Excuse me, but that's not quite the same as seeing a chimera flying down Main Street."

"You're right. I know that. But…"

A rain of sparks erupted from the courtyard, gleaming deep purple in the light from the rising sun. Though they could not see what the source was from their position across the street, they leapt into action. George mounted the Griffin in one giant lunge.

"Get on," he turned, reaching his hand out to pull Chase up. Apollo took off running, in a giant leap his feet left the roof and his wings unfurled in an explosion of feathers. Airborne once again, they headed straight for the source.

CHAPTER 81
ALYX

Alyx remained close to the building, the others closely huddled together behind her. Strength in numbers. Bo had ceased his constant trembling and lay his head on her shoulder, a deep sigh rumbling through his entire body. He pushed his wet snout against her neck. *Trust. He trusts me to protect him.* An unfamiliar feeling settled in her chest, crystalline tears hanging precariously from her lashes. She leaned down, breathing in the woodsy, canine scent of him, and lifted her eyes to survey the scene in front of her. Her small band of rag-tag magicals stood taller when their eyes met. *They all trust me.* One of the tears broke loose to roll in one lone path to her chin. She impatiently swiped at it. *There has to be a way...*

Leaning toward Liz, she whispered, "Why can't we just leave? I mean, they're not paying us any attention ..." Her words fell away when she turned to the door. The first thing she noticed was the wolf-pack, no longer idle, standing in formation surrounding the small courtyard. They blocked every exit, flanking Pavo. It was clear where their loyalties lay.

The second thing Alyx observed was Enzo, moving to stand next to David Moore. The Enfield tossed its head back and howled—so loudly her body flinched and gooseflesh spread up her arms—instantly shattering the silence of dawn. The wolf-beasts returned the call in outright challenge, and the ululations ended with bursts of snarls and growls. Tails standing erect, spines hunched like a spring, the hair on their canine backs stood on-end in clear aggressive behavior.

Her third observation was Liz's eyes. Though moments before she had looked injured and defeated, now her eyes took on a sharpness she hadn't possessed before. As she looked on, Liz rounded her shoulders and her height seemed to expand. She took a step forward.

Alyx's eyes widened, she reached out with a detaining hand. "Liz, wait ..."

Liz did not hear her words, so focused was she on the battle taking place in front of her. While no one paid her an ounce of attention with the exception of Alyx, she made her way to the circular cement pit, pupils gleaming when she looked down into an eternity of magic. The white light from below turned her skin almost iridescent in its paleness, her midnight black hair a stark contrast to the white. Her lips began to move, though the words were lost in the distance separating them.

Bo lifted his head and whimpered once before hiding his face against her neck again. Alyx ran her hand gently over his head, unconsciously soothing. "Shh, Bo. It's gonna be okay. I'll get us out of here, somehow." A small smile turned up her lips when she felt his rough little tongue licking at her neck.

She turned to her small group. "We might as well be invisible right now. Let's try a portal. If we combine our powers it will be stronger, and maybe we can get out of here."

Brian was shaking his head. "No. If we portal out of here, it won't solve anything. We need to end this. Today."

Alyx turned to the others. "What do you think?"

Dawn sat on the ground with Ty in her lap. Huge charcoal-colored rings outlined her eyes, exhaustion plain all over her face. "I don't know how much more help I can be at this point. And I don't want Ty to be involved in all of this. I'm for portaling directly to my living room."

Colin intervened, "What about our parents? We can't just leave them here, Bri. Anna," his voice broke on his dead sister's name, "said she restrained them inside. We have to search for them."

Brian nodded. "We're not leaving. You can go if you want, but we can't. Not without Mom and Dad."

Alyx took a moment, then nodded. "Okay. Maybe we can portal inside to search for them. We won't get past the wolves that way." She pointed toward the door.

"Now *that* I can agree to. I'll cast the circle." Brian began chanting the familiar words, and Alyx joined in. She could hear Dawn's, Colin's, and even Ty's voices combine as the wind swept their hair to dancing.

Just then, black sparks flew in their direction, breaking their magic. Though their chanting gained intensity, the portal refused to form.

Alyx stood, pacing their small circle. "What now? We can't just stand by ..."

Ty lurched to his feet, pointing upward. "What's that?"

Something was coming toward them from the sky. Alyx couldn't quite make out the shape in the new light of dawn, and she squinted, assuming a defensive pose and positioning herself in front of her group.

Enzo, who had previously been solely focused on his master, tipped his head back, letting loose another ghostly howl, unfurled his wings and took off toward the intruder. The two beasts clashed in mid-air, hovering at the highest point of the building, and shouting could be heard above the commotion. She gasped as she recognized one of the voices.

"Chase?" Alyx called out, taking a step out of the circle toward them, head tilted back trying desperately to understand what was happening above them. "Chase?" she called again.

"Alyx?" he bellowed. "I'm ..." His words were cut short as he plummeted through the air toward the ground—and the pit of magic—below.

She began running. "No! Chase!"

"Alyx!" His scream was cut off abruptly.

CHAPTER 82
CHASE

Apollo swooped to the left when he caught sight of Enzo, an eagle's shriek echoed through the morning accompanied by the dip and turn. Chase, unprepared for the sudden movement and unaccustomed to being a passenger on a flying chimera, lost his hold and was airborne in seconds. As if from a long distance away he heard George's shout, "Chase!" but could do nothing except tumble.

Falling. A giddy kind of horror took hold of his gut, as his stomach flipped over and over again.

Arms and legs flailing, one shout escaped his lips before the rushing air took his breath. His body turned, plummeting to the ground after his unplanned dismount. An eternity fit into those few seconds of time, and Chase could see he was falling directly toward some kind of enormous pit. Living lights shone up out of the cavernous hole, and it seemed to go on and on—maybe all the way to the center of the Earth. Turning his head, he saw Alyx, and her name was torn from his lips. That one word spoke of so many things. His heart swelled at her answering yell, "Chase!"

There must be a way. A spell or something that can...

He fell past the ledge of the cement ring surrounding the glowing pit, chanting a spell as he flew. What good was invisibility now? His strength in magic couldn't help him now, but he had learned a few other spells in his time here. Before he could finish the words of his spell, he was sucked into a small opening. As if flying down a sliding board, his body sped to the side and the portal spit him out in the grass at Alyx's feet.

"Chase!"

"Alyx! What ...?"

She reached down to offer him a hand and he clasped it, bracing on her to stand. "How?"

A laugh escaped her, "I sent a portal to you. I didn't know if it would work, but I had to try. And it did!" she clapped her hands, smirking. "What would you do without me to rescue you at every turn?"

Reaching out, his fingers intertwined with hers. "I don't know." Pulling her closer, he laid his forehead against hers. "Thanks. I don't know what we'd do without each other."

Brian humphed. "Again. Really? Do you see that we're in the middle of a magical war here? We don't have time for this lovey-dovey crap." Holding his hand up to his face, he mimed gagging.

Alyx took a step back. "He's right. We have to help finish this, somehow."

"Okay, so I see Pavo is back. The hunter," Chase pointed.

"I have a lot to tell you." Her eyes found the two chimeras, now circling each other warily. "And apparently, so do you."

George joined the group, his eyes never leaving the two beasts, a frown causing creases on his forehead.

"Alyx, meet George. George Apollo. His family has the keeper bloodline. Like ours."

In the ever-brightening sky, they caught each other up on the highlights of what had happened since they'd seen each other last.

. . .

"George can help us. He's, like, really powerful with magic. How do we get out of here, George?"

The older man frowned, his eyes on the chimeras. "I'm more worried about Apollo right now. He's not a fighter."

Chase's eyes followed the beasts. As he watched, Apollo snapped his beak into the flesh of Enzo's shoulder, ripped his predator's head back and forth, then spit out a chunk of flesh and fur. The Enfield backed up, a yelp torn from its throat, then turned to lick at its bleeding wound. "I think he's doing okay."

Just then both creatures took to flight as the fight continued overhead. They rolled and ducked, crashed into the side of the building, and plummeted back down, tumbling to within inches of where their group now stood. Chase waved his hand, squinting through the flutter of fur and feathers left in the beasts' wake.

The dark wizards David and Pavo continued the deadly battle on the other side; tiny, razor-sharp black sparks continuing to rain down around them, impaling the ground at their feet creating a field of deadly ebony blades of grass that slanted upward. It was impossible to deduce who was winning their fight.

Liz still stood at the pit's edge, streams of blinding light seemed to crawl out of the pit and merge into her body. She had the look of a puppet waiting for its master to breathe life into it with a flick of the wrist and a tug on the strings. Her unseeing eyes suddenly looked their direction, and thin streaks of black crawled across her eyeballs as if trying to worm their way into her brain. She mouthed the words, "Go." Teeth clenched, she threw back her head and a scream tore from her mouth as her body started shaking. "Go!" she screamed as her body began shaking uncontrollably, her eyes turning more and more dark with each passing second.

"We have to get out of here while we still can. I don't know how much longer Liz will be with us. She's struggling."

Reluctantly, George nodded. "Yes. She's fighting her own battle. She won't win." He turned back to the courtyard. The wolves, suddenly interested in their small group, turned as one. The black wolf with the brown streak of fur on its side—the pack leader—stalked toward them. After two quick barks, they were surrounded, any chance of leaving through the door was gone.

"Portal. It's the only way. Everyone, together now."

With Alyx and George combining powers along with the others, the portal appeared almost instantly. They were sucked through one by one. When all except George were safely through, he stuck his head through the opening. "I can't leave Apollo. I'll find you if I can. After."

Chase lurched to his feet, reaching toward the opening. "No, George! You can't..."

With a *snap*, the portal was gone, and he looked around. A small juvenile giggle broke through his panic, and he turned to see Sammie, her arms stretched out to Dawn. "Ma-ma-ma-ma-ma-ma!" Another jubilant laugh filled the living room, and Dawn swept her baby into her arms while Ty jumped into his father's outstretched hands.

Bray's voice broke. "You're safe, thank God. I was just about to go to the realty shop..."

Carson stood back, saying nothing.

Brian and Colin jumped up to pace. Colin demanded, "What about our parents? I thought we were portaling inside the realty shop." He turned to Brian. "We left them there. We have to go back."

Chase stood on shaky legs, looking slowly around the room, disoriented from the sudden change in scenes. "And where's Mason? We didn't see him at all."

Alyx stepped forward. "Do you still think David Moore can be saved?"

His eyes broke away from hers, and he stared at the crack between the wooden floorboards before answering. "Everyone can be saved." He glanced at his watch. "But will we have the chance? Or the time to help him?"

Time seemed to pick up its pace. Why was it that minutes fly by like seconds when you're on a deadline? And this—the deadliest of countdowns.

12:09 pm.

Exactly twenty-one hours before the jump.

CHAPTER 83
CHASE

"I have a plan." Chase paced the tiny living room, leaning down, he snatched up Alyx's backpack that she'd left there just last night, gripping it so hard his knuckles turned white. "We'll use this."

Alyx was shaking her head. "Chase, how are we … ?"

Reaching into the bag, Chase pulled out a weapon, and held it up.

Pausing, Alyx tilted her head. "That might actually work. Why didn't we think of this sooner?"

Bray interrupted, "What is that thing?"

"It's called an Inferno Ray," Chase said. "We brought it with us. I guess you could say it has a, sort of, magical ability. The target implodes on impact. Back home, I used it on an ancient, towering pine tree and it just disappeared. One minute it was standing there in the shade of the giant tree, the next minute I was blocking the sun with my hand as if it had never been there at all. *Poof.* Just like that." He snapped his fingers.

Dawn sighed. "So just what do you plan on … imploding?"

Chase looked around the room meeting each pair of eyes, landing on Alyx. "Is it strong enough to take out the whole realty building?"

She shrugged. "I don't know. I saw it take out a helicopter once, but I just don't know about an entire building. And there's the small possibility that it won't work in this world …" She tilted her head. "Though I did fire it at the shield back at Dune Haven, and the laser was absorbed into the shield wall."

Bray added, "What about this magical pit you've been telling me about? Why can't you aim your … what did you call it? An Inferno Ray? Aim it at the magical hole in the ground."

Dawn placed a gentle hand on her husband's arm. "That could remove all the magic from this world. None of us would have magical abilities anymore."

He looked at her. "Is that such a bad thing?"

"Hon, you don't understand what it's like. I can't imagine not having magic at my fingertips. I just don't know…"

"But you would be safe. We all would be a lot safer without the magic, don't you think?" Bray laid a hand on his wife's arm.

"Maybe..." Her brow wrinkled in a frown that seemed to encompass her whole countenance. Dawn began chewing on her bottom lip.

"Wait," Alyx interrupted. "If we aim for the building, maybe the pit would remain intact. We don't know if it'll work unless we try."

Chase added, "Yes. Or if not the building, why not just aim it at the Sovereign Warlocks? If we take them out, then things would go back to normal around here, right?"

"Maybe. But are you okay with taking out Mr. Moore? Will you be able to do that?"

"I think so. If there's no other way to save everyone in this town, then I won't have a choice. I could try to take out Pavo first and give David a choice..."

"You saw how he handled the power before, Chase. Why would he react any different if you hand him the power again?"

"Well, then there's always the pit. I could give him a chance to change, and if he doesn't take it then I could remove his power source. With no magic, he'll go back to just being plain old Mr. Moore."

Colin spoke, his voice shaking just a bit, "Why does David Moore get to have a choice, but Pavo doesn't? Who decides the punishment? You? Just because you know David Moore, he gets a stay of execution? He's done things just as bad as the other guy." He turned away. "Annabelle didn't get another chance."

Chase paused, the words sinking in. His shoulders slumped. "You're right. Everyone deserves a second chance. You and Brian were trying to give your sister another chance, and she chose not to take it. But we have to stop this power struggle. We may not have a choice, and neither will they."

"I just don't see how we are any different from them. I mean, we're standing here plotting murder like we're talking about the weather," Colin said.

Chase sighed. "In self-defense. Because we want to protect people, and make Dune Harbor safe for the people living here."

Brian joined in. "That's the same thing David Moore says."

The room fell quiet, each one of them lost in their own thoughts as the sun continued its arc across the sky.

Finally, Dawn broke the silence. "I'll fix lunch. We have to eat and build up our strength before we do anything."

"I can't eat."

"Me neither."

Dawn stood, wringing her hands. "Well, I'll fix it for anyone who is hungry. I need to do something." She disappeared through the doorway, Brian on her heels.

"Me too. I'll help you."

Chase and Alyx made eye contact across the room, their eyes mirroring the same haunted look of despair.

Finally, Alyx broke the silence, "And what about Liz?"

Carson spoke for the first time since they'd arrived there. "And George and Apollo?"

"And our parents," Colin added.

Chase's sigh seemed to deflate him. "And Mason."

Alyx nodded. "Too many what-ifs."

•   •   •

"It the best we can do," Chase said. "I know there are a lot of variables, but we have to do something. We have to try."

Alyx was shaking her head before he finished. "I don't know, Chase. I don't like you going back there alone."

"I'm the only one who can sustain invisibility long enough to do it. And I won't be alone. You'll be there, too, inside the building." He winked at her. "We don't have time to argue. Who knows what's happened there in the time we've been sitting here in this house."

"I agree," she growled, "but I still don't like it." She held up her arms, ready to begin. "Okay, I'll portal you to the courtyard first, and then Brian and I will follow. We'll be right inside the building if you need us, Chase. As you said, we have no idea what we're walking into."

Chase nodded. "Let's do this."

CHAPTER 84
CHASE

Crouching in the grass behind the overturned lime-green Adirondack chair, feeling the need to hide despite his current state of invisibility, Chase stretched his neck to see.

Not much had changed since they'd left. Liz remained at the pit as if powering up. Her entire body seemed to glow with magical energy, and the air in the courtyard thrummed with it. Her eyes were closed, her head flung back so her shoulder-length ebony hair hung and swayed behind her. She paid no attention to the others around her, completely focused on her task...though her final goal remained a mystery to Chase.

The wolves now surrounded Mr. Moore, snapping and snarling as they approached, inching ever closer to their prey. The sharp blades created by the sparks of battle jutted out of the ground—the only thing holding them back from pouncing. As he watched, one stepped a little closer and a yelp escaped. The animal jumped back to lick at its injured paw.

Chase's heart tripped when he spotted Apollo lying on the ground, Enzo panting beside him with an arrow stuck through his wing. George stood, a bow in his hands, aiming again at the Enfield as it stalked toward him, its fox-like canine jaws bared in a menacing growl that should have stopped a man in his tracks. Blood streaked across George's face, and the older man began chanting under his breath. The wind whipped up around them, tossing their hair, and Enzo stopped in his tracks and even backed up a step. Suddenly, George raised his hands and the beast was lifted off the ground so smoothly Chase almost looked for high-wire lines above its head. George flung his hand to the side, and Enzo's body flew the same direction, slamming into the brick wall, where it lay yelping. George ran to the pit, but called over his shoulder, "Apollo needs help."

Still invisible, Chase wondered how he'd known of his presence. Turning from George, he squinted at Apollo, streaks of blood turning his feathers crimson, and breathed a sigh of relief when he saw that the beast's chest was moving sporadically up and down.

Just then, Enzo stood. Its head whipped in his direction. *Can he see me, despite the Invisibility Spell?* The creature rose, limping directly toward him. Its wing was definitely broken and he'd lost a lot of feathers baring the thin membrane of pale skin underneath. The animal was clearly in pain, but kept advancing.

Chase slouched down, clutching the inferno ray closer to his chest. Walking in an awkward squat, he moved as slowly as possible in a duck-walk around the other side of the chair just as Enzo rounded it, pushing its snout onto the ground in the exact spot he'd been in just seconds before. Chase continued moving, slowly making his way toward Apollo. The Griffin's pupils followed him, looked directly at him. "Shh. Reinforcements are here, buddy," he whispered against its feathered head.

Across the way, Enzo was still rooting around at the chairs and tables. It clearly could not *see* Chase, but could definitely sense his presence.

Chase ran his hands over smooth feathers and soft fur, feeling for the source of blood on Apollo's neck. Though healing was not his strength, he had learned a few things from the Heck brothers. A sharp pain had him pulling his hand quickly away to suck at the tip. His mouth filled with the bitter taste of copper. Carefully, he felt through the feathers again, this time pulling out a shard of black glass that had been embedded in the creature's neck. Tossing it aside, a barely audible chant fell from his mouth. Though the wound did not knit completely, the spell staunched the flow of blood. It would have to be enough. Slowly, he raised the Inferno Ray toward the first Sovereign Warlock, Pavo. Despite what Colin had said, right or wrong, he had no intention of giving this man a second chance. He'd seen what he was capable of in other worlds.

The two battling wizards were almost connected by the shiny black stream of electricity. Sweat beaded on their brow, and they were focused solely on each other. It was a battle of wills. A battle of magic. A war to the death.

The purple-black sparks continued to fly, creating a circular ring around them that nothing seemed to be able to penetrate. As he watched, the arch shrank in size. Pavo seemed to have taken the upper hand, and a slight cocky smile turned up the corners of his mouth. "Concede, and I might let you live."

Through gritted teeth, David Moore ground out, "Never."

"Ha! Stupid man. I never would have let you live after what you did to me, anyway." He pushed more power into the battle with each word, causing David to back up yet another step.

Enough.

Chase lifted the Inferno Ray, aiming directly at Pavo. His fingers, lined up precisely, squeezed the multiple triggers just as Enzo knocked him backward. The laser, that had been intended for Pavo, hit Enzo instead. *Pop.* The chimera shimmered for just a second before turning in on itself and then disappeared with one howl that was cut-off midway.

Gone.

In his fall, the weapon was flung from Chase's hands. Looking down at himself, he could still see through himself. Still invisible. He renewed the chant just in case.

But the blast had alerted the others of his presence.

David Moore's eyes broke away from Pavo, his eyes searching the courtyard. The small distraction gave Pavo the advantage he needed, and he took it. Shards of black glass rained from Pavo's fingertips, piercing David Moore's chest. Mr. Moore sank to his knees, his breathing labored.

Chase gasped, jumping to his feet. "No! Mr. Moore!"

"Dad!" Mason, bursting through the door of the building, ran to his father, placing his own body in front of him. He challenged the other man, aiming his magical abilities—combined with all of his hatred—toward Pavo. His father lay at his feet with his breath rattling in his chest. The older man placed a bloodied hand on his son's leg. "Mason. You came to me."

"Yes. You're my father. I'm not going to let him kill you."

"Even after all I've done?" His eyes seemed to clear for the first time in months. "It's too late for me, Mason. I'm already dead. Save yourself. I couldn't save your mother, but I can save you. I'm sorry. For everything. I love you, son."

With one last blast of power, a white dagger flew from David Moore's hands and into Pavo's chest.

"Dad, no!" Mason fell to his knees, clutching at his father's still body, willing him to live.

Liz stepped forward. "Pavo."

"Help me, Ursa. Help." He fell to the ground, clutching at the knife impaled deep in his heart. With his last act of magic, David had chosen to wield the power of the light.

Ursa barely glanced his way with her black eyes, so black the whites could no longer be seen. "I will help you. As I should have done long ago."

A blinding light, so bright it shone through his closed eyelids so that Chase had to shield them with his hands, filled the space. When he could finally open his eyes again, one word tore from deep within him, "No."

Liz stood alone; Mason, Pavo, and David Moore all crumbled at her feet. The wolf-beasts' bodies littered the courtyard, fallen at the precise moment their creator fell. George now stood at the precipice of the source of all magic, his hands soaking in the power in much the same way Liz had. The pit seemed to pulse with her power; power only for her, but George reached further down into the cavernous hole and found just a fraction of the power for himself.

Chase could feel both the light and the dark swirling around him, the air was thick with it. Glancing down, he saw that he was no longer invisible. The magic that had struck down the others must have broken his spell. Ursa-Liz no longer fought the power but embraced it, wielded it, bent it to her will. The power did not control her. She controlled the power, completely.

She turned slowly, meeting his eyes. Raising her arms, pointing her power now at him, an electric stream flew out of her fingertips directly toward Chase, but at the same time George aimed his own power at her, breaking her concentration. The lightning bolt fell into the ground at Chase's feet, knocking him backward.

He did not know when he retrieved the weapon, or when he'd raised it to point at her chest. But without another thought, his fingers once again pushed down on the Inferno Ray's trigger.

Liz gave one quick nod, a smile turning up the corners of her mouth, and he thought he saw, in that final moment, a look of peace on her face. *Pop.* Like a cork releasing air from a wine bottle.

And then she was gone.

He leaned on Apollo, who nuzzled at his neck.

Alyx, along with Brian and his parents burst through the door, then stopped to look around. Chase got up, slowly approaching the bodies of Mason, his dad, and Pavo.

Dead, all three. The wolves, too. No amount of magic could help them now.

George fell to his knees, alive but battered.

The pit pulsed quietly once again.

It was over.

CHAPTER 85
CHASE

There was no celebration of the events that had transpired in the small town of Dune Harbor. No news reports covering a magical war, or a tribute to the lives lost on September 8th.

The townies went about their day as if nothing had happened, heading out for a morning jog, casting their lines in the surf, or picking up seashells on the beach. And of the reported wolf sightings in town, the local zookeeper quickly squashed the panic by admitting some of his animals had escaped but had been quickly and humanely recovered overnight. No need for worry. Everyone was safe as they had always been in the small coastal town by the sea.

And so it went. The magical community covered up all evidence of magic as they always did, and the townspeople accepted the stories because the alternative was, well, unbelievable and uncomfortable.

By the light of the almost-full moon, a small group dug graves and placed markers in the shape of a cross for the Moore family, for Bea, and for Liz and Pavo. They said a prayer for their souls, and hoped that was enough.

It was hard to come face-to-face with the realization that people could make all the worst choices throughout their lives, but in the end somehow find the strength to make the one right choice when it mattered most. And that the opposite could also be true. Was anyone ever really completely good, or completely bad? Or with motivation and circumstance, do we all have the potential for both the light and the dark? Are we strong enough to make the right decisions in the face of adversity? Do we ever really know which path is the right one?

Chase struggled more with his brooding thoughts than Alyx did. She accepted the choices they'd all made, and was at peace with their decisions.

She reached for his hand, and he looked up to meet her eyes. Leaning over, she kissed his cheek. Just a light touch, her soft lips barely touching his whiskered face, but it was everything. He reached for her, leaning his forehead against hers, he breathed in the scent of her. And his heart lifted.

"I love you, Alyx."

She reached up, her fingers stroking the necklace she wore around her neck, the smile shining from her eyes. "Here you go again. Talking about love, and getting all mushy."

Brian put his hands on his hips. "Do you two ever give it a rest?" he teased.

Colin bumped his shoulder into his brother. "I hope you never act like that, bro."

"No worries. There's no girl alive that would make me act like a love-sick loser." Chase sat back, winking at Alyx. "Hey, don't knock it until you try it, *bro*."

Dawn and Bray stood with their arms around each other. "Yeah, don't knock it."

Carson shook George's hand. "Thanks for all your help, George. I always know I can count on you."

"You got it. But I have to admit I hope you don't need me again any time soon." In one movement, he was sitting astride Apollo. Brian had finished healing the chimera, and it pranced in anticipation of the flight to come. "I need to leave before daylight." He looked from Alyx to Chase. "It's been my true pleasure meeting you two. I always regretted not being able to carry on the legacy of a keeper, but now that I've seen what it's really like, I think I'm happy in my forest. I wrote down a spell in your journal for you to use during the jump. It may help." He nodded, patting Apollo's flank. The beast needed no other words, but trotted a few feet and took off in a flash of wings.

"Don't think I'll ever get used to that. I wonder what he means by help during the jump?" Chase asked.

Alyx shrugged, watching the two merge into the dark sky.

Ty also watched the take-off, and tugged on his mother's hand. "Mommy, who will control the magical power now?"

"No one will control it. As it should be." She smiled down at her son.

"I think, maybe, someone should. To protect the town, I mean. I could do it," Ty said.

Dawn gave Ty's hand a gentle squeeze. "Nonsense, baby. We'll all protect the town together."

Ty's eyes narrowed, a faraway look in them.

A shiver traveled up Chase's spine, and the bone-deep frost tingled at the base of his neck long afterward. It was something he'd seen in Ty's eyes that held a certain kind of foreboding. A look much like he'd seen in Mr. Moore's eyes. He could only hope that the boy's parents could guide him in making the right choices in life.

He was still so young.

Surely there was time for him to see the right path and follow it?

As they walked away from the graves, a frown wrinkled his brow.

CHAPTER 86
ALYX

On the morning of September 9th, Alyx and Chase sat at the small table in Dawn's kitchen. Sammie smeared some kind of orange goo all over her tray, babbling the happy chatter of a toddler. Every now and then she slammed her hands down, sending bits of baby food flying in every direction and freckling her face along with anyone else who stood close. Her sweet giggle filled every corner of the small room.

"Oh, Sammie, I'm gonna miss you." Alyx laughed, taking a bite of her toast. Looking at Ty, she said, "You too, Ty." She glanced at her watch. 9:00 am. "Almost time."

Dawn sighed. "I'll miss having you two around. You're the reason my husband knows about magic. I'm in your debt."

Bray placed a hand on her shoulder, and laughed. "Not sure I want to thank you for that. And I'm not sure I'll miss you in my home, either." He laughed again. Reaching out his hand, he grasped Chase's hand in one brisk shake. "Be safe."

"Thanks. Take care of Ty. And Sammie, too, of course. But it's Ty who will remember and have to live with all of this. Guide him on the right path."

Bray frowned. "Of course we will. He'll be safe. We're his parents. It's our job to keep him safe."

Chase nodded. "I know you will. Okay." He flung his backpack over his shoulders, holding the journal in his hands. "Here it is. The Relief Spell. I wonder...?"

"We better start since we only have five minutes to go." Alyx was already wearing her purple backpack, had given hugs to go around, pausing to ruffle Bo's fur and plant one loud kiss on his head, and quickly pushed out the back door off the kitchen into the backyard. One by one, everyone followed behind her.

The two of them sat on the soft grass, legs crossed, so close their knees bumped, and began chanting the words of the spell in unison. Dawn held onto Bo. The group stood back, careful not to get too close to this unknown power.

Alyx felt Chase's hand on hers, and intertwined her fingers with his. They'd realized in the last jump that they needed to be touching during the transition in order to land in the same location in the next world. A tingling began in her toes and traveled the entire length of her body and up to her head, a sort of numb euphoria taking hold of her. Glancing at Chase, she saw he was having similar effects.

9:08.

Glancing at the small bon voyage party sending them off, tears gathered in her eyes. "Thank you. All of you. For everything."

As if through a tunnel, she heard their murmurs of returned thanks. It was time.

9:09.

The two silvery, mercurial pools appeared over them like personal rainclouds, one above her and the other hovering over him. Moving and dancing, the two at first clashed against each other until, with an electrical jolt, joining as one. Lightning flashed in the sky—one blue streak and one purple—the electrical hum causing the hair on their arms to stand up. As always, their signature colors combined when they joined, veins turning a deep mulberry color that traveled throughout their bodies and crawled across their faces like a crack spreading across porcelain.

This was the first time they had traveled from an open, outside space, as well as the first time jumping in front of an audience, always previously choosing the cover of a house to jump from. The mass above them spread and receded, spread and receded, until all at once it lowered in one quick movement. Bo, in that last instant before the pool engulfed them, leapt out of Dawn's embrace and ran to pounce onto Alyx's lap, her free hand automatically reaching out to hug him to her chest. Eyes opened wide, and one word could be heard before her voice was cut off. "Bo!"

As it enveloped all of them—two humans and one chimera hybrid—they disappeared from head to toe, until all that was left was the indentation in the grass where moments before they had been sitting.

•　•　•

Floating.

Drifting on air, hurtling through a flying tunnel.

Bright lights and sunbeams interspersed with the occasional gentle lightning flash caused her to close her eyes, but there was no pain. Only peacefulness. She squeezed Chase's hand and felt his answering pressure, and hugged Bo closer. Even with her eyes closed, she knew where she was. She heard voices, children at play, seagulls calling in the distance. Ocean waves lapping at the shore. The soft hum of a small plane.

When the wind and light faded, she felt the give of the sand underneath her, and pushed herself up. If only every inter-dimensional entry could be this way.

Forcing her eyelids open, she squinted into the sunlight, then forced herself to focus on Bo. He lurched up, licking her chin with his tiny sandpaper tongue. "Oh, Bo. What are we going to do with you?" She looked up, meeting Chase's eyes. "How will we explain a chimera in a non-magical world?" She glanced around at the people enjoying a beach-day, thankful no one was paying attention to them. "We have to hide him."

"I don't know, but that was awesome! Do you think we can use that spell every time we jump?"

"I doubt it. Unless this is another magical world, but the chances of that are…"

"Yeah. Pretty much non-existent." He caught Bo in mid-flight as the animal leaped from her lap to his. "Wait. Where are his wings?"

"What do you mean, where are …?" Her eyes widened. "He looks different here."

"Yes, he just looks like a dog. A mixed breed mutt. I guess you need magic to see him as he really is. It seems this is not a magical world, after all."

"Do you think we can still use any of it? The magic, I mean?"

"There's only one way to know." He began chanting, then looked at Alyx. "Unless I'm invisible right now, I don't think so."

"I can see you." She sighed. "I think I'm going to miss the magic."

"Me, too."

"Check the journal."

Chase removed it from his backpack, flipping to Dimension 8. The page was blank, as it had been at the start of their journey.

"What about the next page? Dimension 9?"

Chase turned the page, and his eyes widened. "This page has lots of notes. The Young family seems to be mentioned a lot here. I think that's where we need to start." He stood, extending a hand to Alyx. "After I check on Mason."

Brushing sand off her pants, she surveyed the ocean waves rolling in and out on the horizon. "Sounds like as good a place as any. To start, I mean."

"Let's head to his house first this time." He reached for her hand, and they walked toward the residential section of town. Bo struggled in her grasp until she lowered him to the ground. "We need to buy him a leash."

He nodded. "Put that on the list." Chase surveyed from under his lashes as they strolled. "Seems like home. I don't see anything weird, do you?"

"No. You're right. Seems like everything is normal."

He winked. "I think we could use a little bit of normal."

Suddenly, Bo took off running. "Bo!"

"Bo! Come back here!"

They ran after him, glad for their status as keepers and the stamina that came along with it. After ten minutes of sprinting, they still couldn't catch the pup. "Why isn't he listening?"

"I guess this is all new to him, too." Their sneakers slapped on the street, and Chase recognized where they were. The Gull Street bridge. "I wonder if he knows where he's going?"

"Seems like maybe he's just getting some exercise."

"Wait. Is there someone up there?"

"Up where?"

"On the bridge." He pointed, then took off as fast as he could to reach the person who was climbing up on the bridge's railing, his intent clear. "Wait! Don't jump!" Chase screamed, Alyx right behind him.

"Oh no. No! Don't jump!"

The person let go just as they reached the railing and Chase grabbed for the boy's arm wrapping both his hands around the jumper, hanging over the side bent in half, his precarious hold the only thing keeping this boy from falling to his death on the freeway below. Wind from the cars zooming by below blew into his face making him squint, he flinched when one stopped to honk its horn before continuing on. The overpowering odor of exhaust flared his nostrils, but he held the answering cough inside for fear of moving even that much. A burning tore up his arms as he held the dead weight, clasping the boy's arm with one hand and a fistful of shirt in the other.

He looked down at a patch of red hair just before the jumper looked up. He could feel the wetness on his palms and his grip began to loosen.

Recognition dawned and Chase redoubled his efforts, his shock almost causing him to let go.

His own voice was raspy, the words torn from his throat, "Mason? Oh, Mason. Why? Why would you do this?"

To be continued...

I hope you enjoyed reading Book Two in the Keeper of the Watch series as much as I enjoyed writing it! This story, and these characters, are close to my heart because they were inspired by my dad and his love of watches. I truly had a blast continuing this story—and in Dimension 8, I've discovered my love of writing, living, and creating magical worlds!

If you like my books, you can help by simply spreading the word. One way to do that is posting a review on Amazon, Goodreads, or Barnes & Noble. Follow me on social media to stay up-to-date on my latest projects and author visits, or sign up for my blog.

Keep on reading!

Kristen

https://kristenljackson.wixsite.com/kristenjacksonauthor
Facebook: @kristenjacksonauthor
Twitter: @KLJacksonAuthor
Instagram: @krisjack504
Follow me on LinkedIn, Pinterest, Goodreads, & Tumblr too!

NOTE FROM THE AUTHOR

Word-of-mouth is crucial for any author to succeed. If you enjoyed the book, please leave a review online—anywhere you are able. Even if it's just a sentence or two. It would make all the difference and would be very much appreciated.

Thanks!
Kristen

Thank you so much for reading book two of the
Keeper of the Watch series.
In case you missed it, don't forget to check out book one.

Keeper of the Watch: Dimension 7 by Kristen L. Jackson

"This is an exciting and enjoyable read, and I would thoroughly recommend *Keeper of the Watch* to lovers of action-packed science fantasy. Bring on book two!" *–Readers' Favorite*

Available in paperback, eBook, & audiobook

View other Black Rose Writing titles at
www.blackrosewriting.com/books and use promo code
PRINT to receive a **20% discount** when purchasing.

www.ingramcontent.com/pod-product-compliance
Lightning Source LLC
Chambersburg PA
CBHW011129100726
47898CB00009B/2907